Three-ti... ...Beckett learned t... ...e she learned to read. Born to a military family, she has lived in the United States, Puerto Rico, Portugal and Brazil. In addition to travelling, Tina loves to cuddle with her pug, Alex, spend time with her family, and hit the trails on her horse. Learn more about Tina from her website, or 'friend' her on Facebook.

Cursed with a poor sense of direction and a propensity to read, **Annie Claydon** spent much of her childhood lost in books. A degree in English Literature followed by a career in computing didn't lead directly to her perfect job—writing romance for Mills & Boon—but she has no regrets in taking the scenic route. She lives in London: a city where getting lost can be a joy.

Also by Tina Beckett

How to Win the Surgeon's Heart
The Trouble with the Tempting Doc
Starting Over with the Single Dad
Their Reunion to Remember

Also by Annie Claydon

Greek Island Fling to Forever
Falling for the Brooding Doc
The Doctor's Reunion to Remember
Risking It All for a Second Chance

Discover more at millsandboon.co.uk.

ONE NIGHT WITH THE SICILIAN SURGEON

TINA BECKETT

FROM THE NIGHT SHIFT TO FOREVER

ANNIE CLAYDON

MILLS & BOON

First Published in Great Britain 2022
by Mills & Boon, an imprint of HarperCollins*Publishers* Ltd,
1 London Bridge Street, London, SE1 9GF

www.harpercollins.co.uk

HarperCollins*Publishers*
1st Floor, Watermarque Building,
Ringsend Road, Dublin 4, Ireland

One Night with the Sicilian Surgeon © 2022 Tina Beckett

From the Night Shift to Forever © 2022 Annie Claydon

ISBN: 978-0-263-30117-5

02/22

MIX
Paper from
responsible sources
FSC® C007454

This book is produced from independently certified FSC™ paper
to ensure responsible forest management.
For more information visit www.harpercollins.co.uk/green.

Printed and Bound in Spain using 100% Renewable Electricity
at CPI Black Print, Barcelona

ONE NIGHT WITH THE SICILIAN SURGEON

TINA BECKETT

MILLS & BOON

To my husband, who is always there for me.

PROLOGUE

UGH! SHE WAS so tired of waiting. Especially with the questions rolling around in her head and the nausea that had pooled in her stomach.

Breandan Frost started as the door behind her creaked, a sense of trepidation sweeping through her. He was here. They could have things out before the wedding. If there was even to be a wedding.

Her long white dress hissed around her ankles as she turned quickly. Not Sergio.

She forced a smile as her dad's worried face came into focus. He wore his dark tuxedo in the same way he'd always worn his military uniforms, his bearing proud and unflappable.

"Dad, I can't talk about this anymore. Please. Not right now."

Her father had come into her dressing room about an hour earlier and, kissing her mom on the cheek, had asked if he could have a few moments alone with his daughter.

Instead of the pep talk she'd been expecting, he'd pulled out a tabloid with a headline that screamed an accusation.

Hotel Mogul Accused of Money Laundering!

All of a sudden, Sergio's secretiveness about his business dealings, an evasion that had made her more and more uneasy over the last month, seemed to click into place. Buried in the article was a picture of him at a New York restaurant with a beautiful blonde, his electric smile on full display. The second picture had been cropped to show the woman's bare foot curled around Bree's fiancé's ankle. The paper was still sitting on the vanity where she had sat and done her makeup.

When and if he arrived at the church, his explanation would determine whether she walked down that aisle as planned or walked out the door.

"I'm sorry, sweetheart. I'm not here to talk about what Sergio has or hasn't done."

Something else was wrong. Very wrong. "What is it? Is Mom okay?"

"She's fine, she just…" He dragged a hand across his silver hair. "Sergio was parked out front and—"

Her teeth clenched as another wave of sickness hit her system. She gave a half laugh. "I halfway thought he was standing me up. Maybe it would have been better if he had."

Growing up the child of an American military officer stationed in Italy had been confusing. At times, she'd felt kind of lost, like she didn't fit in on either side of the Atlantic. But she loved Italy, and eight years ago she'd made the difficult decision to stay and do her education in the place she'd come to love. Her first position as a perfusionist was set to begin soon after she came back from her honeymoon.

Honeymoon. The word sat like a rock in her brain.

Tabloids were all fake, weren't they? Except they'd known about her engagement before they'd even told their parents.

Her father didn't say anything.

Sometimes those gossip papers got it right. She forced out the words. "Where is he?"

"Come sit down, honey."

"No, I don't want to sit down. Just tell me." Her wedding dress suddenly felt tight, constricting her torso and forcing the air from her lungs. Dragging her veil away from her face, not caring if she damaged the delicate lace, her voice dropped to a whisper. "Tell me, Daddy. Please."

"I don't know where he is. Maybe he saw the papers. He drove away about twenty minutes ago and hasn't come back." The growled words made her wonder if her father had been hoping to waylay Sergio before he ever made it back to her.

The love she'd once felt for her fiancé—the love that had seemed to be faltering lately—went down for the third time.

He'd left her here to fend for himself.

She blinked, trying to process what her dad was saying. She'd always had problems committing to people or things, knowing that her dad could be transferred at a moment's notice, even though they'd been in Italy for close to twenty years. But Sergio, the CFO of a top chain of hotels, had swept her off her feet. Their whirlwind romance had been featured in one of Naples's many newspapers, much to her chagrin.

"I tried calling his cell, but he didn't pick up."

The wedding was already running late—very late—and there were journalists outside with cameras and microphones who'd surely seen him arrive and then drive away. Her mom had tried to diffuse Bree's nervousness earlier, fussing over this and that until Bree had finally sent her out to her seat so that she could regain her composure. Her three bridesmaids were already in the foyer according to the text from her mom she'd received a few minutes ago.

"Does Mom know? About everything?"

"No. I didn't have the heart to tell her. She looked so happy this morning." A muscle in her dad's jaw worked as he tried to contain his emotions.

A blaze of anger scorched through her. Sergio wasn't just doing this to her. He was doing it to her family. To his!

Spinning around to the dressing table, she snatched up her phone and found her fiancé's name, punching the call button. It rang four times, and then he picked up.

"Serge? Where are you? You need to come to—"

"I'm sorry, *Signorina*, this is Officer Cardulla. Who am I speaking with, please?"

That wasn't her fiancé's voice.

Although she'd lived in Italy most of her life, her brain suddenly couldn't decipher what the man was saying. Then the realization dawned—Sergio was with the police. She started shaking.

So he'd been arrested? The reports were true?

Switching to Italian, she answered. "Th-this is his fiancée, Bree Frost. Can I speak with Sergio, please?"

"I'm afraid that won't be possible."

"Wh-why not?"

"Because fifteen minutes ago your fiancé was killed in a single-vehicle accident. Please come, so we may speak in person."

Killed? Sergio was dead?

All her questions disappeared in the mist that swept across her eyes. Seeped into her soul. Sergio wasn't coming back to the church. Not now. Not ever.

A ludicrous thought came to her. Would the blonde in the picture grieve his death?

The phone fell from her hand, clattering on the tile surface of the floor and spinning away. She could hear the officer still calling out to her as tears filled her eyes and spilled over.

When her dad pulled her to him without a word, the floodgates opened, and she turned and wept into his brand-new tuxedo. Wept for the dreams that would never happen. Wept for Sergio's family and friends seated in the huge, ornate cathedral expecting to see his wide smile at any moment.

But most of all, she cried for the fact that she hadn't been able to see through his pretense.

But never again. She wasn't being taken in by a handsome face and convincing lies.

From now on, Bree was going to be on her guard, with her defenses on high alert. And before she pulled her heart off emotional bypass, she was going to block up whatever artery fed the so-called love center of her brain. From now on she was operating off pure reason.

Except right now, everything inside her was telling her to run as far and as fast as she could.

CHAPTER ONE

SICILY. BREE STEPPED off the plane in Catania less than six weeks after coming back from her honeymoon trip. The trip she'd made alone. Her father had had to whisk her out a back entrance of the church to avoid the photographers out front. In her desperation to get away and avoid having to talk to anyone, she'd decided to catch a plane to the island and hole up in what would have been their honeymoon suite.

But that first night had seen her in the hotel bar, downing one too many drinks. When a dark-haired man with intense eyes had pulled up the bar stool next to hers, she'd turned toward him, needing to drown out the pain of betrayal. One thing led to another, and she'd lost herself in the arms of a stranger on her honeymoon bed.

Strangely, that encounter had gotten her through the worst of the continued gossip columns, which also reported Sergio had had a lover on the side who'd come · forward and said he'd planned to abandon his fiancée for his one true love. His family had declared everything to be a lie, suing multiple tabloids.

But it didn't matter. Naples and the life she'd planned with Sergio were now behind her. On a whim, she'd applied at a hospital in Catania and had been shocked when she'd gotten a call the day she returned from her honeymoon. They wanted her.

And she wanted them. Desperately.

So here she was.

Wisps of smoke had sifted from Mount Etna as her flight had neared the island. Whether the volcano was welcoming her or warning her away, she had no idea, but she'd probably find out soon enough.

The double doors at the front of the airport opened, and a wave of heat hit her, making her pause before she wheeled her bags outside. Okay, well, here she was. And not a moment too soon. Her first shift started just two days from now. But flights had been booked with tourists all clamoring to see the famous island. At least she'd made it and had even found a hotel that had an opening for a few weeks.

But this time, she'd be smarter about her stay on the island. No more one-night stands with strangers or being romanced by powerful men like Sergio. She was here to work. To avoid thinking about her past mistakes. She'd been so jittery, her stomach had been tied up in knots until she'd stepped on that plane. But at that moment, everything seemed to fall into place.

She was here now. And she was determined to make Sicily her home. No matter how hard it might prove to be.

Diego Pintor swept into the operating room for his first major procedure of the morning: replacing the aortic valve of thirty-year-old Sara Nirvana. With freshly scrubbed hands held away from his body, he waited as one of the surgical nurses helped him glove up. Then he moved over to the table, his eyes taking in his normal team, nodding to each of them before shifting his gaze to the panel where the new perfusionist was already in place, adjusting dials. She was from Naples, from what he'd been told. When she glanced up, he was surprised to see vivid green eyes peering at him…eyes that widened slightly as she took him in. Her cap and mask were already in place, so he couldn't tell anything else about her, but something jiggled in the back of his head before he forced his attention away from her.

The patient was already sedated, the drape over her chest revealing where the first incision would take place. "Let's get her prepped."

The room went into motion with people taking their positions, instruments gleaming under the bright lights in the space. He glanced again at the perfusionist, realizing he probably should have introduced himself and welcomed her to the team and to the hospital. But that could come afterward. Right now, he had a job to do.

He moved closer to the sedated patient and glanced down, saying a quick ritualistic prayer over the person before asking for his first instrument and making an incision. Then all thoughts were on the surgery at hand. Fifteen minutes later, he was through the sternum and the patient's beating heart was in view. It never failed to fill him with a sense of wonder at how deeply the body relied on this one organ to sustain all its functions, even the brain.

The perfusionist was watching him with expectant eyes. He nodded to acknowledge her. "Are you ready for bypass?"

"Whenever you give the word."

The sentence was spoken in precise Italian, and the quick Neapolitan accent confirmed her being from the Naples area, but there was something else just below the surface. Something tinglingly familiar. He could have sworn he'd heard that voice somewhere before, but that was impossible. He'd been born and raised in Catania, leaving only for some of the highly specialized portions of his surgical degree, so their paths couldn't have crossed. He shook off the weird sense of déjà vu as he prepared the patient to be transferred onto the bypass machine.

Five minutes later his patient's heart was still and un-beating in her chest, receiving oxygenated blood from a machine rather than pumping it through her body.

"I'll need the donor valve as soon as I get the pulmo-nary valve moved over." Diego was the only surgeon in Sicily who'd performed the complicated Ross procedure where the patient's own pulmonary valve was used to replace the aortic valve. A donor valve was then used to replace the pulmonary valve. The advantage was the donor valve wouldn't have to withstand the stress of the blood volume handled by the aorta.

He carefully freed the pulmonary valve from its po-sition and sutured it into its new location. He glanced up at the perfusionist. "How are we doing?"

Those green eyes met his, and a flicker of panic went through them. "Doing?"

He realized she wasn't sure what he was asking. Hell, that's right. This was her first real position. He struggled to tamp down his impatience and clarified the question. "How long has she been on bypass?"

"Oh, of course." Her eyes went to the clock. "Forty-five minutes."

The longer a patient was on bypass, the more chance there was of something going wrong or the heart not restarting. He was still well within the limits. He nodded at her, frowning as he studied her again, before dismissing whatever it was that was bothering him about the newest member of his team.

She was replacing Miriam Steffani, who had just had a child and decided not to return to work for an indefinite amount of time. He'd long ago made a decision not to have children. Not to have permanent relationships. Medical school had taught him more than just medicine. As had his father.

And as the only surgeon on the island who performed this particular procedure, he was in high demand, and Diego wasn't willing to do what his dad had done and keep impossible hours while leaving his two young sons with his wife and expecting her to raise them.

Diego loved what he did, and after missing a girlfriend's birthday due to his hectic schedule, and discovering she'd found solace in someone else's arms, he knew he couldn't have it both ways. And to think otherwise would be selfish. That resolve had cost him his last relationship and probably any other relationship he might have in the future. Although he tried to make it clear that he wasn't interested in more than sharing a bed. Dammit. Not the time or place to think about this. Nor what had led him to have a one-night stand in a bar several weeks ago. A very hot one-night stand. His eyes shifted to the perfusionist before he yanked them back to the open chest in front of him.

"I'm ready for the donor valve."

Sometimes a valve taken from a pig or cow was used, but a human heart had come available at the last minute, so Diego had opted for that. It was the easiest transition and meant that blood thinners might not be needed.

The nurse in charge of the valve carefully transferred it out of the insulated container and handed it over. "Okay, here we go." This was the most delicate part, hoping that the replacement valve—which wasn't always an exact match size-wise—could be grafted into place with minimal adjustments.

He eyed the opening in the heart and the valve. The new valve was pretty damned close, maybe a hair too big. But that was better than it being much smaller than the patient's own valve had been.

Carefully setting the valve in place, he made a slight adjustment and then called for the suture material. With fine, even stitches, he tested the tension of each one as he went, making sure there were no gaps that could cause a bleed later on. He also wanted a smooth joining that wouldn't encourage the formation of blood clots the way a puckered surface might. Twenty minutes later, the new valve was secured in place. He checked and double-checked both valve replacements before preparing to transfer control from bypass to the patient's own heart.

"Let's restore blood flow." He glanced up in time to see the perfusionist nod. Together they walked through the sequence of events, and within a minute the heart began beating on its own, even though it wasn't actually pumping blood yet. That would come in a minute. Diego gave another check to make sure the rhythm was even before saying, "Diverting flow to heart."

The first chamber of the heart filled and pumped with no leakage in any of the sutured vessels. They waited another minute or two and Diego said, "Let's wean her off the support."

The transfer of power was smooth, with the perfusionist handing the work back over to the patient's repaired organ. He allowed a smile. "Good job, thank you."

Then it was all about removing the rib spreaders and wiring the sternum back together before suturing muscle and tissue in layers.

There. Done.

He glanced at the clock. Five hours. Not bad for replacing two valves. He took a step back and let the nurses start clearing away the surgical field.

"Excellent work, people." He let his gaze travel the room, noting the exhaustion on several of the faces. The perfusionist was busy at her table, flushing lines and discarding consumable items. She didn't look up this time. It was as if she'd dismissed him now that her part of the surgery was over. That was okay—he'd catch her when she left the room. He really had been rude not to formally introduce himself, and he couldn't keep referring to her as The Perfusionist. He should have at least looked up her name before stepping into the room. Yet another misstep on his part.

Once the patient stirred from the anesthesia and answered a simple question, he stripped off his PPE and exited the room. He would check on her again in recovery. But for now, he waited outside the door to the surgical suite, waiting as the patient was wheeled out, followed by each member of the team. Then there was

no one. There was no way she could have made it past
him without him seeing her, so with a frown he reen-
tered the room. There she was. Still in her mask and
surgical cap.

He went over to her, wondering if she was okay. Normally once the patient left, there was no need to keep
on face masks. Except she'd removed her gloves. When
she saw him, her eyes closed for a second before reopening…as if she'd been hoping he was already gone.

"I was rude," he said. "I didn't introduce myself or
welcome you. I'm Diego Pintor. And you must be…"

There was a marked pause before she said in a low
voice, "I'm Bree Frost."

There it was again, the strange undertones to her accent he'd noticed earlier, especially when she said her
name. It wasn't a traditional Italian name, either. He put
the pieces together.

He frowned, realizing what it was. "You're American?"

She nodded, and a weird churning started up in his
gut. "My father works on the military base in Naples."

Naples. He'd been right about that. Then he backed
up to the part about her father. And the fact that she
was American.

Oh, hell, no. It couldn't be. The person from that
night six weeks ago had been American. It had come
through in a few of their more intimate moments. Suddenly he had to know. "Surgery's done. You can take
off your hat. Your mask."

She blinked, then slowly reached up and tugged her
mask down. Pink lips appeared. Lips he vividly remembered kissing. Lips that had kissed him…and more.

Then came the hat, and red hair came into view, although it was pulled back in a bun this afternoon. But there now was no mistaking who she was.

A tiny hint of anger spiraled up his chest. He'd had women throw themselves at him before, once they realized who he was. But he could have sworn there'd been no sense of recognition on her face that night in the bar. But there was only one way to find out. "Did you know who I was when I came into the bar?"

"What? No." Her teeth came down and bit her lip. "I had no idea. And I certainly wouldn't have…"

Her voice faded away, leaving him to fill in the blanks. He switched to English to prevent anyone who walked by from easily understanding the conversation. "You wouldn't have what? Slept with me?"

She stared at him for a moment. "Of course not. I had no idea we would be working together—or that we would even see each other again. I was in the middle of a crisis the week I was here on the island. I hadn't planned on coming back once I left, but then again—" her fingers clenched together, twisting as she continued "—I hadn't planned on applying for a job when I was here, either."

"So why did you?" He knew he sounded abrupt, but the thought of working with someone he'd slept with? Whom he thought he'd never see again? Well, it was damned inconvenient. Especially with the way the memories of their bodies straining together were flickering through his head like an old movie. And those memories were having a strange effect on him. One he didn't like.

"I—I needed a change of scenery."

Surely she hadn't come back hoping to somehow find him. "A change of scenery as in location? Or people?"

"Location." She closed her eyes for several seconds before reopening them. There was something about the color of them that made him want to stare at her. Her voice, though, pulled him back. "And people. Listen, I had no idea you worked at the hospital. In fact, I thought you might be a tourist, too, and that our paths would never cross again. To realize the doctor doing surgery was the same person who…" She glanced away.

"Which is why you didn't want to come out of the operating room. And why you kept your mask on. Surely you realized I would eventually see your face?"

She sighed. "I knew you would. I just hoped you wouldn't recognize me. And if you did, I wanted time to decide what to do."

"Do?"

"I think maybe I should resign. Go back to Naples. Or at least go somewhere else."

The thought that he might have made this hard for her—hard enough for her to give up a new job—didn't sit well with him. "Don't do that. We slept together. So what? As long as you don't want more than that, we're fine."

"Of course I don't want more than that." This time the anger was on her side. "Why do you think I wouldn't tell you my name that night?"

That was right. She hadn't. He'd introduced himself as Diego but hadn't included his last name. Then again, he'd been drinking. And so had she, so things were a bit muddled in his head. At least about what had transpired before they left the bar. What they had done afterward remained crystal clear. So clear that he had dreamed about her for a couple of weeks after their encounter.

"Let's reintroduce ourselves, then. As colleagues, this time." He held out his hand in the American form of greeting. "I'm Dr. Diego Pintor, chief of surgery here at the hospital."

She smiled and took his hand, the turning up of lips doing crazy things to his head. And when a dimple formed on the left side of her cheek, giving her an impish air, he had to release his grip to keep himself from reaching out to touch that mysterious crease.

"Nice to meet you. I'm Breandan Frost. Most people call me Bree, though, and I don't normally wear a mask when not working."

"Except in front of me."

"Evidently." Her smile widened. "And thanks for not getting any weird thoughts."

Weird thoughts. Did picturing the way she'd looked naked come under the category of weird? Yes. And inappropriate. But this situation was going to be salvageable. At least he hoped it would.

"No weird thoughts other than it's nice to finally know your name. Mystery solved."

Was it? There was still that life crisis she'd talked about, whatever that had been. But he wasn't going to ask. He'd been going through a type of crisis of his own. Or more like a reaffirmation of what he didn't want out of life—like a repeat of his own childhood. So he and his latest girlfriend—who had broached the subject of having a family and moving in together—had called it quits, and Diego had gone to the bar to seal that decision. And sleeping with someone else had seemed the perfect way to do that.

"Yes. Mystery solved." Some odd expression came over her face, and she blinked. "Would you excuse me, please?"

"Yes, of course."

Bree Frost whirled away from him and started down the hallway, her steps quick and light. A moment later, she disappeared around the corner, leaving him standing there puzzling over this whole strange encounter and wondering what had fueled her decision to leave Naples and come to Sicily. But that was something he had no intention of asking her.

CHAPTER TWO

BREE DRIED HER face with paper towels, glad that the splash of cold water had chased away the nausea and dread that had surged up as she'd been talking with Diego. She hadn't actually gotten sick, but for a second she'd thought she might, which was why she'd felt like she had to get away.

Leaning her hands on the sink, she stared at her reflection in the mirror. She was paler than normal, but other than that, there seemed to be nothing out of the ordinary.

Just this morning, though, her father had texted her letting her know that a formal investigation of Sergio's financials was underway. He wanted her to know before she read about it in the media. She'd immediately googled Serge's name and seen the report. Evidently the tabloids were telling the truth. Except this time, rather than the blonde, this report had included a picture of them from the day of their engagement party. She was smiling up at him, wholly unaware of what was going to happen in a few months' time.

She vaguely wondered if this meant his family would drop their lawsuits against the other papers.

No wonder she didn't feel well. The news combined with the shock of seeing the man she'd slept with less than two days after her fiancé's death… What kind of person was she?

Never make life-changing decisions when you're grieving.

Wasn't that the advice they gave people? And now she'd made two—having a one-night stand and moving to an island where she knew no one.

Except only one of those decisions was a life changer, and that was moving to Sicily. Right now, though, she was glad she was far away from Naples. Glad she hadn't told anyone except her family where she was going, and she knew good and well they weren't going to reveal where she was. Hopefully the papers wouldn't renew their interest in her.

That shook her. Would they?

"Sergio, why?"

She swallowed. Was the car accident that claimed his life…? Had he…?

No. The Sergio she knew had loved life. It had to be a freak accident. He'd been trying to outrun whatever demons had been chasing him and had lost control of his car.

Well, nowadays newspapers were almost passé, even in Italy. Undoubtedly someone would eventually figure out who she was, but hopefully whatever the investigation was, it would blow over, since they couldn't prosecute a dead man.

And if didn't?

Another wave of nausea surfaced, making her drop her head and close her eyes until it passed. Fortunately, she didn't have any more scheduled surgeries today. She wasn't sure she wanted to face Diego or anyone else until she pulled herself together.

If she didn't know better, she'd say she was having an anxiety attack. She'd only had one other one and that had been the night of the wedding, when she'd found out her groom had not only lied, had not only fled the scene leaving her standing there in a state of shock, but he'd also cheated on her.

So what did she do?

For one thing, she was going to spend what was left of the day familiarizing herself with hospital policy and do some of the exploring she hadn't been able to do yesterday. And she was going to try not to think about the fact that six weeks ago, she'd spent her very last night with Sergio and soon afterward she'd had to face the reality that she was never going to see him again. Ever.

Once she got through this, she'd feel better. At least, that was her hope. If she didn't, then the next several weeks were going to be filled with trying to keep people from seeing the dark circles under her eyes and trying to feign that all was right with the world when it wasn't. And when she wasn't sure it ever would be again.

Diego booted up the computer on his desk and waited as it shifted through a screenshot of some kind of natural wonder of the world that was supposed to tempt you to click on it to learn more. Mount Etna was the only point in nature that he wanted to keep track of. One of the world's still-active volcanoes, it deposited quite a bit of ash on the island, sometimes more than others. And the plume of smoke coming from one several craters was thicker today that it had been yesterday.

His valve replacement patient from yesterday was doing fine—he'd checked on her in recovery about an hour ago, and she was stable, no signs of complications so far. And he had a two-hour lull before his next set of patients, unless he was called down for an emergency.

He clicked past the opening screen, typing in his password. Today's news flashed across the screen. His finger pulled the cursor to the top right of the screen to get off the internet when something caught his eyes. The CFO of one of the major hotel chains was under investigation for something. That's not what had grabbed his attention, though. Instead, it was the image just under the headlines.

Manache! A red-haired woman smiled up in adoration at a man, her hand splayed across his abdomen. On her ring finger was a huge rock. He froze. It was an engagement ring. His glance swept back to her face, hoping against hope that he was wrong, then he spied a telltale dimple. Even if she was just a lookalike, what were the chances that she'd have that exact dimple on her left cheek?

He'd slept with an engaged woman? There'd been no ring on her finger that night. The chill turned to anger.

His eyes raced back to the headline:

Dead CFO of Exclusive Marquis Hotel Chain Under Investigation.

The man was dead. Car accident. Diego slumped forward half in relief, scouring the story to see when the man had died. Did it make a difference? Hell, yes. It was the difference between Bree cheating on a troubled fiancé and her drowning her grief in booze and sex.

A day. He'd died a day before their encounter. A day after she was supposed to have married this man.

She'd said she was going through a life crisis. No kidding.

Had she found out about the investigation and called off the wedding? Unless he planned on asking her that question, he would probably never know. What he did know was that other people at the hospital were going to find out about this, so he hoped she was ready for sympathetic noises coming at her from all sides and maybe some hard questions. Maybe he should make sure.

Why? It was none of his business.

But her face and the way she'd tried to hide her identity from him had sent a wave of compassion through him. And that undulating emotion was back, urging him to warn her. She might not welcome it, but at least he would feel like he'd given her a heads-up.

He picked up his cell phone before realizing he didn't have her number. So he dialed the central number to the hospital and waited for someone to respond.

"This is Diego Pintor. Could you page Dr. Frost for me and ask her to give me a call?"

"Certainly."

"Thanks." He set his phone down on the desk and read the article from top to bottom. Sergio Morenz had managed the hotel with his dad for the past fifteen years. It looked like his father was denying that his son could be involved in skimming funds from the chain, but evidently the police thought the story had some

credibility. And he'd stood Bree up at her wedding before running his car into a telephone pole. Suicide? The
thought went through his head, even though the story
didn't spell that out. But he pictured Bree in her wedding gown waiting on a groom who never showed up.

Accidenti. He could see why she'd needed to get
away, saw why she'd wanted a change in venue. Was
she involved in whatever her fiancé had been up to?

He didn't think so. The story was dated yesterday
morning and made no mention of her other than a brief
paragraph about their wedding.

His phone chirped, and a city code from outside Sicily appeared across his screen. That had to be her.

"Pintor here."

"Hi, this is Bree. You wanted me to call?"

"Yes." He paused, the words on the tip of his tongue
before swallowing them down. This wasn't something
that should be done over the phone. So he changed what
he'd been about to say. "Would you have time to come
up to my office?"

"Your office?"

The surprise he heard in her voice…

Dio Santo! Did she think he wanted her there for sex?

"I need to speak with you about something. I'd rather
not do it over the phone."

There was a long pause, then she said. "Okay, can
you tell me where you're located?"

"Third floor, number three twenty-two."

"I'll be there in about five minutes."

He said goodbye and then sat back in his chair,
staring at his computer screen. Was he doing the right
thing? His fingers scraped through his hair in a rough

gesture, and he realized he hadn't gotten it cut in a while. Not that it mattered. He'd always worn it a little longer than was conventional. More out of lack of time than anything else.

It was almost ten minutes before she knocked on his door. "*Entrare.*" He switched to English. "Come in."

Bree barely opened the door, sliding in and pressing her back against it to shut it with a soft click. "You wanted to see me?"

She was pale, her face drawn, looking very different from the woman in the photograph. There was no dimple. No smile. In fact, she looked almost…ill.

"Are you okay?"

She made a sound that he took to mean yes.

Now that she was here, he had no idea how to broach the subject. A subject that was very much not his business.

"Sit." Realizing it sounded like a command, he softened the word. "Please."

Gliding over to one of the no-nonsense chairs in front of his desk, she did as he asked, although she didn't lean back and make herself comfortable. Instead, she looked like she could take flight at any moment. She didn't have on scrubs, like she'd worn in the operating room. Instead, she was wearing a floral blouse with some kind of fluttery little things that might have passed for sleeves, leaving her smooth shoulders on display, freckles scattered across her skin. The island summers were going to do a number on her.

Her hair wasn't confined in a bun today, but instead flowed down her back. This was the woman he recognized from the night at the bar. "No surgeries today?"

"Not so far. But perfusion is used for more than just surgical procedures."

"Of course." ECMO had been used during COVID to help rest lungs ravaged by the virus, and it could do the same for heart conditions like infective endocarditis and some lung diseases. The idea was to give tissue time to heal.

"Do we have another patient?" she asked.

"No. Before I say anything, I want you to know I'm not trying to pry, but this came up when I opened my browser." He refreshed his computer screen and turned the laptop to face her.

If he'd thought she was pale before, now her face drained of any remaining color.

"My dad called to warn me yesterday morning, and I looked it up."

So she already knew.

"I just want to say I'm sorry for your loss." Hell, he was doing the sympathetic noise thing that he'd been trying to prepare her for.

"Thank you." Her hands gripped together on the edge of his desk. "His death was sudden, and I had no idea about…that." She motioned toward the screen. "We were supposed to be married the day he died."

She didn't say anything about her fiancé standing her up.

He nodded, choosing his words carefully. "I wanted to let you know, in case other staff members see it. I thought you might want to prepare yourself for the possibility."

"I will. Thank you again. I didn't advertise that I was coming to Sicily, so hopefully reporters won't be able to find me and cause trouble for the hospital. I can't imagine why they would want to. I had no clue about Sergio's business dealings, although maybe I should have."

"Let me know if there's anything I can do. As head of surgery, I have a little bit of pull as far as the hospital goes."

"Thank you. I appreciate that. The last several weeks have been hard."

"I imagine. What made you want to come to Sicily?"

"After the wedding that never happened, I had the airline tickets in my purse, and the hotel reservations had already been made. I needed an escape, so I came. That was supposed to have been our honeymoon."

Before he could stop himself, he leaned forward in his chair and covered her hand with his. "Again, I'm so sorry. If I did anything that night that was inappropriate…"

"You didn't. Like I said, I needed to escape. You helped me do that. At least for part of a night." Her lips tipped up for a second before returning to neutral.

It was on the tip of his tongue to tell her that he'd needed to escape as well, but this was about her, not him. "How can I help now?"

She shook her head. "I don't think there's anything you—or anyone else—can do. I just have to hope the press loses interest quickly. Or at least in anything to do with me." A frown marred her brows. "If you think this will cause problems for the hospital, please tell me and—"

"It won't cause problems."

"And if someone finds out that I came here six weeks

ago and remembers us leaving the bar or arriving at the hotel?"

He hadn't thought about that. But that wasn't her responsibility. She hadn't forced him to spend the night with her. They were both responsible for their actions. But it might make working together tricky. Fortunately, he didn't do the hiring and firing at the hospital, so it wouldn't look like some kind of pay-to-play situation where she slept with him to gain favor or vice versa.

"We tell the truth. That we're two consenting adults and that it's none of their damn business."

Her dimple reappeared. "I like the way you think."

He realized he was still touching her, and a current of electricity sizzled up his arm, arcing toward places that had the words *Consenting Adults* written all over them. He took his hand away under the pretext of turning his computer back around to face him. "I've always felt it better to play it straight with people."

He'd made it a point to do that, especially in his encounters with the opposite sex.

"I agree. And if Sergio had—" her shoulders twitched in what might have been a shrug "—well, wishing won't change anything at this point. So your thought is that we don't volunteer information, but if someone guesses, we don't bother denying it, either. Is that right?"

"That's what I'm saying. Are we in agreement?"

"Yes."

"Great." He leaned his elbows on his desk and looked at her. "If you start getting harassing phone calls, you'll let me know?"

"It's not your job to take care of my personal life."

"No, but it's my job to make sure you're not kept from doing what you need to for your job."

Bree sighed. "I really appreciate it. But I certainly hope it won't come to that."

"So do I. But you'll let me know."

"I will, I promise." She paused. "How is our patient?"

"She's doing great." With that, the conversation turned back toward the professional realm, and Diego was relieved. He'd done his duty, and that was that.

All he could hope was that they could leave what had happened in the past, where no member of the press— or anyone else—would dig it up again.

A week later, the nausea that had been like background noise for Bree was back with a vengeance.

She'd been under a lot of stress as the news of Sergio's exploits seemed to loom larger and more horrible by the day. Not only was the press digging into his professional life, but they'd discovered the juicy tidbits about his private life as well. And these weren't just the tabloids, but respected outlets. He hadn't had just one woman on the side, he'd had lots. Most of them call girls.

While he and Bree had been together.

And she'd had no idea. How could she have been so blind?

Even thinking those words made a flood of bile rush up her throat. She'd slept with him the night before the wedding. Thank heavens no one had expected her to go to his funeral, since too many people knew he'd been seen leaving he church parking lot on his way away from the wedding, not to it.

On the way to one of his escorts' houses?

Thinking like this would do her no good at all.

It was a horrible mess. She'd had her IUD removed two weeks before their wedding because Sergio had wanted to start a family right away, as soon as the wedding was in the books. She'd been so excited about the thought of a baby.

What if she'd gotten pregnant during that time? Thankfully, he'd used a condom so that people wouldn't try to count months…after all, his family was highly respected in Italy.

Ha! Maybe they were, but Sergio? Not so much. Not anymore. How could he be so very different from the man he'd portrayed himself as?

The queasiness got stronger. Ugh. Wandering into the bathroom, she opened the door to the vanity to get a washcloth and saw a box of unopened hygiene products. She'd bought them before arriving on the island.

She hadn't had a period since her IUD had been removed. That would have been…

She counted back to her doctor's appointment. Eight weeks ago. She swallowed. Her doctor had told her it could take up to six weeks for her periods to start up again. She'd passed that threshold by two weeks now.

Oh, God, she couldn't be pregnant. Not after everything that had happened. How many times had they had sex since it had been removed? Seven? Eight times?

Another thought came to mind, causing her to press the back of her hand against her mouth. She'd had sex with Diego during that time as well. More than once on that night. Three times. They'd used condoms, but what about the time spent swapping them out? She'd been so used to the extra protection afforded by her IUD that she hadn't given it any thought.

Until now.

With shaking hands, she grabbed the washcloth and wet it, drawing the cool cloth over her face and pressing it against her temples.

Surely not. Surely her body was still just adjusting. Six weeks was an estimate. She was just an outlier on that scale of norms. Right?

There was a history of blood clots in her family, so she'd opted not to go on the pill after having the device removed.

Because Sergio had wanted children right away.

And so had she.

But now? With the scandal surrounding him?

No. She did not want a kid growing up with that stigma. And the thought of carrying his child, with everything she knew now? She sank onto lid of the toilet, burying her face in her hands.

"Okay, Bree, don't panic."

She needed to get a pregnancy test and take it, just to reassure herself that all was well.

And if it wasn't? Well, she would cross that bridge when she came to it. Or maybe she would just burn it to the ground and not cross it at all.

With that thought in mind, she exited her hotel and went to look for a taxi. Walking around in this heat didn't really appeal to her, especially not with how shaky she was suddenly feeling.

She also needed to start looking for an apartment if she was going to stay on the island. She couldn't stay in the hotel forever.

Motioning to a passing taxi, she took it to the nearest grocery store and went inside, plucking up a basket as she went. She might as well pick up a few things for dinner since her hotel room had a mini kitchen in it. Except her stomach just didn't feel like food right now.

Okay, maybe just the test. She found the aisle and perused the selections, her stomach getting tighter and tighter as she thought about the possibility that she might actually be pregnant. It would certainly explain the nausea. But so could a lot of other things.

All she could do right now was hope for the best. And plan for the worst.

Deciding to forgo the food, she grabbed a test and threw it into the basket and made her way to the front of the store. There were a couple of people in line in front of her, so, hooking her basket in the crook of her arm, she used her other hand to fish around in her purse for her wallet. Finding it, she removed it, glancing to see where in line she was. The person at the register was done, so the guy in front of her moved forward, putting the things from his basket on the conveyor belt, glancing back at her.

Oh, no!

No, no, no*!* The words screamed through her head.

Diego stood there, a smile coming to his face when he saw her. "Hi. Getting something for dinner tonight?"

Her tongue stuck to the roof of her mouth, and no amount of trying would get it to budge. He glanced at her basket and stood there as his items slowly traveled away from him on the conveyor belt. For a minute no one moved.

Then his eyes slowly came up and met hers.

CHAPTER THREE

SOMEHOW, HE MANAGED to pay for his items and make his way out of the store. But *porca miseria*, there was no way he was going anywhere without some kind of explanation.

She'd had a pregnancy test in her basket.

His mind flew back over the weeks until he arrived at a number. Seven. Seven weeks since they'd slept together.

Words whipped through his head that he could not say out loud.

Maybe the test wasn't for her.

Who the hell else would it be for? She'd only moved to the island, what? A week ago?

She'd been engaged, so maybe she was worried she was carrying her fiancé's baby. Well, *merda*, Diego was worried that she might be carrying *his*!

The last thing he wanted was a child. He'd already thought that through and had come to a firm decision. No kids for him. Zero. Nonnegotiable. It was what had ended his first relationship—the one he'd had in medical school. And the mention of it had ended his last relationship. Well, he and Bree certainly did not have a relationship.

They'd used protection. That thought chanted in his head over and over again. He'd been responsible, just like he always was. But Selina had also used protection, so they'd been doubly protected.

Surely Bree had as well.

She finally came out of the store after what seemed like an eternity.

He wasted no time. "I think we need to talk."

There was no sign of her purchased item, but it was probably hidden away in her purse. Her eyes closed for a second before reopening. "Yes. I guess we do."

His insides did a quick twist that made him break out in a cold sweat.

"Not here. We can either go to a restaurant or go to my place or yours." The last thing he wanted was for what he said to be overheard.

"I don't want a public place, either. We can go to my hotel."

Had he really been hoping she would insist that this had nothing to do with him? Evidently, she wasn't so sure, because right now she looked like she was being led to the gallows.

Well, hell, that was where he felt like he was going. All that time of being so damned careful. Of being so sure he was never going to father children.

How would he even be sure it was his, if it turned out she was pregnant? He wouldn't, unless her fiancé had been sterile. Or she agreed to a paternity test.

Maybe she wasn't even planning to keep it.

Rather than bring relief, that thought made a part of

his chest tighten. He should have had a vasectomy as soon as he'd made his decision, but with his work schedule, it was hard to find the time. If he had, though, none of this would have had any bearing on him.

He swung his two grocery bags into the front seat of his car. "I'll follow you since I have no idea where you're staying, unless it's the same place you stayed the last time."

"No. It's not. I'm at the Grangier."

"Okay, I'll meet you there." He knew where the place was. It was purported to have an excellent view of Mount Etna, although he'd never stayed there, so he had no idea.

But he was glad she wasn't staying at the hotel where they'd spent the night together. He didn't want those memories clouding his judgment.

They made their way to a quiet area of town that was less touristy than some of the beach side resorts. There it was, the Grangier. An older building, there were three floors and all of them had balconies that looked fairly private. It looked more like an apartment complex than a hotel, actually. Finding a parking place in the shade and glad he hadn't bought anything at the store that would spoil in the heat, he got out of his car and met Bree in the parking lot.

"Did you buy it?"

She didn't ask what he was talking about, but instead gave a quick nod, her fingers tightening around the handle of her purse. "My room is up on the third floor."

They went up the elevator, and Bree reached in her purse, bringing out the key card and inserting it into the slot on the door. Something clicked and it swung open. Immediately Diego saw that this was more like a *monolocale* than a hotel room, since there was a kitchenette and living/bedroom all housed in the same space.

"Is this where you're planning to live while you're here?"

Her chin went up, and she stared at him for a second. "Is that a hint?"

"A hint?"

"That you would rather I leave?"

He frowned, having no idea what she meant. "Why would my question suggest that?"

She pulled in a deep breath and then let it out all at once. "I just thought if I ended up being pregnant, you might not want me working at the hospital."

"So you think you are."

She set her purse on a side table and motioned him to one of three pieces of furniture in the room, a futon and two upholstered chairs.

Choosing a chair, he sat and waited for her to do the same. When she sat on the futon, she sent him a shrug. "I don't know. Maybe. It's complicated."

Complicated was definitely one word for it. "If it turns out you are, any idea of whose it is?"

"Exactly how many partners do you think I've had?"

"I was not implying you've had many. But I can think of two."

For all he knew, it could have been months since she'd slept with her fiancé. Especially with some of the things he'd read about the man.

She bit her lip and leaned forward in her chair, bracing her forearms on her legs. "Let's not get ahead of ourselves. I might not even be. The doctor said it might be six weeks before I—"

He instantly recoiled, and she must have noticed, because her words stopped in their tracks.

"Were you on fertility drugs?" The thought that she might be trying to get pregnant—on purpose—hadn't even crossed his mind. Until just this second.

"No, but Sergio wanted children right away, as soon as we married, so I had my IUD taken out two weeks before the wedding. She said it might be six weeks before I got my period."

He did the math in his head. "And it's been eight." He didn't even want to ask this question. It was intrusive and low of him, but he needed to know. "Were you and Sergio…?"

"Intimate? Yes. And then there was you."

And then there was him. A man who'd stupidly noticed a woman in a bar who looked like she was in distress and had gone over to her. The rest was history. Or maybe not, depending on the outcome of that little test in her purse.

"We used protection."

"Yes. So did Sergio. Every time. He didn't want us getting pregnant until after the wedding so there'd be no hint of scandal." Her lips twisted. "It all seems kind of ludicrous now, after all that's happened."

He bet it did, since the dead man's name was linked to all sorts of other scandals. "What would you have done if you'd married that night, before all of this came out?"

Her eyes came up and met his. "I honestly don't know. Probably filed for an annulment. I had no idea he was involved in anything." Her hand went to her stomach in a protective move that she probably wasn't even aware of. "Does it sound awful if I say I hope it's not his?"

She was asking the wrong man. Because if it wasn't Sergio's, that only left one other possibility.

"I can understand why you wouldn't want it to be. What will you do?"

"I think I'm going to wait until I know for sure before I head down that road." She looked at him. "I'm really sorry, Diego."

"You didn't do anything wrong." But he had. There were consequences for everything in life. He'd found that out the hard way. Found out the hard way that he was just as capable of missing important occasions, just like all the band concerts, sporting events and family vacations that his father had opted to skip because of his work schedule.

And Angela had seen firsthand that the apple hadn't fallen far from the tree when he'd missed her birthday party their first semester of medical school. Only she hadn't put up with it, like his mom had. But she had paid the emotional price for his actions. And so had he.

What would his dad say if he knew he was the reason Diego didn't want children? Probably nothing. His death of a heart attack three years ago hadn't been a surprise, with the hours he put in at his job. But his mom had gotten smart after Diego and his brother were out of the house. She'd divorced him. And even then, it didn't change his father's behavior. He was just as distant toward his two boys as adults as he had been when they were younger.

"Do you mind if I take the test now, so we can get any awkwardness out of the way?"

He hadn't even considered being here. But then again, he hadn't considered this situation ever arising. Maybe it was time to make that appointment and put paid to this ever happening again. "You do what you feel you need to do."

In the end, it wasn't up to him to decide what she did if she was pregnant. What he did get to do was decide what part he would play if the test came back positive and if she decided not to terminate.

Those green eyes looked into his for a long moment, and it was all he could do not to look away. One thing he knew was he wasn't going to opt for his father's route and be an absentee parent. He was either all in. Or all out.

She finally broke the silence. "Do you want coffee? Something to drink?"

So she was going to do it. Take the test. Right here, right now. "I think I'm good. Thanks."

"I'll be back in a few minutes." Picking up her purse, she headed toward a door at the back of the room. It clicked shut, and he took a deep breath, blowing it out to release some of the tension that had been growing in his head. Except it was still there. Still revolving around a central question.

Did he have it in him to actually be a father? A real one?

He had no idea right now. So all he could do was wait and see what the results were.

* * *

Bree stood in the bathroom after taking the test, not sure why on earth she'd suggested he wait. She could feel his presence out there in the other room—had seen the trepidation in his eyes when he realized it might be his.

When she'd said she wanted to get this over with, she thought she could answer both their questions in one fell swoop, but since she wasn't sure what she wanted to do if the test were positive, or what she even *could* do here in Italy…

God. She'd wanted a baby just as badly as Sergio had seemed to. But could she carry through with it, knowing it might be his? How many partners had the man had over the course of their engagement?

But this baby would be half hers and wholly raised by her. Surely that would cancel out Sergio's influence other than just contributing DNA to the process.

The stick sat a foot or so away from where she stood. Ten minutes had passed. She was going to have to look at it at some point. And poor Diego was sitting out there waiting to hear the verdict. So, leaning over, she pulled the test toward her. One line would mean life would go on as it had for both her and Diego. Two lines would mean…

She looked at the readout. One bold blue line and… one slightly lighter line.

Pregnant. She was pregnant.

Gripping the test, she sank to the floor and stared at it, eyes blurring.

No crying, Bree.

There were noninvasive paternity tests nowadays that could be done during pregnancy that might at least put Diego's mind at ease. And she could know once and for all who the father was. But would it change her decision?

She didn't think so. But it would undoubtedly make a difference to Diego.

All she could do was go out there and face him, taking the test stick with her to prove she wasn't lying.

Why would he think she would? She didn't even know Diego. Not really. He'd been a wonderful lover the night they'd been together, but that didn't mean he wanted to father a child with her.

In fact, she'd never even asked him if he wanted kids. And the look on his face in the supermarket…

Holding the test down at her side, she quietly opened the door.

He hadn't heard her, that was evident in his posture, so she took a few seconds to study him. He was no longer in his chair. Instead he was over by the door to the balcony, looking out. He was unmoving, hands balled up by his sides, and his spine was rigid. It wasn't the view of Mount Etna he was thinking about. It was the result of the test.

She'd kept him waiting long enough.

"Diego."

He immediately turned around, his gaze on her face rather than what was in her hand. "It was positive."

It wasn't a question. It was a statement. "Yes. I am more than willing to do a paternity test."

He gave a visible swallow. "You're going to have the baby."

She realized she'd already come to a decision.

"I think so, yes." She walked over to him and touched

his hand. "But this is a choice I'm making on my own. I would never presume that you agree or disagree. Or to play any role in the child's life, unless you want to."

He dragged a hand through his hair, causing the waves to turn riotous, making him look much younger than he probably was. Yet another thing she didn't know about him.

"How can I just sit back and do nothing?" he said.

Bree didn't think the question was directed at her, but rather at himself.

"You don't have to make any decisions right now. But think it through. Deliberately. Carefully. Did you plan to have children at some point?"

He hesitated, his glance going to her midsection before returning to her face. Then he slowly shook his head. "I'd decided not to."

He hadn't wanted children. At all?

"Then don't let this change that. There are a lot of single mothers out there."

"You are sure this is what you want. To have this baby, knowing what you know now about your fiancé?"

She paused before answering. "I think I do. I'm not getting any younger, and I have a lot of love to give. I have a stable position that I can continue to work at up until I'm ready to give birth. I'll need to get a house, of course, but there'd be plenty of time…"

She realized she was babbling, but it was something she tended to do when nervous. If she had thought about it a little more, she realized she could have just kept quiet about being pregnant until later, and then when it was obvious, she could have pretended the baby was

Sergio's and not put the decision on Diego at all. But would lying have been fair to him?

Besides, he'd seen that test in her basket and her brain hadn't been fully engaged when he'd told her they needed to talk. To have claimed Sergio as the father might have come across as totally unbelievable. He was a very intelligent man.

But he also didn't want kids.

Bree had always been a free spirit, not feeling the need to settle down with any man. She'd been fully fine with adopting or going to a sperm clinic when she did decide to have kids. But somehow Sergio had changed those plans. She realized she'd become almost a different person when she was with him. One she didn't necessarily like.

Little by little he'd made more and more of the decisions for her. And she'd let him. That wasn't like her at all.

When had that happened?

She wasn't sure. But what she did know was that it was time to take back control over her life and destiny and be true to herself. No matter what Diego chose to do. Or not do.

"Listen. No one knows we were together that night. We can just assume the baby is Sergio's and go about our lives. No one will know anything different."

"I would know."

Those words hit her in the pit of her stomach. They were low and rumbly and filled with just enough accusation in them to keep her knees from turning wobbly.

What did he mean by that?

"But if you don't want kids, wouldn't it be better

to leave it ambiguous so that no one knows for sure who the father is? I don't know why you decided kids weren't for you, and I don't need to know. But I don't want you to feel pressured to take on a role you don't want. In fact, I'd rather you didn't, unless you're very sure you want to."

When he just looked at her, she bit her lip and continued. "Look, I know this is a lot to take in. And we don't even know that it's yours, is what I'm trying to say. We could leave it that way. Or we could meet again later and talk some more. No pressure."

He turned and glanced back out the window. "Yes, I think meeting again is a good idea. Maybe in a more neutral location. Have you been out to see Mount Etna yet?"

The change in subject threw her for a second. "No, but I thought I'd take a trip up there on one of my days off."

"Why don't we have our next meeting there?" He turned back to face her and then stepped closer, his hand touching the one that still held the pregnancy test. "And for what it's worth, I'm sorry for whatever part I played in this. Truly."

The warmth of his fingers took away some of the chill that had nothing to do with the air-conditioning in the room. "Don't be, Diego. I think what happened that night helped clear my head. Helped me see things with different eyes."

It was true. She'd been trapped in a fairy tale that wasn't rooted in reality. Coming to Sicily alone and sleeping with Diego had helped pop that bubble once and for all, setting her free.

His palm cupped her cheek. "I'm sorry that life dealt you such a sucky hand in Sergio."

The sincerity in his voice made a lump form in her throat.

"At least something good has come of it. I got a job in a place I'm coming to love." She leaned into his touch for a moment before pulling away, afraid she would get caught up in yet another fairy tale. This time one that couldn't come true. She didn't want to be with a man who didn't want kids. Because she did want them. And whether she parented those children on her own or with a partner was something that wouldn't be decided in these few moments. That partner wouldn't be him, so she did not need to get emotionally involved with someone who was out of reach and who wanted different things than she did. "I think going to Mount Etna is a good idea. How long do you want to take to think things through…to decide whether you want to know the baby's paternity or not? To me, it doesn't really matter."

Not entirely true, but true enough not to be a complete lie.

"How about next Tuesday?" He took an audible breath and then said. "But one thing is sure. I *do* want to know, Bree. And if I am the father, I want to bear some of the financial burden, even if you think it's best that I'm not actively involved in the baby's life."

"Absolutely not. I'm fine with you knowing who the father is. But if *you* choose not to take an active role in this child's life, then that's on you, not me. And if that's the case, I'd rather you not have any role at all, financial or otherwise."

CHAPTER FOUR

HE TEXTED HER two days later and asked if she'd be willing to go to Palermo to do the paternity testing. He'd done some research into the timing, and it appeared they could do it this early in the pregnancy. They didn't have to go together. And they probably wouldn't have the results back in time for their trip to Mount Etna, but at least they would be on their way to getting an answer. And he could think through what she'd said about it being on him if he didn't want to take an active role.

Did he really think it was okay to bear some of the financial burden while shouldering none of the emotional burden? Wasn't that exactly what his father had done?

He'd said it to be helpful, but her response had been right on target, and it had been the correct one. If he couldn't be all in, then he shouldn't dip his toe into the pool at all.

How had he felt, knowing his dad had left money for his education? He hadn't wanted it. Had in fact given the entire sum to charity and had worked his way through medical school entirely on his own.

So how could Diego have made that kind of an offer? Guilt? He wasn't sure.

His phone pinged, and he glanced down at his desk where it lay. It was Bree.

Yes, I can do that. Do I need to make an appointment?

Even wanting the test done far away from his hometown was telling. But if the baby wasn't his, it would prevent rumors from making their way through the hospital. And with Selina living in the same town, it could turn ugly. After all, she'd mentioned children, and he'd shut her down. Had stopped spending time with her.

And if it turned out he was the father?

Then let the rumors fly. And he would tell Selina the truth—that it was an accident.

He picked up the phone.

We don't have to go together if it would be easier for you.

Yes. That might be easier. If you could make the arrangements, it might make it less complicated, since I'm sure I'll need your permission anyway for the results.

They settled on a day that would be better for her.

Don't forget to keep your schedule clear next Tuesday.

This time his phone rang. It was Bree. "Hi."

"I thought this might be easier than continuing to text. Are you sure you still want to go?"

"I am. I don't want to put things off too long." He didn't. The longer he drew this thing out, the harder it was going to be. Not just for him. But for her, too, as she made plans for the future.

"All right. Do you want to leave from the hospital?"

"How about if I pick you up and drop you home afterward? It would save you a trip and your hotel is on my way."

There was a pause. "I've been looking at houses, actually, so I'm not sure I'll be here on Tuesday."

That was fast. So she was going to move forward with or without his decision. But it made sense, since she'd want to have a more permanent space for the baby. "Any luck?"

"I saw a couple of nice ones yesterday. I'm kind of partial to the view here at the hotel, but I know that's not likely to happen wherever I live."

"Don't count it out just yet. My house has a view of the mountain."

"Interesting. I'll keep looking, then."

The thought crossed his mind to ask her if she wanted to move in with him, but he froze his jaw. That was crazy. He didn't know her. And he liked living alone. It was another of the reasons he and Selina had broken things off. She'd wanted to move in together, and the fact that that thought had never crossed his mind was telling.

Maybe because he'd moved in with his girlfriend from medical school and that had been a disaster. He'd barely had time for her. And then on her birthday, when he'd told her he didn't have time to celebrate with her, he'd changed his mind at the last minute and had come home to find her with someone else. That had shown him just how terrible he was at relationships.

And yet here he was about to make a life-changing decision about another kind of relationship—this one involving a child—in less than a week's time.

He couldn't offer to let her move in, but maybe he could steer her in the direction of available houses, if she was willing to let him help. "Do you want me to go with you to look at houses?"

"Why?"

The question was blunt but not unexpected. "Because I know this city and have a good idea what fair prices should look like."

There was a pause. "Let's talk about that on Tuesday, too."

Meaning she didn't want to talk about it now. "Sounds good. Are you scrubbing in on my surgery today?"

He had a heart bypass patient scheduled who might or might not need to go on a heart/lung machine. It depended on how close to the heart he would need to get in rerouting the blood supply.

"I am, so I'll see you this afternoon?"

"Yep. I'll see you then." With that, they said their goodbyes.

Diego leaned back in his chair and looked at the phone. If he decided not to parent, he needed to stick to that decision and not waver. Because it wasn't fair to Bree or the baby to have him duck in and out of their lives. And he was pretty sure she would cut him off the first time he tried to do that.

So if ever he needed to detach his emotions and make a rational, thoughtful decision, it was now. And that's what he planned to do.

* * *

The surgery yesterday had gone well. So well that they hadn't needed to put the patient on the bypass machine, so she'd been able to watch Diego work. His hands were sure and confident. No second-guessing with this man. So she could bet when he made a decision, he didn't back down from it.

That actually helped her to feel better. Because whereas she could be all over the place as far as thinking and rethinking and triple thinking, Diego evidently didn't. So she wouldn't have to worry about him changing his mind midstream.

After the surgery he'd told her that he'd been able to get them both appointments for paternity testing today. They could drive separately, since he knew that was her preference. But in keeping with her personality, she told him it was okay, that they could ride together if he thought that would help the process.

So here she was standing in front of the hospital waiting for him to pick her up. It didn't take long to see someone creeping up to the curb in a sleek sports car. Sergio had been all about those. In fact, speed had been a factor in the single-car accident that claimed his life. She tensed. Would Diego feel the need to go fast as well?

She slid into the passenger seat, the leather cradling her in a way that somehow reassured her. Buckling herself in, she glanced at him. "How far is Palermo from here?"

"About a two-hour drive. I thought we might stop on the way back and get something to eat."

"Thanks, that would be great." She hadn't felt much

like eating today, but having him drive actually took some of the pressure off her to get there and find the place.

"Looks like it's blood draws for both of us, since it's still early in the pregnancy."

She turned to look at him. "Are you sure you want to do this?"

A hint of a frown appeared. "Do what? Find out who the father is? Absolutely."

It would undoubtedly save him some angst in decision making if it turned out the baby wasn't his. And if the baby was?

Then Diego had a decision to make. She'd already made hers. And this was one decision she wasn't waffling on.

The bangles on her wrist jingled as she clasped her hands together.

"You were smart in bringing a change of clothes to work."

"You look fine," she said. "I had on scrubs and clogs. At least you look like an ordinary citizen."

He did. He had on a white button-down shirt that was loose and flowing and reminded her of an artist's attire. All he lacked were the cream linen slacks and bare feet.

She'd like him barefooted.

A shiver ran over her as her mind conjured up an image of Diego with his curly hair mussed from sleep, sitting on a bar stool with the clothes she'd just thought of. Only the shirt would be undone, revealing a hint of the dragon she'd seen tattooed on his upper right arm the night they'd been together. His feet—tanned and naked—might be propped on the stool's footrest. He would reach for her hips and pull her toward him, his eyes searching hers. And as their bodies connected, she would feel every inch of his...

She shook herself back to the present with a sense of horror, her face burning as she realized he'd asked her something.

"I'm sorry, I missed that."

"I asked if you'd had any luck finding a house?"

"Oh, I think so. I was going to run it by you, since you said you know about pricing and the areas in the city. Maybe when we're waiting on them to call us in for our tests." And she needed to check on whether or not the house had bar stools.

A laugh came out before she could stop it.

"Something funny about that?"

"No, sorry." She needed to stop this before he figured out what she was thinking about. Maybe she would do better to worry about what the results of the test would be. She hadn't wanted it to be Sergio's, but maybe it was better that it was. She could honestly tell her son or daughter that their father had died in a car accident, rather than figure out how to explain that Diego simply hadn't wanted to be a father.

He glanced at her. "Where is it?"

"It?"

"The house."

Of course. What else would he be talking about? "About three blocks west of where I'm staying now."

"That's not too far from where I live. We can drive by it when we're done in Palermo, if you'd like."

Maybe coming together wasn't such a good idea. Her nerves were acting up. But at least her stomach had been stable so far this afternoon. "I don't want to inconvenience you."

"It won't be. Is the view what you were hoping for?"

"Yes, it has a nice big balcony off the upstairs bedroom. There's even a ceiling fan out there and plenty of shade."

He glanced over. "It sounds ideal. There's another bedroom for the...baby, I take it."

There'd been an awkward pause before he said the word. If he couldn't even bring himself to utter *baby*, how would he be when there was an actual human being to go along with that word?

She fiddled with her bracelets, the clinking sound helping to calm her.

"Yep, it has three bedrooms. It'll be nice to have a little more space than the hotel, which is more like a studio—what is the word in Italian?"

"*Monolocale* is I think what you call a studio. You have a great view at the hotel, though."

"It is pretty spectacular. The house I'm looking at has a view of Etna, but it isn't as clear a line of sight as the hotel. Probably because the house is only two stories high and is attached to neighboring homes on both sides."

"A lot of the homes here are. Mine is as well."

The road went up as they neared one of the mountains, and the green that surrounded them was spectacular. "It's gorgeous here. Mainland Italy is as well, but this is different."

"It's hard for me to see it through the eyes of someone who hasn't lived here their entire life. If you haven't been to the beach in Catania, it's worth the trip."

"But is it worth the sand?" She grinned at him, nose crinkling with feigned disgust.

"You don't like sand?"

"Let's just say if I had the choice between a beach or a mountain, the mountain would win hands down."

"Oh, but the beach has its charms. Especially at night. In the dark." He smiled back at her, and the sight made her shiver. The man was so intense that even his smile carried that aura. And he was far too sexy.

The image in her brain shifted from Diego on a bar stool to Diego ankle-deep in the ocean, beckoning her toward him. Suddenly the idea of sand didn't seem so heinous.

She swallowed. "Does it?"

"It does. But good thing we have that trip planned to Etna on Tuesday. No sand."

She suddenly wanted to see the beach he was talking about. At night. With that sand she claimed to dislike clinging to the bare skin of Diego's back.

What was with her picturing him without clothes?

God, she was having a baby. About to find out who the father was. How could she think about anything other than that? She couldn't control much about the situation, but she could damn well concentrate on what she could control. Like where she was going to live and what she was going to do about childcare once the baby was in her arms.

A wave of love swept over her. She was actually going to get to hold this child. Cradle it deep in the night. In the end, did it really matter who the father was? This was *her* baby. *Her* responsibility. A fierce sense of protectiveness burrowed into her chest. She was going to do the absolute best she could to make sure this child never doubted her love. Never doubted that she would give her or him her all.

Out of the corner of her eye, she noted that Diego had looked her way several times. She realized he was waiting for her to respond to his earlier comment about the beach. "Yes, good thing we're going to Etna instead."

If their reasons for going up the mountain weren't so serious, she would be excited about the trip. As it was, it felt like he was going to render judgment on whether or not he was willing to be his baby's father. Of course, he'd never actually said he wouldn't. In fact, she was the one who had given him an ultimatum of sorts. But she needed to know. For sure. She didn't want Diego to start out strong and then disappear from his child's life two or three years down the line. Wasn't that part of focusing on what she could control? Suddenly she needed to know.

"How much farther is it to Palermo?"

He glanced at her in concern, his smile fading. "Are you feeling okay?"

"Yes, I'm fine." She decided to be honest without sharing her reasons. "I'm curious, that's all."

"About twenty-five minutes. So not much farther."

They arrived in the city, and it was a lot bigger than Catania, both in size and in feel. And the roads were crazy busy. Worse than in Catania. She was glad she hadn't attempted this alone. She would get used to the crush, and Naples had traffic problems of its own, just like every big city. "Do you know where the hospital is?"

"I do. I did part of my rotation here. It was an option

when I was in medical school, and I wanted to see how things worked in hospitals outside Catania."

"And yet you decided to stay in Catania?"

"I can't imagine living anywhere else, honestly."

That statement gave her pause. And if he were the father and she decided she wanted to move back to the mainland? He would stay in Catania. Why wouldn't he? Just because he might be the baby's father, that didn't mean they were involved with each other. He didn't need to live near her to be a part of the child's life. Right?

So why did that thought leave her so deflated?

Ten minutes later they were pulling into the parking lot of a large, modern-looking hospital. "Nice."

"It's one of the best hospitals in Sicily." He parked the car, and they got out, walking toward the entrance.

Nerves were sending a herd of elephants into her belly that seemed to stomp with every beat of her heart—which was getting quicker by the second. She only realized she'd slowed her pace when Diego had to stop for a second to let her catch up.

"Okay?"

"Just nervous, that's all."

One side of his mouth went up. "Me, too, if that helps."

Not really, because the reason for his nerves was probably different than hers. She was nervous about him being or not being a father. And he was probably nervous that he *would* be a father.

More and more she was wondering if she'd done the right thing. Not just about coming here together, but about telling him she was pregnant. Kind of hard to hide when you're caught with the test in your basket.

But she could have quit and moved away, never letting him know where she was. That felt dishonest, though. And if the baby grew up and went looking for him?

She shivered at what his reaction might be.

Some of that fear must have made itself known, because he reached for her hand, squeezing it and then letting it go. "It shouldn't take long. Did you eat lunch?"

She thought back and came up blank. "No, I just grabbed a snack from the snack bar."

"Then I'm doubly glad we're stopping on the way back."

They arrived at the lab, and she went up to the desk with Diego, somehow feeling embarrassed. Most women knew who the father of their child was. But the receptionist was kind and professional, not looking at her any differently than she might anyone else. That helped settle her nerves.

"We'll call you back in just a minute."

She was really hoping they called them back separately.

Almost before they found seats in the crowded waiting room, Bree heard her name. She avoided looking at Diego as she headed toward the open door where a woman dressed in scrubs waited.

"Right back this way."

She did her best to smile at the woman. "With the number of patients out there, I'm surprised it was this quick."

"Most of them are here for other types of testing. And we're quick back here in phlebotomy."

"Thanks."

The nurse's kind nature and wide smile helped put her at ease. "How long have you been in Sicily?"

"That obvious, huh?"

"Your accent." She motioned Bree to a seat, putting the arm up so she could rest her right forearm on it. "And your name, actually."

"I was born in the US but have lived in Naples for much of my life. I decided to get my education here and have actually just started working at Ospedale Maria di Concepción."

Her brows went up. "My best friend works there."

Bree immediately tensed, but the woman put her hand on her arm. "Don't worry. I won't say anything. I wouldn't even if there weren't laws in place. I know how it feels to go through this."

"You do?"

"Yes. I'm Teresina, by the way." She smiled. "And my test came out the way I needed it to. I hope yours does as well."

"Thanks." Bree wasn't sure how she wanted her test to come out. But she was hopeful that whoever the father was, it would end up the way it should.

After that, Teresina was all business, cuffing her upper arm with elastic tubing and sliding the needle home with the ease of someone who had done this thousands of times. She probably had. She drew one vial of blood then pulled the syringe free, putting a Band-Aid over the site. "There you go. You should get the results back in a week. You filled out your contact information?"

"Um, I didn't, but…" She licked her lips. "Could you read me what you have down for me?"

"Certainly." The phlebotomist went over to her computer and pulled up the file, reading off the address. Diego had a good memory. He'd only been to her place once. Or maybe he'd looked it up through Human Resources. No, she didn't think he would have done that, because it probably would have shown the search and his access would have been noted. At least at the hospital she'd trained at it would have been.

"That's correct. Thanks for checking."

"Not a problem." Teresina paused, then said, "It is absolutely none of my business. But if something violent happened…if you need help…"

It took her a second to puzzle through what the woman was saying. Then her heart ached, remembering what she'd said about her own test coming back the way she'd needed it to. "I'm fine. My pregnancy is the result of a failed condom. Nothing more than that."

"Okay, good. My stomach knots up every time someone comes in for one of these. Because in my case…" The woman's eyes watered.

Bree nodded. "I'm truly glad your results were what you wanted."

"Me, too. My husband's a good man and told me I didn't need to have it done, that it didn't matter to him. That maybe it would be better if I didn't know. But it mattered to me." She blew out a breath. "Anyway, I have no idea why I just shared all of that. If you're ever back in Palermo, please look me up."

"Thank you. I'll do that. Do you have a card?"

Teresina produced one from the pocket of her scrubs and handed it to her. "I'm serious."

"I really appreciate it, and I think I'll take you up on

it." Despite the circumstances, Bree felt like she'd just met her first friend in Sicily. And God knew she needed one. One who was totally separate from her hospital.

When she returned to the waiting room, Diego was gone. For a second, her stomach clenched, and she wondered if he'd taken off and left her, just like Sergio had. No. That was ridiculous. Teresina had said that her department was in a lull, so he'd surely been called back.

Sure enough, three minutes later he was back, and despite all her rationalizations, she breathed a sigh of relief.

"All done?" he asked.

"I am. Teresina said it would take about a week to get the results."

"Teresina?"

She could have kicked herself for saying the woman's name. "She drew my blood."

Who knew? She might decide to have her baby at this hospital, well away from any prying eyes. Especially if Diego decided to bow out.

"Ah, okay. I was told a week as well."

"So now we wait." Somehow saying the words gave them a finality that lodged in her chest and stuck there long after they'd left the hospital.

A week. A week to figure out how to be a dad.

Hell, if he hadn't been able to figure it out in all those years since his medical school romance, why did he think he could figure it out in seven short days?

Well, technically it wasn't seven days. If the baby was his, he'd have until the child was born before making plans. But it wasn't fair to Bree to make her wait that long. She needed to prepare for this baby. With or without him.

Diego had never been one to shirk responsibility. If anything, it was the opposite. But this time it wasn't just about him. It was about Bree and the baby as well.

If Angela, his girlfriend from med school, had gotten pregnant, it might have been a more straightforward path. He could have just married her and muddled through the best he could. But after seeing what his absence had done to her, what she'd needed to do to get what she needed, he'd realized even as a partner, he hadn't been the best choice.

And it was why he'd ended things with Selina as soon as she started wanting more. Because he just didn't think he had more in him. He was in surgery or planning a surgery on most days and Selina, just like Angela, would be stuck with what was left of him at the end of a long day. Which wasn't much.

He could have cut back on his schedule and sent some of his caseload to other area hospitals, but he'd chosen not to. Maybe because he'd wanted Selina to see the reality up front.

So, if he wasn't marriage material, how did he expect to be father material?

Except in a relationship there was an out. You could never undo the ties of fatherhood.

Maybe the best idea was to go through this next week with the assumption that the baby was his. He could mull through things as if this were the real thing. Figure out how he could play it differently than his father, or if that was even a possibility for him.

Then if it turned out the baby was Sergio's, he'd

be off the hook. Ha! And if that didn't sound like the thought of a selfish bastard.

But wasn't he?

And if he was selfish in his thoughts, what would make him different in the life of an actual living human being? Was selfishness programmed into one's DNA? He had no idea, but God, he hoped not.

To take his mind off his musings, he glanced over. "There's a town not far from here called Campofelice di Roccella. I know you're not much of a beach person, but it's a cute little beachside town that has a great restaurant with a view."

She smiled over at him, that dimple giving a flirtatious wink that she was totally unaware of. "Does 'beachside' mean we would have to eat on the beach and pick sand out of our teeth?"

"Nothing like that. Trust me?"

Her head tilted, and she looked at him for a minute. "Yes. I do."

The words sent a shiver through him. Such trust, so easily given. It had gotten her hurt not too many weeks ago by a man she should have been able to trust. She didn't deserve to be hurt like that again. So he needed to tread lightly. Starting with those words.

"I promise no picking sand out of your teeth, how's that?"

"That will work."

They arrived in the town and Diego drove partway up a mountain to get to Pasta in Mare, a place where they made homemade pasta and had a spectacular view of water and mountains alike. He found a parking place, and they got out of the car. Bree went over to the rough wood railing and looked out, leaning her forearms on the banister.

"This is really lovely, Diego. A mountain with a view of the beach. What more could anyone ask for?"

He came to stand beside her, a strange, sharp longing coming over him. He pushed it to the side. Just because you wanted something didn't mean you should have it. Hadn't he proved that by sleeping with Bree? He'd wanted her and had thought it was something flip, something he could forget about the next day. The problem was, he hadn't forgotten. And to see her again…

Well, he needed to be careful. His dad had evidently wanted marriage. Had wanted a family. So what had happened? Had the reality of the day-to-day grind worn him down? Or had he simply done what was expected of him by society and had kids? Things in the world had changed since then, but there were still societal pressures.

So as he stood there looking at the beautiful view, next to an even more beautiful woman, he needed to make sure he separated wants from shoulds and was very careful that he kept them as far apart as he could.

CHAPTER FIVE

IT DIDN'T TAKE long to be seated, since they'd arrived at the restaurant in between the lunch and dinner rushes, when the wait times could be phenomenal. Not only to be seated but also to be served, since this place was famous for its pasta and the view, which Bree had had a hard time pulling herself away from.

He was glad she liked it.

The waiter came over and presented them with wine menus. Diego glanced up in time to see pink infusing Bree's face. He knew exactly why. She wasn't supposed to drink because of the pregnancy. And although wine could be ordered by the glass, it was more customary to order a bottle.

Diego took the lead. "I'll just have a water, please."

"Yes, I'll have the same." The relief in her voice was palpable. A sense of warmth went through him. One right choice down. A million more to go.

Or maybe it wasn't because of pregnancy. Maybe she was worried that he might drink too much. Look at how he'd been the night they'd slept together. They'd both drunk more than was safe for driving.

He looked at her. "Just to be clear, I would never do anything to put my passenger or other vehicles in peril."

"Oh, I didn't mean… It's just I can't…"

This time it was Diego who felt relief. "I understand. I just wanted to make sure you knew."

"Thank you."

Car accidents were probably a difficult subject for her anyway, because of her fiancé's death.

The waiter had left food menus as well, and he passed her one.

She glanced at it. "What do you recommend?"

"The swordfish is very good, as is *sarde alla griglia*. Italian sardines are nothing like the canned ones from America, however."

"I grew up in Italy, remember? I love the sardines here."

"Good. The squid is also very nice."

She laughed. "Okay, I grew up in Italy but still haven't gotten past anything with tentacles."

He liked when she laughed. The bangles on her wrist jingled with the movement like the wind chimes from his mother's porch. Soft. Comforting.

And the way her mouth curved, showing off white teeth and that treacherous dimple. It was no wonder he hadn't been able to resist her at the bar that night.

"I bet you would like these." As much as he liked her smile? He doubted that was possible.

"I don't know…"

He grinned, leaning forward. "I could order some for myself and you could take the tiniest of bites."

Dios, those words had come out in a husky voice that

he didn't recognize. And they made all sorts of images slide through his head.

"Hmm…maybe. How about if I order the sardines, and you order your tentacles, and we share." Her dimple winked again. "Unless I don't like yours, then all bets are off."

"Somehow I think you will like mine very much."

Her face bloomed with color, making him realize he wasn't the only one who was feeling these odd vibes—ones he was having trouble controlling. Thankfully the waiter came with their glasses and a large pitcher filled with water, sliced lemons and plenty of ice. It was hot outside, and the windows to the restaurant were open. But with the sea air flooding the space and the large ceiling fans above them, it was warm but not uncomfortably so. And he loved the smell of the water.

The waiter asked if they were ready to order. He raised his brows at Bree. "What do you think? Are you willing to share?"

"Let's go for it."

His eyes met hers. "Yes. Let's."

Diego placed their order, asking for stuffed mushrooms as an appetizer. Once the waiter left, he poured water in their glasses. "Seriously, if you don't like the squid, don't feel like you have to eat them."

"Don't worry. I won't." Her bangles sounded again as she reached for her glass, making something inside him tighten. "I'll try them. Just no promises."

"I'd never ask you to promise."

They talked about work for the next fifteen minutes until their appetizers arrived. Bree cut into one of the mushrooms and popped it into her mouth. Her eyes widened, and he looked at her in alarm.

"You don't like it?"

She finished chewing and swallowed. "It's amazing. I love it! Seriously."

"You know raw seafood is not recommended during pregnancy." The words that came out of his mouth were ones he didn't even recognize, and he had no idea why he'd said them.

"I didn't order my food raw." She drew the words out in a way that said she was puzzled. As well she should be.

"Sorry. I have no idea why I said that, other than being a doctor."

"It's okay. I already figured that, like alcohol, sushi was off the menu. But thanks for your concern."

The words were said in a light tone, but there was a hint of warning behind them. And she was right. Unless he could convince her to let him be a part of this child's life—and hers—he had no right to dictate anything to her. Actually, even if he did take an active role, it wasn't his job to police her food or anything else. Which wasn't what he was trying to do, but he could see how she might take it that way.

There was a subtle shift in atmosphere that made conversation difficult for a few minutes before she asked about the decor on the walls. Once they made it back onto neutral ground, things seemed to be okay. At least for now.

They finished the plate of appetizers just as their main dish arrived at the table. The sardines were nicely grilled to a golden color, and in the Italian way, their heads were still on. "Wow, these look fantastic."

"They taste as good as they look, if I remember right."

She glanced at his plate. "Okay, that doesn't look as scary as I expected. If I could just have a part of it that isn't curled and doesn't have suckers…" She bit her lip as if knowing it was a strange request. But it was an endearing gesture that made him smile, glad things between them seemed to be back on decent footing. He didn't know why that was so important to him, but it was.

"Not curled and no suckers, coming right up." These particular squid did not have long tentacles, and so it was easy to cut several chunks from the upper portion of the seafood, passing them over to her and allowing her to put one of the large sardines onto his plate. His mouth watered.

Campofelice di Roccella was one of his favorite towns, although his last girlfriend had never been a big fan of the place. Somehow he liked that Bree could find the beauty in the town.

She expertly slid her knife between the flesh and bones of one of her sardines and laid it on her plate, cutting off a portion.

"It's so strange," he said, "to see you do that with no hesitation."

"Why?"

"I'm not exactly sure."

She smiled, somehow seeming to guess that it was because she was American. "I've lived in Italy a lot longer than I ever lived in the States." She finished a bite of her fish before continuing. "But it's weird to feel like I somehow have a foot in two places but don't truly belong in either of them."

She'd used a typical Italian expression when she said it. "I think you're more Italian than you give yourself credit for. If not for your name and the tiniest difference in inflection when you talk, I never would have guessed you weren't from Naples."

"I think people outside Italy have this caricature in their heads of what people here look like. It's not like I'm the lone redhead in the country."

She was right. Just like in any nation, Italians came in all shapes, sizes and colors. It's what made the human race beautiful. "You're right. Just like the stereotypes people attribute to Sicily."

"Those stereotypes are nothing close to reality. It's beautiful here. Even more than I imagined."

"The beauty here is more than I imagined, too." He was talking about Sicily, but he was including the woman seated across from him in that statement. She was gorgeous. With the light of the sun behind her, it gave her hair an almost golden appearance.

Her eyes met his for a few seconds before traveling back to her plate. "Moment of truth." She speared a piece of the squid on her plate and took a deep breath before sliding it into her mouth. She chewed a second or two, her brows going up as her throat moved to swallow. "Well, okay, I didn't expect that."

"What? Do you actually *like* something you'd once claimed you never would try?"

He said the question and immediately tensed. Wasn't that what he'd done with the idea of having kids? Said he never would? Eating squid and taking on a lifetime commitment and doing it justice were two different things, though.

Her grin was spontaneous and contagious, making him forget his moment of reflection. "It's definitely not as tough as I expected it to be. Almost like a scallop."

"Yes. The trick with calamari is to either cook it quickly, before it has a chance to get tough, or to cook it for a long time until it becomes tender."

Maybe Diego was in the second category. Maybe he needed to be flung into the fire for a long time before he could become tender. Before he learned how to be nurturing. Except that took time. And he just wasn't sure he had enough of it.

"I'm not sure I could ever get used to the tentacles, but the squid itself is quite good." As if to prove her point, she ate another piece, followed by an olive from a little bowl on the side of the table. "I'm going to be very full, though."

He thought of something. "How's your queasiness?"

"It's been okay, except in the mornings or when I'm placed in a stressful situation."

So she didn't find being here in the restaurant with him stressful. He liked that.

They ate for a few more minutes, and the mood between them had lightened considerably since they'd left the hospital. He could understand why. They'd taken the tests and there was nothing they could do to change the outcome, so worrying accomplished nothing.

Do you actually like something you once said "never" to? If only it were as easy as he'd made it sound.

The waiter appeared at their table with another, smaller, menu. *"Vuoi un dolce?"*

Diego looked at her in question. "What do you think? Dessert?"

"I don't think I can eat another bite, but you go ahead."

He shook his head at the waiter. "I think just the bill, please."

Bree looked conflicted, as if she was going to contradict him, but she didn't say anything until after the waiter left. "I'd planned on buying my own meal. So we can just split the check."

"Please let me. I enjoyed showing you one of my favorite spots in Sicily."

She hesitated before nodding. "Okay. This time. But next time is on me."

Was there going to be a next time? Something about the thought of that made a warm wash of pleasure run through him. Of course, they were going to Mount Etna on Tuesday, so it was likely they would eat together then as well.

He paid the bill, and then they were out of the restaurant. The sun was beginning to sink on the horizon, turning the sky to an assortment of reds and pinks, painting the tips of the mountains in the same colors.

"Look at that," Bree murmured, standing at the railing. "It's so beautiful. Can we stay here for just a minute?"

Yes, they could. They could stay for as long as she liked. Anything to keep from returning to the reality of his life, which had now taken a turn that was…unexpected. Although, that word sounded too tame for the wild ride he was about to embark on.

And what about her? What was she thinking?

He half turned toward her, propping his hip against the low wall. "Are you doing okay, Bree? I didn't think to ask."

She stared out at the horizon. "I'm not sure. I've always wanted children, but this wasn't quite how I envisioned having them. When Sergio died and I realized who he was, exactly…well, who knows how long I would have waited if left to my own devices? Maybe it would have been too late by the time I was finally ready to try. I'm hoping this will work out the way it should have." She turned to face him. "And I'm serious about not expecting anything from you. If I hadn't married, I might have had this baby through a donor."

"Will Sergio's parents want to be involved, if it turns out to be his child?"

"Probably, and I'm not sure how I feel about that, although I've always liked both of them. I'm hoping his father wasn't involved in anything shady."

"That hotel has a pretty good reputation, but things aren't always what they appear to be."

"No, they're not." Her voice had a musing quality to it. Was she thinking about Sergio and wishing he'd survived? Although, under the circumstances, he couldn't see her staying married if what he'd read about the man was true. "Things could be much simpler if…"

Her voice faded away, maybe forgetting whom she was talking to. Because he could have sworn she'd been about to say that things would have been much simpler if the baby was Diego's rather than Sergio's. Ha! Simpler for her, but definitely not for him. Or her baby.

She took a deep breath and shook her head. "I guess we should be getting back. You have an early day tomorrow, right?"

"I do. Don't you as well?"

"No, I'm on call in case they need me, but I'm planning to go look at that house again. The one I told you about."

"Oh, right. Right. Let me know how it is."

"I'm going to try to take some pictures. It'll be good to have a place of our own."

For a second he froze, then realized she was talking about her and the baby. Not her and Diego.

She moved to go and stumbled, dropping her purse, which tumbled down several of the steps. He gripped her elbow. "Are you okay?"

"Yes, just a klutz."

He smiled. "You are anything but." He jogged down the steps and retrieved the item, coming back and handing it to her.

"Thank you."

"You're welcome." A quick snatch of something went through his mind. A snapshot of Bree, well into her pregnancy, her long hair flowing around her shoulders as she gripped his elbow as they made their way down these very same steps. Something burned in his throat, something he tried to will away, even as they trekked down the shallow stairs until they reached the parking area.

She slid into the passenger seat and waited for him to get in and start the vehicle. "How are the roads at night?"

"They're pretty good. Although, when the A19 was shut down a few months ago, it took a lot longer to get from Palermo to Catania because of the mountains and winding roadways."

"It's probably a nice drive, though."

"It is. Especially if you want to get off the beaten path."

She laughed, and he glanced at her. "What?"

"I don't know. Just something about that struck me as funny. I think I'm off the beaten track right now. I've exited the highway and am going through some pretty rocky terrain."

He smiled, despite himself, feeling a camaraderie with her that he didn't expect. "I think we both are."

"I really am sorry, Diego. If only I hadn't stopped in that bar…"

"I stopped in there, too. We both made the same choices. Made the same mistakes."

"Mistakes." Her voice was low and sad. "I don't want this baby to ever think he or she was a mistake."

Merda. That wasn't what he'd meant to say.

"I phrased that badly." He glanced over to see her hands gripped tightly together.

"No, you said exactly what I was thinking. But I want to change that. At least on my part. I want to give this baby the best parts of me."

That was just it. The best parts of Diego were related to his job. It was the one thing he knew he was good at. And he'd poured himself into that at the cost of everything else.

Just like his father had.

And just like his dad, he was terrible at relationships.

Terrible at spending time outside the hospital on anything except sleeping and showering. Even his friendships were mainly formed around people he worked with. Going to the bar that night by himself had been out of character for him. His relationships were always pretty clear-cut. And he chose women whose end goals were the same as his—as in nonexistent. So when Selina had mentioned children, it had ended the relationship. Maybe she'd hoped she could change him. But Diego hadn't wanted to change. At least, not at that moment.

Because he knew—*knew!*—the truth about himself, even if the world at large hadn't guessed. It's why he'd had that dragon emblazoned on his arm after the breakup of his first relationship, as a reminder to himself that his nature was not what most women were looking for. Tangle with him and you were apt to come out on the losing side emotionally.

Bree, on the other hand, was the polar opposite of him.

"You're going to make a very good mother."

She looked at him but didn't say anything for a minute. Didn't give him any empty assurances that he would make a great dad as well. Because he hadn't even said whether he'd be willing to be a father to this child.

"I hope so. I'm pretty scared, actually."

There was a raw vulnerability in her tone that pulled at something inside him. He wished he could say something profound that would help her feel less afraid, but there was nothing. Because the thought of actually becoming a dad was...terrifying. To be in the very same position his dad had been when he'd been born and stand there and…decide if this tiny human would get some of his time—or not. He wanted to be the kind of person who could make those sacrifices with gladness, but in some ways he didn't know who he was outside work. Was that how his father had felt, too? That gnawing uncertainty of who he really was?

He reached over and gripped her hand, his thumb brushing over her skin. "I'm sorry, Bree. I can't even imagine." He couldn't. He was having trouble grasping what was happening right now. If his response could be what it needed to be. And it was tearing something inside him into tiny pieces. Pieces he wasn't sure could be reassembled.

He wanted to be the kind of man his child could be proud of but, was he that man? Oh, he was good at his job. Very good. But he didn't know if he was a good person.

He hoped so. But until he was sure… Did he have a right to play a pivotal role in this child's life?

He didn't know. And that fact was giving him a whole boatload of regret. So he said the only thing he could think of. The only thing that was true.

"I'm scared, too."

A day later Bree sat at her perfusion table on what was supposed to have been her day off watching as Diego worked his magic on yet another heart. With steady hands and a determined jaw, it was hard to equate the man he was this morning with the one who'd admitted to being scared.

He'd never seemed more confident than he did right

now. But then again, this room was a place in which he felt at home, a place where he knew his way around.

But to wrap his head around being a father? Yes, she could see how that might seem pretty terrifying.

She was scared, too. And strangely, his admission was he first time she'd felt a real emotional tether to him. Oh, he was sexy and the things he'd done to her that night at the bar had been surreal. But the softer side?

Honestly, saying he was scared was the first time she'd seen that softness. Or even believed there might be something more to him than a brilliant heart surgeon and a gifted lover.

"How are we doing?"

His words yanked her thoughts back to the task at hand. Only unlike her first surgery with him, she knew he wasn't using the word *we* to mean him and her. It was about their time clock. And it was her job to know how long the patient had been on bypass down to the minute.

"Two hours, eleven minutes on bypass."

His eyes met hers for a moment. And she was right. There was no fear there. No emotion whatsoever except a steely determination that was contagious. His team fed off his energy, and it was kind of amazing to watch. Even Bree, who considered herself pretty self-contained and separate from the actual surgical team, got caught up in that energy.

He set the world around him on fire. Just like that fire-breathing dragon inked on his arm. Maybe that's what it represented. That fiery energy that consumed everything in its path. She just had to be careful that it didn't consume her, too.

He was asking for some specialized tool, and since her board had been Steady Eddie this whole time, she took a few seconds to study him, trying to figure out what it was about him that was so captivating.

The individual pieces of Diego's face could tempt a sculptor, but there were some slight imperfections that made the overall package come across as rugged and sexy rather than pretty. She couldn't quite put her finger on what it was, though. It wasn't his crooked smile that lifted higher on the left than on the right. Or his nose that had a slight bump on the bridge. Or his hair, which could be sleek and tame or wild with riotous waves.

Unpredictable. That's what the man was. It wasn't just his physical presence that overwhelmed her, but his nature. He could morph from a colleague into a fierce boss in the space of a few seconds, one that demanded that jobs were done well, including by him.

He glanced up again and caught her staring. "Something wrong?"

Fire licked at her face, and she could have sworn that tattoo under his sleeve was glowing with heat, ready to spew its flames in her direction.

She swallowed. "No, I just wondered how things were going."

One brow went up, but he didn't challenge her. He'd caught her and they both knew it. "It's going *meravigliosamente*."

Marvelously. Her blush deepened. She was pretty sure, judging from a couple of chuckles from the people around him, that adverb wasn't one he normally used.

But at least he'd seemed amused rather than angry. But it wouldn't do to let her attention wander again.

She gave a quick nod and this time focused on the readings in front of her until Diego needed her to do something else. Which he did around forty minutes later, when he was ready to wean the patient off her machine.

The switch from bypass back to the patient's own heart went without a hitch. It was as if Diego had written the book on every heart surgery in existence and excelled at them all. She was sure that wasn't the case, but right now it seemed that way.

She was in awe of his skill.

I'm scared, too.

She could not picture this man saying that. Not about a surgery. Not about much of anything.

"Preparing to close up."

For Diego, the exciting part of surgery had to be over, kind of like when she turned the patient's circulation back over to the team. But if so, you couldn't tell it by the meticulous way he wired the sternum back together. By the small, even stitches that she'd seen on every patient she'd worked on with him. Not that there'd been all that many. But each one told a story. That there wasn't any one part of the surgery that was more important than another. It all mattered.

Diego asked for a different type of suture once he'd finished stitching the muscles together. He was preparing for the final step: closing the skin. It was funny how even though Bree didn't have a clear view of what was happening from where she sat, she could still tell exactly what Diego was doing. Not just by his running commentary, but by the instruments he asked for. From scalpels to cauterizers to sponges, each part had its own special place in the process. Just like every person did.

And he was good at letting people know that. At making them feel special and needed.

She'd felt it that night at the bar. But she hadn't been looking for special or needed that night. She was looking for something that would numb her pain. Instead of numbing it, however, Diego had brought an ecstasy that had accomplished the same thing. But the next morning they both went their separate ways, and there'd been nothing to make her think they would ever see each other again.

Ha! She glanced up again, making sure she didn't pause too long this time. Who would have ever thought she'd be sitting in an operating room working less than fifteen feet from that very same man?

Certainly not her.

The snip of scissors sounded, as if putting a period on the act of surgery.

He instructed the surgical nurse on how he wanted the site dressed and which medications were to be administered when. The nurse charted everything on her tablet and read the instructions back to him.

"Yes, that's correct."

Diego glanced around the room in that way he did, his gaze touching each person present, including her.

Heat surged into her face all over again. There was no good reason for it. The man just affected her in ways that she'd rather he didn't. But hopefully he wasn't aware of it.

"All right. I think we're about done here. Any comments? Suggestions?"

His eyes skated over the room again. "No? Well, good job everyone. Signor Moseli's bypass should give him quite a few more years. I appreciate you coming in on a weekend."

Several people murmured that they didn't mind. Bree bet they didn't. Who wouldn't want to work with the renowned surgeon?

Regardless of her personal issues with Diego, she was smart enough to know that she could learn a lot from the man. And that this was a great opportunity. She just had to be careful not to let her emotions run rampant and turn her into some kind of fangirl. She was pretty sure he wouldn't appreciate or welcome that kind of fawning. Not that she would. She didn't normally wear her heart on her sleeve. But that didn't mean that things couldn't affect it. They could. So she would be cautious about opening up around him.

"I hope everyone has good rest of their weekend. I'll try not to drag you down here again. See you all again on Monday."

Diego smiled, and when he did, it seemed to be aimed right at her, even though she was sure that it probably wasn't.

But heaven help her, even after swearing she wouldn't fawn over him, she couldn't stop what happened next: she smiled back.

CHAPTER SIX

Etna was being a naughty girl today.

A deep plume of smoke was roiling from the top of her, making it almost impossible to see the mountain peak.

Diego was knocking at her door first thing Tuesday morning. "Are you sure you want to do this today?"

She motioned him in. "I'm fine with going. If you think it's too dangerous, we can always just go partway up."

"It's not that it's dangerous. The visibility just won't be very good. And it'll be worse the higher we go, and the air quality will go down." He moved into the space. "How did your house looking go?"

"Great. I think the one I told you about is the one I'm going to get. I put a deposit on it and took some pictures. Do you want to see?" She wasn't sure why she was so excited, but she was. Maybe because she'd barely seen Diego since their trip to Palermo. The trip where he'd admitted to being scared, too. That admission had moved her in a way she hadn't expected. And she'd hoped to run into him at the hospital, just to see him.

And boy, was the guy a hunk today in a short-sleeved

brown polo and a pair of cargo shorts. His legs were very masculine, with a light dusting of hair and a deep tan that said he spent time in the sun, although she'd heard he didn't have much of a social life. At least not that the people at the hospital knew of.

Not that she tried to pump people for information. But whenever his name came up somewhere in conversation, she found her ears immediately pricking, even when she didn't want to listen. He was an enigma, even to those who'd worked with him for years, it seemed.

He sat on the futon with her, and she immediately realized that was a mistake. His shampoo or aftershave or whatever it was smelled amazingly delicious. Or maybe it was just him. But it was distracting, and she found herself fumbling with her phone, trying to find the pictures while acting as nonchalant as she could—not an easy feat. Especially with the bottom edge of his tattoo peeking from below the sleeve of his shirt. She knew exactly was inked there. She'd actually kissed it, running her lips over the lines of it.

There! Finally!

She scrolled through the pictures, answering his questions and trying her best not to move deeper into his personal space.

"What's that?"

She glanced at the screen. "It's the balcony off the bedroom."

"Nice. It's very private." His words were low. Husky. "Just like the one at your hotel room."

Her belly quivered in response. Until he added, "You'll be sitting out there with a book and a cup of coffee before you know it."

Squelch. That's not what she'd been picturing doing out on that balcony. She hurriedly moved to the next picture, which was…the bedroom. Ack!

"Does it come furnished?" he asked.

"Yes, everything in it stays, which is a good thing, since I don't have any furniture of my own."

Two more pictures and they were done. Finally! She stood up, trying to make it look as casual as possible. He did not need to know that her knees were shaking and her head felt slightly off-kilter. As did her heart, which had begun pounding when he'd mentioned how private her balcony was. She was going to have a hard time getting those words out of her head.

"I made a lunch. I wasn't sure what they have up there in the way of food." She motioned to the backpack sitting on the table. "I put it in there in case we were going to hike up the mountain."

He walked over and slung the rucksack onto one shoulder with ease, despite the fact that it had a couple of liters of water stuffed in there as well as sandwiches and some fruit. "Thanks. I have some water in the car as well. There are spots to park as you go up, so we can get out and move around and decide how much of it we want to walk."

"I know we're planning on talking about things, but thanks for offering to do it on the mountain. It's really the one place I wanted to see while in Sicily."

"While in Sicily? Are you not planning to stay here?"

She blinked. "Well, I'm not assuming I'll be moving anytime soon, but you never know what the future holds."

"I see." But she didn't really think he did, because

his brows had come together in a way that suggested he wasn't happy about something she'd said. It was about moving. And his reaction was exactly what she thought it might be, since he'd once said he couldn't imagine himself living anywhere but Catania.

But if he, for some reason, decided he didn't want to be a part of the baby's life, what did it matter where she lived? And she might want to be closer to her mom and dad, if that were the case.

Her mouth tightened. He couldn't have it both ways. He was either all in…or he was out. Completely out. Her father had been there for her for every step of her life. Ballet recitals. Graduations. And in the most heart-breaking time of her life, he'd been right there to pick up the pieces. She couldn't imagine anything less for her child. She wouldn't *allow* for anything less. "We can talk about that, too. We each have plans for the future. I'd like to know what yours are."

"My plans are to remain here in Sicily."

There'd been no softening of his gaze, but there had been a weird strangled sound to the words. As if they'd been forced out of him against his will. So if he decided he wanted to be a part of the baby's life and she eventually needed to move for a new job opportunity, was he saying he wouldn't come?

"My plans for the moment are to do the same, but circumstances don't always allow us to do what we want."

"Yes. I know."

Great. They were not getting off to the best start. Maybe a change of scenery would help. "Are you ready? Maybe we should go while the weather is still nice."

Thankfully, he agreed immediately, probably feeling the same uncomfortable tension that she had. Diego carried the backpack and a quilt she wanted to bring and loaded them into the back seat of the car.

Then he started the vehicle, put it into Drive, and they were off.

She might move? That thought had not even crossed Diego's mind. But it should have. She hadn't been born in Sicily—in fact, her family was in Naples, and she probably had other family in the States. Why would he think that she would stay here forever?

Maybe because she might be having his baby.

Except Diego was still wrestling with the ramifications of that. Bree's words had made him realize that being involved with his child might prove to be complicated. There could be decisions—hard decisions—on top of the main one in question: How hard was it going to be for him to change his ways? To give time that he'd never learned to give?

The drive up the first quarter of the mountain was done in silence. Until he heard Bree gasp and, looking over at her, saw that she was staring out over the terrain. Right before the road curved to the left, it looked like the mountain peaks had lined up, going from short to tallest. He relaxed. She said she loved Sicily. The longer she was here, the more likely it was to grow on her.

And the more she would grow on him. He could feel it happening already.

And if this baby *wasn't* his? He wasn't positive he could back away from her the way he'd once thought he could.

And that scared the hell out of him.

So was he hoping the child was his?

For once he allowed himself to relax. To forget about everything but being up here with her. "It's amazing, yes?"

"Yes. I don't think I've ever seen anything like it. And the smoke seems to have dissipated, or maybe it's just blowing in another direction."

"That happens sometimes. I'm glad we're able to see. There will be a spot to pull over in about a half a mile. Do you want to do some walking? Or..." His gaze ventured to her stomach, which was still flat. For a second he imagined what it would look like in six months' time, with a cute little bulge where their baby was growing and a—

Their baby?

"I'd like to walk. It's still cool outside, and my sandals are comfortable. I can carry the backpack, if you want."

"I'll carry it." He sent her a smile, hoping that didn't sound chauvinistic.

They got to the stopping place. They weren't the only ones who were going to do some exploring. There were several other cars here as well, and a few people milling around the area.

He parked and got out and grabbed the pack while Bree hesitated. "How long are we going to be out? Do you want me to bring the quilt?"

"I thought we might come back to the car and go up farther. There's a pretty overlook where we can set up everything. I just thought we might want some water. I also brought a cooler and some ice."

"That sounds great. Thanks."

Maybe by the time they got to their ultimate destination, he would have figured out how to explain what his thoughts were. He figured she didn't want a testing period. She wanted a black-or-white, yes-or-no answer. But what about a compromise that tested the waters before the baby was actually born? Maybe he could put himself on trial and let Bree give him a verdict on his performance. If he couldn't make himself better than his father, then she had the right to say no to him being involved.

He had to be careful how he worded it, because it would be easy for her to take it the wrong way and cut him off without giving him a chance. He'd kind of done that to himself, hadn't he? Cut himself off by deciding not to have kids.

And now fate had laughed that decision into the dust and set him on a path there seemed to be no coming back from.

They hiked over to an area that allowed them to see off into the distance. Her pink denim backpack was smaller than the one he normally carried, so slinging it over one shoulder had been his best bet. But it worked.

And he liked shouldering a tiny portion of her burden. It wasn't a baby, but spending time with a woman like this was out of his norm. This took a lot more time than just falling into bed with someone and fixing them breakfast the next morning before heading back to work—like he'd done in recent years. This required a lot more…effort. And he didn't resent it. In fact, he'd looked forward to today. It was a tiny step, and God only knew if it was sustainable for him in the long haul. But he wanted to try.

"How far up the mountain can we go?"

"We can drive up to about the two-thousand-meter point. To actually hike to the top, we'd have to be part of a group headed by a professional tour guide. They have safety equipment and climbing gear in case of an accident. I didn't think to reserve a spot—sorry about that."

"It's fine. I just wondered." She glanced out over the mountainside before tilting her head. She held a hand to her brows to shade her line of vision. "What's that?"

"Where?"

"That black ridge. There's not much growing on it."

He glanced out to see what she was looking at. "That's a lava field."

She blinked. "As in real lava?"

That made him smile. "Yep. Produced the natural way, by a volcano. I don't think they're interested in manufacturing lava just for tourists."

"Ha! Okay, I guess that wasn't the brightest question. It just surprised me. Can I touch it?"

"I don't see why not." He'd just started to move that way when they heard someone scream and then cry out in pain.

Bree whipped around, looking for whoever had made the distressed sound. "There! Someone's on the ground."

They made their way closer, only to have someone motion them back. "There's a snake."

"Venomous?"

"I think so, judging by the head," said the man. "I'm pretty sure it's an asp viper."

Asp vipers were the only venomous snakes in the area. Bree slid past the man. "We're medical professionals."

"Be careful. Please," the concerned man said. "We don't need anyone else getting hurt."

A young woman dressed in shorts and a T-shirt lay on the ground staring at something. Her hands were wrapped around her lower leg.

He spotted it. A beige snake with black markings and the familiar anvil-shaped head of a viper lay about twenty feet away. It looked like the victim had scooted back from it, but the snake was still coiled and looked ready to strike again. But at that distance it wouldn't be able to reach her.

Diego put a hand on Bree's shoulder. "Let me find a stick."

"The hell with that." Before he could stop her, she removed one of her sandals and went over to stand right beside the victim, then she cranked her arm back and let the shoe fly. It slammed into the ground near the snake hard enough to send dirt flying in all directions. Evidently the reptile decided it had had enough excitement for the day, because it slithered through a rocky pass, disappearing from view.

She knelt beside the woman. "Let me see your leg. Diego is a doctor, and I'm a Perfusionist. What's your name?"

"Oh my God. Thank you. I think you saved my life. I'm Lydia." She took her hands off her leg, where blood trickled freely. There were twin marks that definitely looked to be caused by fangs. Then Bree turned her attention to Diego. "What type of venom do they have?"

He heard her question but was already phoning in, asking that an EMS squad be sent to their location. They were about twenty minutes out. Until then they would have to do first aid and pray that the snake didn't decide to pay them another visit. Bree had saved some valuable time by tossing that shoe. But it was also a risk. One she'd been willing to take when no one else had. "Asp viper venom is a hemotoxin," he said. "It affects the clotting system."

He crouched down with her and zipped open her backpack. "Do you have something in here I can use as a tourniquet?" They needed to at least slow the flow of venom to other parts of her body.

"No, but I have this." She stood up and took off the belt around her waist and handed it to him.

"Perfect." He wrapped the slim band of leather twice around the woman's thigh and buckled it in place.

The woman pressed a hand to her mouth and moaned. "It's starting to really hurt."

"I know. Are you here with anyone?"

She shook her head, tears coming to her eyes. "No. I broke up with my boyfriend last week and decided to come on vacation anyway to get back at him. We already had reservations here."

He saw Bree's teeth come down on her lip. Maybe thinking of her own reasons for originally coming to Sicily.

"Is it supposed to hurt this much?"

At first, he thought she was talking about the breakup, then realized she mean the pain in her leg.

His own breakup as a young medical student had been devastating and had sent him spinning into an orbit from which he'd never returned. And hadn't wanted to.

Until now?

He pulled his mind back to the work at hand.

The venom was already causing damage. Soon some of the tissue would start turning dark as mini hemorrhages began to erupt near the site of the bite, spreading as the toxin moved through the limb.

Bree took the woman's vitals. "It's important to stay calm, Lydia, even though I know it's the hardest thing you've ever done."

Diego had to admit that looking down the barrel of a pregnancy was one of the hardest things he'd ever done. But it wasn't death. Or the possible loss of a limb. And if this woman could sit here and not be a screaming wreck, then he could damn well face the toxin of his own past and stay calm, working on it until he found the right treatment.

Bree wrapped her arm around the woman's shoulders. "Emergency services will be here soon to take you to the hospital."

Her eyes widened. "Am I going to die? I need to call my boyfriend. Well, my ex-boyfriend."

"No. You're not going to die." Bree said it softly but firmly as Diego kept track of the time on the tourniquet. It would have to be loosened periodically so that blood flow was not completely interrupted from her leg. "You can call him later. Once you're feeling better."

Five minutes later they heard the sound of a siren coming up the mountain road.

The perfusionist gave Lydia a squeeze. "See? What did I tell you? They'll take you to get some antivenin. It'll counteract the snake's venom."

Lydia moaned again, trying to look down at her leg. "I had no idea there were snakes in Italy."

Diego glanced at her. "You're not from Italy?"

"No." She sucked down a deep breath. "My parents are Italian, but I was born in Switzerland. It's where my boyfriend and I live. It's always been my dream to come to Sicily."

He patted her arm. "Don't let this change that. We really are a pretty nice lot." He nodded in the direction the snake had gone. "Most of us, anyway."

The woman actually laughed, and Bree smiled her approval at him. His insides turned to quicksand, trapping him in an impossible grip. He stared at her for several seconds as her smile continued to shine.

Dios, he would make every person in the near vicinity laugh if it would get her to look at him like that again. It was like at the bar where they'd first met. She'd turned and smiled at him, and it was as if something in those upturned lips and dimple had bewitched him, causing him to act in ways he might not ordinarily have. He'd never picked up a woman in a bar before. Ever. And from the sound of it, neither had Bree. Two people acting out of character and look what had happened. A baby.

His baby.

He clenched his teeth. No, it would only be his child if Bree determined he was good enough. The last thing he wanted was to be like his own father and make a mess of his child's life. He'd once heard his mother arguing with his dad, saying that all he was was a sperm donor. Diego had been young at the time and had gone to his ten-year-old brother and asked him what those strange words meant.

All his brother had said was that it meant his father

wasn't really their father. Diego had taken that literally until he was old enough to work out what Antonio had meant.

He did not want to be a father who wasn't really a father. So if he wanted to change things, he was going to have to work damn hard to prove to Bree—and himself—that he could.

Someone motioned the pair of EMS workers over to them. They were carrying a portable gurney with them. Diego quickly filled them in.

"Where's the snake now?"

"He's gone, but several of us saw it. It was a *Vipera aspis* for sure." He glanced at his watch. "It's been three minutes since the tourniquet was last loosened. It was put on a total of seven minutes ago."

The man looked at him, eyes wide. "You're a medical worker?"

Yeah, it might have been nice if he'd identified himself first thing. "I'm a cardiac surgeon." He motioned to Bree. "She's in medicine as well."

"Well, thanks for making our job easier by not trying to suck out the venom."

Diego smiled. "No worries there."

They got the woman loaded up, who despite the pain flaring across her face had reached for Bree. The perfusionist took her hand and squeezed it. "Go and feel better. I'll come by the hospital later and see how you're doing." She glanced at the EMTs. "Where are you taking her?"

"Concepción."

"Perfect, that's our hospital. They're very good at what they do. We'll meet you there."

So Bree had gone from checking on Lydia later to meeting her at the hospital. He had a feeling it had something to do with the breakup. Maybe she really was comparing it to what she'd gone through.

Evidently that ended their trip up Etna. But that was okay, because he still had no idea what he was going to say to her.

Diego watched them load the frightened woman up. "I take it we're abandoning our trip."

"I think it's for the best. I really do want to see how she's doing. Besides…" She wiggled the toes of her right foot. "I don't think I'm going to want to hike around with one shoe on and one shoe off."

The shoe had skipped to the edge of a downward slope. "I'll go get—"

"No." She shuddered. "I'm actually terrified of snakes. I don't want to take the chance of it being over that ridge somewhere watching. And I don't think I can ever wear that shoe again, knowing where it's been."

Said as if it was somehow contaminated. "I'll tell you what. I'll get you to the car, and then I'll come back for the shoe." When she acted like she was going to argue, he shook his head. "You don't have to wear it again. I'll put it in a bag and throw it away, but we can't leave it there."

She shut her eyes. "I know. I just don't want it near me."

"It won't be. You never have to look at it again." He turned his back to her. "Hop on."

There was silence behind him. He turned his head to look.

Her mouth was open, and she looked shocked. "Excuse me?"

"You can ride on my back. How do you say it in English?"

"A piggyback ride? I don't think so. I can walk."

He glanced at the terrain, which was strewn with pebbles, some of them sharp black volcanic rock. "Your feet will be cut to pieces before you've gone ten feet. And we've already walked a couple hundred yards." He grinned at her. "Unless you'd like me to throw you over my shoulder like a *pompiere* would do." He reached down and picked up her backpack and the quilt, holding them in one hand, the other arm ready to do exactly what he'd said.

"But you're not a fireman." She took a deep breath, looking at the ground. "Okay. I'll get on, but don't you tell *anyone* about this."

"I won't. Promise." Even if she hadn't made him promise, there was no way he was going back to the hospital and telling everyone within hearing distance that he'd carted Bree around on his back.

He felt her hands go to his shoulders, and she leaped, her legs wrapping around his hips in a way that made things shift and then...tighten. His free arm scooped under one of her bare legs to hold her in place before realizing they weren't going to make it without him holding on to her better. "Can you take the quilt? Drape it around my neck or something."

Somehow, she managed to take the cover and lay it

over his shoulder, along with the strap of the backpack. Then, wrapping his arms beneath both of her legs, he started back down the hill.

CHAPTER SEVEN

OH, GOD, WHY did you have to wear a skirt today of all days?

With her arms wrapped around his neck, trying to make sure her forearm was holding the quilt in place, there was no way to rescue the hem of her skirt, which was riding higher and higher on her thighs. Thighs that were becoming sensitized by rubbing against his lean hips. She could hear him breathing from the exertion of going down some of the steeper parts of the hill, and one time his foot slid on some loose gravel and she closed her eyes, expecting to crash to the ground. But she didn't. He'd righted himself and kept on walking.

"I should have let you find a stick."

"I don't think I could hold a walking stick."

She shook her head, even though she knew he couldn't see her. "I mean a stick to throw at the snake."

"No," Several more steps. "You did the right thing."

"Why don't you stop and take a rest?"

His head swiveled from right to left as he shook it to mean no. "If I put you down, I know you well enough to know you'll never get up again. Not that much farther."

He was right. There was no way she'd make him

carry her again. If she'd realized how far they'd come, she'd have never agreed to this stupid plan in the first place. But here she was. And he was still going back for the shoe afterward.

Why hadn't she just let him pick it up? Thinking about it, she'd probably sounded extremely childish, saying she wouldn't wear the shoe. But she had a phobia of snakes. She didn't know what had possessed her to try to scare the thing away anyway. Maybe because she'd pictured Diego picking up some kind of stick and getting close enough to its fangs to get bitten, too. If it had come toward them, would she have stood her ground? Or abandoned her patient? Thank heaven she hadn't had to make that choice.

"I'm sorry, Diego. It was stupid of me to leave my shoe behind."

He gave a chuckle. "I'm rather enjoying this."

His breathing didn't quite sound like he was enjoying it. Then again, her breathing wasn't exactly steady, either, but there was a completely different reason for that. With his arms looped under her legs, it was as if he were holding her in place—holding her tightly against his body. If he'd been facing her rather than having his back to her... Her thighs rubbed again, and sensation arced with lightning speed to the area he would have been touching. Oh, man, it didn't bear thinking about.

She tried to pull air in and out of her lungs in slow deep breaths, but her brain had already shifted onto another track. She wasn't going to survive this.

Even now her nipples were tightening, every jostle of his body providing a delicious friction that made her want to whimper and press closer. Instead she tried to lean slightly back to take the pressure off.

"Hey, what are you doing back there?" His voice had a gurgling quality to it. "You're choking me."

"Sorry!" She pressed against him again, loosening her grip on his neck.

Scrape, scrape went her thighs. And her blouse against her sensitive nipples. Every footfall he made just upped the ante. And now that central area between her thighs was beginning a familiar tingle that spelled disaster.

They came upon another couple who were walking in the opposite direction. The man was on his phone. He looked at them twice, eyes going wide. Before she could say anything, Diego said, "Missing shoe. It's a long story."

"You're that woman who threw her shoe at the snake, aren't you?"

"I—I..." She couldn't think of a thing to say.

As the couple passed them, the woman smiled at her. "Well done. I don't think I would have been courageous enough to do that."

Thankfully they had already passed them by the time her tongue was able to free itself from the roof of her mouth.

Oh, God, the car. She saw it! If she could just survive another fifteen feet, she would soon be...

They got to the hood of the sports car, and she took the quilt from his shoulder and tossed it onto the vehicle. "You can put me down now." *Please, please put me down.*

Instead of letting her slide down, his arms tightened. "Are you sure that's what you want? For me to let go?"

Had he felt her reaction to him? Maybe she'd bored twin holes into his back.

"Yes. Thank you for carrying me, though."

Thankfully, he released her legs, and she scrambled down his body, doing her best to keep her skirt from riding all the way up. Once down, she made sure her arms were over her chest before he turned to face her.

He glanced at her face and then moved down to her crossed arms. When his eyes came back up, one side of his mouth twitched slightly.

Oh, hell. He knew. He *knew*! Her face heated to something that would rival Armageddon as she stood there. She was so tempted to look to see if there was any answering response on his part, but he would know exactly what she was doing if she did. And right now, she preferred to pretend she had no idea what he was thinking.

"You're very welcome. Anytime."

Not very likely. "I don't think I'll be throwing my shoe again."

He smiled. "Speaking of shoes. You'll be okay here while I go retrieve it?"

"Oh, Diego, first you have to carry me down the mountain, now you have to make that trip all over again."

"It's not a problem. Get in the car, and I'll turn the air on." He retrieved two of the water bottles from the cooler when he threw the quilt and backpack onto the back seat and handed her one of the bottles. The water was super cold and hit her system with a welcome jolt that would hopefully ice down some of her earlier thoughts.

He climbed in the driver's seat and cranked the engine, keeping the parking brake on while shifting the vehicle into Neutral. It didn't take long for the air to cool the space, drying the sweat on her and making a chill rush through her system. She couldn't suppress a shiver.

"Too much?"

"No, it's perfect."

"Okay, lock the door when I get out."

She nodded. "Please be careful. You don't know where that thing went."

"Will you come and throw your other shoe at it if it gets me, too?"

This time she laughed. "And how will you carry me back down the mountain if you're bitten, too?"

"I would find a way."

With those enigmatic words, he was gone, slamming the door and leaving her to stare after him. He would, too. Find a way. Or at least try to. He was that kind of man. So why was it so hard for him to commit to a child that he might have had a part in conceiving?

She could just as easily ask herself why it was so easy to expect him to, when he'd had no say in whether she kept the baby or terminated the pregnancy.

Why hadn't she considered that?

Because something inside her was already attached to this little bean—or whatever size the fetus currently was. She wanted it. And she didn't want Diego to feel like he needed to want it, too. Even though in her heart that's exactly what she was hoping. It was stupid. And it was selfish. And she needed to try to prepare herself for the reality that he really might not want to be a father. Who was she to dictate how he felt or didn't feel?

Maybe he would choose to walk away, just like Sergio had. God, she hoped not. She didn't know why, but she wasn't quite ready for him to be out of her life.

A half hour passed before he finally returned. But there was nothing in his hands. She frowned, waiting for him to climb inside. "What happened? Couldn't you find it?"

"I did." He looked at her. "Did you want it?"

"No. Where is it?"

"In a rubbish bin on the path. I can go back and get it if you've changed your mind."

"No, I definitely haven't. Thank you. I know it's stupid, I just—"

"You just can't stand looking at it every day and remembering its significance. I understand all too well."

Its significance? Was he thinking about how, once she had this baby, he wouldn't be able to stand looking at him or her every day without remembering the child's significance? That he or she was conceived as the result of a stupid one-night stand? What had he called it?

A mistake.

A spear of pain went through her. Just like carrying her down that mountain, was she putting a burden on him that she had no right to make him bear? Maybe demanding he take part in raising this baby was wrong. Maybe it was downright cruel.

But what else could she do? She had to think of her baby, too.

I would find a way.

Wasn't that what he'd said? But carrying her down a mountain was different than taking on a lifetime commitment.

"Would you mind swinging by the hospital before you drop me off so I can check on Lydia?" She realized there was another answer. One that would make it easier on him. "Sorry, I guess there's no reason why you couldn't take me back to the hotel and let me drive over."

"I'd like to make sure she's okay, too, so we'll go to the hospital first. That is, if you can stand being in the car with me a little while longer."

Had he guessed her thoughts from a few seconds ago? No, she was pretty sure he had no idea what she'd been mulling over, and she was glad. She had a lot to think about tonight.

"Of course I can. I do need a shoe, though. I don't think the hospital would approve of one of its employees traipsing around barefoot. If you could just find a store and let me run in on the way?"

The trip to the hospital seemed to take a lot less time than their trek down the mountain on foot. After a successful shoe mission, Diego found a spot and pulled the car into it. She wiggled her toes in her new jewel-encrusted flip-flops. It was all they'd had in her size.

They got out and headed up to the front entrance. "I didn't get her last name," she said.

"I'm pretty sure all we have to say is snake bite victim and they'll know where she is."

Diego went up to the information desk and took a minute to chitchat with the person manning the station before he came back. "She's not in ICU, so that's a good thing. She's on the third floor."

They went up the elevator, and she followed him down the hallway until they got to the room. Diego knocked, and a woman's voice called for them to enter.

Diego opened the door and held it so she could pass through it. Once they got inside, they saw Lydia sitting up in bed, the area around her ankle stained with a black permanent marker, showing the spread of damage over her leg. But the lines were close together, and it had been over an hour since the ambulance had left the scene.

Bree smiled at her. "You look remarkably well."

"They've given me some lovely painkillers." Her face contorted. "They said I was lucky. Very, very lucky. And I have you two to thank. The damage to my leg could have been so much worse. And it if had spread…"

Diego moved closer. "Emergency services were there in fifteen minutes. They had a lot to do with it."

"I'm just glad you were both there. Thank you. I truly mean that. If you hadn't acted quickly, who knows what might have happened."

Bree laid her palm on the woman's shoulder. "It looks like there's not much progression up your leg."

"No. Everyone was surprised. I might not even need another dose of whatever they used to counteract the poison."

It was a common mistake. Calling it poison rather than venom.

"I'm glad the antivenin is doing its job. Some of that depends on how much venom the snake injected. There's even such a thing as a dry bite, where no venom is released, although from your pain levels and the marks they've made on your leg, that wasn't the case this time."

Diego said, "Is there anything we can do? Anyone you'd like for us to call?"

She gave kind of a sheepish shrug. "I called Patrick—my boyfriend. He's trying to get a flight out right now."

She hadn't used the qualifier *ex* this time when she talked about him.

"That's wonderful," Bree said. She forced her voice to sound cheerful, even though she couldn't help but think of Sergio and wonder what would have happened if he'd chosen another path. If things had been different. They might have been starting their own family.

But they weren't. And now he was gone. Along with his deceit and lying.

She'd been thinking so much about Diego and his plans as far as the baby was concerned. But it might not even be his. She kept forgetting that one little fact. And if he wasn't, then all this angst she'd been going through—that she'd been putting Diego through— might all be for nothing. Because if the baby wasn't his, there was no way he was going to want anything to do with it. No way he would want anything to do with her. No chance…for anything.

Was that what she wanted? A chance for something? How did she know that Diego would stick around? That he was any more honest than Sergio had been?

He'd been honest about not wanting to be a father. He could have told her exactly what she wanted to hear and then skipped out. But he hadn't. And he was standing here right now. That was worth something, wasn't it?

She had no idea. And unfortunately it had become kind of natural to think of him as the father. As somehow being in her life, even after such a short period of time. Was she fantasizing about things that would never happen?

Like she'd fantasized about him on the way down from that mountain?

Oh, yeah. She'd been on fire. For him.

The fantasy of spending one more night with the cardiac surgeon was going to be a hard one to banish. Because once she knew whose baby it was, one of two things was going to happen. He was either going to walk away with a huge sigh of relief, or he was going to stay because he had to.

He wasn't entirely immune to her, though. At least she didn't think he was.

So what would he say if she propositioned him to stay with her tonight? Would he think she was manipulating him in order to get him to stay in her life? Or would he take it at face value, as the request of a woman who desired a man? Physical desire. Not emotional.

God, at least she hoped it wasn't.

She glanced over at where he was talking to Lydia. As if sensing her eyes on him, he turned toward her. He blinked. Frowned. "Are you okay?"

"Yeah. I am, Diego. Really fine, actually."

He must have seen something in her face or heard it in her words, because that frown faded, and his head tilted as he studied her. Then a devastating half smile took its place. The same one he'd given her when he'd turned to look and saw her covering herself up with her arms.

Was she that easy to read?

He murmured to Lydia about how glad he was that she was feeling better and that someone was coming to be with her. That they'd check in on her again tomorrow.

They?

And that's when she knew. He was not only open to spending a few hours with her tonight. He might not be planning on going home at all.

Diego could have sworn he'd heard an invitation in Bree's voice a moment or two ago. But he waited until he got to the car before actually turning to look at her.

Disappointment sloshed through him. Whatever he'd seen was gone now. As if it had never been there at all. And maybe it hadn't. Maybe he'd imagined all of it.

"How are your new shoes feeling?"

"They're fine." She fiddled with the fabric of her skirt before looking at him again. "Hey…um, do you want to come up once we get to the hotel?"

Okay, so maybe it hadn't been wishful thinking after all.

"Yes, I would like that." Only this time, he didn't want to guess what she meant. He leaned forward so he could look at her. "Just to make sure…this isn't for coffee or tea…or to eat those sandwiches you made, as delicious as they might be, right?"

"I wasn't planning on offering you any of those things."

His brows went up as a whisper of anticipation

crouched low in his belly. "And just what were you planning on offering me?"

She hesitated for a minute before placing her hand on his knee and squeezing. "Me."

The word was simple. Unadorned. And it moved him in a way not much could. In a way that nothing had in a very long time. Not with Angela. Not with Selina.

Without a word, he turned his key in the ignition and backed out of the space before he was able to answer. "I accept your offer."

The trip to her hotel found the roads congested, just as they'd been on the trip into town. But this time there was an impatience in him that hadn't been there a half hour ago. The whole time he'd carried her down that hill, he'd been hyperaware of her weight on him, had remembered how it had felt to have her splayed across his hips in an entirely different way. And her breasts mashed against his back? That had been heaven. Sheer heaven. He'd had a hard time making it down without giving himself away. Had been out of breath and out of sorts, almost stumbling once as they continued their trip. He'd been glad to have to go back after her shoe, hoping it would give him time to compose himself before he had to face her again.

And he had done a decent job of it. Until she'd told him she had no intention of offering him coffee or sandwiches.

He'd be a fool to turn her down. Especially since both of their lives were about to change forever. This time there was no worry about pregnancy. Because Mother Nature had already taken care of that.

They could go back to his place—it was closer—

but something kept him from going that route. She'd already inserted herself into his life—even though it hadn't been intentional—and he'd rather control the setting. And she'd already suggested her hotel. It was easier. Less personal. For both of them, since it wasn't a space either one of them would inhabit afterward. She had a place she was getting ready to move into. This event could just fade into both of their pasts, just like the previous hotel visit had done.

Except that hadn't faded into the past. Because Bree was here. And she was expecting his—or Sergio's—baby.

He decided to follow up on something. "It's okay? You're feeling okay?"

"Yes. I'm actually feeling better than I have in a couple of weeks."

He was glad. Not just because it meant they were going to sleep together again, but for her sake.

They got to her street, and Diego turned onto it. If he was going to back out, now was the time. Except he didn't want to. The other night he'd spent with her had been fantastic. Better than any night he'd ever spent with a woman. Something he really didn't want to examine too closely. Maybe that had been because at the time he knew there were no strings. No next-morning angst or regrets. Or at least he'd thought there'd been none.

But even that didn't deter him from wanting to be with her again, as evidenced by how fast he'd leaped at her offer. It was embarrassing, really. But that fact wasn't enough to make him want to back out. He didn't think anything would really make him want to do that. Unless she changed her mind.

Then they were out of the car and up the elevator, her hand clasped tightly in his as if he was afraid she would fly away if he let her go. He had a feeling it wasn't that. But more that he was trying to assure himself that this was true. That he wasn't dreaming this.

The second her front door swung shut behind them, he hauled her to him for a long kiss, eyes clenched tight as her remembered taste poured through him. Sweet. Like the sweetest wine. And the most potent tequila.

Her arms wound around his neck, and her breasts were again pressed tight against him. And it was still heaven. He sighed, leaning back slightly to look at her. "I thought about this on the way down the mountain, you know."

"You did?" She smiled, that dimple hitting his gut and sliding down to the part of him that was already aching for her. "So did I. I was afraid you'd notice."

He decided to let her in on a little secret. "I did. But then I thought maybe I was imagining it. That I was just projecting my own thoughts onto you."

"Oh, there was no projecting going on at all." She grabbed his hand and started to lead him back to where he suspected her bedroom was, but he countered the move with one of his own.

"Let's save the bed." He looked at her. "For later."

She blinked at him.

Kissing her mouth again, he whispered. "I thought I saw a nice little balcony out there the last time I was here. The picture you showed me of your new place has one that's similar. Just as private."

Her breath washed across his mouth. "I like the way you think." She bit her lip. "I do have neighbors on either side of me, though. They can't see, but..."

They could hear. He caught her meaning. His cheek brushed against hers as he moved over to her ear. "We'll have to be very, very quiet, then. Can you do that?"

He didn't think she'd been the noisemaker the last time they were together. That had been all him. But the thought of trying to contain himself—to pour all his energy into loving her—was a heady thought. One he was pretty sure he could do, but that tiny hint of doubt...of having to purposely restrain himself from yelling out... It was a huge turn-on.

"Yes." Her whispered confirmation was all he needed to grab her to him with a growl and kiss her the way he'd been dying to all the way down that mountain.

She giggled. "I thought we were supposed to be quiet."

"Oh, believe me, I can be perfectly silent." His tongue touched her lower lip. "Perfectly. Still."

The shiver he felt against his chest hadn't been his imagination.

He scooped her up in his arms and carried her over to French doors that opened onto the outside space. Bree reached down and twisted the handle of the one to the right and pushed it away from them. With her still in his arms, he went through them, setting her down next to the railing, where walls extended out past the barrier, ensuring that no one on either side of them could see anything. And in front of them was nothing but the mountain.

CHAPTER EIGHT

BREE COULDN'T BELIEVE this was happening. And yet it was.

Diego was behind her, arms wrapped around her waist, his lips slowly brushing across the sensitive flesh of her neck. The sensation was slightly tickly, mixed with a whole lot of sensuality. This time there was no mistaking his reaction to being close to her. No need for her to look. She could feel him pressed tight against the top of her butt. She swallowed. She wanted to bend at the waist and let him slide her skirt up her legs, up her thighs…over the curve of her bottom. Her teeth sank into her lower lip as she struggled to contain a whimper that rose in her throat as she thought about what he was going to do to her. What she was going to do to him.

No sounds. She tried picturing her neighbors sitting on the other side of that partition enjoying their demitasses of Italian coffee.

Italian coffee. Pah! There was no comparison to the Italian she was currently enjoying.

His hands slid up to cup her breasts through her blouse before sliding down and with deliberate motions tugging the shirt up and over her head. There was no one in front of them to see, except for the mountain, and Bree was pretty sure Etna wouldn't be sharing anything that she saw.

Even so, she felt very naughty standing there in her bra. Then, that, too, suddenly went loose, the straps carrying the entire garment down her arms before dropping to the ground.

But she didn't have time to debate what to do, because no sooner had the slight breeze washed over her bare skin, causing her nipples to contract, than his hands covered her again, the warmth of his palms rivaling the heat of the outside air.

He nipped her ear, fingers moving from her breasts down the bare skin of her torso before finding her hips. He pulled her back against him, the hard ridge behind her making her gasp.

"Shh…"

Lord, she wanted to reach behind her and grip the backs of his thighs and keep him right where he was, but she'd have to let go of the railing to do that.

Then the very thing she'd fantasized about began to happen. Her skirt began inching up her legs.

Diego whispered in her ear, the Italian low and raw. *"Voglio te."*

He wanted her. Well, that wanting was mutual, only hers was wild and desperate. At this point, it couldn't happen fast enough. The anticipation had been building ever since the trip down the mountain, and she was pretty sure the second he touched her, she was going to explode. She squirmed against him, wishing he would hurry. Not because she was afraid someone would discover what they were doing, but because she needed to feel him again. Wanted that intimacy that only sex could bring.

And it was sex, right?

Nothing more.

Don't think about it, Bree.

So she didn't. Instead, she allowed herself to revel in the little things. The sound that her skirt made as it continued its whispered ascent. The breeze as it rustled the leaves of the plants that surrounded the space. The way her heart pounded in her chest.

Then her skirt was around her waist. She wasn't sure why he hadn't pushed it down her legs, but she didn't care. This was just as sexy. Maybe more so, since she now caught the sound of his zipper as the tab snicked across each tooth, separating them.

One hand cupped her chin and tipped her face to look at him before he kissed her deeply, his tongue filling her mouth. Her nerve endings went wild as she closed her lips around him, holding him in place before she felt him slide free.

Down went her panties, and his hands were back on her hips, tugging slightly to encourage her to take a step or two back. She took the opportunity to step out of her underwear as well.

She was tipped forward, exactly the way she'd imagined it. The sound of a packet being ripped open distracted her for a second before she shook off the sensation. Of course he would protect himself. Sergio had had who knew how many partners? But still there was a frisson of disappointment that she would not get to feel him skin to skin.

But it was okay. It was more than okay. He was still here with her.

And when she felt the touch of him against her, her eyes shut and she savored the sensation of him entering her, stretching her. His shaky breath blew across her ear. "I'm trying."

She had no idea what he was trying to do. To be quiet? To hold on?

Diego set a slow, languorous pace that made her squirm. And then his hand reached around to cup her, fingers touching sensitive places that sent her reeling toward madness.

She wanted to tell him to go faster, to push deeper, but she'd taken a vow of silence. So she tried to tell him with her body, pushing back against him with each thrust of his hips, arching into his hand to deepen the pressure there.

He got it. He wrapped his free arm around her waist and jerked her back to him, changing the pace inside her, increasing the friction in front.

Her nerve endings became a mass of activity, each electrical signal trying to catch her attention. And they did, quickly overloading her senses. The rush to the top happened with a speed that robbed her of breath, stole her thoughts. All she could do ride high and let the vortex overtake her. She exploded around him, somehow managing not to scream or moan or do any of the other things her body yelled for her to do.

His movements matched hers, and when he thrust deep into her and strained and strained, she knew he was reaching his release as well.

Moments went by, and she was vaguely aware of her

heart rate slowing. Her ragged breaths easing back toward the normal range.

A sense of despair shivered along the nerve endings that had once carried ecstasy.

It was over. And this was probably the last time she would ever be with him.

She let go of the railing, and her fingers trailed along the arm that was still around her, needing a connection that didn't have anything to do with the sex they'd just had.

His fingers caught and gripped hers as he eased from inside her. He held her there for another minute or two. Then he smiled and scooped her back into his arms. The sense of loss was brief as he kissed her forehead. His words were still spoken in hushed tones. "Do you want to eat? Or visit that bedroom that was mentioned earlier?"

Relief washed across her. Maybe it wasn't over after all.

"Can we eat *after* the bedroom?"

Standing there whispering back and forth was somehow as intimate as what they'd just shared, maybe more.

"Yes, I think that would be my preferred order as well."

With that, he carried her back into the hotel room, closing the balcony door firmly behind him. At least now they were no longer committed to silence. They could both be as loud…and as free…as they wanted.

Diego was gone when she woke up. And he hadn't answered the question she'd asked as they lay in bed together after making love. What the tattoo on his bicep meant. Instead, he'd distracted her with kisses that led to more.

She wasn't surprised to find he'd disappeared. She'd half expected it. In fact, she was glad she wasn't going to have to go through the morning rituals of trying to find small talk that meant nothing and trying to avoid subjects that meant everything.

It had been a night to remember. And she, for one, would remember it all. Every touch. Every whispered word.

Every climax.

She shuddered before showering and getting dressed for her day at the hospital. She and Diego didn't have a joint surgery today, but he had mentioned going to see how Lydia was doing. So she checked her phone for messages—there were none—before driving herself to the hospital and found a spot. Then she hurried into the main entrance of the hospital.

"Well done, Doctor."

The words from Geraldo at the information desk stopped her midflight. She froze. "I'm sorry?"

"What you did yesterday. Everyone's talking about it." The man gave her a huge, goofy grin.

Oh God! How? How could he know? And not just him! Everyone?

Maybe they hadn't been as quiet as they'd thought.

"I—I'm not sure what you're talking about."

Geraldo pulled out his phone and scrolled for a second before turning the screen to face her.

Doctors from Ospedale Maria di Concepción Save Snakebite Victim

Right underneath the caption was a picture of her… and Diego. Not a respectable picture of them at Lydia's side, trying to save her life, but one with her clinging to Diego's back like some kind of sex-starved leech as he'd carried her down the mountain.

Oh, no!

"Where did you find this?" Maybe it was some obscure site. Except he'd said everyone was talking about it.

"It was the first thing that popped up on my browser this morning. I didn't realize the victim was here at the hospital."

"Was?" She and Diego were supposed to visit her this morning.

"She was released a few minutes ago. They said she gave a nice interview."

Oh God. Lydia had talked to the press about what happened? Bree pressed her lids together. Well, the snakebite victim certainly hadn't taken that picture of them, though. She'd been long gone by the time they'd left the scene.

She thought about that couple they'd come across on the path. She thought she remembered the man looking at his phone. But maybe he'd been taking a picture of them instead. *Jeez, Louise*—the expression her mom liked to use popped into her head. It probably didn't look good that the chief of surgery was giving piggy-back rides like some sort of sappy boyfriend.

What about a not-so-sappy lover? God, this was a mess. And someone was probably going to guess if they didn't cool things down.

"I—I lost my shoe and couldn't walk."

Geraldo turned the phone around and refreshed the screen. "Ah, I didn't notice you were missing a shoe when I saw it the first time. I thought maybe you guys were celebrating saving that woman."

No, the celebrating had come later.

The thought made her face heat. "It's a long story." She started to say goodbye and walk away, but instead she said, "Thank you for letting me know."

Better to hear about it right as she walked into the hospital than to have no idea their day at Etna had made the papers. Was Diego at work yet? If not, maybe she should warn him before he walked by Geraldo. She moved a short distance away and dialed his number.

He answered on the first ring. "Pintor here."

"Diego, where are you?" Her words came out as a whisper.

"Bree? Why are you talking like that? I'm in my office."

Maybe somehow he'd gotten through without anyone stopping him. Except his words were clipped and blunt—no hint of a greeting there. Or an apology for leaving before she woke up. She raised her voice to a more normal volume. "Have you heard, um...?"

"Heard the news? Yes. Hard to get through that entryway without Geraldo divvying out the latest gossip. This time the gossip just happened to be about us."

Except this wasn't gossip. It had really happened. And if people got the wrong idea about them, they wouldn't be entirely mistaken. There had been more to it than that picture had shown. Much more. Except the sex part wasn't permanent. But a baby certainly was.

"Hey," he said. "Can I call you back? I have some-one in my office at the moment."

Had he gotten in trouble for that picture? It wasn't his fault.

"Is it about what happened? Do you need me to come up and explain?"

"No. I don't think that would help in this case."

She shut her eyes, imagining HR sitting in Diego's office demanding an explanation of their conduct. Well, good thing the powers that be hadn't seen the conduct that had happened later that evening. They'd probably both be out on the street, pink slips in hand.

Surely not. What doctors did outside office hours was none of anyone's business, right? Not really. If the heads of Concepción decided she and Diego reflected badly on them, they were allowed to take action. That had been a clause in the hiring document she'd signed. A sense of humiliation engulfed her before she brushed it off angrily. She didn't have anything to be embar-rassed about. There was nothing in her paperwork that forbade relationships between coworkers.

A voice that wasn't Diego's came through the phone. "Is that her?" It was a woman, and the tones were clearly peeved. Accusatory. It sounded personal in nature rather than professional.

Was that his ex? His mom?

She heard murmurings that she couldn't make out. Diego must have put his hand over the phone to muffle whatever he was saying. Then he came back. "Let me call you back in a few."

Then the line went dead. Whatever was going on up there wasn't fun. If his ex was upset about a picture, imagine what the woman's surprise would be when she found out Diego had fathered a child with the woman from the picture. *If* the baby was his. Hopefully by Friday they would have their answer.

She waffled from one side to the other as far as who she hoped the father was. It would be a whole lot less complicated if Sergio turned out to be the father. Yes, his parents would want to be in the baby's life, and that would be heartbreaking for her and for them. Especially if the accusations surrounding Sergio turned out to be true.

And if the baby was Diego's?

She'd never even met his parents. Or even knew if they were still alive.

In reality, they didn't know much about each other. Except she knew that Diego was a dedicated doctor and a thorough lover, taking as much care for her pleasure as he had for his own. She'd tried to add to what he was doing, but at times she'd felt like she was floating in a pool of sensuality, so overcome that all she could do was lie there and absorb what was happening.

No wonder he'd taken off. She swallowed. Maybe she owed him an apology.

Five minutes later her phone went off. It was Diego.

"Hi," she said.

"Sorry if you heard any of that."

She tried a guess. "Your ex."

"Yes. She was a little…surprised that I seemed to have moved on so quickly. Not that she doesn't already have a new person in her life."

"Oh." What else could she say? "I hope you got everything worked out."

"There's nothing to work out. We never could agree on a certain point. She asked for permanence, and I didn't want that."

Her belly squelched as she realized she might have given him exactly what he didn't want. And unlike his ex, Bree hadn't asked. But she hadn't tried to corner him into giving something he didn't want. She'd made it more than clear that she didn't expect him to be a permanent fixture in her or the baby's lives.

"I'm sorry, Diego."

She heard him expel a breath. "Don't be. My issues with her have nothing to do with you. Well, maybe they do. Anyway, do you have time to meet for a few minutes so we can decide how to handle all of this new attention?"

"Sure. Do you want to come down here? Or do you want me to go there?"

"Let's meet outside the hospital, if that's okay. I don't really want anyone to see me disappearing into your office right now."

Ah, she got it. No more secret rendezvouses for Diego. She should probably be just as concerned, but she wasn't. Eventually her pregnancy was going to make itself known, and everyone was going to be wondering the same thing—whether or not Diego was the father.

What a mess. What she'd thought could be hidden was going to be yanked from behind the curtain and put on full display. All she could do was say the father was no longer in the picture and hope for the best. So much easier to do if Sergio was the father.

"There's a little patio with some tables outside, although people will probably see us. Unlike..."

Last night?

She wasn't going to say it, although there'd been no way to keep it from running through her mind.

He went on. "I'd rather people see us talking and being friendly rather than avoiding each other. That will just make things look worse."

She agreed with him, although, boy, did avoiding him ever sound attractive right now. "Okay, the patio it is. Five minutes?"

"Yes. I'll meet you down there."

Bree ducked into the coffee shop on her way to her destination, being stopped a couple more times by colleagues congratulating her on her quick thinking.

Damn, it wasn't like she'd grabbed the snake by the throat or anything. Even the thought of that made her shudder. She glanced down at her feet, glad she hadn't worn her new thong sandals. She wasn't sure she would wear those anywhere around Diego again. Because when he'd finally removed her shoes last night, he had massaged her feet and toes, giving her an entirely different kind of pleasure. It had been tender and romantic and nothing like she'd experienced before. But the sweet and the sexy had all kind of merged into one blissful night. Even looking at those sandals made those memories come into sharp relief.

Her coffee in hand, she pushed through the door to the outside patio area. A huge pergola covered the space; its canvas covering could be pulled to give shade to those out there or retracted to bring warmth in the winter. Diego was already out there, hunched over one of the tables. There were only a couple of other people on the patio, and they were seated quite some distance away. Glancing at the coffee in her hand, she wished she'd asked him if he wanted anything. Moving over to him, she picked the seat across the table from him. "Sorry that this thing kind of blew up in our faces."

"Yeah. Me, too. I was focused on the talk we were going to have yesterday, and it never dawned on me that anyone would find out and misconstrue things so completely."

"Misconstrue them how?"

"That we're in a relationship."

It was exactly what she'd feared when Geraldo had waylaid her this morning. And even though she knew in her heart of hearts they weren't emotionally involved with each other, the words still stung with a sense of rejection. "All we can do is tell them, if they ask. Just say that I asked you about Mount Etna and that you felt obligated to take me on a tour. The rest is history."

"So lie, in other words?"

She shrugged. "What do you suggest we do, then?"

"I have no idea."

"Does this have to do with your ex coming to see you? Does she see that article as somehow confirming something?"

"No. She doesn't. I think she was just feeling me out to see if I'd changed my mind."

"About what?"

He gave a hard laugh. "About having children. That me saying it wasn't her, it was me had been something I'd made up so I could go out and make a child with someone else."

"You broke up with her because you didn't want

kids?" Her heart seized. "Did I miss you telling me this? I thought you said it was about permanence."

"Is there anything more permanent than having a child together?" He squeezed the bridge of his nose between his thumb and forefinger. "Anyway, I didn't think it was relevant. But it wasn't the only reason Selina and I called it quits."

But it was the main one, or the woman wouldn't have come looking for him. "She has another boyfriend?"

"Yes, and she didn't hide the fact that they're trying to get pregnant."

God, Bree and Diego hadn't even *tried* to have kids. It had been the furthest thing from either of their minds, and yet here they were.

"Did you tell her? About my condition?"

"No. I didn't see the need."

Because it might not be his. Or maybe because he wasn't planning on sticking around. The sting from earlier came back stronger than ever.

"So what did you tell her about that picture? And what do you want me to say when people stop and ask me?"

"Just tell them the truth. That we were hiking up Etna and came across someone who needed help."

He was right. Said like that, it seemed about as innocent as you could get.

"Well, that's what I told Geraldo. And I told him I'd lost a shoe and that's what the picture was showing. He hadn't even noticed, he said. Hopefully that will help head off a lot of gossip."

"You and me both."

She decided to say something that she hoped would

help him feel less pressure. "I don't expect you to make any kind of decision until after we find out the results of the test, which is just two days away—if they're on time with it."

"I have thought about it, and what I'd like to propose is this. That if this baby has my DNA, we use the pregnancy as a testing ground for you to see how I do. To see how I handle the pressures involved with being a father. And then sometime before the baby is born, you can make the final decision about what role I play."

If this baby has my DNA... That phrasing was about as impersonal as you could get. It rubbed her wrong and kept rubbing until a raw spot opened up in her heart.

So he was going to act like the baby's father during the pregnancy, but he was going to be passive about it? Was going to make *her* choose whether or not he was involved? What about him? What did Diego want?

And if it wasn't the rosy experience he wanted it to be? She wasn't sure why, but that suggestion just made the DNA comment even worse. He'd said the wrong thing...on the wrong day. And she wasn't having it.

"I'm sorry, Diego. But that is absolutely not an option. You're either in this baby's life or you're not."

CHAPTER NINE

DIEGO WASN'T SURE what he'd been expecting her to say, but that wasn't it. She'd cut him off without even giving him a chance.

"Don't you think it's better to do the test run now before the baby is born than after he or she has come into the world?"

She frowned and took a big drink of the coffee she'd brought. "I don't understand you. You were just worried about people thinking we were in a relationship, so you going with me to prenatal visits isn't going to look the least bit suspicious?"

He leaned back in his chair. "I wasn't exactly going to advertise that we were going together."

"I don't think we exactly advertised our trip up to Etna, either, and look what happened with that."

"What do you expect me to do, Bree? Suddenly confess to being the baby's father after he or she is born?"

"No." Her voice was low and firm. "I don't expect you to do anything. And I really don't want to make any kind of decision until after we get the results back from the paternity test."

"And then what? We were supposed to make plans

when we were at Etna, so why the sudden about-face?" He'd just had a completely exasperating meeting with Selina, and now to have to sit here and hash out things about the baby he thought he'd never have? It wasn't sitting well.

"I don't know. Maybe we weren't supposed to talk on Etna. The bottom line is I don't want to make plans for what I don't know. Not yet. And I certainly don't want to make plans for you."

Two women came out onto the terrace area, trays with food in their hands. They sat down at the next table, looked at them and then leaned across to say something to each other. Great. So much for talking this out. It looked like everyone else was talking about Bree and him...except for Bree and him.

She tipped the cup up, taking what must be the last swig of coffee and swallowing it. "Why don't we hold off on this until I go on Friday?"

This was the first he'd heard of this: that she was going in person to get their test results. Well, if she could be there, then so could he.

So, very aware that there were people at the next table, he murmured. "Great. So what time should I pick you up?"

Her eyes widened as she, too, glanced at the next table. "You don't have to do that."

"That's where you're wrong, Bree. I want to. And then we can decide things right then and right there." He stood up and gave her a smile that felt grotesquely fake. But he wasn't going to give her a chance to argue about it any more than she'd given him a chance to argue his point about trying fatherhood on for size. "I'll see you then."

* * *

Bree had been a little hasty in shooting down Diego's idea. And once she had a chance to think about it, she saw that it had merit. Hadn't she been afraid he would suddenly disappear from the baby's life like Sergio had disappeared from hers? And how could she ask him to decide on something he couldn't try on for size? Something he'd have no idea how he'd feel about until he experienced it. She'd been able to make a choice about having the baby. Wasn't it only fair that she allow him to make the best choice he could under the circumstances?

But she also didn't want to take another two-hour trek over to Palermo trapped in a car with him. So she'd called Teresina, the friend she had made over at the other hospital, and asked if she could have the results delivered to her house. Because if they drove over there together, her mind was going to drift off into areas she shouldn't revisit. That she couldn't revisit. The last two days had been torture as far as her work at the hospital went. She had been approached by person after person and given congratulatory words, when any one of them would have done the same thing under the circumstances. Worse, the hospital had blown up a copy of the story and put it on one of the bulletin boards, where patients could see it. Including the picture of Diego packing her around on his back.

But fortunately, HR had never called her in to ask her about that day. For that she was very glad. If Diego was to be a father to this child, then that would have to change. They would have to go together to talk to the people who handled personnel matters and inform them. And what then? Would they ask her to resign?

Things could get ugly if she and Diego ever disagreed over things like custody or visitation. Because although they weren't romantically involved, they would have to come to a consensus on how they would make decisions. Would the baby have her last name? Or Diego's? A million choices that never would have had to be made if he hadn't seen the pregnancy test in her basket that day.

Would she have told him if he hadn't been there that day? She wasn't sure. Although, she was almost certain he would have asked at some point because of the timing, and because he'd known next to nothing about her relationship with Sergio. Of course, now he knew a lot more than he'd bargained for.

Bree was supposed to call him once the results were couriered to her hotel, and they would meet and discuss them. Was she going to look at them ahead of time? Probably not. The last thing she wanted was to be tempted to back out of meeting him. And if she found out the baby was Diego's, she might. So her plan was to open them together.

Probably another mistake. But honestly, she didn't want to be alone when she found out.

But she didn't want to be with Diego, either.

So it was a no-win situation. But she would get through it the same way she'd gotten through the day of her wedding, the way she'd gotten through the results of that pregnancy test. They way she'd gotten through the news of their trip to Etna being broadcast far and wide. She'd weathered all those things. She would weather this, too.

The hotel's reception desk called and said she had a

package down at the lobby. Her heart skipped a beat. This was it. The moment of truth.

She went downstairs and picked up the official-looking envelope, glad that the paper was thick enough to keep prying eyes from seeing what was inside. Including hers.

Then rather than go back upstairs, where the temptation to tear it open and look would be too much, she went and sat in one of the chairs in the lobby. They hadn't talked about where they would meet to find out the results. But she didn't want to be upstairs in her room. And she didn't want to go to Diego's house.

In fact, the sooner she could move her things out of this hotel, the better. The memories here were just… overwhelming. Every time she went out onto that balcony, she felt him all around her. And damn if it didn't hurt. In a way that it shouldn't hurt. Unless she cared about him more than she wanted to admit.

Pulling her phone from her purse, she dialed his number. He picked up on the first ring. "Did you get it?"

"I did. Where do you want to meet?"

They sounded like two spies planning some kind of covert op. And maybe they were, kind of. They were trying to keep something from people at the hospital, although after that fiasco with Etna, she wasn't sure it was even possible. But at least they could keep this part between just the two of them.

"How about at the lower parking area of Etna? We can talk in the car. In private."

Yes, that would work. In fact, she couldn't imagine a better place to do that. "Okay, do you want to meet there?"

"Why don't I just pick you up and we'll go from there. Fifteen minutes?"

"Sounds good. I'm already in the lobby, so just pull up in front of the hotel. I'll be watching for you." With that they hung up, and Bree prayed they could work this out. Because the sooner they could do that, the sooner they could put all this behind them. At least, she hoped they could.

She was outside when Diego pulled up. She slid into the passenger seat and hoped he couldn't see the worry swirling around inside her. Well, judging from his tight jaw and the muscle working in there, she wasn't the only one. Whatever was in that envelope wouldn't change things for her as much as it would for him. Unless he decided to walk.

Only she was going to wave a white flag and suggest they do what he'd wanted to do and give things a trial run, but more for his sake than hers. He needed to be sure about this more than she did.

So that meant they would need to travel to Palermo together for her prenatal appointments. Which she assumed was part of what he'd meant when he talked about that.

He glanced at her. "Do you know?"

She knew what he meant. "No. I…" Suddenly it was hard for her to see. "I didn't want to open it on my own."

A hand touched her, fingers lacing through the one in her lap. "I understand. We'll get through this together."

"I haven't even told my parents. I wasn't sure how to. I thought I'd wait until after I had the results, but if the baby's not Sergio's…" She swallowed a ball of regret. "I'm not quite sure how to explain it."

"Maybe you won't need to."

She shut her eyes. She had made such a mess about everything. Maybe she should have terminated, even gone to another country if necessary to have it done. But even the thought of that made her belly ache deep inside. She'd longed for a baby, and Sergio had felt an equal desire to have kids. Despite everything, this seemed like the right thing to do. For her. Whether or not it was the right thing for Diego was another subject entirely.

I would find a way.

His words on Mount Etna came back to her. Except he'd broken up with someone he cared about because she wanted kids and he didn't. It had been a deal breaker for him. And Bree wanted more than one. Whether that would ever happen or not…

But she would need to be honest with Diego about that as well. Because that might cause even more complications for him. How did you take one child—your child—on outings and leave the other behind? As a mom, how could she allow that? And if she found someone who would love them all equally and married him? So many hard, hard things to wade through.

"Maybe you're right and I won't have to." But in the pit of her stomach was a growing fear that this child might very well *not* belong to her late fiancé. And might belong to a man she'd spent a single night with.

Well, make that two nights. And actually, the baby was the whole reason they'd spent that second night together.

They got to the parking area and Diego found a space

at the far back corner, since they weren't going to get out and hike this time. He left the car running and shifted in his seat to look at her. He'd unlinked their hands to shift gears a few minutes ago, but he reached over again and gave hers a squeeze. "I want you to know that even if this baby isn't mine, I will support you in any way I have time to."

In any way he had time to? That was an odd way to phrase things, but she nodded and said thank you. She had a feeling he'd be a lot more empathetic to her situation if the baby was Sergio's and not his. What did that say about his chances of seeing this thing through to the end? It was one thing to explain why "Uncle" Diego didn't come around to visit anymore, but to explain why Daddy didn't care—or couldn't care? They were both equally damning.

"Well, I guess I should open it." She pulled free and held the envelope.

But when her hands were shaking too much to get her thumb under the flap, he took it from her and set it on his lap, then, cupping her chin, he looked at her. "It's going to be okay, Bree. I promise."

How could he promise that when he couldn't even guarantee he was going to be there for the baby? But she would be there. And she had love enough for two people. So she nodded at him. "I know it is."

And for the first time, she thought maybe it was.

Diego had no idea why he'd said that. But watching Bree struggle with her emotions, listening to her talk about her fear about telling her parents and then seeing those hands so skilled in perfusion shake at the thought of this baby's fate had gotten to him. But she was stronger than she knew. And she was good at everything she did. He had no doubt she would be equally good at being a mom. His own mother had raised two boys practically on her own with minimal help from his father. If his mom could do it, Bree could, too.

And what about you?

A question he couldn't answer. Not yet.

"Ready?" he asked her.

She nodded.

Diego ripped open the envelope and pulled out the sheet inside. On it were a bunch of numbers in two columns. He held it down so Bree could see it, too, as he tried to make it out. Then he realized one of them was for Bree and the other was for him. At the bottom of the test were the words *The alleged father is not excluded as the biological father of the fetus.* The percentages were listed as ninety-nine point…followed by a bunch of other nines.

Well, now he knew. Now they both knew.

He was this baby's father.

A big part of him had hoped he wasn't. No decisions. No responsibilities. No angst.

Instead, he was faced with all three.

But there was something else there. Some weird thread of emotion that he'd never experienced before. But he was absolutely not going to set Bree up for disappointment by impulsively jumping in with both feet. He was going to do what he did before any surgery. Deliberate. Think about what could go wrong. About what could go right. Plan out each step and have an exit strategy in mind if one part didn't go as planned.

Exit? This wasn't surgery, where he could just abort the procedure if things started going wrong. This was a baby's life. It's happiness.

Still, it was the only strategy he knew. He could approach And if it turned out this was inoperable because of who he was as a person?

Well, then, yes, he was going to have his exit strategy planned out far in advance, when it would do the least amount of damage to Bree or the baby.

"Well, it looks like Sergio didn't get the winning ticket this time."

She gave him a look that bordered on a glare. "You didn't think of it as much of a winning ticket, either, from what I remember."

"I phrased that badly. I'm sorry."

Closing her eyes for a second before looking at him, she squinched her nose up. "I'm the one who's sorry. None of this is your fault."

"It's not yours, either."

"So it's neither of our fault, and yet here we are." She stared at the paper for a minute before taking it from him and stuffing it back in the envelope. "Thoughts? Or do you need time to process?"

"Yes. To both questions."

"Okay, let's hear the thoughts part."

"I know you said you didn't want to take me on a test run as a father and see how I do—and for *me* to see how I do, but—"

She held up a hand. "Right after I said that, I realized I was wrong to shoot you down like I did." She licked her lips. "So how would this 'test run' play out, exactly?"

"I would go to your appointments with you. See how my schedule can be rearranged." He decided to be honest with her. "My dad was not there for my brother and me. Ever. My parents were married, but my mom raised us single-handedly. Oh, he handed her a check every week and took care of us financially, but he was barely home. Maybe three or four hours a week."

"A week? And your mom put up with that?"

"I think she was scared to leave him and not have a safety net, since her parents were both gone already. But once we were out of the house, they divorced. My father remarried less than a year later. And he had another set of kids, twins this time. We never knew them. Because my dad wasn't there for them, either. This time, though, his wife didn't wait around for them to grow up. She left him and moved to a different part of Italy, and none of us heard from her again."

"Why did he even have kids, if he didn't want them?"

His eyes came up and met hers. "That is the question, isn't it? I think he thought getting married and having kids was an expected part of life. But it's a mistake I don't want to make. I am invested in my job probably just as much as my father ever was. I see it. I know it. And yet it's hard for me to let go. I do not want my kids to have the kind of father I would be at this point in my life. Which is why I wanted to see if I could change my priorities."

"Where is your father now?"

"He's dead."

Bree went pale. "He died?"

"Three years ago. Of a heart attack."

"And that's not reason enough for you to make a change?"

He sighed. "I have made some. The question is, can I make enough of them to do some good for someone other than my patients?"

"I see. So this trial period is to see if a leopard can change its spots."

"That's it in a nutshell."

She nodded. "Well, this is your chance to try. Only I promise you, if I think you aren't going to be able to hack it, you won't need to step in and fire yourself. I'll be there to personally hand you that dismissal form." She smiled, as if to take some of the sting out of it. And it did. It also gave him some reassurance that she didn't need him for a paycheck like his mom had done with his dad. This woman was strong enough to push him away if she thought it was best for her and her child. And she'd already told him she didn't want his money.

So he was going to take her at her word and let her stand back and observe how real his commitment turned out to be. Surely with both of them wanting what was best for this baby, they would come to a decision. The right one. For everyone involved.

"I'll hold you to that dismissal form. I don't want you to cut me any slack. Because I'm not going to cut myself any, either. Okay?"

"You've got yourself a deal, Probationary Partner. Now let's see if we can get this kid and his or her mother something to eat. Because she is starving."

"One dinner coming up. How about if I take you to a swanky little place I know that's not too far from here?"

"As long as they have food that won't poison us, I'll take almost anything."

CHAPTER TEN

BREE'S PHONE RANG. Peeling her eyelids apart, she rolled to the side and struggled to focus the clock. It took three tries before the lighted numbers made any sense.

Two a.m.

She came fully awake. No one called in the middle of the night unless something was very wrong. Her parents? She spun her phone toward her. If this was a crank call...

Diego's name showed in big white letters.

It had been almost a week since they'd had their talk at the base of Mount Etna and, so far, life had carried on as normal. She saw him in passing, and they smiled at each other. And the ruckus at the hospital over piggy-back-gate was slowly winding down. Like her eyelids, which were drifting back together. The phone buzzed again.

Wake up, Bree!

Panic started swirling through her, memories of talking to a police officer after Sergio's accident.

The confusion. The fear. The numbness afterward.

She snatched the phone up and pressed the answer button even as she was sitting up. "Hello?"

Her voice was high-pitched and unsteady. She tried to punch back the sensation of fear.

"Bree, we need you down at the hospital if there's any way you can get here."

"Diego…" She went slack with relief when she realized it was his voice, not some stranger's. "It's you."

"Yes, of course it's me." There was a curt impatience in his tone that she didn't understand. "Can you come?"

"You need a perfusionist at this time of night?" Normally heart surgeries were scheduled during daytime or afternoon hours. If they needed her now… Her fingers tightened on the phone.

"We have a patient with infective endocarditis in her mitral valve. Severe regurge. She's not going to make it without immediate surgery." There was a pause. A long one, where she thought she'd lost the signal. Then his voice came back. "She's also twenty-one weeks pregnant."

Her stomach lurched, and her free hand went to her lower belly and pressed. Twenty-one weeks. The baby wasn't old enough to deliver before surgery. Her mind ran through the case studies she'd read of pregnant women who'd been put on cardiopulmonary bypass for surgery or other reasons. There was a narrow margin of error, and sometimes the baby didn't make it. The mortality rate could be as high as eighteen percent.

If Diego was calling her, it meant that he was the only one who could tackle this and be successful, since he was the best heart surgeon on the island. He was this woman's best chance for survival. Her baby's best chance.

"I'll be there in fifteen minutes." Tossing the phone

onto the table, she leaped out of bed and grabbed a set of scrubs from one of her drawers and yanked everything into place. Taking time only to drag a brush through her hair and to brush her teeth, she was out the door in five minutes, rushing down the stairs rather than waiting on the elevator.

She fired up her car and headed north. She'd never seen so little traffic on the streets of Catania, and she made it to Concepción two minutes earlier than she'd predicted. Jamming the gearshift into Park, she got out and sprinted up to the hospital entrance, her mind going through everything she needed to do and the precautions they needed to take.

Diego was nowhere to be seen when she burst through the doors, but she was sure he was either with the patient or already scrubbing in. Fortunately she kept the bypass machine at the ready, checking on it every single time she arrived or left the hospital.

After she took the elevator to the third floor, where the surgical ward was, a nurse met her at the doors. "He said go ahead and get set up. They'll start as soon as you're ready."

"Everyone else is already here?"

"Yes."

How could that be?

Nerves kicked in. She normally had more time to prepare, but these kinds of cases didn't always follow a set schedule. And today, time was of the essence. If the mother didn't survive, then the baby had no chance at all.

She got ready and then gloved up and entered the room. Diego was already there, as was the patient and the entire surgical team. All except her. The nurse was right.

How had they all gotten here so fast? Had she been the last person to be called?

Maybe Diego hadn't thought they'd need to put her on bypass. But with endocarditis and a destroyed mitral valve? That was unlikely.

Getting in her station, she checked that they'd gotten everything she needed. Diego must have arranged to have this set up already, too. He came over. "Are you okay to do this?"

"What do you mean by okay?"

He frowned above his mask and said in a low voice, "I mean because of the patient."

She still had no clue what he was talking about. Wait, did she know this person?

No, she didn't see how she could.

Oh! Realization dawned. Because the patient was pregnant! Was that why she felt so late to the game and why everyone else was already here? Had he scrambled around trying to find any other perfusionist before calling her?

Her nerves unwound, and a thin thread of anger took its place. Yes, Bree was pregnant. But Diego was going to be a father, too. Did he feel he was somehow immune from feeling fear for their patient and her baby? Bree was certainly able to put herself in the patient's shoes and, hell yes, it scared her to death to think of something like this happening to her and her baby. Diego should feel that, too. Shouldn't he?

She sat up straight and looked him in the eye. "I'm fine. Just tell me what the plan is."

The surgeon filled her in, letting her know the specific changes they would make for this particular surgery. The goal was to not only save the mother, but to maintain the pregnancy as well.

"You have the replacement valve here already?"

"Yes. Porcine this time."

"Okay. Anything I should know about her blood work?" She needed to focus on the patient and not on what Diego had or hadn't done.

"Because of the severity of the regurgitation, there's some evidence of hypoxia."

"And the baby?"

"So far, the fetus is hanging in there."

Hanging in there. But not thriving. "Let me check a few more things. Is there a neonatologist here, just in case?"

Diego looked at her, and she could have sworn she saw something flicker behind his eyes. The first indication of true empathy, although if so, he'd hidden it admirably. "Yes, he's standing right over there by the fetal monitor, but at twenty-one weeks..."

"I know. So let's do all we can to have a good outcome."

His expression returned to the stoic neutral man she was coming to know. "That's all I ever want. A good outcome."

The words gave her pause. Yes, he'd been repeating her statement, but there was an inflection there that made her wonder if it was just about the surgery at hand. But right now she couldn't worry about that. Or about anything other than doing her job.

Less than a half hour later, Diego was making his

first incision. It was hard not to let her gaze keep drifting to the fetal monitor, which was keeping track of variations in the baby's heart rate. The real test would be when the patient went on bypass. Surgeries like this one were not done every day, and the thinking was to hold off, whenever possible, until late in the third trimester, when the baby could be delivered by caesarean before valve-replacement surgery was performed. That was the best option. But the best option wasn't always available. Sometimes you had to salvage what you could from a bad situation.

She shifted on her stool as inferences from that statement coiled around her brain's amygdala, squeezing emotions from it that she didn't want or need right now.

Forcing her attention back to her job and away from Diego and her pregnancy, she settled in for the long haul. She could hash this out with her heart and her brain later. And she needed to leave the patient in the hands of those who knew what they were doing. The ones who would pay attention to the baby's stats and the mom's. She just needed to do her very best to give the team what they needed.

So far, things were progressing the way they should. Diego was in the chest cavity, getting the vessels hooked up for bypass. Her part was coming soon. And she was right where she needed to be. Where she wanted to be. In this room.

She tried not to think about his possible reasons for trying to lock her out of this case, if he'd even done that. She wouldn't know unless she asked. And that would have to wait.

Sergio had wanted her to be a stay-at-home mom, but

when she'd stood up for herself, he'd given in, maybe realizing he would be dooming their relationship if he tried to push the matter.

And Diego. What did he think? After all, Bree was replacing a woman who'd made that very decision: to stay home with her baby. There was no right or wrong path here, each individual had to do what was right for them and their family, but Bree knew she needed to be in the operating room. It was part of her DNA.

"Ready for bypass."

Diego's voice brought her back to the task at hand. Twisting some knobs and checking levels, she glanced up at him and nodded. "Commencing bypass."

Blood flowed through the lines and through the machine, which would oxygenate it and push it through a heat exchanger as it prepared to pump it back into the patient.

There were a tense few minutes while everyone waited to see how the baby would handle the CPB. So far, the heart rate hadn't fluctuated, but that could always change if the baby didn't get exactly what it needed from the machine. It was up to Bree to make sure that baby got every molecule of oxygen it required.

She kept her eyes on her panel readings, watching for problems, signs that something was going wrong.

So far, everything was steady. Which worried her. It was going a little too well.

"I'm ready for the valve."

It was amazing how quiet it was in here today. It was as if everyone knew what was at stake. A lot of times there were jokes or light camaraderie to relieve tension, and some surgeons liked to have music on. For some, the louder the better. But this particular room was bathed in concentration. It was palpable.

She glanced up to see the pig valve being handed over to Diego. She watched him examine it for defects, those long fingers turning it this way and then that. Then her attention was right back on her instruments.

The neonatologist's voice broke through the silence. "There was a blip. And now a slight drop in heart rate. A little more."

He was talking about the baby's heart rate, not the mom's. She hurriedly checked the fluid reservoir, knowing if it dropped too low, air could enter the chamber, causing a fatal embolism. But it was fine. Nothing had changed on her table. Oxygen saturation levels were steady.

Diego stopped what he was doing and waited.

Finally the other doctor said, "We're coming back up. Not sure what that was, but we need to keep this moving."

"I need another half hour to forty-five minutes. Okay to continue?"

The neonatologist nodded. "You have to. I don't see any exit strategy that carries a positive outcome for either of them."

Out of the corner of her eye, she saw Diego's head whip up to stare at the man. That was strange. She'd never seen him do that before.

His jaw was tight for a second or two before he responded. "Neither do I. We have to do what's best for both of them. And that's to remove the damaged part and take it out of the picture."

There was an air of resignation about the way he

said that that made a bubble of uneasiness rise up in her stomach before popping. Another took its place, and then another and another. Just like the air embolism she'd been worried about.

He got back to work, giving his commentaries as he went through each step. Part of that was so that everything was on the official record, but in Bree's experience, they were also crossing things off their grocery list of items that had to be completed during surgery.

"Valve is in place. Checking suture line." He paused. "How's the fetus?"

"Holding steady."

Diego glanced at Bree and then looked away. "Ready to restore blood flow to the heart."

A few more tense seconds went by, and then the patient's heart monitor started registering activity. "I've got a heartbeat."

"Baby is hanging in there." The neonatologist sounded relieved.

It was funny how different people referred to an unborn child. Because she was pregnant, she tended to think of her own baby as a...well, baby.

It doesn't mean anything that Diego is using the word fetus. *It's the correct technical term. Right? The one most medical professionals use.*

But there had been something about the way he'd looked at the neonatologist earlier when he'd talked about exit strategies... About how he said they needed to do what was best for them, meaning mother and baby.

"Let's wean her off bypass."

Her. The mother. As if that was the only individual who mattered.

Could a leopard really change it spots?

Her words to Diego came back to her.

She shook off the growing number of worries that now seemed to be lobbed at her one after the other as she did her best to deflect them. Maybe Diego had been right to try to find someone else.

No. If anyone would work hard for this patient and that precious cargo she was carrying, it was Bree. And she had every right to be in this room.

"Weaning off now." She turned the knobs, slowly transitioning her machine's duties back onto to the patient. The baby's heart rate spiked for a couple of seconds, and she closed her eyes, breathing a silent prayer. Hopefully it was due to the normal change in blood pressure after coming off bypass. Then the heart rate slid back to normal once again.

"Oxygen sats are holding steady. Normal sinus rhythm. No leakage." Diego glanced around the room but skipped over her. Just like he had during their very first surgery together. She swallowed hard. Had she wanted him to give her that secretive smile she loved so much? A slight nod to let her know everything was okay?

Yes. But there'd been nothing.

God. So much had happened since that first surgery. So very much.

But had anything really changed?

She didn't know. But right now it felt like her stomach was being squeezed in a vise that kept tightening with every beat of her heart.

"And baby is doing fine, thank God."

The words of the neonatologist echoed in her skull.

Yes, thank God. This time Bree let her own forearm press on her lower belly. Her baby was fine, too. And he or she would be fine. With or without Diego.

But holy hell, she wanted him there. And that seemed to be the biggest tragedy of all.

"Okay, let's close her up. We'll need her on IV antibiotics for a few days and by mouth after that to make sure the other valves stay safe."

Diego's low, reassuring voice continued as they worked to close things in stages, ending with the skin.

Only it didn't reassure her. Not like it once had.

And when the surgeon was finished and all his checks had been completed, he left the room. Before she'd finished cleaning up her station. Only this time, she wasn't stalling. And this time, she knew Diego wouldn't be standing right outside the room waiting on her. He had fled the scene. Just like Sergio had on their wedding day. And she had no idea why.

Diego sat in his office, staring at the computer image of a patient's file. Lorenzo Portini's words during his surgery had sent an electric shock through him. He knew it was common for doctors to talk about exit strategies, but to hear it so soon after he'd mentally gone through his own checklists of being a father had sent him reeling. Was it coincidence? Or was someone trying to tell him something?

Dios! His patient had survived the surgery. So had the fetus. But there were other things that could happen even afterward. Preterm labor. Premature delivery. Oxygen deprivation to the fetus despite their every effort. Those blips on the monitor had meant something. Except no one knew what. Not yet. Maybe not ever.

A knock sounded at his door. "Come in."

Bree slid through the door, and his heart sank. He should have stayed after the surgery. He'd just needed time to…process. But what he was supposed to be processing, he wasn't sure.

This time Bree didn't wait to be asked to sit. She walked over and sank into one of the chairs, looking at him with steady eyes.

"Can I ask you a question?"

"Sure." He said the word, but the last thing he wanted right now were questions.

"Did you try to find another perfusionist before calling me?"

Dannazione! Had someone told her he'd scrambled for almost a half hour before dialing her number? "What do you mean?"

She leaned forward. "I don't think it's a difficult question, Diego. Did. You. Call. Someone. Else?"

"Yes." He wasn't going to lie to her.

"Why?"

He'd asked himself that same question. "I'm not sure. It was a pregnant mom. I thought it might…" He paused for a long time before saying the words, realizing for the first time how they sounded. "I thought it might upset you."

"You thought it might upset *me*. But it wouldn't upset *you*?"

"Of course it did. Any time someone comes in with heart problems, there's always a chance that—"

"No." Bree rubbed a thumb along the sharp edge of

his desk, the way she might check to see how damaging something could be. "I'm not talking about the upset that comes with a generic case. I'm talking about the concern that comes with putting yourself in the other person's shoes. Of wondering the normal what-ifs that come with the thought that it might be *your* baby whose life is on the line. I certainly thought it."

"I had a job to do."

"Yes. Well, so did I. One that you tried to keep me from doing."

He leaned back in his chair and crossed his arms over his chest. "I'm sorry if it seemed that way."

The second he said the words, he realized it wasn't a real apology. He was pushing it back onto her, saying it was all about her perception. But it wasn't. She was right. He had called around, trying to get someone else. And had wasted valuable time in the process.

Before she could call him out on it, he sighed. "No, you're right. I did try to keep you from coming. And I don't know why, other than what I've already told you. That I wasn't sure how hard this case would be on you."

"That's for me to decide, don't you think?"

He decided to move to the heart of the matter. "Look, Bree. When my dad wasn't there for us, my mom always was. She was there. Every single time I or my brother needed her."

"Are you saying I won't be for our child?"

"No, but if I somehow can't..."

Bree went completely still when his voice trailed away. "If you can't what?"

"I want to make sure that someone will be there for this child."

"Which child? *Ours?*" Her lips thinned. "There will be someone there for the baby. I will be. Whether you are or not. But that doesn't mean I'm going to sit at home 24-7. Or avoid cases that might prove to be painful. I want to work. I love my job, and I want my son or daughter to know that it's okay to go after your own dreams. That you can have both. You can love someone *and* be there for them while still pursuing your goals. They're not mutually exclusive. It's all about balance."

"What if you can't? What if *I* can't?"

She shrugged. "I don't know. I guess you're going to have to do some soul-searching and see how you want to spend the next fifty or so years of your life. Is work enough to fulfill you? If it is, then... Well, I'd rather know that now." She closed her eyes. "No, not now. But soon. Think about it. And when you've decided, come and talk to me."

With that she stood and came around to his side of the desk and dropped a kiss on his cheek. One that burned like fire and seared his soul.

"And if you decide you can't, I'll be okay. We both will."

She left his office with a quiet click of the door, leaving him staring at the chair she'd just occupied. And wondering what the hell was wrong with him.

CHAPTER ELEVEN

IT HAD BEEN more than a week since she'd left Diego's office, and she'd heard nothing from the cardiac surgeon. Worse, she'd noticed on the staffing board that he'd performed two surgeries since then. One was another valve replacement and one had been a triple bypass. Bree had been called in for neither of them. She'd been devastated. She thought he cared about her. At least on some level. Evidently she was wrong.

Horribly, over the last week, she'd come to realize she loved the man. Loved everything about him.

But that didn't mean they were destined to be together. She couldn't force him to love her back. Or to want to stay with her. Or even to love their child.

He was an honorable man, so she felt like he would try like hell to be in the baby's life, but how fair was that of her to expect something he didn't feel he could give?

And if he didn't even feel like he could work with her in surgery— Well, that wasn't a good sign.

She'd had other work, so it wasn't like she was out of a job if Diego never wanted to work with her again. There were a couple of other cardiologists attached to the hospital. And she'd gone to a neighboring hospital in the middle of the night to help with a difficult surgery while their perfusionist was on vacation. The feeling of having a foot in two worlds had shifted over the last week to having a foot in *three* worlds—Sicily being the newest member of that club. And yet she belonged to none of those clubs. Not really.

She'd reached out to her parents last night via video chat and told them about the pregnancy and shared a little bit about what had happened since then. Once she started, she hadn't been able to stop the tears from flowing. Her dad had offered to come and beat up whoever had hurt her. That had finally gotten a laugh out of her.

"I don't need violence," she'd said. "I need advice. What should I do?"

"Come home." Her parents had said the words in unison.

Home. Where there were people who loved her and would help her with the pregnancy and all that came afterward.

So today, Bree was sitting at the small table in her hotel room with the papers for the house she'd planned to buy laid out in front of her. The deadline for putting pen to paper and closing on it was today. If she went through with it, she would be entering a contract that would be difficult to withdraw from. She would already lose her deposit. But if she signed, she stood to lose a lot more.

Yes, she did. And not just monetarily.

She stood to lose emotionally by staying in Catania.

And what if Diego decided he wanted to be in his child's life?

How long did she intend to wait? It had been a week.

Did she wait a month? Wait until after the baby was born? Wait until he or she was eighteen?

No. She wasn't going to allow her life or the life of her child to remain in some kind of limbo. She needed to move forward. With or without Diego.

And from the looks of it, he was going to choose the "without" clause. What had he said during that surgery? Something about doing what was best for the mother and fetus. And that meant taking the damaged part out of the picture.

She'd thought it was a weird way to word it at the time. In fact, he'd seemed agitated, jerking to look at the neonatologist as if coming to a realization. Diego had struggled and struggled hard, from the sound of it, with how little involvement his dad had had in his life. Maybe that's what he'd meant in his office about wanting to make sure her baby had someone he or she could count on. Because he wasn't expecting the child—or Bree—to be able to count on him.

A spear of pain went through her.

Well, at least he'd been honest about it. Painfully honest, unlike Sergio. And what had he gotten for it? Lambasted by her and prodded to hurry up and decide.

Had she been unfair to him? Maybe. But looking back, she thought some of her insistence might have come out of fear. Fear of being alone. Fear of a second person who seemed to be all in and then suddenly exiting her life. Although, what she felt for Diego eclipsed what she'd ever felt for Sergio. It was awful and made her realize she'd had no business getting engaged to him.

So no more prodding Diego or going to him to ask

for a commitment. This time, she was going to be the one who let go.

So what did she do about the house? Did she go forward with it and face the next seven months of her pregnancy wondering if she was going to be able to find a birth coach? Going to prenatal appointments by herself? Answer awful, probing questions about whose baby it was?

And seeing Diego as they passed in the hallway, when she was as big as a house? When he was thanking his lucky stars that he'd gotten out while he still could?

God, she couldn't do it.

Come home.

The words whispered through her head like a siren's song. It wasn't true that she didn't belong anywhere. She had a family who loved her, and she was about to form her only little family, consisting of her and the baby. And maybe she would add to that number after a while using a sperm bank.

And suddenly she knew what she was going to do. She picked up the contract and slid it—unsigned—back into the envelope it had been delivered in. Then she got up from the kitchen table with the envelope and her phone in hand and made the call.

It was answered on the second ring. "Romildi Realty."

"Hello, Tania? Do you have a few minutes to meet with me this afternoon? I'm afraid I have some bad news."

Diego exited the nondescript gray building he'd been visiting for the last couple of weeks. There was no sign advertising who resided in there or what they did. In fact, if he hadn't gotten the center's name from a friend, he would have never known about the meetings that went on inside every Monday, Wednesday and Friday. It wasn't that he was ashamed to be seen there. He wasn't. But what he had needed was to understand what was going on inside his head. And why he seemed dead set on embodying the same traits that he'd claimed to hate.

He wasn't the only one in that situation, it seemed. And when he'd talked to his mom, she had agreed to come to one of the meetings with him. Afterward, she'd hugged his neck, whispering, "I am *so* proud of you."

He wasn't done figuring things out. That would take a long time. But as he got in his car and sat there, thinking about all that had happened with Bree, he wondered if it was possible… With the baby…

He swallowed. A baby. *His* baby. His and Bree's. He was going to be a father, and yet he had managed to hold himself completely aloof from that reality as if he was peering through a window and coveting a life he could never have.

Except there were people who thought he could. People who had overcome bigger obstacles than his.

He thought about Bree's smile. That bewitching smile that he'd loved so very much. He remembered carrying her down that mountain and the reaction he'd had to her proximity. Her laughter. And making love on that balcony. Little by little, something had crept up on him. Something so quiet that he hadn't noticed it until it was far too late.

He loved her. And by God, he loved that baby. He just

didn't know if he deserved either of them. If he could do right by either of them.

But other people had done it. They'd come out on the other side and had gotten their happy endings, despite the pain of their childhoods. Why couldn't he?

On that mountain, Bree had asked him how he would carry her down if he'd been bitten by that snake. It had been a light question. One that had made him laugh until he really thought about it. And he'd responded, "I would find a way."

Maybe he should start doing that. Start finding a way, before it was too late.

He swallowed. Maybe it already was. She'd been pretty upset when she left his office three weeks ago. But she had also said when he decided what he wanted to do to come and talk to her. So surely that meant that she'd left the door open.

At least, he hoped she had.

If not, he had to at least go and try. He couldn't make any black-and-white promises. But he could tell her he loved her and that he would do what he'd said: find a way. He could call her, but this wasn't a conversation he wanted to have over the phone. Or have at the hospital. He wanted to sit and look in her eyes and tell her exactly what he'd learned about himself. And exactly what his plan was to fix those areas that he didn't like.

He'd finally done the hard work that he'd told himself he was going to do and had approached this like a surgical plan. He'd gone in expecting to find that he was doomed and would be the worst thing possible for Bree or the baby. Had expected to be like that damaged mitral valve that he'd replaced in that pregnant woman during his and Bree's last surgery together. So far gone that it had to be surgically removed and discarded—replaced.

But he wasn't. And with the right counselor and a whole lot of blood, sweat and tears, he might just be able to make himself into a man his child—and Bree—could be proud of.

Starting his car, he headed to where she'd told him her new house was. It was about twenty minutes away. But when he pulled up in front of it, an eerie stillness washed over him. There was a For Sale sign in the yard out front. Shouldn't that be gone by now?

He got out, and as he headed up to the door, a woman with a notebook came out of the house, followed by a young couple who were probably in their mid- to late twenties. The woman held a child's hand, complaining about all the things they would need to fix if they bought this house.

The first woman eyed him. "Can I help you?"

"Wasn't this house already sold? I know the woman who was supposed to be buying it."

The man frowned and glared at the Realtor. "I thought you told us it was available."

"It is, I assure you. Can you excuse me for a minute?"

"Forget it," the man said. "We didn't like it anyway."

The couple skirted them and went through the open gate.

The woman planted her hands on her hips. "Okay. You have my attention. Now what is it that you want?"

"What happened to the woman who put a deposit down on this house? She showed me pictures of it."

"Are you talking about Signorina Frost?"

"Yes, did something happen?"

The woman's brows went up in a haughty way. "Yes, as a matter of fact, it did. She backed out at the last second. And I'll tell you, I didn't appreciate—"

Her voice droned on for several more sentences, but all he heard was that Bree had backed out of buying the house at the last minute. Backed out.

"Did she say why?"

A frown appeared on her face. "Like I said, she said she was going home to Naples and would no longer need it. Said I could keep the deposit. I told her I surely would."

Dios. There'd been something said about Naples some time ago, and he remembered how it had made him feel back then. Uneasy. Unsure.

Well, what he felt now was light-years from that lukewarm sentiment.

Desolation. Bleakness. Hopelessness.

Those were a few of the words that came to mind. And he didn't like any of them.

He'd avoided her like the plague at the hospital, and she must have done the same, because he hadn't caught sight of her in over two weeks. Maybe more.

"Did she say when she was going?" He held up a hand and looked back at the house. "Never mind. So since that couple evidently wasn't interested in the house, does that mean it's still on the market?"

Her demeanor changed in an instant, going from accusatory to saccharine sweet. She gave him a big smile and opened up her notebook. "Yes, it is, as a matter of fact. Do you want to take a look?"

He smiled and hoped to hell he was doing the right

thing. "That won't be necessary. I've already seen it through someone else's eyes. Someone whose judgment I trust completely."

Bree finished packing the last of her belongings into suitcases. It was surprising how few things she'd bought since arriving in Catania. It was as if she'd somehow known she wouldn't be here all that long. Two months. And yet some pretty profound changes had happened in her life since her arrival.

And as much as she'd thought otherwise, she wouldn't change any of them. Because they had all helped her to grow and change and to learn what was truly important in life: this baby. Her life. And her family.

Something black and glittery caught her attention from under the foot of her bed. She frowned and bent to retrieve whatever it was.

The black flip-flops she'd bought on their race to the hospital. She brought them to her chest and hugged them tight. She hadn't had any problems throwing her other sandals away. But this pair?

"No. You're staying with me." They would be a reminder of a very magical time in her life. One that, despite the heartache it brought, she didn't want to forget.

She would still be in Catania for another month, or until the hospital could secure a new perfusionist, but she would be moving from this hotel to another, since the room was already booked for someone else. She was supposed to have been in her new house by now and had given the front desk a checkout date. She was lucky she'd been able to stay for an additional week until she could find a spot in another hotel.

She rang down and asked the front desk if they could call her a taxi.

"Actually, Signorina Frost, there's someone at the front desk to see you. Should I send him up? It's the gentleman you were with a few weeks ago."

Gentleman?

Her heart stuttered in her chest when she realized whom they were talking about. She should tell them to send him away. Tell him she was no longer interested in anything he had to say.

But she couldn't. It seemed like so long since she'd seen him. In reality, it was three weeks. Oh, she'd seen the back of his head once or twice. But the hospital was big enough that it had been easy to avoid each other.

But she wanted to see him. To talk to him. To share the same space with him. One more time.

And then she'd be free of him.

Liar. Well, lie or not, she wanted to hear what he had to say.

"Signorina?"

She realized she'd kept him waiting for longer than she should have. "Yes, please send him up. Thank you."

Hanging up, she glanced around the room. Her suitcases were strewn every which way, one on the couch, two on the floor. And those black shoes were still clutched in her hand. She carefully laid them on top of one of the bags on the floor.

She thought about trying to throw everything in a closet, but so what if he saw them? It was really none of his business where she went or when.

Had he heard that she was moving back home and coming to say his goodbyes?

God, she hoped not. Their last goodbye had been hard enough. To stand here while he muttered some platitudes and said she'd be missed would be excruciating.

She could always stand in front of the door and make him say whatever it was in the hallway, but she wasn't going to do that, either. He could come in and sit on the futon and be offered coffee and cookies. And she could drink in his presence one last time. Once she left Catania, that was it. She would consider whatever this had been to be over.

A knock sounded on her door, but she barely heard it above the knocking of her heart. She suddenly felt breathless and faint and wondered if she would even make it through his visit without completely falling apart. But she had to. She did not want him to see how horrible these last three weeks had been. Wishing things could be different while knowing they would not be.

She opened the door, and there he was. The man she loved. The father of her child.

But he didn't sweep her off her feet or get down on one knee. Not that she'd thought he'd come for any of that. But still, it was like some remote part of her had still held on to a modicum of hope.

Sorry, hope. Not today. Maybe not ever.

"Come in."

He followed her into the room and glanced at the bags she'd packed. "So it's true."

She nodded. "Did they put that in the papers, too? Is it pinned on the bulletin board with a cute little picture?"

"No. I was surprised when I heard. And it wasn't

from anyone at the hospital." He sat down beside her big suitcase and looked at her. "Why are you going?"

"Why not? My parents are still in Naples. They think I should be near them during the pregnancy. I tend to agree." Her initial impulse was to remain standing, but her knees were shaking so much she might as well sit before they rebelled completely and dumped her onto the floor.

"Bree, what if I asked you to stay?"

That modicum of hope grabbed the molecules around it and consumed them, growing a tad larger. But she and Diego been down this path before, and he'd wavered back and forth. She didn't know if she could bear going through that again. "Why would you do that?"

"Because I've come to the conclusion that I'm not beyond hope."

That simple phrase was not what Bree expected him to say. And her heart cramped into a small, hard lump that cried for him. Cried for whatever dark place inside him that had told him he was. She reached across the space and grabbed his hand and held on tight. "I know you're not. If I ever gave you that impression—"

"You didn't. You didn't need to. I've said it to myself almost my whole adult life. That having a real relationship was beyond my capacity. That having a baby was not even in the realm of possibility. So when you said you were pregnant… You have no idea." His fingers curled around hers. "I looked down at the ruined valve in that endocarditic heart, and it was like I was standing outside myself. I used my scalpel and carved it away—removed every trace of that part. A part that would only create death and destruction if it stayed. And in my head, I was carving away me."

The raw emotion in his voice was her undoing. She got up and climbed into his lap, held his head against her chest as words poured out of her that made little sense, only needing to reassure this man that he would not bring death or destruction. Not to her. Not to his baby. Not to himself.

"Look at me, Diego."

When he did, she said the words she should have said to him as soon as she discovered the truth. "I love you. I realized it a couple of weeks ago. I never wanted you to feel forced or trapped. It's why I gave my notice at the hospital."

He leaned up and kissed her. "You never made me feel trapped. I put myself into a cage years ago and locked the door behind me. I've met a group of people that have helped me search for the key. And I think I found it. I've been going to counseling. Learning how to deal with my past." He smiled. "And I'm learning how to plan for the future. A future I would very much like for you and the baby to be a part of. I love you, too. And I want you to know, I've renewed the vow I made on Etna. I will find a way to carry you down that mountain."

He was getting counseling? Oh God, that meant he was serious. Serious about being with her. Confident that they had a chance to make it, or he wouldn't be here, would he? "How about if neither of us carries the other? How about if we prop each other up when we're weak and encourage each other along when we feel we can't go on anymore."

His fingers threaded through her hair. "I think I can

do that. With your help. Would you be willing to go to counseling with me? It might help us both."

"Yes." She would do whatever it took to have a chance to be with this man. To make their home on this island.

Home. Her brain froze.

"Oh, no!"

"What is it?"

"I let the contract go on the house I was looking at."

He frowned. "I know. I went over there to find you, but you weren't there, and the house is no longer on the market. And my place really isn't suitable for a baby."

"I wasn't expecting to move in with you. Not this soon. But I can't live in hotels forever. I'm already having to move from this one to another one because the room is reserved for someone else starting tomorrow."

"You might not have been expecting to move in, but I would very much like you to. I know it can't be today, but I'd like it to be sometime before the baby is born. You decide the when. But I already know the where."

"You do? But I thought you said your house isn't suitable."

"It's not. But I know one that is. It's the perfect house for you."

Hope surged inside her, growing to monstrous proportions. "It is? But how could you know that?"

"Because it's the one you picked out. The one you backed out on."

"But I thought you said it was no longer on the market."

"It's not, because I bought it. Before anyone else could."

Her head tilted, a smile coming to her face. "You bought *my* house?"

"I did."

She snuggled in closer. "I suppose you expect me to pay rent."

"No rent. But I would like us to design the nursery together. And I want us to pick out the baby's name. And I want us to make a life together. One that we'll both share in, equally."

It was too much. Her heart was set to burst in a million pieces, and she buried her face in his shoulder to keep him from seeing. But this kind of heartbreak was the good kind. Because those pieces would all knit back together, and in the cementing process, it would become stronger than it ever was before.

"I want that. All of it. And I want to live together sooner rather than later, once we work out all of the logistics."

She slid her hand beneath the sleeve of his shirt, where his tattoo lay hidden. "Don't you think it's time I hear the story of your dragon? You didn't want to tell me the last night we were together."

When he hesitated, she stopped him. "It's okay. It doesn't have to be now."

"No, it's okay. I want to. I got it as a reminder to myself that I can be hard to get along with. The hope was that I would temper myself. I'm not sure it worked."

"Hard to get along with. Really?" She nipped the side of his jaw. "I think your tattoo is very sexy. But I think you're more like a calamari—a lot more tender than one expects. And very delicious."

"Delicious, huh? I don't know about that." But his smile said he appreciated her words.

He placed his palm over her lower belly, filling her with a sense of wonder and love. She could trust him to stay. To work through his problems and to love her and the baby.

His words came back to her: he would find a way. But not just him. They both would. And if they couldn't *find* the way, they would forge a brand-new way. A path on which she, Diego and their children would journey. Together.

And that was enough.

EPILOGUE

A SLIGHT SOUND made Bree glance up from the ultrasound. She found Diego propped in the doorway of the clinic. "What are you doing here? I thought you had a surgery this afternoon."

"I asked Martini to step in and replace me."

Her eyes widened. "You did?" He had been true to his word and was working hard to make sure he made time for her and the baby. But she didn't want him to feel he had to cancel every surgery to do that. He had more than proved they had what it took to stick as a couple. And Diego had become a facilitator at the counseling center they'd both attended. They were doing a wonderful work and had given her new husband the courage he'd needed to break the cycle of his childhood. They'd forged that new path. And it was wild and crazy and filled with a truckload of happiness.

"I did." He came in and sat on the edge of the bed and toyed with a lock of her hair before looking at the image on the screen. "She looks like you."

Bree snorted and then laughed. "That's her behind."

He tilted his head and scrutinized the picture before ginning. "In that case, she looks like me."

This time the obstetrician gave a choked laugh, which she tried to cover with a cough. She reached over to the machine and pressed a button to print off an image. Of the face this time.

They'd found a clinic near their home in Catania, since it no longer mattered who knew about their relationship. In fact, they'd gotten married in the hospital chapel. It was a small intimate affair, nothing like the lavish wedding she'd planned with Sergio. She didn't need it. Didn't need the trappings. Didn't need hundreds of guests. All she needed were her parents, and Diego's mom and brother, and a handful of friends. Teresina, the phlebotomist from Palermo, had stood with her as her bridesmaid. The two had become fast friends over the intervening months.

Bree looked at the obstetrician. "Is everything okay?"

"Yes. She's perfect. She is poised to come any day. But if you could have a little chat and ask her to come during daylight hours, I would appreciate it."

"Any? We still have a week to go before her due date."

"You're completely effaced and two fingers dilated. If I were a betting woman, I'd say you aren't going to make it another week."

"Dios!" Diego's face changed, the color draining from it.

"What is it?" Were the old fears coming back to haunt him again? If so, they could tackle them, just like they had with every other blip that had come their way.

"I haven't finished painting the nursery, and the crib is only—"

"Oh!" Bree blinked as something strange was released inside her. She reached over to grip Diego's hand. "I think it's too late to do any of those things."

"What? Why?"

"Because I think my water just broke."

The obstetrician looked from one to the other with a smile. "Too late? No, it's not too late. This is only the beginning. The start of a beautiful new life. For all three of you."

Diego reached down and kissed the top of Bree's head. "Yes, it truly is."

* * * * *

FROM THE NIGHT SHIFT TO FOREVER

ANNIE CLAYDON

MILLS & BOON

To Maggie, with thanks for tea and inspiration!

CHAPTER ONE

IT WAS JUST another Friday night in A & E. Busy, sometimes frustrating, sometimes heart-rending. Tears, drunkenness and pain. But Dr Joel Mason wasn't in any doubt that this was exactly where he wanted to be. He was hoping an angel might arrive at any moment.

North London Nightshifters was a local charity and one of the first things he'd been told about when he started work here, six weeks ago. If you were running low on something, they'd find it for you and deliver it. They worked at nights when the usual supply chains weren't operating, and an emergency case might otherwise mean a set of frantic phone calls, trying to locate what you needed and get it sent over via a taxi service. Many of their couriers were medical professionals, and so they were able to check their cargo and get it to the right place with the minimum of fuss and the maximum of care.

He'd seen the couriers a few times already, coming in and out of the hospital. Two of them had been noticeable only for the Nightshifters logo on their courier bags, but the third had made him turn and look. A woman in motorcycle leathers, with blonde curls and pale skin, ethereal and glowing. Her smile was almost formidably bright, like a warrior angel's...

His phone buzzed in his pocket. It really didn't much matter which courier was coming, just as long as they were here. Nightshifters had located the blood he needed, which in itself was nothing short of a miracle since his current patient had such a rare blood group that most hospitals didn't carry stocks of it.

'It's here.' He turned to the nurse who had been monitoring the young woman he was treating. 'I'll go and collect it.'

He opened the door of the cubicle, just in time to see her. His thanks dried in his throat as the box was shoved into his hands, and the courier took off her motorcycle helmet, her blonde curls falling around her face. He could see now that she had sapphire-blue eyes.

'Don't just stand there.' Her voice had a melodic quality about it and betrayed more than a trace of humour. 'Check and sign.' She unzipped her jacket, producing a docket.

Joel opened the box, looking inside, checking that the quantity and blood type were correct. Then he took the paperwork, scanning it and scribbling his name at the bottom.

'Thanks. You're a lifesaver.'

'That's the general plan.' She gave him the merest hint of a smile and then turned her back on him and walked away.

Joel hesitated for one moment, resisting the urge to run after her and ask her name. Then he too turned, taking the lifesaving cargo back with him into the cubicle.

* * *

Robbie Hall walked back out of the A & E department, signalling a goodbye to the receptionist. Then she unzipped one of the pockets of her leather jacket, taking out her phone.

'Hello, Nightshifters, how can we help?'

'You can tell me I don't have any more calls for tonight, Glen.'

Glen's low chuckle sounded in her ear. 'Nah, we're done. Haven't you seen the time?'

The traffic on the roads had gone from non-existent to light as she'd made her way here, and the sun had been up for a while. Robbie took a guess.

'About seven o'clock?'

'Nearer eight. And you've finished for the night. We've no more calls.'

'Great, thanks. I'm going to the cafeteria to get some breakfast.'

'You caught up with the new doctor?'

There wasn't any particular doubt about where Glen was going with the question. In addition to daylighting as a paediatric physiotherapist and moonlighting at Nightshifters, Glen was a confirmed matchmaker. Lately he seemed to be viewing Robbie as his most troublesome challenge.

'Two heads. Breath that would make a dragon faint, and I thought I spotted a tail under his white coat...' Robbie sent up a silent apology for the undeserved injury to Dr Mason's reputation.

'You're far too picky, Rob. Breakfast for two makes you see someone in a completely different light...'

Breakfast for two wasn't on Robbie's agenda. Not

this morning or any morning. She'd seen Dr Joel Mason from afar, when he'd been given a whistle-stop tour of the paediatric A & E unit. A couple of the nurses who'd had the benefit of an introduction had told her his name and that he was the new doctor for general A & E, confirming at some length that he looked just as good close up as he did at a distance. Robbie could now privately confirm their assessment, but that was as far as it went.

'I'm not thinking about getting lucky at this moment. I'm too hungry. Want me to bring you an egg-and-bacon sandwich?'

'He'd be the one getting lucky, Rob. And no thanks to the sandwich, Carla's packed me soup and pasties.'

'Stop. Right now…' Glen's wife was a great cook and Robbie's stomach began to growl with envy.

'They smell pretty good. Even better when I warm them up in the microwave…'

'I'm hanging up, Glen. Actually, I'm never speaking to you again, so have a nice life…' Robbie heard Glen's laughter as she ended the call.

The staff in the cafeteria were getting ready for the morning onslaught as the night shift came off duty. The toast was freshly made and when Pete saw the motorcycle helmet and leathers, he gave her extra bacon and eggs done the way she liked them.

'Had a good night, Dr Hall?'

'You've just made it a great night, thanks, Pete. A large coffee would round it off perfectly.'

Pete had the coffee ready and put it onto her tray, waving her away from the cash register. 'It turns out that one of your visits last week was for the daughter of a posh bloke. He got in touch with the chairman of the hospital board and he's set up a tab for the Nightshifters.'

Robbie nodded. The posh bloke was an MP and his daughter had needed a ventilator. 'Use the tab for the others—I'll pay.'

Pete looked affronted. 'I've worked out a rota and everyone gets three free breakfasts. Don't mess with my system.'

Upsetting Pete's system was more important than Robbie's embarrassment at being well able to afford to pay. She grinned, picking up her tray. 'Okay, thanks, then. I'll enjoy this even more.'

A table in one corner was free and she sat down, peeling off the thin protective gloves she wore underneath her motor cycle gloves. The small patch of eczema on the back of her hand was fading fast and didn't itch at all now. And an egg-and-bacon sandwich was like a taste of heaven at the moment.

By the time she got to coffee, Robbie was beginning to relax. She'd go home and sleep, then let the rest of her Saturday take its course. Maybe spend a bit of time cooking, instead of just pulling something out of the freezer. She'd taken up cooking as her new and relaxing hobby, and if the results weren't always great the making of mess and then cleaning it up again did the trick for the relaxing part. It was all sounding pretty perfect when a shadow blocked the light from the window and made her look up.

He really *was* handsome. Or, on closer inspection, not quite perfectly handsome, because then he would have had a symmetrical smile. The crooked grin that

Joel Mason was giving her now was far, far more attractive than perfect features could ever be.

'Hi. May I join you?'

She'd almost finished her breakfast so it would only be for a few minutes. Robbie leaned forward, catching her motorcycle helmet up from the seat opposite and tucking it next to her on the bench.

'Sure. How's your patient?'

'Looking a lot better now. She'd lost a lot of blood and we were keeping her stable with fluids. Now we can risk sending her down for surgery to set her broken leg.'

His dark-eyed gaze seemed to be pulling her in, to a place of warmth. Robbie struggled to escape it and didn't quite succeed. The mental effort was unsettling, because it made her want to jump to her feet and move, rather than just watch as he sat down and unloaded his tray onto the table.

'Great. We're here to help.' Robbie toyed with the last crust of her sandwich, trying to use it to divert her attention.

'I'm new here. Joel Mason.' He reached across the table and Robbie picked up her coffee, nodding a *hello* instead of shaking his outstretched hand. Don't touch what you can't have…

'I know. Robbie Hall. I work in the paediatric A & E department.'

'Here? I'm sorry, you must be one of the million people I was introduced to.' He shook his head slightly, as if wondering how he could have forgotten.

'We weren't introduced. I saw you from the other side of the room.'

That sounded as if she'd been staring at him across

rooms. The slight quirk of Joel's lips didn't help Robbie's discomfiture. 'I was dealing with a four-year-old boy who'd swallowed a twenty-pence piece.'

'Was he okay?' The medical detail was enough to divert his attention.

'Yes, we X-rayed him and it was in his stomach. When he came back a few days later for another X-ray it was gone.' Robbie took a sip of her coffee and Joel grinned suddenly.

'I imagine you see that kind of thing more often in Paediatrics than we do in general A & E.' He picked up his knife and fork and started to tuck into the full English breakfast in front of him. 'I'm interested in Nightshifters...'

That was good to hear. It took her mind off Joel's square jaw and broad shoulders. His thick dark hair, cut short, which lent a touch of the unyielding to his soft, mesmerising eyes. And it was always nice when someone expressed an interest in Nightshifters because Robbie had put a lot of work into setting it up, and she financed most of its costs from her trust fund. It was her creation, although she didn't want any credit for that, preferring to stay in the background and get on with the things she really wanted to do. Apart from Glen, even the volunteers didn't know that Robbie provided most of the funding.

'You're thinking of helping us out?' She might as well throw a challenge his way.

Joel's fork paused in mid-air, halfway towards his mouth. 'Maybe. What do you need?'

Good question. It was the one that the Nightshifters always asked. 'Lots of things. People with some medical knowledge, who can find their way around the system and track down whatever's needed. Drivers, who can check the consignment they're carrying and make sure it's right. It helps if you know London as well—we don't usually have the time for getting lost.'

'And that's what you do? Someone like me calls you and asks for something, and you track it down and deliver it.'

'It's slightly different with blood—there are established channels that we use. At night we can often transport what's needed quicker and more reliably, so that an urgent request like yours doesn't have to rely on a regular taxi service. We're not the only charity doing work of this kind, there are different groups all around the country. We're locally based and serve the hospitals in this area.'

'What hours do you work?'

'We're open from eight at night until eight in the morning, but everyone gives what time they can. I usually do either a whole night, or midnight until eight in the morning, because I work nights at the hospital. People who work days tend to prefer eight in the evening until midnight.'

'How many nights a week?'

'I work one, sometimes two. But Glen, our coordinator, makes sure that no one takes on more than they can comfortably sustain. Everyone has commitments and a lot of people do just one night every two weeks or a month.' When she said it like that, it sounded as if she didn't have a life outside the hospital during the week and Nightshifters at the weekends. That was largely true.

If that had occurred to Joel, then he wasn't saying. If he was *really* interested in helping out, then they could always do with more volunteers. Robbie would just have to forgive him the good looks and the stomach-stirring sensuality.

'And...you use motorbikes?'

'That's just me, actually. The charity owns a couple of cars for deliveries, but a lot of people prefer to use their own and claim a mileage allowance. A lot of our delivery teams work in pairs.'

He grinned suddenly. 'But not you.'

'I prefer to work alone.' And the bike was a pretty good excuse for Robbie to do so.

He nodded, slicing into the toast on the side of his plate, and dipping a piece of it into the runny yolk of the eggs. Robbie waited as he chewed thoughtfully, and then gave in to her own impatience and asked the question that meant rather more to her than it should.

'So, are you interested?'

'I'd definitely like to know more.'

Good answer. In Robbie's experience it was the people who wanted to know more before committing themselves who were really interested in helping. Plenty of people promised a lot, on the basis of a five-minute conversation, and then you never saw them again.

'Then you should speak to Glen. He's the boss.' That was true, in terms of the day-to-day running of the operation. Glen had known Robbie's father for years, working with him on a number of charitable projects, and he knew how wealthy Robbie's family was. When Robbie had first started to develop her idea for Nightshifters, Dad had introduced her to Glen and they made a great team. He'd accepted Robbie's offer to run North London Nightshifters, and allowed her to make her own safe place there, where she was valued for what she could contribute on a practical basis, rather than how much money she could spend.

'And how do I get in contact with him?'

'I can get him to call you. Or you're welcome to pop into the office and see for yourself what we do.'

'I'm free this evening. Any time after eight.'

Joel didn't waste any time in putting his decisions into action. But Saturday night was a good time to come because Nightshifters was always busy and he'd see some of the challenges of what they did. And Robbie was planning to be in the office, as well.

'This evening's fine. Glen's expected at nine, so that's the best time to come. I'll be there too, so I can show you around.' She reached into her jacket for her notepad, writing down the instructions to get to the office. That was generally the second stumbling block. If Joel could find his way to the office, then he was serious.

'Great, thanks. I'll see you later on this evening.' He folded the paper without looking at it and put it into his pocket.

Robbie emptied her coffee cup, gathering up her jacket and helmet, ready to go, 'Yeah. See you later.'

It was the strangest address that Joel had ever seen. He'd gone home and slept for eight hours, then found the piece of paper that Robbie had given him. Then he'd puzzled over it for a while, and decided that the only way he was going to arrive was by starting out.

Orton Road was easy, ten minutes' walk from the Underground stop before the one for the hospital. Joel walked to the end of the road as instructed, and then turned left onto a footpath that led between a high wall and the side of the last house in the street. Then right onto a footbridge that spanned a small waterway, one of the tributaries of the Thames.

The steps at the other side of the bridge led down onto a wide riverside path, well lit and still busy, with a row of narrowboats moored on one side. Joel consulted the instructions again.

Walk down until you get to a corrugated iron building, painted turquoise.

Now that he was actually here, a corrugated iron building painted turquoise didn't sound quite so impossible. He'd driven across the road bridge a little further down many times, and was vaguely aware of the fact that there were boats here. But this looked like a whole community, living in the heart of London and yet to all intents and purposes hidden. Joel kept walking and caught sight of a flash of colour up ahead, set back from the river path.

The one-storey building, with a pitched roof and a small porch over the door at the front, was painted a particularly bright shade of turquoise. As he got closer, it also looked as if it were made entirely of corrugated iron, but there was an arched wooden door, and the windows that stretched along the side had wooden frames and shutters. Joel had never seen anything quite like it, and the overall effect was both odd and enchanting.

There was a sign beside the door bearing the charity's name, and, reassured that he was in the right place, he reached forward and knocked on the front door. He could hear the sounds of activity inside, and was just wondering whether he should wait or go inside when the door was flung open suddenly. Robbie was wearing a pair of jeans and a chunky knitted red sweater, which swamped her slim frame. Her hair curled around the side of her face, and she had a pencil propped behind her ear. The effect was enchanting and not even slightly odd.

'Hi. Don't bother about knocking, no one ever does. You made it, then?' She stood back from the doorway, and let him into a large, open-plan space. Lights hung from wooden beams that supported the V-shape of the roof, and the walls were clad in white painted timber panels. She was quite alone, but the comfortable seating and the two L-shaped desks at the far end of the space indicated that the office was designed to hold more than just one person.

'I said I would. What *is* this place?'

Robbie grinned, shutting the door behind him. 'It's a Tin Tabernacle. Haven't you seen one before?'

'No. You mean there's more than one of these?'

She laughed suddenly. Joel wanted more of that. Her laughter seemed to brighten the well-lit space around her.

'They were built in the mid- to late-eighteen hundreds and designed to provide low-cost churches and community halls, which could be taken down and put back up again to follow moving communities, such as construction workers on the rail and canal networks.'

'Hence the wooden doors and windows.' Joel turned to inspect the door. It was solid oak, and the dents and scratches were obviously touches of character that had been developed over many years.

'Yes, they all have these really good quality doors. If they're well maintained they'll last for ever. This one was used as a community hall and it's on brick footings so it's survived pretty well. We were lucky to get it. They're in quite a bit of demand as architectural curiosities, but the owners put a condition on the sale that said it had to be used for community purposes.'

'And they let you paint it turquoise?' It was a great colour, fitting in with the characterful nature of the building, but Joel wondered what the historians might think of that.

'They're all painted in these bright colours. Yellow, sky blue…a lot of them are various shades of turquoise—it's all part of their charm…' The phone rang and Robbie's head spun around. 'Uh, hang on a minute. Make yourself comfortable.'

She shot over to one of the desks, answering the phone. Joel sat down on one of the comfortable sofas, looking up as two men entered.

'Hi. You're Robbie's doctor?' One of them came forward, holding out his hand, and Joel got to his feet to shake it.

It would be nice to be Robbie's anything and doctor would do for starters. Joel dismissed the thought, because belonging with someone had never been one of his goals. A wide and varied group of friends, colleagues and acquaintances was a good thing. Friends with benefits was an occasional option, but anything approaching a real relationship took a great deal more trust than he was comfortable with.

'I'm Joel Mason. I work in A & E at the London Fitzrovia hospital and I met Robbie briefly this morning, when she brought some blood supplies we needed.'

'Glen Taverner, I'm a paediatric physiotherapist over at St Stephen's Hospital. And that's Dan Wright, he works at St Stephen's too.' Glen jerked his thumb towards the other man, who signalled a hello.

Glen was tall and bulky, the kind of guy that looked as if he could dead-lift the average person. But he had the gentle air and ready smile that most kids responded to.

'You have a great set-up here. And you came to my rescue this morning.'

Glen chuckled. 'That's the general plan. You're thinking of joining us?'

Joel didn't get a chance to answer. Robbie put the phone down, calling over to them.

'Guys, sorry… I know you've only just got here but I've got someone from St Stephen's who needs some milk for a preemie baby.'

'I'll go.' Glen responded to Robbie and then turned to Joel. 'Sorry about this, but Dan's just done three deliveries without a break, so I should do this one. If you'd like to leave your contact details, I can get in touch with you during the week.'

'We can talk later, maybe. I was hoping to be able to see a bit of what goes on here, if that's okay?' Joel replied.

'You're welcome to stay as long as you like.' Glen

turned towards Robbie, grinning at her. 'Robbie can tell you all you need to know.'

Glen walked over to the desk, putting down the large plastic food box he was carrying, and taking the docket that Robbie had just filled out from her hand.

'Thanks, Glen.' Robbie tapped the box with her finger. 'Carla hasn't sent coffee and walnut cake, has she?'

'Yep. And if it's all gone by the time I get back, I'll know who to blame.'

'You'd better hurry up, then.' Robbie chuckled, turning to Joel. 'Glen's wife, Carla, is *the* most amazing cook. I love her coffee and walnut cake.'

'There's banana bread in there too...' Glen was halfway to the door, waving over his shoulder. 'Never say that I don't do anything for you.'

'Tell Carla that if she ever gets tired of you, I'll marry her,' Dan called after him, and Glen's easy laugh sounded as he closed the door behind him.

'Right, then.' Robbie turned to Joel. 'Coffee and walnut cake or banana bread?'

'Banana bread.' He felt in his pocket. 'Is there a kitty for cakes?'

'No, that's okay, you can put your money away until January. We have a whip-round for Carla's birthday and I only take notes.' She grinned. 'The board makes sure that Glen and Carla aren't out of pocket for all the baking she does for us.'

'Okay, thanks. There's a board in charge of all of this?'

'Every charity has to have a board of trustees. But Glen's the one who's actually in charge here—whatever he says, goes. While we're waiting for him to get back,

I'll show you the ropes and then you can talk to him about whether you want to join us or not.'

There wasn't really any question about that. Joel had already seen the difference that the Nightshifters were making, and the easy camaraderie here made him feel instantly at home. And then there was the added bonus of Robbie's smile.

He was already sold. He wanted to be a part of this.

It was turning into a busy night. The three women and five men who were on courier duty tonight barely had time to introduce themselves to Joel and grab a coffee before they were sent back out again. Robbie was expecting him to just watch, and wait until Glen returned, but instead he came to sit at the desk next to hers and offered to take over the phones while she located some equipment that was needed by one of the hospitals in the area.

He was still there at midnight, when the pressure suddenly lifted and there was a lull in the calls. Joel stood up, stretching his shoulders, and Robbie tried not to look at him. She reckoned she'd done a fine job of pretending not to notice when his fingers brushed hers as he passed the call information across to her to distribute amongst the drivers. But the way he'd snatched his hand back made it very clear that he'd noticed, and that he knew all about keeping his distance.

Everyone had their own reason for working nights, but maybe Joel's were the same as hers. There wasn't too much time for meeting people and if you did then the unsocial hours were enough to keep things uncomplicated. It seemed that Joel shared her reservations about acknowledging the moments when two desks hadn't been a significant enough barrier to prevent Robbie from feeling that she was falling into the warmth of his gaze.

'Shall I make coffee?' He grinned at her.

'You're a…' Sweetheart? Tower of strength? The available evidence was indicating that he was both, and that he could probably be a great lover as well. 'Good timing. I could murder a coffee right now.'

Joel glanced around, including the four drivers who were sitting in the easy chairs in his offer, and took their orders. Glen ambled over towards her, sitting down on the other side of the desk and planting his elbows on it.

'Is this a volunteer opportunity? Or a date?'

He murmured the words so quietly that even Robbie could hardly hear him. Joel was at the far end of the office, chatting amiably with Rosie as she showed him how to operate the cappuccino machine, so there was no chance that he could be privy to the conversation.

'I've known him ten minutes. It's a volunteer opportunity.'

Glen grinned. 'When I met Carla it took me about ninety seconds to know.'

'That's you and Carla, you were made for each other. If I ever had a Prince Charming, I think he must have left my glass slipper on the train on his way home.'

'Lost Property's always an option.' Robbie waved Glen's suggestion away, and he abandoned it. 'Whatever. So you'll ask Joel if he can join us?'

'That's up to you. You're the North London coordinator.' Robbie pressed her lips together. She didn't want to have anything to do with asking Joel to stay, because she wanted him to so much.

'You're the founder, Rob. And our largest source of funding...' Glen practically mouthed the words at her, careful that none of the other volunteers should hear.

'And you're in charge, Glen.'

Robbie had said it enough times, but Glen was never slow in voicing the opinion that she should at least take some credit for her involvement. But he knew that Robbie was more comfortable with the way things were, and he went along with it.

'If you're so intent on me being the boss, then I should remind you that I'm allowed to delegate, Rob.'

Robbie shot him a smile. 'But you're so much better at it than I am, Glen.'

Glen clearly wasn't convinced. He flapped his hand dismissively, muttering something about excuses as he got to his feet. Walking over to Joel, he started to chat to him, and, while Rosie took the coffees back to the group in the seating area, the two men seemed deep in conversation. Finally they shook hands, and Joel walked back to the desk next to Robbie's.

'Looks as if I'm on the team.' His grin told Robbie that he was pleased about that, and she felt a shiver run down her spine.

'That's great.' She smiled across at Glen, who had taken a moment to speak to one of the other drivers and was now heading back towards them. 'When are you starting?'

'I've got to get a copy of my driving licence and various other documents to Glen first, so he can do the paperwork, but he says next weekend would be fine.'

Glen joined them. 'I'd like you to take Joel in hand and show him how everything works, if you would, Robbie. Since you'll be here next weekend.'

Glen didn't give up on an idea… But Robbie had told him that he was the boss, and she could hardly veto any of his decisions now. And something about the melting look in Joel's eyes made her feel that she wouldn't mind taking him in hand one bit.

'Next Saturday, then…?'

Both Joel and Glen nodded, and suddenly the gap between now and next Saturday opened up into a wide chasm. Robbie reminded herself that counting days before she saw Joel again wasn't on her agenda.

The phone rang and she reached for it. But Joel was quicker, grabbing it and giving her a delicious smile as he answered. 'Hello, Nightshifters. How can we help?'

CHAPTER TWO

RESISTING THE TEMPTATION to walk over to the Paediatric
A & E department to find Robbie, was made a great
deal easier by knowing that he'd be spending the night
with her next Saturday.

Spending the night… He shouldn't really think of
it as that; maybe working a shift was a better way of
looking at it. Learning something from her. Even the
word *learning* was problematic, because, despite Robbie's very obvious attitude that she was interested in
him only as a fellow volunteer, he reckoned that she
could teach him a few things about softness. About the
yielding nature of a kiss…

But Joel wasn't up for yielding to that kind of thing,
he never had been. He'd learned that particular les-
son young, finding out that his father was unfaithful
when he was only seven years old. He'd been sworn to
silence, and told that if he didn't keep the secret from
his mother, his family would break in two and it would
all be *his* fault.

So he'd stayed silent. By the time he'd been able to
apply an adult mind to the matter, it was a completely
different decision. What was the point of hurting his

mother with the revelation that his father had been unfaithful more than ten years ago?

But the torment hadn't ended. There had been times when he hadn't gone home because he couldn't face his mother and brother, and didn't want to face his father. When his mother had died suddenly, during his second year at medical school, guilt had made grief so much harder to bear. He'd lost precious time with his mother, and he'd lost the chance to make things right now.

The practice of medicine had filled the void in his heart. The secret that he kept meant that he hardly saw his own family, and he didn't feel qualified to make a new one for himself. Working at night was an easy way to keep his relationships uncomplicated and he'd taken the new job at the London Fitzrovia hospital on the understanding that the night shift was where he was most needed.

But when he'd seen Robbie he'd known that a short-lived affair with no strings attached wasn't going to work as a modus operandi this time. And that was going to be a problem.

He could convince himself that he'd volunteered because he wanted to be involved with the good work that Nightshifters were doing, and he had some time to spare. But as he came off shift on Friday morning, he couldn't truthfully tell himself that the excitement in the pit of his stomach wasn't something to do with seeing Robbie again.

As he wearily walked to his locker, his phone rang. Joel glanced at the screen and answered, expecting that Glen had thought of yet another piece of paper he needed to bring with him this evening, to keep the records straight.

'Hi, Joel. Are you still at work?' Glen sounded unusually terse.

'Yes, just finishing. What can I do for you?'

'I need a favour. Robbie's come off her bike at the side entrance to the hospital. She called saying she was all right and she's making her way there on foot with a delivery but she didn't sound all right to me. I don't suppose—'

'I'll find her and call you back.' Joel ended the call, hurrying out of the staff exit and scanning the curved slip road that led from the side entrance of the hospital to A & E.

He saw her almost immediately, just yards away from the main entrance, walking slowly past one of the ambulances that was parked up outside. A courier bag was looped across one shoulder and her crash helmet was nowhere to be seen. Her other arm was hanging limp against her body.

Joel reached her at a run, and she looked up at him as if she'd been caught doing something she shouldn't.

'Hey. Glen said you came off your bike. Where's your crash helmet?' If she'd lost it or it had been damaged, she needed to stop moving around, right now.

'I took it off. No head injuries.'

That was no substitute for a proper examination, but it put his mind at rest a little. The next, most obvious area of concern was her shoulder, and he gently took the courier bag from her other shoulder. That seemed to afford her some relief and she straightened a little.

'Take it inside…' She still seemed to be struggling to stay on her feet.

The delivery was of secondary importance right now. But when he quickly looped the bag across his chest and held out his arm to support her she drew back, wincing as she did so, her hand flying protectively to her shoulder.

'Take the bag, Joel. I'll follow you in.'

She was obviously hurt and very probably in shock. Sometimes the direct approach was the best one.

'Do I need to remind you who's in charge here? Take my arm, it's just a couple of steps. Can you manage that?' He spoke as kindly as he could, but he wasn't going to allow any arguments.

'Yes.' She was surveying the short distance from here to the main doors as if every inch was going to be a challenge and she took his arm, gripping it tightly. That more than anything convinced Joel that she really wasn't okay. He walked her slowly through the automatic doors, and carefully sat her down in the first available chair.

'Give them the bag, Joel.'

It was obvious that the sooner he made the delivery, the sooner Robbie would allow him to tend to her. He consulted the label attached to the parcel she'd brought, finding that it was milk for a premature baby, and hurried over to the reception desk. The receptionist asked him to wait, and Joel rapped out a brisk instruction for the woman to take charge of the delivery herself, and make sure that it got to the right place. Then he turned back to Robbie.

'My bike…'

She was blinking away tears, and cradling her arm against her body. Apparently this was the next thing on her list of concerns before he would be allowed to examine her.

'Stay there.' Joel hurried to fetch a wheelchair, and when he returned Robbie's eyebrows shot up as if this were the first time in her life she'd ever seen such a thing.

'I can walk.'

'Hospital regulations.' Joel had no idea what the hospital regulations said about recalcitrant doctors on their way into A & E, but perhaps his no-nonsense tone did the trick. Robbie took his arm and stood, then sank into the wheelchair and allowed him to wheel her through to a spare cubicle in the treatment area.

'Should we be going straight in?' Robbie was still in distress, but couldn't conceal her relief at being in a safe place now.

'My medical opinion is that you need to be seen straight away. There's nothing more urgent on the board, and I'm not on duty any more. Wait one minute while I call Glen and then we can forget all about everything apart from your arm.'

He pulled out his phone, and dialled Glen's mobile number. He answered on the first ring.

'Yep?'

'I've got Robbie here in A & E, she's taken a tumble and I'm going to examine her now. The delivery's at Reception and Robbie's worried about her bike…'

'Okay, I'll call the special care baby unit, and make sure they know the delivery's there. Tell Rob not to worry about the bike, I've already got someone on the way and we'll deal with it.'

'Great. Thanks.'

'And don't take any nonsense from her, Joel. She's to shut up and follow doctor's orders...'

'Sure thing.' Joel ignored Robbie's outstretched hand, her fingers signalling that she wanted to talk to Glen, and ended the call.

'What did he say?' Robbie looked a little annoyed with him.

'Someone's already on their way to see to your bike and he's calling the recipient of the package to let them know it's here.'

She let out a shaky sigh, and allowed him to check her pulse. 'And the last part?'

'He...hopes you're okay.'

Robbie smirked suddenly. 'He definitely didn't say that.'

'No, actually. He said I should tell you to shut up and follow doctor's orders. Stop fighting me, Robbie.'

Tears welled in her eyes. She was beginning to let go, and she was obviously hurting badly. Before he turned his attention to her shoulder, Joel performed a few quick checks to make sure there wasn't anything more serious going on here, trying to ignore the fact that she was weeping silently.

But it tore at his heart. He'd just let her in to the place he reserved for the hurt and the helpless, and there was no denying that Robbie could cause havoc there. But it was too late to go back now and she needed him.

'Am I going to ask, or will you just give me the answers?' He murmured the question, trying to regain some distance. Robbie knew what he needed to know, and having her just tell him was a way of checking how alert she was, as well.

'Someone hit me from behind and I went over the handlebars. I didn't hit my head and my leathers saved me from scrapes but I landed on my right shoulder...' She tailed off, vulnerability sounding in her voice.

Joel nodded. 'Anything else?'

Her eyes were focussed on his raised finger, following its movements. 'That's all, Joel. I *said* I hadn't hit my head.'

'Who's in charge here?'

She glared at him. 'I'll allow you to think that you are.'

'That's good, thanks. Let's see if I can get your jacket off without hurting you too much.'

He would have preferred another smart answer but Robbie nodded quietly. The fact that she had no more fight left in her was the symptom that concerned him the most, and he carefully unzipped her heavy jacket.

If this was what he thought it was, then pain was the most obvious symptom. She was wearing a loose-fitting hoodie underneath, and Joel unzipped that too, thanking his lucky stars that Robbie hadn't chosen to wear anything that he'd have to pull over her head. She knew what he had to do and he saw her press her lips together.

'We'll take it slow and steady. Uninjured arm first.' He helped her slip her left arm out of the jacket and hoodie together, revealing a white fitted T-shirt with long sleeves underneath.

'Well done. Now hold onto me to steady yourself if you need to...'

This was the part that would hurt the most, and he caught her left hand, resting it on his shoulder. Joel gritted his teeth, trying to insulate himself from the whimpers of pain that escaped her lips as he carefully loosened her jacket and hoodie from her right shoulder and threaded the sleeves down her arm.

The heavy jacket crumpled onto the floor and she was still holding onto him, her fingers bunching the material of his scrubs. She let go suddenly, turning her head away from him as if she was trying to conceal her tears. Joel resisted the temptation to comfort her, knowing that making this as quick and efficient as he could was the best way of ending it. He gently probed her shoulder with his fingers, and found what the slight droop of her shoulder had already indicated to him.

'I think your shoulder is partially dislocated and I'll order an X-ray to confirm. But I'm going to need to take a look at it. How fond of that T-shirt are you?'

Robbie nodded, as if that was what she'd expected to hear. 'Will you cut it, please?'

Joel nodded, smiling. 'Yeah, I think that's best.'

He'd been unable to stop thinking about Robbie in the last week, and he wouldn't have been surprised to find that he felt some trickle of the desire that had been threatening to wrap its web around him. Maybe it was their surroundings, but it was also her vulnerability and her tears that left him with nothing but the urgent need to stop her pain. She could have stripped naked in front of him right now, and he probably wouldn't have even noticed.

Correction. He'd notice. But he wouldn't care.

He unlocked the treatment cabinet, finding a pair of

surgical scissors. Carefully, gently, he cut the sleeve of her T-shirt, peeling the fabric back.

'Yeah, I think it is a partial dislocation.' Robbie was craning around, trying to see her shoulder, and he suppressed a smile. He'd probably be doing the same in her place.

'What's this?' He pointed to the small patch of what looked like eczema on her arm.

'You don't recognise eczema when you see it? I may be beginning to lose confidence in you.' There was a trace of weariness in her tone, as if she was used to these kinds of questions.

'I was going to fetch one of the nurses, to help you into a gown. But I'm thinking that you might prefer not to wear anything that's been washed in an unknown detergent.'

Suddenly there was warmth in her eyes. And with it came more tears. Robbie was battling to hold everything together and somehow he'd made her feel safe enough to let her guard down.

'You're right, I would prefer to stick with my own T-shirt.' She managed a smile. 'What's left of it.'

That smile was everything. Joel resisted the impulse to hug her, but couldn't help reaching out to lay a comforting hand on her left arm. 'Would you like something for the pain? Entonox?'

'I might save that for later.' Robbie knew what was coming just as well as he did. 'I'll scream if I want something.'

'You do that. Sit tight, I'll be a couple of minutes with the paperwork and then I'll take you for the X-ray.'

'You don't need—'

Joel turned away, ignoring Robbie's protest. He had no other patients to attend to and he really *did* need to make sure that she wasn't alone.

It had taken all of her single-minded stubbornness to get this far. As she'd turned into the quieter side entrance to the hospital, slowing to make sure that there was no traffic coming the other way on the slip road, someone had come out of nowhere hitting the back of the bike and sending her flying. The bike had ended up on a strip of grass beside the entrance to the hospital, and Robbie had ended up in agony.

But she'd got to her feet. That was the first step. The second step was get to her bike, and the third to get the pannier open and retrieve her courier bag, the pain in her shoulder rendering her right arm useless. She'd hardly noticed the car backing and driving away, leaving her alone, because single-mindedness didn't take account of anyone else's actions. She'd called Glen and then allowed herself to cry out from the pain, because there was no one to hear her. Then the fourth step. It had seemed like a very long way to the entrance of the A & E department, but the only way she was going to get there was to start walking.

And then Joel had found her. She'd almost wept with relief when she'd caught sight of him, trembling as he'd gently relieved her of the bag, and along with it all of the responsibility for taking the next step.

He hadn't pushed things, or tried to be the only doctor in the room. But he'd taken charge, and as Robbie had slowly begun to let go it had been difficult to hold back the tears.

His touch, his scent had been intoxicating enough to take the edge off the pain. And his matter-of-fact attitude to the patch of eczema he'd seen, and practical consideration, had stabbed even deeper. Now that she was alone, she could wallow in the luxury of embarrassment, knowing that Joel was dealing with everything else.

Right now, that embarrassment centred around her T-shirt. Even thinking about pulling it off made her feel slightly dizzy, and the X-ray required any metal to be removed from her clothing. She supposed she could call a nurse, but dealing with this herself, while Joel was out of the room, seemed a better option.

He'd left the scissors on the top of the treatment cabinet, and she reached for them. Using them to snip the bra strap that ran over her left shoulder was a bit awkward but easy enough, even if it did send pain thrumming through her. The right hurt even more, but it meant that she could now unhook her bra and pull it off without having to pull her T-shirt over her head.

The scissors slipped from her lap onto the floor, and she closed her eyes, breathing through the pain. Then she heard a soft rap on the door, and Joel entered, carrying a set of A & E treatment notes, and a temporary sling for her arm. He looked down at the pair of scissors, picking them up, and he must have been able to see the ruined bra that she was still clutching. Robbie felt herself redden.

'You decided not to wait for the nurse.' He grinned suddenly. 'I thought there was a secret trick to taking your underwear off under your clothes.'

Robbie couldn't help laughing. And every time Joel's

warm humour touched her, making her feel safe and secure, she started to cry as well.

'If I told you, it wouldn't be a secret, would it? You need two working shoulders.' Her nose was beginning to run again and she snuffled awkwardly. Joel reached for a tissue, putting it into her hand.

'Too bad. This should make you a bit more comfortable until we get the X-ray results.'

He fixed the temporary sling, and then held her hoodie out so she could put her left arm into the sleeve before wrapping it around her shoulders. The trip down to the X-ray department was made with the minimum of fuss and since there wasn't a queue they didn't have to wait.

Joel spent a moment examining the results on the computer screen in the corner of the cubicle, and then turned to her. 'You want to take a look?'

'Of course.'

He twisted the screen around to face her. Robbie had expected to be able to give an informed and objective opinion about what should happen next, but somehow she couldn't. She stared dumbly at the image.

'This is what I think…' Joel was gently taking charge again, seeming to know that she couldn't. 'You've got a partial anterior dislocation, and it should reduce without too much trouble. You'll be having pain relief because it's going to hurt, and I'd like to do that now if it's okay with you.'

'Yes… Yes.' He was absolutely right, and had put it all into words when she couldn't.

'Right. You said Entonox? I can give you something a little stronger than that if you want.'

'Entonox is fine.' Robbie just wanted to get this over with.

'All right. We'll have this sorted very soon.' He gave her an encouraging smile, leaving the cubicle for a moment and then returning to help her out of her hoodie and the sling, gently supporting her as she lay back onto the bed. Kat, one of the nurses, appeared, bringing with her a bright smile and the cylinder of Entonox, and Joel handed her the mouthpiece.

He positioned himself on her left side. Close. No closer than he needed to be to do this, but it *was* close. She could feel his fingers on her shoulder and around her elbow. Maybe she should have asked for someone else to do this.

'Deep breath.' He nodded at the mouthpiece and Robbie sucked in a breath, feeling her head swim a little from the Entonox. 'Try to relax.'

That wasn't easy. Not when he was so close and she knew exactly what was coming. It clearly wasn't happening, because Joel hadn't pushed the shoulder joint back in yet.

'That's the trouble with doctors.' He grinned at Kat. 'They know what's going to happen next.'

'Nurses too.' Kat returned his smile.

'Yeah, nurses are the worst,' he joked, turning his head back towards Robbie. 'I'd say that this is going to hurt me more than it hurts you but…you can imagine it will if it makes you feel any better. Another breath.'

Suddenly she was floating in the languorous pool of his gaze. The floating part might well be the Entonox, but the warmth and the feeling of well-being were all down to Joel. She hardly registered his fingers tightening around her elbow, or the sharp pain that accompanied his swift, precise movement of her arm.

'Great. Well done.' His smile was everything. Robbie dropped the mouthpiece, almost reaching out for him before Kat put it back into her hand, encouraging her to take another breath.

Don't show yourself up now by clinging to him. Someone will say something and it'll be halfway around the hospital before you know it.

She struggled for self-control and found it, somewhere in his cool, professional touch. Something in Joel's eyes betrayed that hurting her *had* hurt him, and she hung onto that. One small way that she could take control and be the one to offer comfort. She smiled up at him and he nodded.

'One more X-ray, just to make sure everything's back in the right place, and I'll sort out a sling for you. Then you can go home.'

CHAPTER THREE

JOEL HAD BEEN determined that Robbie should have the best. And he'd failed. Because the best involved a doctor who could step back and treat his patient with both care and objectivity. He'd managed the care part, but fallen down badly on the objectivity, although he'd managed to hide that. Robbie's case had been a simple one, and there had never been any doubt about the correct way to proceed.

A & E wasn't busy, and he handed the responsibility for helping Robbie back into her clothes and fitting her with a sling over to Kat, the nurse who had helped with the reduction. She raised her eyebrows when he asked her to reiterate the need for rest and keeping her shoulder immobile for at least three days, but Kat obviously knew Robbie.

'Leave the really tough jobs to the nurses, eh?'

Then everything became easier. While he was waiting in the pharmacy queue for the painkillers he'd prescribed, he called Glen. He changed out of his scrubs on the way back, and by the time he arrived back in A & E he could slot effortlessly into the role of concerned friend, which allowed him a little more lassitude than the role of doctor.

She was sitting in the waiting room, her jacket on the chair next to her. Joel sat down on the adjoining seat, glad of the opportunity to keep a little space between them, because he just wanted to hug her.

'How's it feeling?'

'Much better, thanks.'

'Anything else you want to bring to our notice, before you go?'

She rolled her eyes. 'You gave me a thorough examination when I first got here. And Kat interrogated me just now, in case there was anything you'd missed.'

'Glad to hear it.' Joel leaned back in his seat, shooting her an innocent look. 'Did she manage to get anything out of you?'

'Just that I fell on my hip as well, and I think I may have a bruise tomorrow. And no, you're *not* going to take me back in there, because I showed it to Kat and it's just a bruise, which will be fine. I want to go home.'

Joel nodded. 'I spoke to Glen. They've collected your bike and it's back at the Tin Tabernacle. He says it's a bit scratched up but it doesn't look to be too badly damaged. He said you'd want to know.'

'I do, thanks. Not that I'll be riding it for a while.'

'No, not that you will. I told Glen that I'd take you home.'

Robbie narrowed her eyes. 'Thanks, but there's no need.'

'He seemed to think there was.' It was a convenient excuse, but not the whole truth. Joel had already decided that Robbie wasn't going home alone. 'There's always the option of reporting back and having Glen come down here, if you prefer that…'

Robbie shook her head, wincing slightly at the sudden movement. 'Don't do that. He'll be wanting to get home and have breakfast with Carla and the kids. And I wouldn't mind a helping hand if that's okay. I only seem to have one.'

Joel reckoned that this was about as close as he was going to get to an admission that she could do with some assistance. He respected her bravery and her independent spirit, even if it had wrenched at his heart to see her hurt and yet still putting the delivery she'd come to make first.

'By the way. I phoned up to the special care baby unit. They got your delivery and the baby's doing well.'

For a moment the news cut through her obvious fatigue. 'Thanks. I appreciate that.'

'And the taxi will be here in five minutes.'

She chuckled lazily, leaning back in her seat and closing her eyes. 'You're endlessly capable, aren't you…?'

Robbie leaned on him as they walked out to the taxi and let him help her inside. That was enough to allow Joel to step back a bit from any enjoyment he might have in being close to her, because you just didn't feel that with a friend in need. He had to prompt her for the address, and remind her to shift over to the left-hand side of the back seat, so that he could pass the seat belt over her uninjured shoulder.

The taxi slowed, driving around a quiet tree-lined square, the driver looking for the building number. Then it stopped outside a large mansion house, one of the solid stone facades that Joel generally only ever saw the outside of. He wondered whether there was some mistake, but then he saw Robbie release her seat belt. She tried reaching for her jacket, which lay beside her on the seat, puffing out a frustrated breath when Joel leaned forward to pay the driver.

He grabbed her jacket and helped her out of the vehicle. Robbie walked slowly towards the stone steps outside the building, and he followed her.

'Keys are in the top inside pocket of my jacket.'

Joel unzipped the pocket, handing her the keys, and she promptly dropped them. Robbie was clearly far too weary to do anything remotely practical, and he picked the keys up, trying a few in the lock of the heavy wooden door until he got the right one. Inside, was a lobby, with golden wood panelling on the walls and an air of understated wealth.

He wouldn't have been much surprised if Robbie had lived in some quirky, out of the way place, but this was *not* what he'd expected. She seemed at home here though, letting out a breath of relief when he closed the door behind them. She walked over to the lift, which opened immediately when she pressed the call button and revealed more glowing wood panelling.

'Top floor… You'll need the key…' She leaned against the back of the lift car, closing her eyes. Suddenly all that Joel could see was that she was in pain and couldn't wait to get home. He found the key that fitted the lock beside the button for the sixth floor, and when he twisted it the elevator started to move. When the lift doors opened they revealed just one front door and Joel sorted through the keys again to open it.

Then he saw nothing. Just Robbie's fatigue and her pain. He ushered her inside, and she walked into a large, light-filled sitting room and sat down on the sofa. Joel tried a few doors, finding the kitchen, and got a glass of water for her, opening the box of painkillers and handing her a couple.

She smiled at him wanly. 'Thanks. Sorry...'

'Don't you dare apologise. Take the painkillers, you obviously need them.'

'Yeah, I think I do.'

She put the tablets into her mouth and Joel handed her the glass of water to wash them down. Then he carefully arranged the cushions from the sofa, putting one at her back and another to support her arm in the right position.

'Thanks. Would you like some coffee or something...?'

Joel had been feeling a little like an intruder here, but Robbie obviously wanted him to stay. That was enough to stop him from walking away.

'I'll make it. Or would you prefer tea?'

She nodded. 'I was hoping you might offer. Coffee's good, I think I need to wake up a bit before I can get to sleep.'

He knew that feeling. The exhausted buzz after a busy night that made sleep impossible. She needed to eat something and get comfortable before she'd be able to rest properly.

'Can I get you something to eat?'

'There are some chocolate bars in the fridge. Take whatever you want for yourself.'

Sure. Chocolate and coffee might be a quick fix and

about as far as Robbie could think at the moment. Good food and a warm drink would help her sleep a little better. She was shifting her feet restlessly, and she leaned forward to tug at the laces of her boots, wincing in pain as she did so.

He knelt down, unlacing her boots, and she didn't protest. Then Joel pulled a footrest over, propping her feet up on it and arranging a chunky knitted throw, which was slung over the armrest of the sofa, over her legs.

'Stay there. I'll get you something to eat.' It was gratifying that she hadn't put up even a murmur of protest.

'And coffee…'

'As long as I can work out how to operate your coffee machine.' Robbie's kitchen was smart and gleaming, and he'd noticed a coffee machine that looked as if you needed a two-day induction course before you even switched it on.

'Just pull levers…' She waved her hand, lazily. 'You'll be fine.'

He found a carton of soup in the fridge and heated it up, choosing a large mug from the kitchen cabinet that would be easy for her to manage one-handed. The coffee machine wasn't as complex as it looked, and there was some decaffeinated coffee in the cupboard, along with bread for toast. Joel added some fruit to the tray, and took it all through to the sitting room.

The analgesics had clearly kicked in, and she seemed more comfortable and alert, her cheeks a little less pale. She accepted the food gratefully, and Joel went back to the kitchen to fetch an ice pack from the freezer for her hip. He re-plumped the cushions at her back, just for good measure and because he wanted the gratification of being close to her. Then he sat, watching her drink the soup, as if his life depended on it.

'That's better.' She leaned forward to put her empty cup back onto the tray, and Joel took it from her before she had to stretch.

'You think you could get some sleep now?' He handed her the coffee.

'Maybe this will wake me up enough to move.' She took a sip and then another, as if she was making sure. 'It's decaf, isn't it…?'

He chuckled. 'I thought I was going to get away with that.'

'You can't fool me. When you work with kids you get a whole arsenal of little doctor tricks. You're dealing with an expert.'

Was that what it was? Little doctor tricks? Or little friend tricks? Or just the actions of someone who cared, but who couldn't bring himself to admit it.

'That shoulder's going to be pretty painful for a few days. But you should try to get some rest.'

She nodded. 'It's not too bad. Just as long as I don't do anything drastic like breathing. I feel as if I could just stay here and doze…'

That wasn't going to help much. It occurred to Joel that Robbie's eczema might make her going-to-bed routine more lengthy than just finding her bedroom and taking off her clothes, which was enough of a challenge at the moment.

'Can't face the emollients?' He said the words cautiously. The last time he'd mentioned her eczema she'd reacted as if it was a sore point.

'Something like that. I'm…um…sorry. That I snapped at you when you asked about my eczema. You had a good point about the hospital gown and I wasn't thinking straight at the time.'

It had been one of the things he'd done right. Looking at her as a doctor who could see each of the things that might affect her medically. Forgetting that, as a man, all he could see was Robbie's hard-won smile.

Joel shrugged. 'It's okay. People have done a lot worse. I reckon that anyone who doesn't take a swing at me is a model patient.' Robbie could have done that if it would make her feel better. It probably would have made *him* feel better. The one thing that had been eating at him was her quiet vulnerability, and knowing that she was in a lot of pain.

'You have very low standards. I keep going until I get a smile.'

He'd bet she did. And he reckoned that in most cases she got one as well. He'd seen a new side of Robbie in the last few hours. Determination, certainly, but also patience and the willingness to make the best of things. She'd demanded nothing from him, and that had taken grit.

'You get a lot of that kind of thing? Comments about the eczema?' Joel always worked hard not to assume anything about anyone, but from Robbie's attitude he reckoned she did.

'That's one of the reasons I work with kids. They just ask what that funny red patch is and I tell them and they go *Oh, okay* and move on. Adults can be less forgiving.'

'You need to be *forgiven*?' Joel shot her a pained look and Robbie laughed.

'Me? No. It just makes me a bit weary when people say *Can't you cover it up with something?*' She stared up at the ceiling, as if wanting to avoid his gaze. 'Or that I must be able to afford some proper treatment...'

There was hurt, there. Joel suspected that she wasn't really talking about *people*, but one person in particular. Someone close... He felt himself shying away from the inevitable question, because whatever his remit was, it was definitely outside it.

'As if NHS doctors aren't as good as private doctors.' The attitude always made him frown.

'Yes, something like that. People have a habit of measuring things by how much they have to pay for them.' She turned her gaze on him as if something had just occurred to her. 'You're wondering how I afford this place on a doctor's salary?'

It would be an obvious lie to say no. The simple equation of square footage and location made the large room they were sitting in way beyond his own pay grade, and no doubt Robbie's as well. And it was nice square footage. High ceilings with moulded plasterwork, painted in different shades of cream that emphasised light and space. The furniture was plain but attractive and clearly of good quality. The one thing that wasn't understated was the light that hung from the centre of the ceiling. A huge globe, made up of swirling glass filaments, that fitted the proportions of the space, and gave it focus.

'It occurred to me. I reckon maybe a lottery win?'

She laughed suddenly. 'No. Ice-cold.'

'Rich uncle?'

'You're getting warmer... This was my grandparents' place. My grandfather died when I was nineteen and left it to me.'

She seemed almost apologetic. As if she was going through all the things that people had made her apologise for over the years, her eczema, her beautiful home, and challenging him with them. The thought that Robbie even cared about what he thought sent a tingle down his spine.

'I'll bet it's great for parties.'

Right answer. Robbie smiled suddenly. 'Yes, it is. Thick walls so you can make as much noise as you like.'

And the whole of the top floor of the building, if the single front door outside the lift had been anything to go by. Joel wondered how many other large rooms there were, which he hadn't seen. Right now, the only one he was really interested in was Robbie's bedroom. He shivered at the thought, and adjusted his focus. Her bedroom with Robbie in it and fast asleep, and him somewhere else.

'If you need some help…getting ready for bed…' He felt himself flush and wondered what the professional way to say this might be. 'You've taken a nasty fall, and you're probably still a bit shaky. The last thing you need to do is fall again.'

Her gaze softened. 'You've already done too much, and I'm grateful. You must be tired.'

Nope. Wide awake. 'While I'm here, I may as well make myself useful.'

What was she doing? Testing him, that was what.

Robbie didn't much care what other people said, about anything in her life. Everyone thought what they thought, and as long as they didn't shove their opinions in her face she was happy to let them do that. She'd worked that out with her counsellor when she was a teenager.

Her parents could have sat back and enjoyed their wealth but instead they'd used it, not just sponsoring a variety of medical initiatives, but becoming personally involved with them as well. And wherever they went they took their daughters. She and her big sister, Izzy, had grown up in a world where everyone was taken just as they were, and if Robbie ever gave her eczema a second thought it was to realise that she faced fewer challenges than some of the other kids she knew.

And then suddenly, she'd become aware of it. A newspaper had published a photograph of her family, and drawn attention to the marks on her skin. The two most noticeable patches on her arm and face had even been enlarged in separate images, so that readers could examine them in detail. As if that were the only thing that mattered about her. Some journalist who didn't know her father from Adam had insinuated that it was Robbie's eczema that had prompted him to devote so much time and money to helping other kids.

It wasn't true. But Robbie had suddenly seen only Izzy's perfect skin and the marks on hers. She'd locked herself in her room, refusing to come out.

The matter had been dealt with, in the same way that her parents dealt with everything else that pertained to her and Izzy. Common sense and love. But even though Robbie had learned to appreciate her own worth and feel happy in her skin again, she hadn't quite managed to forget. Her parents had respected her decision to take a step back from the uncomfortable glare of the public eye, asking only that Robbie found her own ways of making a difference.

Then Rory. Dad had never liked him, and Robbie hadn't understood why. He'd seemed a little over-concerned about her eczema, but Robbie could cover it up if that was what he wanted. She'd just never been taught that there was a need to.

But Rory was the kind of person who couldn't feel truly happy if he wasn't better than everyone else. Robbie's trust fund suited him down to the ground on that score, and his attitude to her eczema was his way of making her feel unacceptable to anyone else. He'd chipped away at her confidence, until there was nothing left.

Finally she'd cracked. She'd realised how worthless Rory made her feel, and gone away on holiday without him, to give herself a chance to think.

When she'd returned she was ready to end the relationship with Rory and to hear her father's thoughtful advice. *'Be whoever you want to be, Robbie. Money's only a burden if you allow it to be.'*

So Olivia Roberta Hampton-Hall had adopted the nickname her family had used for her since she was a child, and truncated her instantly recognisable surname, to become Robbie Hall.

All of her colleagues at the hospital and everyone at Nightshifters knew her as that. And it was her safe place, her refuge from the fear that some people would only ever see two things about her. Money and eczema.

Joel had seen both the money and the eczema, even though he didn't know it. Didn't know that her family's money was the reason Nightshifters existed. Regardless, neither had seemed to change the way he acted towards her. Why hide any more?

Because guarding those secrets was what made her feel safe and in control of her life. Loving someone like Joel would be horribly easy, someone who saw the things she kept hidden, but it stripped away everything that made her feel secure.

She was aware that she'd been silent for a while now. He hadn't pushed her, gathering the mugs and plates up, and taking them into the kitchen. From the sounds of it, he was doing the washing up. Robbie put her mind to how she was going to reach the fading eczema patches from her last flare, and even thinking about it made her shoulder hurt. And Joel was here and he'd offered his help.

Robbie swallowed her last gulp of coffee and with it a slice of her hard-won self-reliance.

When he reappeared from the kitchen, she said, 'I think I need some help. If you don't mind.'

He smiled, shaking his head. 'Of course not. What do you need?'

Joel had followed her to her bedroom, stopping abruptly at the door, until she beckoned him in. He'd opened the wide drawers, which wouldn't budge if she tugged at just one of the handles, and she'd found a soft, comfortable nightshirt, which had the added advantage of having long sleeves and reaching down to her knees.

Then came the awkward part. But Joel was well practised in making the very awkward seem hardly difficult at all, sitting her down on the bed and then unclipping the sling and laying her arm on a pillow that he'd placed on her lap. Then he spread the nightshirt out next to her on the bed and drew back.

'Undress your uninjured side first...' He'd retreated back through the open doorway and was out of sight now, but from the sound of his voice Joel was standing right outside in the hall. And clearly attempting to be of some use from a distance.

'I know.'

Getting out of the T-shirt and threading the part of it that Joel had cut away at the hospital over her injured shoulder was easy enough. The nightshirt was a bit more tricky, but she managed to get the sleeve over her right shoulder without too much pain.

'It sounds easier than it actually is.'

She heard his low chuckle. 'I've never tried it. Are you okay?'

'Just about.' She'd forgotten to undo the buttons at the neck of the nightshirt, and it was stuck over her head.

'Do you need a hand? I could keep my eyes closed...'

Robbie gave the nightshirt a tug and felt it give. The button had flown off and clattered against something. That was okay, she'd find it later. She could get her left arm through the sleeve of the loose garment now.

'How are you going to help with your eyes closed? You wouldn't be able to even find me, you'd have to feel your way.'

His embarrassed cough made her smile. And then the incongruity of the situation struck her, and she started to laugh. Two doctors being shy with each other over getting into a nightshirt. Really?

Pain shot through her shoulder, making her yelp and

bringing tears to her eyes. Then she felt Joel, his arms around her, gently supporting her shoulder. She clutched at his shirt, burying her head against his chest.

'Just breathe. You're okay.'

Yeah. Breathe. That was what she'd forgotten to do. The first breath made her whimper with pain but the second one wasn't so bad. The third was positively delicious, as she took in his warm, clean scent.

'Better?'

'Yes.' Great actually, despite the throbbing in her shoulder. 'I didn't knock it back out again, did I?'

She felt his fingers on her shoulder, so gentle that his probing didn't even hurt. 'No, you'd know if you did and it feels fine. This is the *It's going to be painful for a while* part.'

'I might say that with a bit more emphasis in future, when I'm dealing with patients.'

'Being a patient is generally a much tougher job than being a doctor.' He drew back and Robbie glimpsed tenderness in his eyes, before he turned his attention to the sling, carefully putting it back on to support her shoulder again.

That was what marked Joel out. He wasn't just kind, he'd been there for her in a way that was both touching and supportive. He probably didn't take all of his patients home and make soup for them, but Robbie wouldn't blame any of them for being a little in love with him.

He helped her out of her jeans, his deft fingers not once touching her skin, although she wouldn't have minded if they had. Then he fetched the emollients and cleansing creams from her bathroom, laying them out on the bed so she could choose which ones she wanted.

'These two will do for now.' She'd work out a way to continue her usual moisturising routine later.

'Hands, knees and elbows?' He grinned. It clearly wasn't lost on him that, while they were the usual trouble areas for eczema, they were also relatively safe territory.

'Yes, that's good. I have a small patch on my left shoulder that I can't reach, and the one you saw just above my right elbow.' In the warmth of his smile, elbows were taking on a major sexual significance that she'd never considered before.

'Sounds good. I'll just go and wash my hands with your soap if that's okay...'

He missed nothing. And he seemed to find that gentle rhythm that Robbie used when she cleaned and moisturised her skin, not stressed and resentful but using this as an opportunity for leisurely self-care. It would— should—have been relaxing, but her nerve ends were tingling at his every touch.

'Just as well you're left-handed.' His observation was clearly intended to be the kind of conversation that would put her at her ease, but it didn't. Joel had been noticing things about her.

'Yeah, I guess so. I never realised quite how much I use my right hand though.'

He nodded. 'Are you ready to sleep?'

She could spend all day just talking to Joel. But he looked tired and Robbie had to admit she was feeling sleepy now too. A picture of lying down to sleep, curled up in his arms, floated into her head.

It would be safe and secure. Robbie added to the picture in her head—a couple of layers of clothing and bedding between them—but that made it only slightly less delicious. It was still far too good to be a practical possibility.

Maybe she'd wake up in the morning and feel better. She'd wonder why it had ever seemed so necessary to cling to him.

Joel seemed undeterred by her silence. He was plumping pillows and arranging them so that she could sit up comfortably in the bed, and then he drew the duvet back. He seemed to have everything in hand and Robbie went with the flow.

But he was steadily getting ready to leave. When he went to fetch her phone from the sitting room, putting it in reach beside the bed, Robbie made one last effort to make him stay, shifting herself upright on the pillows.

'Don't close the curtains. Not yet…'

He took the hint, pulling the comfortable wicker chair from the corner and sitting down, stretching his long legs out in front of him.

'How did I do? In terms of interesting cases, tonight.' *This* was something they could talk about. Something that they had in common that didn't allow for any thoughts of how it might feel to have him touch her.

Joel grinned lazily. 'Well…good marks for accurate self-diagnosis, before you even arrived. But unfortunately you don't get the top prize for the night. That goes to Edna.'

'I'm mortified. Who's Edna?'

'She's an elderly lady who came in at about two in the morning. She'd fallen and couldn't get back up again, and pressed her personal alarm. When the ambulance brought her in she was wearing her nightie and dressing gown, with a hat. Apparently she'd insisted that the paramedic fetched her hat for her, before she'd agree to come to the hospital with them.'

'I knew I'd forgotten something.' Robbie smiled. Talking about the routine of other people's ailments was surprisingly relaxing. 'Was she okay...?'

CHAPTER FOUR

ROBBIE WOKE AT five in the afternoon. Her shoulder was throbbing, an acute reminder of the feeling of panic as she'd parted company with her bike and felt herself hit the ground. Her hip was stiff and sore as well.

Then she remembered. The relief when Joel had found her. X-rays, soup and then hearing about Joel's night at work, which had made a world that seemed to be spinning out of control more reassuringly normal. She'd started to doze halfway through his story about a practical joke that one of the nurses had played, and Joel had rearranged the pillows so that she could lie down.

Everything was in its proper place, the curtains were closed and the wicker chair he'd been sitting in back in the corner of the room. Had he gone? Her bedroom door was open and she listened carefully. Silence. Of course he'd left.

A dangerous thought entered her mind. A thought she shouldn't give space. She wanted him back. Robbie felt alone and vulnerable, and…she just wanted Joel back. Maybe a good cry would help, but that wasn't her usual modus operandi. She'd feel better if she found something to occupy her.

She got out of bed carefully, wrapping her dressing gown around her without bothering to go through the rigmarole of removing the sling to put her right arm into the sleeve. Knotting the tie was a problem and she left the gown open, walking towards the kitchen. Hopefully Joel had left her analgesics somewhere she could find them.

Then she saw that the sitting-room door was wide open and the blinds were closed, light filtering through them. She padded into the room and found Joel, stretched out on the sofa under the knitted throw, and fast asleep. Just the sight of him was enough to realise that the doctor-patient gratitude effect hadn't worn off yet. He still looked just as sexy and she could watch him sleep for any amount of time.

The temptation to give in to tears of gratitude was indescribable. He'd stayed, and he was obviously tired because the sound of her moving around hadn't woken him. She'd let him sleep a little while longer, secure in the knowledge that he was still here.

Robbie crept into the kitchen, opening the fridge and taking out a bottle of water. Getting the tablets out of the foil pack was a little awkward, but easy enough once she worked out how, and she laid them on the worktop next to the sink. The bottle was a greater challenge, the top stubbornly refusing to turn. Maybe if she ran it under some cold water…

The bottle slipped in her wet fingers and smashed into the sink. Great. And to add to her helpless frustration, she heard a noise from the sitting room and then Joel appeared at the kitchen door, obviously wide awake now.

'Sorry. I was going to let you sleep.'

'Are you all right?' His gaze took in the broken remains of the bottle. 'Did you cut yourself?'

'I dropped it. I'm...' Right now, nothing else mattered, apart from the fact that he was here. 'You stayed.'

'Yeah. You muttered something about a spare room as you were going to sleep, so I reckoned it would be okay with you.' He shrugged, turning the corners of his mouth down.

'It's fine. I really appreciate that you did. I wish you'd taken the spare room—you would have been more comfortable.' His feet were bare but he was still wearing his jeans and shirt, and his hair was sticking out a little. Perfect. Gorgeous.

'The sofa was fine. I reckoned I'd be able to hear you if you got up, but...'

'You were tired. I'm sorry I woke you. And I really appreciate all you did to help me this morning.'

He grinned suddenly, running his hand through his hair to flatten it. It was a great morning look. 'My pleasure. Leave the glass, I'll clear it up. Do you want something to eat?'

'Coffee would be great. With caffeine this time.' Robbie went to the fridge, taking out a fresh bottle of water, and Joel took it from her, opening it. She collected her tablets from the worktop, and sat down at the kitchen table. If she was going to have to submit to being looked after for a little while longer then she might as well enjoy it.

Watching him was *very* enjoyable, and when his back was turned she could do it as brazenly as she liked. Broad shoulders that gave the appearance of muscle when he stretched. Slim hips emphasised by a pair of jeans that looked as if they'd been washed a hundred times, because they fitted in all the right places. She must have been in a bad way when they'd arrived back here this morning, because she hadn't even noticed that.

And he had the best waking-up smile she'd ever seen. A little lazy, with the suggestion that dreams weren't just things that happened when you were asleep. Her immobilised shoulder suddenly became a *lot* more frustrating, because there was nothing she could do in response except smile back.

If he'd had to wrestle with the coffee machine the first time around, he had it under control now. He put her coffee down in front of her and sat down.

'I should be getting going soon, if I'm going to be at the Tin Tabernacle this evening. Is there anything you need?'

Robbie took a deep breath. This couldn't go on; she had to stand on her own two feet. The longer he stayed, the more difficult it would be to let him go, and not letting a guy go wasn't anywhere on her agenda.

'There's nothing I need, thank you.' She gave him a smile. 'I really appreciate all that you've done, but it's time for me to chase you away.' Robbie phrased it as tactfully as she could. What she really meant was that it was time for her to stop ogling him.

He gave her a thoughtful look. 'You can manage?'

Right now she felt that all she really needed was Joel's smile. That was the best reason of all for sending him away.

'I can manage. This is what happens after we decide

that patients don't need to be taken in to the hospital and send them home to get some rest.'

Joel nodded. 'And that's what you're planning on doing?'

Good question. 'I'd prefer to be at the Tin Tabernacle tonight, and back at work on Sunday night.' She saw a flash of alarm in his eyes. 'I'm telling myself right now that's not going to happen.'

'No, it isn't. At the very least you should be staying home until you've seen someone in Orthopaedics for a follow-up appointment—' He broke off suddenly as Robbie shot him a querying look. 'You remember that?'

'Uh…yes, you did say something about it last night, didn't you?'

Robbie wasn't sure that the follow-up appointment was strictly necessary. She was a doctor and she knew what she should do to care for her shoulder. But, on the other hand, it wasn't very likely that she'd be allowed back to work without an all-clear from Orthopaedics.

'Are you working up a list of reasons why you don't need to see a specialist?' He seemed to be able to read her mind without any effort at all.

'I was thinking it through. If my reasons are looking a bit flimsy to me, I imagine you'll be able to knock them over in no time.'

He nodded, amusement showing in his face. 'You might be overestimating me.'

Robbie doubted it. But the idea of putting up a fight, and seeing who got the better of whom, was much too tempting at the moment. She got to her feet, trying to shake off the delicious feeling that when she was with

Joel she was somewhere warm and comfortable, that she didn't want to leave.

It was just doctor-patient infatuation kicking in again. He was a good doctor and he was easy on the eye, and Robbie guessed that many of his patients developed symptoms.

'I can manage. And I'll do as I've been told, I promise.'

Robbie was concentrating on giving him no reason to stay. And Joel was clearly getting the message, because he got to his feet, draining his cup and walking through to the sitting room, to put on his socks and shoes.

'You've got my number?'

'Yes, you gave it to me last week.'

'Use it, then, if you need it.' He paused, waiting for her assent, and Robbie nodded.

She'd left him no reason to stay now. Robbie hovered at the front door while he called the lift, and then decided that gave all the wrong signals. She gave him a final, cheery goodbye and a thank-you and closed the door.

Leaning against it, she heard the lift doors open, and a slight creak as he stepped inside. She closed her eyes, trying hard not to cry. The apartment seemed suddenly very big and very empty, and the safest corner of it was right here, where she was closest to Joel.

'Stupid…' Robbie muttered a reproach, and tore herself away from the door. Joel had been here, he'd been kind, and now he was gone. That was exactly what she wanted, for him to take that perfect body of his somewhere it wouldn't wreak such havoc. The next time she saw him, he'd just be another volunteer, who didn't make her heart swell with longing.

An hour later, Robbie was still going through the process of getting showered and dressed in her head. It seemed like a great deal of trouble if she wasn't going to be going anywhere, and she was warm and comfortable on the sofa, wrapped in her thick dressing gown. Then the doorbell rang, and Rosie's voice floated over the intercom.

Rosie arrived, trailing the scent of a large bunch of freesias behind her, and immediately started to rap out orders. Robbie wasn't to move, while she found a vase. She could indulge in a little light flower arranging, while Rosie made a cup of tea.

'Yes, ma'am.' Robbie grinned at Rosie, glad to have the everyday clatter of activity around her again.

'Don't be smart, Rob.' Rosie clearly had her nursing hat on at the moment. 'Glen said he'd be popping in and, you never know, he might bring something to eat. You need to keep your strength up.'

Glen arrived, with a kitchen container full of food, adding the scent of cooking to that of the flowers. Clearly there was a concerted effort to try and make the place smell like home. Rosie peeled open the lid.

'Oh. Chicken jerk.' Rosie grinned. 'Carla's mum's recipe?'

'Of course, what other recipe is there?' Glen replied. 'Leftovers from lunch, and there's more than enough for two.'

Clearly these weren't leftovers, and Carla had deliberately cooked a few extra portions. Rosie added her thanks to Robbie's and disappeared into the kitchen.

'How's it going?' Glen lowered himself onto the sofa next to her.

'Oh…you know.' Robbie puffed out a breath. 'It hurt, and then Joel administered a sharp crunch and it felt a bit better. I'll be fine in a week.'

'Bit more than a week, Rob.'

'Maybe. Maybe I'll stun you all with my amazing powers of recuperation.' Robbie had picked up her phone to text Carla and frowned at the screen. 'I've just told Carla Thank you for the goofs. Who knew that texting with one hand was so fiddly?'

'Give it here.' Glen held out his hand and Robbie dropped the phone into it. He typed *food* into another text and sent it.

'What time did you get home this morning?' Glen worked the day shift during the week and usually dropped in to the Tin Tabernacle at either the beginning or the end of the night, to check on how things were going.

'About half past ten. Just in time to take the kids to the park before they tore the house down.'

'Not before you made Joel come home with me.' Robbie injected a note of reproach into the words.

'He insisted, actually. Told me I didn't need to come because he was going to see you home and make sure you were all right.'

A tingle ran down Robbie's spine. Joel hadn't mentioned it was his idea. What did that mean? Best not enquire any further.

'By the way, I got a little something for Amelia's

birthday. Would you be able to take it now? I'm not sure whether I'll be able to come to her party next week—'

Glen shot her a warning look. 'Don't even try it, Rob. A dozen over-excited eight-year-olds don't mix well with a dislocated shoulder. If you want to come over, come to dinner another evening.'

'Thanks. You'll take the present, though—I'd like her to have it on her birthday. It's on the top shelf of the cupboard in the hall in a blue and white bag.'

Glen went to fetch it, and returned inspecting the contents of the bag, smiling at the roll of sparkly princess wrapping paper. 'Oh… This is the book she wanted.'

'I hope she likes it. Dad was at a thing, and he got it signed for her.'

Glen flipped open the cover, reading the author's message, wishing Amelia a happy birthday. 'She'll be over the moon with this. Thank David for me, won't you? Have you called your mum and dad?'

'Not yet. They were in Ireland all of last week and they're flying back tonight. I'll give Mum a call in the morning, and no doubt she'll be all over it.'

'Good. So you want me to call the Nightshifters off your case?'

Robbie laughed. 'It means a lot that you came, I'm really grateful. But yes, please do call them off, I can only take so much looking after before I start climbing out of the window and shimmying down the drainpipe.' Hopefully that message would get through to Joel, as well.

'Not on my watch, you're not.' Rosie appeared with the tea and sat down, opening the roll of princess paper so that she could wrap Amelia's present.

It was nice, having her friends here. The comfortable, easy laughter and the good-natured bossiness. It took the edge off missing a man that she had no business missing.

And she and Joel were over. Finished, before they'd even started. It had seemed so real, and maybe he had felt it too, but it was a relationship that wasn't meant to happen. She wouldn't allow it to.

Joel had heard the messages. Glen had popped in, and was satisfied that Robbie was all right and not overdoing things. Rosie would be staying the night with her. After that, Robbie's mother would be coming to stay for a few days.

He wasn't needed. Robbie had made it clear that he wasn't wanted, even though she'd couched it in the nicest of terms—he'd done enough and she had to let him go. That suited him just fine, because he wasn't looking for a relationship with her. He knew himself too well, his relationships had a limited shelf-life and Robbie was the type of woman that deserved much more than something that fell apart of its own accord after a few weeks.

He had some thinking to do. Joel had seen Robbie at her most vulnerable, and he knew from experience that patients acted out of character when they were in shock and in pain. The idea that he should feel anything different from the cool professionalism that he usually brought with him to these encounters was a new one.

Waiting was hard, when he couldn't help wanting to see her. Couldn't help wondering whether she was all right, although he knew she was being well looked after. But he had to do it, because the dynamic between them was all wrong. He'd been a doctor and she'd been a patient, and that had opened up the prospect of all kinds of inappropriate feelings, the kind that they might regret later.

So he would wait. When Robbie was over the initial shock of what had happened, then maybe she would want to be his friend. And he'd be satisfied with that. He'd have to be.

CHAPTER FIVE

ROBBIE EMERGED FROM her consultation, clutching a handful of patient leaflets, her ears ringing. The head of orthopaedics didn't usually bother herself with a simple shoulder dislocation, but she was the firmest person that Robbie had ever met. She was beginning to wonder whether Orthopaedics weren't taking a leaf out of Nightshifters' and her parents' playbook and ganging up on her.

Then a ray of sunshine made her stop in her tracks, almost blinding her. Joel was sitting quietly at the back of the waiting room.

She could have been forgiven for not noticing him, and walking straight towards the exit. But her legs were already carrying her towards him, and she could feel herself smiling, with every inch of her body. Even her shoulder seemed to be doing its own version of smiling, and had stopped throbbing.

'Hey.' She sat down beside him. 'What are you doing here?'

The answer to that appeared to require some thought. 'Glen told me you had an appointment to come and see Dr Thompson.'

'You asked?' The thought that maybe he was here because he wanted to be, and not because Glen had hinted that he should be, was suddenly important.

Joel smiled. 'Yes. I asked. I wanted to see how you were.'

Five days of being without Joel had been enough time for Robbie to convince herself that what she'd felt for him really was just gratitude. It had taken about ten seconds for her to change her mind. Right now, she could think of a dozen different ways to inconvenience him, all of which felt perfectly acceptable.

'My parents came to stay for a few days. It was lovely to spend some time with Mum and Dad, but they've been looking after me to within an inch of my sanity. And now I've been subjected to a thorough talking to from the head of orthopaedics. You should bear Dr Thompson in mind for your more difficult patients— she's terrifying.'

'Yeah?' He raised an eyebrow. 'You don't look all that terrified…'

'That's because I'm annoyed.' Robbie frowned.

'Why? What did she say?' He pulled a face, seeming to regret his questions. 'Asking for a friend, you understand.'

It seemed that he was asking for himself. But Robbie understood why he wouldn't say so, because she was confused too. Caught in the middle of a battle between her instinctive feelings for Joel, and the way she'd planned her life.

'My friend?'

His eyes grew warmer and he nodded. 'Yes, your friend.'

They knew where they stood, now. And friendship

could be any number of things, so there was a way forward for them both.

'She gave me exercises.' Robbie handed him the printed sheets and Joel glanced through them, nodding.

'Looks good.'

'They are, and she'll be giving me a rocket if she thinks I haven't done them every day. And she says that I can come back to work, which is good, but that she's going to call my head of department and discuss light duties with him. I've got to go back and have her sign me off before I can actually do my job.'

'Is there such a thing as light duties in A & E?'

Robbie turned the corners of her mouth down. 'I wasn't aware of that either. I reckoned I'd be okay if I had a nurse with me to help, but apparently I'm not allowed to do that, I have to just talk to people. She says that I can answer their questions and give them general guidance, after they've seen the doctor.'

'Sounds like a great idea. I wish we had someone like that full time, I don't always have the time to go through everything as thoroughly as I'd like with patients.'

'It is a great idea. I just didn't want it to be me!'

He leaned back in his seat, a smile playing around his lips. 'Something tells me that you don't want to hear what I think.'

That was what she liked about Joel. They could disagree without it having to turn into an argument.

'Go on. Say it.'

'You think that Dr Thompson's not assessed you properly?'

'No, she's fierce but she's an incredibly good doctor.' Robbie had to admit that.

'Then… What you did on Saturday morning was incredibly brave. You were in shock from an accident, and a lot of pain, and somehow you managed to get up and collect your courier bag and walk.'

The thought of the effort that it had taken still made her tremble. Robbie turned her head away from him, blinking away the tears that were forming in her eyes.

'Look at me.' His words were gentle, but Robbie responded angrily, glaring at him. The softness in his gaze only made her want to cry even more.

'You can stop now, Robbie. You did it, you made the delivery and you got yourself some help. You've said yourself that Dr Thompson is a good doctor, and you can let her take the strain, and dictate what pace you need to go at to recover properly. That's *her* job, not yours.'

Warmth. The sudden feeling of a weight being lifted. And the equal and opposite feeling that she could do this by herself.

'That's what you think, is it?'

His gaze didn't waver. 'Yeah, it is. You did what you had to do, and there are powerful emotions behind that. It's okay to still feel them, but you can make your decisions on a more rational level now.'

Somehow that sounded like a promise. One that Robbie wanted to make, because it seemed that Joel was making it too. What they felt for each other was too powerful to either dismiss or ignore.

'I'm not going to give you the satisfaction of admitting you're right, Joel, even though you are.'

He chuckled, leaning back in his seat. 'I wouldn't expect any less from you.'

The bustle of the hospital, the familiar world around her, seemed to move back into focus. Normality was piecing itself back together again, and Joel was there, beckoning to her. Robbie could take his friendship and deal with the rest as it happened.

'How do you feel about breakfast?'

He smiled. 'Much the same as usual. I'm always up for breakfast whatever time my body clock's set to.'

'Me too. And I know just the place...'

Robbie directed him through a maze of backstreets, stopping at a small patisserie on the way. He guessed that her other 'job' with the Nightshifters had given her this encyclopaedic knowledge of every shortcut in the area, and he wasn't much surprised when he realised that they were heading for the Tin Tabernacle. He drew up in the small parking area behind the building, next to the two cars that the Nightshifters used, and switched off the engine.

'Couldn't keep away, eh?'

'This is a social call.' She opened the car door, managing to get out of the low seat without any help from him, and Joel grabbed the bag from the patisserie. Whatever was wrapped up inside smelled great, but Robbie seemed to have bought too much for two.

The towpath was deserted, and Robbie led him around to the front of the Tin Tabernacle, opening the door. Walking to the back of the space, she unlocked another door, set into the partition behind the desks.

'What the...?' Joel had thought this must be a small storeroom, but he'd miscalculated the footprint of the building. It was a good-sized area, shelved out and well organised. There was an impressive array of medical stores and equipment, along with handyman's tools and supplies, which he supposed were necessary to keep a building of this age and type in good condition.

Robbie grinned. 'Working at night, we need to be self-sufficient.' She pointed to a neat stack of folding chairs and tables. 'Would you bring these out for me, please? And take two chairs and a table and put them outside on the towpath.'

Joel decided to go with the flow. Having coffee here had seemed a little pointless, when it would be nicer to go to a café somewhere, but Robbie obviously had something else in mind. He did as she asked, moving the tables and chairs out of the storeroom, before Robbie closed the door again and locked it.

He took a couple of chairs outside, placing a table between them, and then went to find Robbie. She was wrestling with the coffee machine, but seemed to be managing, and he waited while she made two cups of coffee, then picked them up along with the patisserie bag and followed her back outside.

It was a little chilly, but she sat down, drawing her jacket around her. Joel took a couple of paper napkins from the bag, along with two of the pastries. They were still warm and he laid them down next to their coffee cups.

'This is nice...' He wasn't all that sure that it was, but Robbie seemed content with the arrangement. Maybe just being here was lifting her spirits, and he wasn't going to argue with that.

A wiry man with a grey beard and wearing a check jacket climbed out of a brightly painted boat moored a little way along the towpath. As he strolled towards them, Joel saw that he was holding a mug.

'Hi, Robbie. What have you gone and done to yourself?' He nodded towards the sling.

'*I* didn't do anything. Someone knocked me off my bike and dislocated my shoulder.'

'Ouch.' The man grimaced. 'I'll bet that hurt.'

'I was lucky, I happened to be turning into the hospital when it happened.' Robbie turned to Joel. 'Joel, this is Roy. He lives over there.'

Roy held out his hand and Joel shook it. 'You're with the Nightshifters? I saw you here the other day.'

'Yes, I've just started here.' Joel couldn't conceal his surprise. No one could miss the boats lining the towpath, but they were just a gaily painted backdrop and he'd walked past them without really considering who might be living in them.

Roy chuckled. 'No secrets around here.'

That wasn't a bad thing. Joel had lived his life trying to shed the burden of his father's secrets and he liked the idea of a place where everyone knew what everyone else was doing.

'Apart from the fact that we're even here?' Robbie chimed in. 'Not a lot of people know that.'

Roy nodded sagely. 'Yes. Apart from that.'

Discomfort trickled down Joel's spine. Maybe it was impossible to live entirely without some kind of secret. But Robbie was grinning up at Roy and he dismissed the thought.

'You know where the coffee machine is.'

'I do.' Roy didn't seem surprised about the offer and strolled round to the entrance of the Tin Tabernacle. A young couple were walking towards them now, and they were introduced as Chloe and Grant, here for the summer from Australia and due to fly home in a month's time. Chloe put the biscuit tin she was carrying down on the table, and followed Roy inside to make coffee, and Grant fetched more chairs and another table.

Joel understood now. People were appearing from the boats to join them, some bringing something with them, others just bringing themselves. Clara and Joan lived here because they liked the river and somehow managed to run a knitwear business from the confines of their narrowboat. Terry worked at the floating restaurant a little further along the towpath, and Kamal with a local theatre group. Roy was a writer, and when he went back to his boat to fetch one of his books for Joel, he realised that he was talking to the author of a string of bestsellers. Someone brought a chess set, and a small group gathered around one of the tables to watch and discuss each move that the players made.

The news of Robbie's accident had spread quickly, and each of the dozen people seated in groups around the tables had come up to her to ask how she was. Clara had gone back to her boat and reappeared with a brightly coloured knitted scarf for her, and she and Joan had insisted that she take it, wrapping it carefully around her shoulders. Joel reckoned that if anything would help heal her, this definitely would.

'This happens a lot?' Joel asked in one of the few moments that Robbie wasn't in conversation with someone.

'Most mornings. Whenever we're here we always open up the Tabernacle, but otherwise it'll be somewhere along the towpath, or on one of the boats in the winter.'

'How does everyone know where to go?'

Robbie chuckled. 'Everyone just knows. It's easy to think that you're alone here at night, but you never are. The Tin Tabernacle was first built here as a place for people working the barges that travelled up and down this stretch of water, and although that's changed we still try to play our part in the community. We hold two afternoon surgeries a week here. We'd like to do more but we can't get the volunteers.'

'I never would have thought...' Joel shook his head.

'Most people don't. They drive over the bridges, or walk along the towpath, and they just see boats. They don't realise that people are here, living their lives.'

'And you like being under the radar, like this?' The question was more important to him than just a way of passing the time, and it seemed to be more important to Robbie as well, because she considered it carefully.

'It's not something that anyone really goes out to do. But yes—that was one of the things that attracted me...' She paused, pressing her lips together as if she'd made a faux pas. 'It suits Nightshifters. Being tucked away here, so that we can get on with what we're aiming to do.'

'But everyone knows about the work that Nightshifters does.' Joel was struggling with the idea that he'd joined some kind of secret society that appeared every now and then to help when there was a crisis, then disappeared again.

She turned her gaze on him, and suddenly he felt

he knew all he needed to know. 'Don't sweat it. We're here, and we are what we are.'

Robbie was right. He didn't need to examine everything so closely, wondering what it might conceal. They were talking about Nightshifters, nothing more.

'Everyone here seems to get along.'

'Not always. It's like living anywhere. There's always someone who'll play loud music all night or be a nuisance. But they tend to either mend their ways or move on, because it's hard living here if you don't have the support of the people around you.'

Joel had so many questions. They could wait, because Robbie was obviously thriving on the chatter around her, and anyway it appeared that a lot of things just happened of their own accord rather than being planned out. It was a bit like being a stranger in a small village, hidden away somewhere—the best thing to do was just listen and watch and the rules became obvious.

It seemed that one of those rules was that morning coffee lasted for a whole hour, but not much longer. The chess pieces were dropped back into their box, plates were cleared away and cups washed, and the tables and chairs were neatly stacked by the door of the storeroom. Everyone said their goodbyes, and meandered back to their boats, blending back in with the people who were toing and froing along the towpath.

'Thank you. I really enjoyed coming here.' Joel turned to her, smiling. 'Time to go home now?'

'Yep. If I'm going to be on time for work tonight, I'd better get some sleep.' Robbie hid a yawn behind her hand.

'Tonight?' Joel tried to control his pleasure at seeing Robbie again so soon.

'Yes, Dr Thompson said she'd speak to my head of department today, and work something out with him. She suggested I switch to working from Monday to Friday, instead of Sunday to Thursday as well.'

'Not a bad idea. Sunday nights can be busy. Would you like a lift into work? It's not much of a detour.'

Robbie laughed. 'I'm tempted to say that I can manage. But even thinking about a crowded Tube train makes me flinch at the moment.'

She was still fighting it. Still refusing to accept what she, as a doctor, should know better than anyone else. Joel had learned one thing this morning, though.

The way he cared about her wasn't just because she was hurt and vulnerable. That had just allowed him to open his heart to her, and when he had she'd swanned in, taking up residence there. He was beginning to wonder whether he wasn't in this for keeps, and, since he could no longer write this off as a passing attraction that would fade with time, he would have to call it a friendship. One that felt stronger and far more urgent than any friendship he'd ever had before.

So much for the theory of being a little in love with the man simply because he'd saved you. Joel wasn't just that any more, and Robbie still had to grapple with the temptation to step a little closer to him. But they'd been important enough to each other to pull away from the doctor/patient dynamic and be friends. They could be important enough to each other to stay friends, and not cross the dangerous line into lovers.

Made all the more difficult because it had been decided that Robbie's new role was most needed in the main A & E unit. The pleasure of being able to see Joel as he walked back and forth, between patients, was mitigated by the impossibility of the task she'd been set. Sitting behind a desk, she had found herself with an unregulated queue of patients all wanting to get home. Joel had noticed the pressure she was under, trying to juggle the questions and the grumbles about having to wait yet *again*, and suggested an amendment to the plan. The A & E doctors should call her into the patient's cubicle when they were ready, which allowed her to deal with one patient at a time, and was a great deal less stressful.

And it was working. Glen had told her that if he saw her at the Tin Tabernacle this weekend he'd take her back home himself, but Joel had promised they'd go somewhere else to eat on Saturday morning. He hadn't said where they were going and Robbie hadn't asked; it somehow heightened the feeling of anticipation.

'I'm not going to ask, because I actually don't want you to tell me where we're going.' She got into his car, settling herself into the passenger seat.

'It's nowhere special...' He shrugged and Robbie held up one finger to silence him.

'I like surprises.'

'You do? I'll bear that in mind.'

Their route out into the suburbs of London was certainly a surprise. After half an hour they drew up outside a row of small two-up two-down cottages.

'Is this where you live?' He helped her out of the car

and Robbie looked around her, unable to see any other reason for stopping here.

'Yep.'

Suddenly the whole street took on a new and rosier perspective. Particularly the house with wooden blinds at the windows and a green front door, which Joel was leading her towards.

She caught a glimpse of pale walls and lots of books through the door into the sitting room as he led her to a large room at the back. The back room and scullery had been knocked together and extended to make a large kitchen with a dining area. There were no frills, but Joel obviously liked the uneven quality of natural and traditional materials because they were everywhere. Seagrass matting on top of stripped floorboards, an original cast-iron stove, and what looked like reclaimed bricks for the patio outside.

'Outside or inside?'

She could see a couple of wicker chairs and a table outside on the patio, and the sun was enough to cut through a little of the morning's chill.

'Let's go outside.'

Robbie settled herself into one of the chairs. The small walled garden was low maintenance, with plants and shrubs in clay pots, but it was like a little oasis of calm. Joel joined her from the kitchen, a bottle and two glasses in one hand.

'I thought we might drink a toast. To how far you've come in the last week.' He put the bottle down on the table. 'It's alcohol free, but it does have bubbles.'

That was just as well, as she was still taking pain-killers. 'Bubbles are the main thing.'

The cork came out with a satisfying pop, and Joel poured the drinks. Sitting down, he tipped his glass against hers.

'To steely determination. And outrageous progress.'

Robbie laughed, taking a sip from her glass. 'That's nice, thank you. Particularly as you don't hold with the steely determination part.'

He shrugged. 'Nothing wrong with determination. It's one of the building blocks of recovery.'

'*Steely* determination, though?' Robbie raised her eyebrows.

'I admire steel, too.'

As long as it had the capacity to bend. Their relationship was all about compromise.

'Well, this last couple of days has been a revelation.'

'Yeah? Enlighten me.'

'The questions that people ask, after we think we're done with them. How they feel about their experience.'

He nodded. 'Maybe you should write it all up. It sounds as if this could turn into something that we could all benefit from.'

He'd been nothing but positive about this. If Dr Thompson had intended Robbie's amended work role as a placebo, then it didn't really matter because Joel had turned it into something that was working, and that had been a learning exercise for both Robbie and the whole department.

'I hope I won't be doing this for long enough to be writing anything up.'

'That's not really up to you, is it?' He leaned back in his seat, looking thoughtfully out at the bird feeder at the end of the garden, where despite their presence a robin had alighted.

Robbie puffed out a sigh. 'I don't do well with things I can't control.'

His grin broadened suddenly. 'A control freak. Tell me more…'

She wasn't going to tell him about how she might bend his body to her will. Or how he might bend hers. Even if the touch of mischief in his melting eyes brought that right to the forefront of her thoughts.

But could she reveal more about why she kept such tight control over her life and her emotions? Why that made things easier.

'I've had eczema since I was a kid. I didn't think too much of it, apart from when it got really itchy. Getting to be a teenager changed things.'

'You mean that agonising feeling that everyone's looking at you?'

Everyone *had* been looking at her. The newspaper article had seen to that, and it had shown her that anonymity was her best protection.

'What were you self-conscious about when you were a teenager?' Robbie couldn't imagine Joel having too much to worry about.

He chuckled. 'Just the normal stuff. I grew eight inches in two years and I was clumsier than a baby giraffe.'

He'd made up for that since. Joel was tall, but he'd knitted together well, with a controlled power that made him a pleasure to look at.

'That's not the same, though. People expect teenaged boys to be a bit gawky.' He seemed to understand, without having to be told. It seemed easy to acknowledge the things she never talked about.

'Yes, that's the thing. Something that's slightly different from everyone else gives some people the idea that you belong to them, and they can talk about you however they like.'

'That's such bad manners,' he quipped.

Joel never failed to make her smile, and she liked that he thought about it like that. 'Yes. All about them and not about me.'

He looked at her thoughtfully. 'But it's you that it hurts.'

'It did hurt a lot, when I was a teenager. Now it just makes me…weary. I can deal with my eczema myself and I can't be bothered about engaging with other people's negative attitudes.'

He was nodding thoughtfully. Waiting. That was Joel's modus operandi; she'd seen him when he was at work. He just waited and people told him things. But this was different. He wasn't gathering information, he just wanted to understand and inhabit the same mental space as her.

'Boyfriends. I found that I couldn't deal with their negative attitudes, actually.'

There was a flash of understanding in his eyes. 'Ah. Yes, it's the relationships that always get you, isn't it? Boys are horrible. You can take my word for that. I used to be one.'

'Don't categorise yourself. Not everyone's like that. Sometimes they are…'

'Yeah. Sometimes.' He was still waiting. Robbie drew in a breath.

'I had this guy... I was in my last year at university and there was a bit of pressure, and my eczema was flaring up a lot more than it does now. He used to make a big thing about me dressing to cover it when I went out, and there were even times he made an excuse about not turning up for things when my eczema was really noticeable. He used to tell me that I needed to change my clothes, or apply more make-up if he could see any red patches.'

'And you gave him his marching orders...?' Joel's face hardened suddenly. 'Didn't you?'

It hadn't been that easy. Robbie had been young and she'd craved acceptance from the person that she'd thought she loved. *Had* loved. It was Rory who hadn't loved her well enough.

'It took me a while. I really liked him, but not being good enough for him as I was didn't do much for my confidence.'

'I'd say he wasn't anywhere near good enough for you.' The way his lips caressed the words seemed to scream the message that the tender look in his eyes was giving.

'I think...it wasn't really about the practicalities, although he made it all about that. It was about him, and the way he was. What he wanted out of things.'

Joel considered the thought. 'What *did* he want?'

'A mouse. Someone who did what he said and reckoned they were lucky to have him.'

He laughed suddenly. 'Okay, you definitely failed at that. There are a lot of words I'd use to describe you, but *mouse* never occurred to me.'

It would be interesting to know what words Joel

would use to describe her. Maybe she was falling into the same trap all over again, and craving his approval. Or maybe it would just be interesting...

Robbie wondered if she should tell him about the rest of it. Her parents' money, and how that had catapulted her into the public gaze. Rory's attitude to the money, and the suspicions that it was all he'd ever really seen in her.

But secrets had saved her life. They were the comfortable cushion that protected her, and which allowed her to be seen for what she did, and not who she was. Letting go of one of them might not be so bad, but letting go of everything was impossibly risky.

'I decided not to be a mouse any more. The funny thing was that when I applied my own solution to the problem, and left him, my eczema improved a lot. It has a habit of getting worse when I'm stressed out.'

He nodded. 'And now you need to be in control of your recovery, because taking things into your own hands is what's worked for you in the past.'

It seemed that he really did get it. Maybe he'd get the rest of it, as well, but Robbie didn't have it in her to explain. How she'd felt that she was disappearing under the weight of other people's expectations. And how actually disappearing had changed all of that, and allowed her to expect other people to take her as they found her.

'I'm working on it. By the time I'm better, I'll be a model patient.'

He chuckled. 'And in the meantime you'll be a terrible patient.'

'Maybe. Sorry.'

'Don't be. I can only take so many good patients in

a day and then I find I need someone to stretch me a bit. You reckon it's about time to eat?'

Yes. She'd told him enough already, and there was such a thing as quitting while you were ahead.

'I'm really hungry. I'm getting far too used to three square meals a day.'

'Good. How do you feel about home-made hamburgers? I'd do them on the barbecue, as a last-ditch attempt to preserve the summer, but I'm not sure how my neighbours might react to barbequing at nine o'clock on a Saturday morning.'

'Hamburgers sound great. And thanks for the talk.'

'I didn't say all that much.' That innocent look of his always made her insides go to jelly.

'You're going down in my estimation if you think that. Quick, go cook...'

He held up his hands in a gesture of surrender, and disappeared back into the kitchen.

CHAPTER SIX

JOEL COULDN'T SHAKE the feeling that Robbie was holding something back. The way she'd thought so carefully during the silences between them, as if choosing her words. He knew all about those silences and the guilty feeling that his parents' marriage hung on what he chose to say next. He knew that he'd never had the guts to say what was on his mind, even though his mother had sometimes seemed to know. Even though he'd wanted so badly for the words to fall from his mouth. And he knew that he couldn't stand the idea that Robbie was keeping secrets from him.

He pushed the thought aside. He could understand being hurt and his heart ached for the way that Robbie had been hurt. That was all there was to it.

He made hamburgers with bacon and cheese, salad, French fries and onion rings. The look on Robbie's face when he brought the plates out was worth the twenty minutes he'd spent out of the reach of her gaze.

'You are a *dream*! Do you always cut your hamburgers into four?'

'No. I thought you might feel that I was singling you out for special treatment if I didn't cut mine up as well.'

Teasing her was becoming one of his favourite pastimes. And Robbie was one of those people who only seemed to take offence at things that weren't said.

'Good thought. My feelings are completely salvaged.' She picked up a quarter of her hamburger and took a bite. 'Mmm. This is so good.'

'Sauce…' Some of the sauce was dribbling down her chin. He leaned forward to hand her a napkin and she stuck her chin out playfully, not letting go of the hamburger.

He rolled his eyes, pretending that wiping her chin for her was a chore. But the look in her eyes was one of sheer nakedness, and it exploded through him.

'I was thinking…'

'Should I be worried?' He grinned at her.

'You tell me. It's been really good of you to bring me to and from work this last couple of days, but I thought that next week I ought to go into work on the Tube. What do you reckon?'

'I think that's a terrible idea. It's a ten-minute detour for me to pick you up. I'd far rather do that than be fretting about whether someone's crashed into you on the Tube and you're howling in agony somewhere. And I've got used to having you around. I quite like the company.'

Sometimes the direct approach was the most effective. It certainly was with Robbie; she looked as if that was the last answer she'd expected from him.

'You're not going to lecture me about taking things easy?'

'You've had those lectures already. And I was listening when you were talking earlier about defining your own needs, rather than responding to someone else's. So I reckoned I'd just tell you *my* needs and let you pitch in with yours.'

Robbie stared at him. And then she laughed. 'You listen far too well, Joel.'

Nice. That was a nice thing to say. He *did* listen to every word that Robbie said. It was difficult not to.

'So what *are* your needs?'

She shot him a look of indescribable mischief. 'I listened to you, too. I need to lighten up and actually get better, instead of pretending there's nothing wrong with me. I'd appreciate a lift to and from work next week, if that's okay with you.'

'It would be my pleasure.'

Something had changed between them and Joel reckoned that it suited them. They were clearing away the old patterns of the past, and it gave them just that bit more space to inhabit together. And right now, time and space with Robbie was all he really wanted.

Joel could hear the little boy howling. The whole of the A & E department could hear him, even though he was with Kat and up till now Joel had reckoned that it was impossible for a child to resist Kat's reassurance, and still continue to cry.

'Bring him back.' The woman he was trying to treat batted his hands away and sat painfully up on the bed. 'He needs to be with me.'

'Sarah, I need to take a look at you.' Joel tried to reason with her.

'No! You don't touch me until I've seen my son.'

Common sense told him that you didn't examine a

woman who'd fallen down the stairs, and who might well have any number of injuries, with her five-year-old son in the cubicle. It appeared that common sense wasn't going to work.

'Okay. Stay here, right? I'll go and fetch him.' Joel glanced at the nurse who was helping him, and she nodded. He left the cubicle, hoping that the child's cries had attracted the attention of the one person he wanted to see.

They had. The door of the next cubicle was open, and Robbie was already there. Kat was kneeling down next to Sarah's son, who was crouched in the corner, sobbing his heart out.

First things first. Joel needed to defuse the situation, before he talked to Robbie, whose experience of dealing with children in distress in the paediatric A & E unit might well come in useful at the moment.

'Kat, why don't you take him in to see his mum for a minute? We can't do anything for either of them like this.'

Kat nodded, bending down to speak to the boy. As soon as she said the word *'mother'* he got to his feet, allowing her to lead him out of the cubicle, his face still bright red and tears still running down his cheeks.

'What's the story? Kat's usually so good with kids.' Robbie looked up at him, concern on her face.

'They came in by ambulance. Mum had fallen down the stairs and her son got out of bed and brought her phone to her so she could call for help.'

'Brave kid. How is she?'

'Difficult to say—she's not letting me examine her. She says that Eliot has to be with her. He's been through a lot and he's obviously upset and worried, but we gave him and his mum plenty of time together and I explained that she was all right. I've never seen this level of separation anxiety before in either a parent or a child.'

Robbie thought for a moment. 'Is he neurodivergent?'

'I asked and his mum says not. There's an issue here that I haven't been able to address and I'd like to be able to calm Eliot's fears, but his mum won't say anything more than he just wants to be with her.'

'They were alone in the house?'

'They were when the ambulance got there. They brought Eliot in because they wanted him checked over by Paediatrics, but every time he loses sight of her he starts screaming and there's no calming him down. I'd really appreciate your input.'

Robbie shot him a smile, and he began to feel a bit more equal to the situation. 'Okay, let's do this. I'll take Eliot through the basic checks you'll be doing on his mum. Maybe he'll feel better if he sees he's a little more in control of the process.'

'Yeah. That works.' It struck a chord with Joel, as well, from somewhere way back in his own experience. Being in control, rather than just responsible for a myriad of bad outcomes, had been something he'd wanted as a kid.

'If it looks as if something's happening that we don't want Eliot to see, then give me some warning if you can.' Robbie nudged him gently back into the here and now.

'Will do.' Joel looked across to the other cubicle. Kat had ushered Eliot inside, and the grizzling had stopped, as if someone had flipped a switch.

An exchanged glance told him that Robbie was concerned too. She followed him into the cubicle and Joel saw that Kat had lifted Eliot up to sit with his mother. Sarah was talking to him quietly and the boy was smiling now, even though his face was still red from his tears.

Robbie walked over to the pair. 'I'm looking for a boy called Eliot. I'm Dr Robbie.'

Eliot eyed her suspiciously. 'You've got a boy's name.'

'Yes, that's right. I'll tell you my real name if you like.'

She whispered in Eliot's ear and he nodded. Joel dismissed the temptation to ask Robbie to share the secret with all of them. It was just a way of helping Eliot feel a little more in control of things, and it seemed to be working.

'Did you hurt your hand?'

Eliot reached out to touch Robbie's arm gently, and she didn't flinch back, as she usually did when it looked as if someone was coming too close. She was wearing a light sling that gave her more freedom of movement but still supported her shoulder, and she lifted her forearm a little, wiggling her fingers.

'No, but I hurt my shoulder, so I have to wear this for a while.' She wrinkled her nose in an expression that Joel always found irresistible. 'I fell off my bike. Dr Joel fixed my shoulder for me though, and it felt much better straight away.'

Eliot nodded. 'My mum fell. From the top of the stairs to the bottom.'

'I heard that you were a very brave boy, and that you went to fetch her phone so that your mum could call for an ambulance.' Robbie leaned in confidingly, her voice dropping to little more than a whisper. 'Dr Joel's going to look after your mum too. He's the best doctor in the hospital but don't tell him I said that.'

'Why not?'

'He'll get a big head. But since he *is* the best doctor in the hospital, then I think it would be okay if he looks after your mum, don't you?'

Eliot looked Joel up and down gravely, and he smiled at the boy encouragingly.

'What's he going to do?' Eliot didn't seem convinced.

'Let's see now...' Robbie pretended to think for a moment. 'Why don't we ask Dr Joel to tell us exactly what he needs to check out with your mum? We'll try it out as well, so that you know whether it's okay.'

The same thing that had occurred to Joel was behind Robbie's suggestion. Eliot had seen someone hurt his mum, and the boy was trying to protect her. To him, Joel wasn't a doctor, but an unknown threat to his mother.

Eliot nodded, and Robbie glanced across at Sarah. 'Is that all right?'

'Yes. Thank you.' Sarah took her son's hand. 'You go with the lady doctor, Eliot. I'll be right here.'

This was the signal to move. Robbie stood back and Kat picked Eliot up, giving him a cuddle before she set him down on a chair on the other side of the cubicle. And Joel took his place next to Sarah.

'I'm sorry...he just needed to see me.'

'That's all right. He's had a fright, and so have you.' Joel smiled reassuringly, raising his voice so that both Eliot and Robbie could hear him. 'Now I'd like to just check your ribs...'

* * *

Sarah's gaze didn't leave her son, and Joel had to catch her attention a couple of times before she answered his questions. But they were making progress. Robbie was carefully following his lead and with Kat's help she was managing to examine Eliot thoroughly in the process. The boy was obviously encouraged by feeling involved with what was happening to his mum, and called across to her from time to time, to tell her that everything was okay. From Robbie's quiet words, it appeared that he had no physical injuries.

Sarah, on the other hand, hadn't been so lucky. Her ankle was swelling badly, and was almost certainly fractured, and so was one wrist. She had badly bruised ribs and a slight concussion and Joel was going to have to keep her in the hospital overnight at least. He relayed the news to her and asked if there was anyone who could take care of Eliot.

'I'll call my mum. She'll take him.' Sarah glanced across at Eliot, who was whispering something to Robbie. 'Oh, dear…'

'What is it, Sarah?' Robbie had been giving Eliot her full attention, but there was something about the way that she was leaning towards the boy, listening carefully to what he was saying, that was ringing alarm bells.

'I don't know what to do…' Sarah looked up at him, biting her lip in agitation.

'Is there a problem with having your mum look after Eliot?'

'No…no, Mum's really good with him and he adores my dad. They only live five minutes away from me, and they look after Eliot all the time.'

'He won't mind leaving you here?'

'No, you've been so good with him and...he had a shock but he's feeling much more confident now. He'll be all right if he's with Mum and Dad. I just...' Sarah's hand moved to her mouth to cover her sobs.

Silences, and the pain that inhabited them. The things that weren't said, which ate into you if you weren't careful.

'Are you and Eliot covering up for anyone, Sarah?'

Sarah nodded, her gaze moving behind him to her son. Joel looked round and saw Robbie curling her arm around the boy's shoulders, and when she glanced up at him their gazes met. In that moment, Joel knew that he was going to have to give a little of himself, to protect the child.

'Sarah, I think that Eliot has to talk about this. There's one thing that you can do to make it easier for him.'

'You think...?'

'I know it's hard for you, but please don't let him carry this on his own.'

'It was my ex... Eliot's father.' Sarah whispered the words. 'He pushed me and Eliot saw. I told him not to say anything. I didn't want him to have to speak up against his father...'

The nurse on the other side of the bed was comforting Sarah as best she could. Joel didn't want to ask, but he had to.

'Has he hurt either you or Eliot before?'

'No. Never.'

It was always best to be honest and clear about what he needed to do next. 'Okay. As Eliot saw his father push you, the law requires that I report that because I have to put his interests above anything else. It's up to you whether you press charges or want to get the police involved, but that might be something to consider.'

Sarah nodded. 'I suppose if you *have* to report it... Just as long as you do what you said. Put Eliot's interests first.'

'That's what everyone here will do. We have a dedicated team here at the hospital and there's a domestic violence advisor on call right now. She's very experienced in dealing with this kind of situation and I'd like to ask her to come down and speak with you, if that's okay.'

'I don't know...' A tear ran down Sarah's cheek. 'It all seems so... I don't think it's really necessary to talk to domestic violence people. He's never done this before.'

'No, but he's done it now. He hasn't just hurt you, he's hurt Eliot and we want to make sure that he can mend, too. No one's going to draw conclusions or try to classify you, but I do think you need some help right now.'

Sarah nodded. 'Yes, you're right. I want to see her, then. On the condition that Eliot's her first concern, because I'm his mother and he's *my* first concern.'

Something about the vehemence of Sarah's whispered words made Joel smile. 'All right. I'll go and call her now, and then we'll get you down to X-ray.'

He left Sarah with the nurse and waited for a moment outside the cubicle. As he'd expected, Robbie came outside to join him.

'What did Eliot have to say for himself?'

She turned the corners of her mouth down. 'That his father pushed his mother down the stairs. He hasn't hurt

Eliot before, and from what I can see that's the case. He's an extremely healthy little boy and he doesn't have a mark on him. Which is pretty unusual, actually, for a five-year-old. Sarah?'

'She said the same. And that Eliot saw what happened.'

Robbie let out an exclamation of dismay. 'That poor kid.'

'And that she'd told Eliot to keep quiet about it, because she didn't want him to have to say anything against his father.' Joel could understand why Sarah had done it, but he knew from his own experience just how agonising it was to be a child with a secret.

'Okay. I can see why she did that, she was trying to protect him, but he did need to talk about it. All I had to do was gain his confidence a little and he just told me. I didn't have to push him.'

'Sarah saw him whispering to you, and she realised that she couldn't keep it a secret.' Joel wondered what it would have been like if someone like Robbie had taken the time to gain *his* confidence as a child. His own story was still waiting to be heard, and he could hardly bear it at the moment.

'You're calling the domestic violence advisor?'

'Yeah. I guess she'll take it from here.' There was nothing more to be said. There were strict procedures, designed to protect both Eliot and Sarah, that everyone would follow from here on. Somehow Joel just couldn't let go of it, though.

'What?' Robbie seemed to know that he wasn't done with this.

'I just… You know how it is. Some cases just get to

you.' He shrugged. 'You must deal with these kinds of cases, where kids are involved, all the time.'

'Not all of the time, but we have our share of them. If I ever get used to it, then I'll know I'm in a lot of trouble.' She took a step closer to him. 'There's a procedure for this. Meet me outside the staff entrance, when it's time for our break.'

'Break? What's a break? We're pretty busy tonight.'

Robbie smiled. 'You'll find the time. Call me when you do.'

Phillipa, the duty domestic violence advisor, was with another family and so Robbie had volunteered to stay with Sarah and Eliot until she was free. Eliot had been snuggling sleepily against his mother for most of the time, but Robbie had managed to coax him away from her for long enough for the X-rays to be taken.

When the results came through, Joel returned to the cubicle and quietly explained to Sarah that the X-rays had shown her ankle and wrist were fractured, telling her exactly what would happen next. His reassuring manner had made Sarah and Eliot feel safe and secure, and when Phillipa finally arrived, Sarah was ready to take the action that was needed to protect herself and her son.

'Two minutes…' Robbie murmured the words as she walked past him, as he strode towards the administration desk to file his notes.

'Three…' He called after her and Robbie decided it would probably be four.

It was five, but just as she was beginning to shiver in the cool night air, he made it. He was smiling but there was an edge of weariness about Joel, as if he'd been fighting with his thoughts.

'Here's what we're going to do. First you take a deep breath.' She sucked in a lungful of air, and puffed it back out again and Joel followed suit.

'Second, you say the first thing that comes into your mind.'

'Are you making this up as you go along?' He raised an eyebrow.

'Yes, I am. Just do it…'

'Your eyes are a deeper blue in this light.'

Were they? 'Is that *really* the first thing that came to mind?'

'Yes. What's yours?'

'I just told you…' Robbie decided that pursuing that would only tie them up in knots and that she should move on.

'Then it's the group hug.'

Joel made a point of looking around for any groups that might have suddenly appeared. There was no one else here. Then he smiled, folding his arms gently around her, careful not to jostle her injured shoulder.

It wasn't *quite* a group hug. For a start there were too few people, but that wouldn't have mattered so much. Snuggling against him, hearing his heart beat… Not wanting to let him go, and being able to believe that he couldn't let her go either. Feeling a heady intoxication, instead of just comfort.

'This works.' He was looking down at her, and Robbie thought she saw the reflection of a kiss in his eyes.

For one heady moment, all she could think about was

that they might run away. That they'd race to his car, and he'd drive to her apartment and if the lift travelled fast enough they'd just about make it to the front door before they were making sweet love.

It was a nice thought, and it was just as well that it hadn't occurred to her earlier because then she would have had to confess that it was the first thought that came to mind. And there were people waiting for them. Not just tonight, but every night. This was what they'd built their lives around; it was what they were. Robbie let go of him, and felt Joel's arms loosen.

'Are we ready to go back...?' She couldn't avoid his gaze.

'You go inside, you're shivering. I can do with a few more breaths.'

'You're all right, though?'

'I'm fine. This really works, thank you. I just want a little time alone.'

These few moments of respite hadn't been enough. They'd been so delicious that they felt like for ever, but Robbie had the feeling that whatever was nagging at Joel had just been submerged, and not completely banished.

It happened. Bad things happened and some of them would push buttons for the medical profession-als who were doing their best to help people. You picked yourself back up again and kept going, be-cause if you didn't then more bad things would hap-pen to more people.

Something about Sarah and Eliot had pushed buttons with Joel, but when she saw him return to the admin desk to pick up the notes for his next patient, he seemed to have pulled himself back together. He caught her staring at him and smiled, mouthing a *thank you* across the busy space. That was all she really needed to know.

CHAPTER SEVEN

NIGHTSHIFTERS HADN'T BEEN busy tonight, and there were plenty of people to deal with the calls that were coming in. Joel had taken Robbie home, on the understanding that the two of them would be on standby, in case they were needed.

Which was why Robbie was cooking at half past one in the morning. That seemed to involve a great deal of mess, a long list of printed instructions, and some crashing and cursing floating out from the kitchen. In the end, Joel decided that staying in the sitting room was far too much to ask of him.

'What the...?' When he walked into the kitchen, the mess seemed to have grown exponentially since Robbie had chased him away. Since she could still only lift anything with her left arm, she'd clearly skipped past the expediency of putting anything away again when she'd found what she wanted, and it looked as if half the contents of her kitchen cupboards were strewn across the worktops.

'I know. This is my sister's recipe, and she says it's really quick and easy. Izzy never mentioned the mess.' She shifted her arm in the sling to hold up her hands in an expression of surrender. Which wasn't really surrender at all; she was holding her hands up because she could. Robbie never missed a chance to demonstrate how her shoulder had been improving over the last week.

'I expect when you've done it a few times, you'll know exactly what you need…' He started to put some of the unused kitchen implements back into the cupboard. 'You have a sister?'

He couldn't help asking. Robbie had given the same smile when she mentioned her sister as she had when she talked about her parents and it seemed that her family were close. Joel was happy for her, and at the same time a little envious.

'Yes, we don't get to see each other all that much because Izzy and her husband live in Ireland. But we talk all the time and she's a great cook. I've been thinking for a while that I might give it a go as a hobby, and since I have some extra time…'

Joel nodded. It was just as well that this was a hobby, because none of the effort that Robbie was putting into it was in the least practical.

'What are you making?' Joel couldn't decide from the array of ingredients and utensils that were scattered around the kitchen.

'Chocolate cake.' Robbie flipped through several sheets of paper, which contained typed instructions and photographs of every stage of the process, and stabbed her finger against the final one. 'I don't think it's going to look like this.'

'I don't see why not. Just follow the instructions and it'll be great. Want me to stack the dishwasher?'

'That sounds like helping to me, Joel. The idea of baking is that I get some time alone in the kitchen to express my creativity. Creativity always involves mess. You can't do it without breaking a few eggs...' She grinned at him. 'See what I did, there?'

He couldn't help smiling. 'Yeah, I saw. Can't hurt to share a piece of your creativity, can it?' Whatever Robbie did, she did with an intoxicating verve. It was impossible to just walk away and cool his heels in the sitting room.

'That was going to be when I presented you with a slice, so you could have the first taste.'

'If I'm going to get the first taste, it's only fair to let me see what you're putting into it, isn't it?' he teased, and Robbie wrinkled her nose.

'It's all there, in the mixer bowl.' Robbie gestured towards a mixer that looked as if it might also make you a cup of tea and sing a lullaby if you selected the correct programme. 'Izzy said it was okay to do it like this, since it's bit tricky to do the mixing myself with only one good arm.'

She consulted a bulky instruction booklet and turned a knob on the top of the mixer. The paddles started to move, and, after squinting into the bowl, Robbie clearly decided it was best to let the machine get on with it.

'What's this?' Joel caught sight of a bowl that contained a dark, chocolatey substance, and wondered if Robbie had forgotten to add it to the rest of the ingredients.

'Oh, that's the topping. I decided to do it first, because it looked the easiest.'

Okay. Whatever worked. Robbie walked over to him,

dipping her finger into the bowl and licking it. That worked too…

'I'm not sure if it's a bit too runny.' She rubbed the side of her nose, leaving a chocolate smear. He could resist that. Then she pushed a stray curl out of her eyes, leaving a trace of the mixture on her forehead. *That* wasn't playing fair.

'You've got it all over you, now. No…don't touch, let me…' He picked up a kitchen towel, wiping the gooey mixture from her face, but when some of it got onto his fingers he couldn't resist taking a taste.

'It's good… The icing's good.'

Then he was lost in her gaze, pale sapphire tonight under the bright kitchen lights. Robbie's mouth curled into a mischievous grin.

'That's not enough to tell, is it?' She dipped her finger in the bowl again, holding her hand up towards him.

A rich, chocolatey taste on his tongue, and the feel of her body against his as she stepped closer. Then Joel did what he'd been aching to do since the first moment he'd seen Robbie, and kissed her.

If he'd had time to consider what he was doing he might have prepared himself for an anticlimax, because it would be logical to suppose that nothing could be quite as good as what had been going on in his imagination. Logical thought could go take a running jump, because this was better. Sweeter. More unexpected and unrehearsed.

She moved against him, curling one hand behind his neck, the other arm tucked against his chest in the sling. Robbie stretched up, standing on her toes, and he felt the delicious slide of friction between them. That intoxicating feeling that he was losing his balance and falling into a place where there was only the two of them, and Robbie was kissing him.

'You taste of chocolate.' She must like that, because she kissed him again. She tasted of…

A different life. One that saw no limit on how he might give himself to her. One that didn't recognise the fear that had bound him and kept him in solitary confinement for years. If she hadn't hesitated before the next kiss, just for one moment, he would have been free.

But she did. And her hesitation allowed the doubts in. Robbie had been hurt and even though she seemed bold in so many areas of her life, she was also cautious. The next step, the one that seemed almost inevitable now, was the one that could hurt her even more if fear made him stick to what he knew and draw back again.

'You are so perfect…' He caressed her cheek tenderly, staring into her eyes. 'And I am…so fearful.'

Her eyes darkened suddenly, with an emotion that he couldn't quite get the measure of.

'Why?'

'I know you've been hurt. I've been hurt too and I can't do this without telling you…'

'Then tell me, Joel.'

He didn't know how to answer. Joel knew how corrosive secrets could be, but it was hard to let go of this one. He knew that he had to, before he embarked on any kind of physical relationship with Robbie.

His phone rang in his back pocket, and he ignored it. He didn't care what Glen, or anyone else, wanted. The whole world could crash and burn, as long as they could have just a few more moments together.

She grimaced and reached round, pulling the phone from his pocket. As she did so, it stopped ringing.

'Missed it…'

He spoke too soon, and his phone started to ring again. Robbie flipped the answer button and handed the phone to him.

'Hello…?' His voice sounded husky and strange.

'Joel? Sorry, were you in the middle of something? It's Glen.'

'No, it's okay.' Joel pulled himself together, the effort greater than it might have been, because his other hand was still around Robbie's waist. 'What can we do?'

'Is Rob with you?'

'Yes, she's here.'

'We need to get an organ donation, from Tower Bridge to Birmingham. Are you up for it? You'll need to have Rob with you, because she's a named person on our agreement to carry organs.'

'Okay, I'll check and call you back.' He glanced at Robbie. 'Transplant organ from London to Birmingham?'

'Yes! Of course…' Robbie stepped back suddenly. Losing her was almost a physical shock, as if something had been ripped away from him. Then he heard Glen's voice at the other end of the line.

'I heard. Call me back when you're ready to go.'

Joel put his phone back into his pocket. 'I didn't know Nightshifters did organ transport.'

'Yeah, we don't do a lot of them, but their usual carriers must be busy. We have an agreement in place, and because we're volunteers we had to submit a list of named people.'

'And this is okay with you...?'

'What do you think?' She grinned at him as if someone had just presented her with a surprise gift. 'Let's go to Birmingham.'

Robbie switched off the mixer, and put the bowl into the sink, reckoning that there would be no salvaging the cake when they got back. Joel had already fetched their coats, and on the way downstairs in the lift he was on the phone with Glen, getting the details of where they were to go and who they should ask for when they got there. They were in the car within two minutes.

Two minutes when everything had suddenly changed again, back to what they'd been before. There was no thinking about that, and they had to postpone whatever it was that Joel wanted to talk about. He understood that the urgency of their work sometimes took priority, just as well as she did, and he knew that there would be time to talk later.

'We'll avoid Covent Garden, cut across to the City and then Waterloo.'

'Okay.' He shot her a grin. 'Directions?'

Joel knew his way around London, but Robbie had a better grasp of which shortcuts to take and how to avoid the traffic. Covent Garden would still be busy at this time on a Saturday night, but the City of London would be deserted.

Tall, glass-clad buildings, and older granite monoliths loomed up on either side of them. Joel was driving at just under the speed limit, and they'd be in good time to collect the kidney that was being removed and prepared for transport in the hospital on the other side of the river.

'This is one of the things I like about working at night. You get to see the same things in a completely different way.' He nodded towards the clear road ahead of him.

'Me too.'

This part of London was usually full of people and traffic during the day. At night, the quiet solidity of the buildings was all that remained of that frenetic activity. They were alone here in their small bubble, and it seemed that all of London was theirs, from tin tabernacles to royal palaces.

Robbie looked to her left as they crossed Waterloo Bridge, to see Tower Bridge, swathed with lights, further up the river. She saw Joel glance that way too, and smile. It was as if it were glimmering in the darkness just for them.

There were IDs to be checked, and paperwork to be completed at the hospital, then a half-hour wait until the kidney was ready to be transported. Then their precious cargo, labelled and sealed, was handed to Joel and they hurried to the car. He secured the organ transport box inside the Nightshifters carrier on the back seat, while Robbie called the Tin Tabernacle to confirm that they were on their way to Birmingham.

They left the lights of London behind, and Robbie settled back into her seat, no longer needing to give directions now that they were on the motorway. Joel had opened one of the windows by a crack, for some fresh air to keep him alert, and she wrapped her jacket around her for warmth.

'Twenty-four to thirty-six hours...' The numbers had been running through her head, since they first took charge of the kidney, and she was hardly aware that she'd voiced the time that a kidney would remain viable for transplant.

Joel chuckled. 'We're not going to need that long. We'll be there in a few hours, tops.'

'We're not there, until we're there.' This was the first time she'd been on a delivery since her accident. The long walk from the side gate of the hospital to where Joel had found her outside A & E suddenly seemed very clear in her mind.

'Hey. We'll be there.'

She had the comforting thrum of the SUV's engine, which was effortlessly eating up the miles. An empty motorway in front of them. And most of all she wasn't alone this time, because she had Joel.

He leaned forward, flipping on the radio. The late-night talk show was about as soporific as the motorway floodlights that flashed past at regular intervals.

'Can you find some music?' He glanced in her direction, and Robbie smiled back at him.

'Driving music?'

He chuckled. 'Of course, driving music. What else?'

They arrived in Birmingham just over two hours later, and Joel was still humming the last track that had been playing in the car as they hurried to the transplant unit at the hospital. They'd called ahead to say when they'd be arriving, and a junior surgeon was waiting for them at Reception.

The box was checked for any damage, times and

dates were recorded and Robbie scribbled her signature at the bottom of a form. The young man hurried away, the next link in a chain that would bring hope to someone.

'Is there somewhere we can get a drink and something to eat?' Robbie asked the nurse who'd been there to witness the handover document.

'You could try the cafeteria, but at this time of night it's all leftover sandwiches. Turn right out of the main gates and go three hundred yards and there's a little takeaway café. It doesn't look much from the outside, but it's much better.'

'Great, thanks. Have a good night.'

'Wait…' They'd already turned to leave but the nurse called them back. 'I heard that you're both volunteers?'

'Yes, we work with a charity called Nightshifters in North London.'

'Thank you, on behalf of a great kid and their family.'

Joel grinned broadly. This meant as much to him as it did to Robbie. The nurse couldn't say any more, but she'd given them all the information they needed.

'It's our pleasure. Thank *you*.'

They parked outside a rather ramshackle-looking café, and Robbie wondered whether Joel would be straight back out again after he'd seen the inside of the place. But when he returned to the car he was carrying coffee and a brown paper bag.

'That place is amazing inside. It's got the old-style green and white tiles on the walls, with scrubbed wooden tables and stools—it's like stepping back in time. It's spotless though, and they have a great selection of food.'

Robbie laughed. 'Another little hidden gem of the night.'

'Yep.' He handed her his purchases and started the car.

He seemed to know where he was going and he drew up, five minutes later, by the side of a large warehouse building that had been repurposed into smart flats. On the other side of the road there was a railing, and beyond that the glint of water.

'A river?'

Joel rolled his eyes. 'No. Birmingham doesn't have any navigable rivers. It has loads of canals, though.'

'And you knew how to get here by instinct?' Robbie followed him out of the car, and onto a small footbridge.

'No, I worked in Birmingham for a couple of years. How does standing and eating sound?'

'Like heaven.' They'd been in the car for long enough now, and Robbie wanted to stretch her legs.

He stopped in the middle of the bridge and propped the coffees on the curved iron parapet, then opened the bag. Just the smell made her mouth water. She opened the greaseproof-paper package that Joel had given her and took a bite from the toasted cheese and tomato sandwich.

'Mmm. That's really good. So what were you doing in Birmingham?' Joel hardly ever spoke about anything other than the present and the future, and she'd never heard him mention his family.

'Just working. There was a good job here, and I took it.'

'And London?'

He shrugged. 'Same, really. There was another good job and I took it. I like London and so I stayed. Then the job at the London Fitzrovia hospital came up, and I couldn't pass it up. There are so many good initiatives going on there.'

He didn't seem to mind her questions. Robbie ventured another.

'Where do you come from?'

'Surrey. I went to medical school in London and there weren't any good jobs in Surrey when I left, so I didn't go back.'

She should stop. She hadn't told him everything about herself, and if Joel wanted to keep something back it was his right to do so. Robbie fell silent, watching the reflection of the streetlights in the dark water below her.

She finished her toastie, rolling the greaseproof paper up into a ball and putting it into her pocket. Joel reached for her coffee, handing it to her.

There was one thing she needed to know, though. He'd kissed her and she'd kissed him back, but she wasn't so naïve as to believe that they would have been waking up together if Glen hadn't called. Joel had already been drawing back from her when his phone had rung.

'What's going on between us, Joel?'

'I kissed you and I meant it.' He seemed to be savouring that moment in his mind as he stared out over the water. 'We've both got our reasons for being cautious.'

'It probably wasn't a good idea.' It had felt like a pretty darn fantastic idea to Robbie, but she sensed that Joel needed a bit of space.

'Maybe not.' He turned the corners of his mouth

down. 'Sometimes the bad ideas are the ones you like the most.'

Always the gentleman. Not so much gentleman as gentle man, Joel wouldn't let her feel embarrassed about kissing him.

Maybe it was the eczema…

That came from another place, one where she'd allowed Rory to see only the money and the eczema and not look past either of them. Joel wasn't like that, he never thought about how her eczema affected him he would have found the idea laughable. He only cared about how it affected her.

'Could we make a course correction?' He seemed suddenly embarrassed.

'You mean… Pretend it never happened?'

Joel shook his head, smiling. 'No, let's not do that. Just think of it as something we did on the way to becoming friends?'

He was right. It was what Robbie wanted in her head, it was just her emotions that were running away from her and wanting to beg him to reconsider. That would be a mistake, because she still couldn't shake the way she'd felt when she'd been with Rory.

'Friends is good.' She took his arm as they walked back to the car. But as soon as he unlocked it, opening the passenger door for her, Robbie knew. Things weren't going to be the same between them from now on.

CHAPTER EIGHT

IT HAD BEEN a good night's work. It had been great for Robbie too, a chance to get back to doing something that she valued. Joel regretted the kiss, though.

Regret was the wrong word. It had been wonderful, and finding that it was a great deal more wonderful than he'd ever imagined just opened the floodgates on a whole raft of possibilities. What it might be like to wake up with Robbie. To go to sleep with her. All the things they might do together in between waking up and going to sleep.

But he couldn't. The secret that had stood for so many years between him and his family still seemed to surround him. He'd kept lovers at arm's length, and refused to dream about a family of his own because of it. If he couldn't bring himself to see the reproach in Robbie's eyes when he told her, then the secret would just corrode their relationship, the way it had corroded all the others in his life.

They played the same music on the way back to London in the car, but neither of them sang along. Joel dropped Robbie off at her apartment just after dawn and she smiled the way she always did. But he stayed in the car, and she didn't ask him up.

They did all the same things. Joel brought Robbie to work and then took her home again. They exchanged notes on patients, and in the brief moments when there was time for a break they even found themselves drinking coffee and grabbing a sandwich together. But something was missing. They were both being far too friendly, far too polite, and the light in Robbie's eyes had died.

Then Tom and Babs happened. Right at the start of their shift, Joel saw Robbie ushering a middle-aged couple into a cubicle and there was something about the way they were walking close and Robbie was walking right behind them as if to shield them from view that caught his eye. Then he saw a couple of nurses, laughing behind their hands. And then Robbie approached him.

'Got a minute?'

'Yeah, I'm just waiting for some X-rays to come back. What is it?'

'I need a bit of help. I have to lift a patient and I can't do it. But you mustn't laugh.'

'Okay…' Laughing at patients wasn't the norm, although every A & E department had its share of stories about unlikely injuries.

'So… I'm just going to say it. Tom's hand is glued to Babs's bottom. I need to help Babs into a comfortable position where I can get at them to dissolve the glue.'

'Right. This is what we spent seven years studying for, isn't it?'

'Yes, it is.' The corner of Robbie's mouth twitched. 'They're so sweet. If anyone should be glued together it's Tom and Babs, but I'm really worried about the possibility of burns. I looked at the clothing label on Babs' skirt and it doesn't contain cotton, but I still think it's best to get them apart as soon as possible.'

Robbie had a point. A cyanoacrylate adhesive could cause cotton to smoulder or ignite, and he'd seen some nasty injuries where people had dripped glue onto clothing.

'Do we know what kind of glue?'

'No, Tom said it was his model-making glue. His hand's stuck fast, though. The good thing is that neither of them are experiencing any discomfort.'

He followed her to the cubicle. Babs was perched on the side of the couch, trying not to put too much of her weight on Tom's hand.

'Hi, I'm Dr Joel Mason.'

Both Tom and Babs smiled at him. 'Tom Freestone. And this is Babs, my wife.'

'I think Dr Mason better take a quick look, if that's okay, Babs. Just so he can see how best to get you comfortable.'

'Yes, of course.' Babs beamed at Robbie, sliding off the couch. 'I bet you're wondering how we managed to do this.'

'We see a lot of unexpected things in A & E.' He glanced at Robbie, who was clearly trying not to laugh.

'Yes, he's wondering.'

Babs chuckled and started to explain, while Joel looked at Tom's fingers. 'Tom loves his model aircraft, and I made him a cup of tea and sat down to see what he was doing…'

'And she sat on the glue.' Tom interjected.

'Yes, there was this pop as the tube burst. I realised what I'd done and jumped up, then Tom managed to get the tube off my skirt.' Babs flicked her hand to indicate an urgency of motion. 'But he didn't realise how much glue there was on my skirt. It had soaked through my skirt to my skin and when he put his hand there…well, here we are.'

Tom nodded. 'I suppose if we were going to glue ourselves together, we may as well have a story to embarrass the kids with when they come over to lunch on Sunday.'

'Yes. Good point,' Babs agreed.

Joel was beginning to see what Robbie meant. Tom and Babs were dealing with what might well have been an embarrassing situation in the best way possible.

'Right, then. As Dr Hall's said, you're stuck pretty fast, and Tom's hand is at a slightly awkward angle to do this standing up. I think that if we can get you onto the couch and you'll be comfortable lying on your tummy, Babs…?'

'Oh, yes, that's perfectly fine.'

'And then we'll find Tom a chair…'

Tom nodded. 'Thanks. Sitting around with your hand on your wife's bottom seems far better manners than standing, eh, Babs?'

Babs snorted with laughter. 'Always the charmer, Tom.'

Robbie giggled. That was the last straw for Joel's composure and he grinned. He saw the light in Robbie's eyes rekindle and warmth flooded through him.

Robbie adjusted the couch to the right height, and Joel practically had to lift Babs onto it to avoid ripping the glued skin. Then he fetched an adjustable stool, for Tom. A nurse brought a bowl of warm soapy water and a bottle of solvent and Robbie settled down on the other side of the couch, ready to start carefully prying Tom and Babs apart.

'I have to go.'

'Yes, thanks, Joel.' Robbie gave him one of her dizzying smiles.

'Thank you...' Tom and Babs chorused as he left the cubicle.

He couldn't help going back. By the time he'd finished dealing with his patient Robbie had managed to prise Tom's fingers free and just the palm of his hand remained stuck. The indomitable pair were still smiling, and Tom's fingers were a little red but there was no real damage to the skin. Robbie flashed him a grin.

Joel went back again, after he'd dealt with his next patient, and found Tom and Babs finally separated. Babs had clearly had the foresight to bring a pair of trousers along with her to wear on the way home and had changed into them.

'Hello again.' Babs gave him a bright smile. 'I'm glad you came back. Robbie says we can go and I wanted to say goodbye and thank you.'

'You're very welcome. None the worse for wear, eh?'

Babs leaned towards him. 'I've got a handprint on my derriere.'

Robbie chuckled. 'The skin's just a bit irritated from the glue. It should fade in the next day or so.'

'More's the pity,' Babs said in mock dismay. 'Thank

you so much, Robbie. And for the advice on moisturis-
ers, that was all very handy to know.'

'My pleasure. I hope I don't see you back here any
time soon.'

'I'm going to keep well away from him in future.'
Babs smiled up at Tom and he put his arm around her
shoulders as they left the cubicle.

The door closed, and Joel turned to see Robbie shaking with laughter. 'Oh… I'm so glad they're all right.'

Joel chuckled. 'Me too. How on earth did you manage to keep your hand steady?'

'I have *no* idea. They were both cracking jokes the
whole time. And when Babs saw the handprint…she
was so pleased with it.' Robbie was laughing and fan-
ning her face at the same time.

Her hand moved to her shoulder and her laughter
subsided. Joel suddenly couldn't bear being this far
away from Robbie, and moving closer to her wasn't as
hard as it had seemed during the last few days. 'You all
right? That was a pretty long consult.'

'Yes, I'm okay. I shouldn't laugh so much.' She
smiled up at him.

In that moment, Joel knew that he'd been wrong. Acceptance wasn't about the nature of the difficulty, it was
about the person you shared it with. He would bide his
time, but he *would* tell Robbie his secret, because he
trusted that she wouldn't judge and condemn him out
of hand. And maybe he'd finally feel free of its burden.

'Yeah. No heavy laughing.' Even if hearing her laugh
was the most wonderful thing in the world, right now.

'It's just that… I thought for a moment there that
Babs was actually going to show you the handprint, she

was so proud of it.' She started to giggle again, and this time Joel couldn't help but laugh with her.

It had been an up and down kind of week. It had started off badly, with awkwardness solidifying into stultifying politeness that felt as if it were freezing Robbie's heart. And then Tom and Babs had turned up. Laughter couldn't cure every ill, but their affectionate jokes and their determination to squeeze humour into their situation had been the catalyst that healed the rift between her and Joel.

The following night Robbie had had to go home early, after a recalcitrant ten-year-old had yanked at her arm when she was trying to examine him. He'd been suffering from a feverish cold, and had probably come out of their encounter in better shape than Robbie had, even if he was a little sleepy and a lot grumpy at being taken from his bed and brought here by his parents.

There was no I-told-you-so from Joel, just the acceptance that accidents happened, and his quiet assurance that the pain would subside. Robbie knew that he was watching her when she returned to work the next night, but she couldn't find it in herself to be indignant. It was just good to have him there and to know that he cared enough to do it.

When he dropped her home after their Friday night shift, she asked him to come inside with her. She had a bottle of prosecco in the fridge, ready to be opened, and she ushered him into the book-lined snug, which was much cosier than the larger, more formal sitting room. They sat on the long sofa together.

'What's this for again?' He twisted the cork out of the bottle, grinning at her.

As if he didn't know. 'Three weeks. I've done my exercises every day, and, apart from that slight setback the other day, my shoulder feels so much better than it did. And I'm not taking the painkillers any more so I can celebrate with a drink.'

She tipped her glass against his, and they drank together. As lovers did, each not taking their gaze from the other.

He nodded. 'That's a fine piece of progress. It's downhill all the way, now.'

'Downhill? Don't say that, it's supposed to be uphill.'

'Nah. Downhill's a lot easier than uphill. You just take the brakes off and coast.'

'I'm going uphill. Reaching greater heights.'

Joel smiled. 'Whatever floats your boat. Have you read all of these books?' He nodded towards the bookcases that lined the walls.

'No. That's terrible, isn't it...? Having a load of books just sitting here that I haven't read yet.'

'Why? Are you working your way through them?'

'Yes, slowly. Those on the right are mine, and on the other side, the ones with the nicer bindings are my grandparents'. They both read a lot and they had all of the classics.'

'They're a wonderful thing to keep, then, aren't they? You can spend years enjoying the very same books that your grandparents have read. When you've finished, you could go right back to the beginning and read your favourites again.'

'I do think of them sometimes, sitting in here and

reading the same things that I am.' Robbie stared at the bubbles that were floating gently upwards in her glass. 'I know how lucky I am.'

He flashed her a quizzical look. 'You make it sound like a bad thing.'

'I don't mean it like that. Just that I'm grateful, because I know that a lot of people aren't given the start in life that I've had.'

'You're one of the hardest-working people I know and you spend your time helping people. If you think you have anything to apologise for, then I'd take issue with that.'

His attitude was like a breath of fresh air. Joel was one of those people who valued someone for what they did, not what they had. It was what Robbie's parents had brought her up to believe.

'I'd find life pretty boring if I didn't do something.'

'Try not to get any more interesting. I'm not sure I can take it, and there aren't enough hours in the day.'

He smiled, raising his hand to brush her cheek with the backs of his fingers. Robbie shivered. They'd come full circle and were back again in the moment before she'd kissed him, and he'd kissed her back. It was exactly where she wanted to be, but she dreaded the thought that this might be one more iteration in a spiral of intimacy and then disappointment.

She caught his hand in hers. Wanting to keep what she had right now, but not at the cost of losing Joel again. When she looked into his eyes, she knew that they were moments away from repeating a kiss that might be the best thing that could happen, or the worst mistake.

'I don't need to know what's going to happen next,

Joel. But I do need to know whether we'll see it through together. I'm sorry if that sounds a bit control freaky...'

He laid his finger across her lips. 'It's nothing of the kind, and I'm just grateful that you're willing to give me a second chance. I won't throw this one away.'

'I know you're cautious and... I like that. I'm cautious too.'

'You should be. You've been hurt before.'

'So have you.' Robbie wanted Joel to know that it was all right to talk and that she'd listen.

'It's...complicated.' He smiled suddenly. 'I think that *complicated* means you have a right to know before we go any further.'

'No, that's not what it means at all. It means you have a right to talk about it if you want. Whenever you want.'

'Then it's my decision to talk about it now.' He reached forward, taking her hand in his. 'Robbie, I don't know where this is all going to lead.'

'Of course you don't. Neither do I. I can't see into the future. But I would very much like to find out.'

CHAPTER NINE

HER EYES WERE sapphire-blue in the firelight. This moment had been inevitable, since the first time they'd met. Waiting to happen, pushed closer by everything they'd said and done.

'When I was seven, I found out that my father was having an affair.'

Shock registered in her face. 'Ouch.'

'Yeah. He swore me to silence, and told me that if my mum ever found out I'd be responsible for breaking up the family.'

'Oh, a nice guy, then.' Her hand flew to her mouth. 'Sorry. He was your father...'

'Don't be. They're my sentiments exactly. It went on for years, and he used me as a smokescreen. Used to tell my mum that he was taking me out somewhere, and he'd drop me off in the park and disappear for a couple of hours. When I got back home I'd have to say what a nice time we'd had together and Mum always used to ask exactly what we'd done, as if she had some idea that I was lying. I used to dread it.'

'That's outrageous, Joel. It's abuse.'

Joel shrugged. 'I didn't think of it like that...'

'You were being intentionally harmed by an adult. You were manipulated and threatened, and made to feel that you'd be to blame if you spoke out. I work with kids and that's one definition of abuse.'

The heat of her outrage warmed him. Joel wondered again what it might have been like if he'd had an adult like Robbie in his life. Maybe this secret didn't have as much power over him as he'd thought. Maybe Robbie would be the one that set him free.

'I just felt guilty. I had this secret that I knew would hurt my mum, and I couldn't bear to tell her. But not telling her was hard to bear, too.'

'I'm so sorry that happened to you. And I'm really sorry that you were made to feel guilty about it, because it wasn't your fault.'

She was saying all the right things. And she said them with such passion, such implacable certainty, that they struck straight into his heart. He believed her.

'Did your mum ever find out?'

That was the worst admission of all. That he'd never put right the things he'd done as a child.

'Not from me. When I got a place at medical school I left home, and I wasn't very good at going back. It was just all too difficult, and I made an excuse not to go home at Christmas because I didn't want to see my father. My mum died suddenly the following February and…it's too late now. I didn't know how to tell her the secret, because I'd kept it for so long, and it drove us apart. It ate away at my relationships with the rest of my family too, my younger brother and my mother's sister.'

'They don't know what happened?' Her gaze held

him warm and soft in its embrace. Somehow it was all right to tell Robbie.

'No. My brother doesn't understand why I've stayed away, and I haven't seen him in a long time. I pop in to see my aunt from time to time but…' Joel shrugged. 'It's hard. This is the one thing I want to talk about but can't and it's driven a wedge between us.'

'Your mother and her sister were close?'

'Very. That's what makes it so difficult. I don't want to hurt Aunt Carrie.'

Robbie thought for a moment. 'Has it occurred to you that…' She seemed suddenly at a loss, pressing her lips together tightly as if she was making up her mind whether or not to say something.

'There are probably quite a few things that haven't occurred to me. Give me a clue.'

She nodded. 'It's just that my sister and I are close, and we generally know when something's the matter before it's even said. Are you *sure* your aunt Carrie didn't know—or at least suspect that something was up?'

That hadn't occurred to Joel, but when he thought about it, it didn't seem so unlikely. 'Maybe. Perhaps it's not too late to mend some bridges with Carrie, but I can never put things right with my mother.'

Robbie reached forward, taking his hand and squeezing it tight. 'Some things aren't yours to put right, Joel. It was your parents' marriage. It doesn't matter what your mother knew or didn't know, and it makes no difference what your father wanted to cover up. You had no responsibility for anything, not to keep quiet when you were a child, or to tell your mother later on.'

It all sounded so simple when Robbie said it. 'You think that's so?'

She rolled her eyes. 'You're asking me because I'm so good at relationships? I don't know, but I do know that what your father did was very wrong, and that everything that's resulted from that is his fault and not yours. I'm not surprised you're cautious in your relationships.'

The weight was lifting from his chest, and with it Joel's need for euphemism. 'Maybe cautious doesn't cover it. That implies I actually *have* relationships.'

'You mean…' She gave him a confused look. 'I don't even know how to ask.'

She was grappling with something. Robbie had already listened to the worst thing that he could think of to say about himself, and she'd made the first time he'd spoken about it easy. There was nothing she couldn't say to him now.

He picked up her hand, bringing it to his lips. The sensation of being close to her, of being able to touch her and show her how he felt, was almost overwhelming and he could see an equal and opposite reaction in Robbie, pushing back and making him want more.

Her cheeks began to flush a little, and Joel tested their smooth heat with the tips of his fingers. Was this where he finally took the plunge, and let his feelings for someone complicate the simple satisfaction of sex?

'Does this make it any easier?'

She swallowed hard. 'Not really. Are you telling me that you've never been with anyone before?'

Robbie had it wrong. This might be a first, but not that kind of first. 'You mean have I had sex with a woman before—'

'It doesn't matter.' She interrupted him, reddening furiously now.

Joel couldn't help laughing and he saw a flash of indignation in her face. This was already far more fun than the cool exchange between two people who knew what they wanted and were sure that commitment wasn't on the list. More awkward and much more entrancing.

'Yes, I have.' He resisted the temptation to say *plenty of times* and that they'd all merged into one take-it-or-leave-it experience. 'I'm a relationships virgin, though.'

Her eyes widened and she pushed him away. Clearly that was a little more of a problem to her and Joel had to admit that he was liking the challenge. Perhaps a little more than he ought to.

'You're sure I'm the one, Joel. I work nights…' Her fingers had wandered to her neck and she was rubbing the skin. 'I don't go to bed before I've spent half an hour in the bathroom, and if my eczema does flare there are times I don't want to be touched. I'm probably not the one to get involved with as a first… And don't smile at me like that, I can't think properly.'

Good. That was exactly how he felt. Joel pulled his face straight, but he couldn't stop smiling on the inside.

'I know what having friends is like, Robbie. I have plenty of them. It's about valuing someone for what they are and reckoning that it's your privilege to compromise as much as you need to for them. About knowing what hurts them and respecting their boundaries. Knowing what pleases them.'

She stared at him, the flush mounting on her cheeks. Joel reached forward, taking her hand. 'Do I please you?'

'Yes.' She seemed certain of that, at least. 'You please me…a lot. Much more than a lot…'

'That's about how much I want to kiss you right now.'

That made her smile. She leaned forward, brushing her lips against his. This was a courtship, with all the bear traps and pitfalls and all the exquisite pleasures of finding that he *could* please her. When he kissed her back he felt a shiver run through her whole body.

'I have to…um…stop.'

The one word that would put an end to it, immediately. It wasn't as frustrating as Joel might have thought, because doing what Robbie wanted was what *he* wanted.

'Sure. We'll stop.'

Seriously. Joel thought he knew nothing about relationships? He knew everything he needed to know, which was a great deal more than she did. He leaned back on the sofa, his arm on the cushions behind her back.

'I didn't mean stop. I meant…pause.' He hadn't asked why, and Robbie was sure he wouldn't if she didn't volunteer the information. 'That half an hour I said I needed to spend in the bathroom…'

He nodded, understanding now. 'Robbie, you owned my secrets and you took them and made them something different. If I tell you that I want to be with you, it's not a tactful way of saying that I want to make love to you. I mean that I want to be with you.'

Joel was just too good to be true. Robbie hoped that wasn't a reason to disbelieve him. 'I'd like that.'

'Then will you wait for me, just for a moment while I fetch my shaver from the car? Then we can do whatever we need to do together.'

Whatever *we* need to do. There was no you or I, no impatience in his tone. And she hadn't even had to mention that beard burn wasn't a good look for her, he'd already thought of it.

'The keys are on the hook, behind the door.' She leaned forward, kissing his cheek, and Joel got to his feet. He gave her the wickedest look she'd ever seen and then he was gone before she had a chance to demand that he hurry.

Those few moments of quiet were enough to break her nerve. Robbie hurried into the bathroom, staring at her own face in the full-length mirror. What if he couldn't do this? What happened if Joel retreated into the safety of a throwaway affair and they lost the friendship that had become so important to her? What if the secret that she hadn't told yet came back to slap her in the face? Who she really was, who her family were.

'Hey...' She hadn't heard the front door open again. She must have been lost in her thoughts. Joel was standing at the bathroom door, and the sudden rush of desire swallowed everything else up.

'Second thoughts?'

'No.' There was only one thought in her head now: she wanted him to kiss her. Or just touch her.

But it seemed that Joel had other ideas. He walked into the bathroom, propping his shaver on the shelf above the basin. Then he pulled his sweater and T-shirt over his head together. Nice. She reached for him and he took a step back, grinning.

'Is this look but don't touch?' She smiled at him. 'Don't get me wrong, I'm liking what I see.' She liked it better that Joel was even doing this. That he had the confidence to stand half naked before her, without needing anything back.

'It's whatever you want it to be.'

'You should know that I'll be doing all kinds of touching in my head.'

'So will I.' The idea was clearly turning him on. 'You can tell me all about that, later.'

She turned, twisting the taps of the large bathtub. 'I like this game. Your move.'

He knew just what she wanted him to do. His shoes came off, then his jeans and socks and then his underpants. His body was beautiful, there was no doubt about that, and becoming harder by the moment as if her gaze had the power to actually touch him. He liked the game too.

Joel got into the bathtub and she perched on the rim of it, soaping her hands. Robbie could feel the muscles tighten in his shoulders as she began to wash him. Suddenly he slid forward, ducking his head beneath the water and then resurfacing with a splash.

'Can I see a little more of you?'

'Fair's fair.' Robbie wriggled out of her loose sweatshirt and T-shirt, dropping them on top of his clothes. She could unhook her bra with one hand, and the knowledge that he was watching sent tingles racing across her skin. Whatever happened next, they didn't need to stop for anything, because sex with Joel clearly wasn't something you could only do in a bed with the lights turned off. It was anything and everything, the practical blended with the sensual, all bound up in a growing arousal that *could* wait but might not.

They washed each other, and then Joel got out of

the bath, wrapping a towel around his waist and help-ing her out. He carefully rubbed emollient cream into her back, stopping to gently press his thumbs on either side of her spine in a tingling massage. She shaved him, carefully, her fingers caressing his cheek as she did so.

When she led him into the bedroom, there was no question of closing the curtains because the morning sun caressed every line of his body. He sat down on the bed, and Robbie took the condoms from the drawer. When she stood between his outstretched legs he could reach every part of her body, and that was just the way she wanted it.

'Here…' He guided her hand onto his shoulder and lifted her a little so she could tuck her legs on either side of his body. Then he shifted back. 'You like this?'

'Maybe a little too much.' She kissed him. If they weren't careful it would all be over too soon.

'Is there such a thing as liking it too much?' She felt his hands tighten on her hips, stopping her from mov-ing, and Robbie caught her breath. When he kissed her, holding her tight against his body, all she wanted was what he wanted.

He wanted a great deal. He wanted to make sure that she was ready for him, before he gently lifted her so that she could guide him inside. Sighs weren't enough, he wanted to hear her call his name. He wanted to feel her shake with passion and he wanted her to look into his gaze so that they could share each moment of it.

He made her come so hard that she cried out, and as the aftershocks were still pulsing through her body she felt him stiffen and swell inside her. One move-ment of her hips, and his head snapped back. She held him tight, feeling the shock waves that were travelling through his limbs.

Then he lifted her off him, his body still shaking. Robbie curled up in a ball next to him, her legs still twitching involuntarily, and Joel flopped back onto the bed. His hand reached for hers, holding it tight. That one small contact was enough, because she knew that Joel belonged to her, and that she belonged to him.

She heard his breathing begin to steady and felt him move. He rolled onto his side to face her. 'I'm sorry... I'm not that guy that rolls over and falls asleep.'

Robbie was still trying to gather her scattered wits, but she knew one thing for sure. She laid her finger across his lips. 'Don't you *dare* say sorry, Joel. I like it that you're the guy that gave so much he needed a moment to catch his breath.'

'You felt it too?' His mouth curved into a broad grin. 'When I said I'd done this before, I didn't actually mean *this*.'

'Me neither.' This was a first for Robbie, too. Knowing that someone wanted to share everything and allowing them to do it. It had formed a bond between them that had been strong enough to contain the fiercest desire. 'Must have been something you did.'

'No. Definitely wasn't me, it must have been you.' His fingers skimmed her cheek, moving slowly down to her neck and shoulders. Robbie could feel the tingling murmur of her skin, still reacting to his touch.

And she could still feel the heat of his gaze, as their bodies slowly began to wind back down again. When she shivered, finally sensing the cool touch of the air around her, he drew back the covers of the bed, propping a pillow on one side of her to support her shoulder.

She didn't want to lie on her back, staring at the ceiling. She wanted to curl up in his arms to sleep, however stiff her shoulder might be as a result. But he hushed her protests, curling his legs under hers and taking her hand in his.

'Just sleep.' He pressed her fingers to his lips.

She was already warm and comfortable, and beginning to relax. 'We're not doing that again, Joel. Not until…this evening at least.'

She heard him chuckle quietly. 'No. Definitely not. I don't think I could take it…'

'Me neither.' Robbie's eyelids were drooping and she was half asleep now. This evening couldn't come too soon.

CHAPTER TEN

JOEL WATCHED HER sleep until the warm languor in his limbs made him unable to prop himself up on his elbow any longer. Carefully keeping hold of her hand, he curled around her in the bed as best he could without disturbing her.

So *this* was what a relationship was like. He dismissed the thought. It was what Robbie was like. Full of sweetness and strength, and there to share all the things he'd never spoken about before. Sharing her doubts and fears with him. He drifted off to sleep, wondering if he'd ever be the same and knowing that she'd already made him into a better man than the one she'd found.

One who couldn't get enough of her touch. He woke early in the afternoon, to hear rain beating against the windows. And Robbie was already awake, whispering in his ear.

'Don't move…'

'Uh? Why not?' He decided that he didn't really care why not. If Robbie wanted him to stay still, then that was what he'd do.

If he could. Her head popped beneath the covers and

he felt her lips on his chest. Desire flooded through him and he reached for her, feeling her push his hands away.

'Are you leaning on your shoulder?' He tried to focus on the practicalities and managed to get one sentence out.

'No.'

He felt her tongue circle his nipple and Joel groaned. This was just too sweet to stop her, and he clasped his hands behind his head, waiting for whatever was going to happen next. When Robbie was done with him, there would be plenty of time to return the favour...

They'd been in bed for maybe twelve hours. He'd made sure that Robbie had been resting comfortably for eight of them, and for the rest of the time they'd been talking and making love. Rather more making love than talking, because actions spoke a great deal louder than words.

But it was time to get up. The Nightshifters phones were covered until midnight, by a volunteer who worked the day shift, but they were on the rota for the following eight hours. Robbie showered and got dressed while Joel made egg-and-bacon sandwiches, and they hurried out to the car in the rain.

The sound of rain on the roof in the Tin Tabernacle was already moving from a soothing patter to a deafening roar. Ava, who had been covering the phones for the first part of the night, packed her things up and ran out through the pelting rain to her car, leaving them alone. Robbie closed the door behind her and turned, grinning at Joel.

'Don't you love the sound of the rain? When I was

little we had a tree house, and when it rained it sounded just like this.'

Robbie's memories of her childhood were obviously happier than his. 'I'll take here and now. With you.'

She nodded. 'Me too. Rain on the roof is all yours from now on.'

That might be a little rash, because their relationship wasn't even twenty-four hours old yet. But rain on the roof would always be Robbie's, even if the next thing she did was walk away from him and he never saw her again.

And that wasn't going to happen. He couldn't let it happen.

Joel unwrapped the sandwiches, which were still warm inside the greaseproof paper, and made the coffee, while Robbie took a call. Then the phone fell silent and they could tuck into their food.

'Who was that?' Robbie hadn't made any of the usual follow-up calls to find out if a driver was available.

'Glen. He won't be in tonight, the kids both have a feverish cold that's been going around at school, and Carla's caught it now as well. Probably only a matter of time before he goes down with it, but until then he's on hot lemon and cuddling duty.'

'And wondering how we're managing?'

'Yes. I told him we were fine, that you were here and he was to shut up and go away. He does enough already.'

Joel nodded. 'Yeah, I can always do a few deliveries...' He forgot all about deliveries as a crash sounded behind him followed by the sound of dribbling water. Robbie was staring up at the ceiling, her hand over her mouth, and when he turned to see what she was looking at he could see why. Water was trickling through one of the joints in the wooden panelling of the pitched ceiling and onto the floor, next to one of the sofas.

'Oh, no! We just had the roof done last year…'

'Sounds as if something's fallen on it.' Joel got to his feet, looking around. 'Do we have something to catch the water before it gets everywhere and damages the floor?'

'There are buckets in the storeroom.' Robbie opened the door behind her, disappearing into the storeroom that had everything, and reappearing with a large bucket in her hand. She placed it under the leak in the roof, while Joel looked under the sink for a cloth to wipe up the mess.

'That'll hold it for…' He glanced at the bucket, which was already beginning to fill.

'About half an hour. Tops.' Robbie sighed.

'I'll go outside and see what's happened. Torch?' There *had* to be at least a couple of torches in the storeroom.

'Yes.' Instead of fetching a torch, Robbie had reached for her waterproof jacket and was threading her arm into it. 'I'll go.'

'You will not. Keep an eye on the phones, and I'll go.'

'This is *my* place…'

That wasn't entirely true, but Robbie was clearly very attached to the Tin Tabernacle. All the same, Joel wasn't going to allow her to go out in the pouring rain to inspect the roof.

'Your shoulder is still weak, Robbie. And you're…' He thought twice about what he'd been about to say. 'We're in a relationship.'

She glared up at him. 'Oh, and because we're in a

relationship, that makes me the little woman, does it? Think again, Joel.'

She'd been *all* woman with him today and if he was totally honest that had changed his view of her slightly. Joel decided not to mention that. Robbie was already cross enough.

'No. It makes us a team. You're shorter than I am and I have greater reach, even supposing your shoulder was fully healed, which it's not. It's about each of us doing what we can do best.'

Robbie narrowed her eyes. 'That makes sense. I'm very cross with you for it, though.'

'Fine.' He grinned back at her. Robbie's fiery independence was one of her most attractive traits. 'You can watch the phone while you're being cross. And tell me where I can find a torch.'

She turned on her heel, marching back to the storeroom and fetched him a large lantern torch. Joel zipped his waterproof jacket up, pulling the hood over his head, and made for the door, turning when Robbie called him back.

'Be safe, darling.' She was smiling, waving a paper handkerchief from the box on her desk. Joel started to laugh, and she poked her tongue out at him.

'Just do a little light dusting with that hanky... While I'm gone.' He turned before Robbie could throw something at him, making his way outside to the relative safety of the storm.

Wonderful. Robbie looked at her watch. Sixteen hours in, and she'd already allowed her fears to get the better of her judgement.

Of course, Joel was taller and stronger than she was. Of course, she wasn't going to be much use, when her arm still protested when she lifted it above shoulder level, or put any weight on it. And how was he to know that the Tin Tabernacle really was hers and she'd put her heart into renovating it, if she'd never told him?

But she'd reacted to the situation with all of the hurt that she'd felt when she was with Rory. He'd seen only that she was weak and flawed, and had decided that making her dependent on him was a project that carried some financial reward. He'd crushed her confidence, and she'd fought back by deciding that she could do anything. Mending a broken roof in the rain was nothing...

She stared at the phone, almost willing it to ring so that she could prove to herself that she could do something useful. That was ridiculous. Joel had never said she was useless, and she knew that wasn't what he thought, either.

There was a rattling at the door and it opened. 'I'm sorry...' The apology died in her throat when she saw that it wasn't Joel. Clara and Joan were both shrouded in knee-length waterproof jackets, which were dripping onto the floor.

'Come in. Close the door.' Robbie got to her feet. 'Are you okay?'

'Yeah, we're fine.' Clara pulled down her hood, her mass of red hair spilling out over her shoulders. 'We've pulled the tarps over the front and rear decks on the barge and slackened off the mooring ropes, so she'll be fine. But she's rocking like Elvis.'

'Well, make yourselves at home. You might not get

much sleep here with the phone ringing, but it's warm and dry.'

Joan smiled, taking off her jacket to reveal a thick multicoloured sweater. 'Thanks. Being at the same angle for more than five seconds is a huge improvement.'

Clara had caught sight of the bucket. 'Roof leaking?'

'Yes, it's only just started. Joel's out there trying to see what the matter is. We might be able to fix it from the inside.'

Clara and Joan both looked up at the ceiling. People here were used to making and mending and the small, self-sufficient community was one of the things that had first drawn Robbie here.

'Yeah, I reckon you probably could. Can you remove the wooden cladding?' Clara gave her verdict on the situation.

'Yes, it's designed so that the panels will slide out, so we can get to the roof from the inside. Specifically with leaks in mind. The old roof leaked like a sieve. We've got some sealant and stuff to patch it with in the storeroom.'

A creaking sound came from the roof and then a sharp bang. All three women stared up at it. Then the leak slowed.

'It looks as if he's done something.'

'Yeah.' Clara walked over to the bucket, her gaze fixed on the ceiling. 'It's definitely not dripping so fast now.'

The roof creaked and another, louder bang made Robbie jump, clutching at her shoulder as she did so in an instinctive expectation of pain. Then she forgot all about the slight tremor that ran down her arm, because the dripping slowed again and then stopped.

Clara gave a nod of approval. 'He's done it.'

When Joel appeared in the doorway, wet and wind-blown, Robbie had to stop herself from running over to him and hugging him.

'How's it looking now?' He pulled back his hood and saw Joan and Clara. 'Hi there. Everything all right?'

'Yes, it's just a bit choppy out there,' Joan answered and he nodded.

'And the drip's stopped.' Robbie grinned at him. 'What did you do?'

'There was a branch lodged between two of the cor-rugated panels. It's pretty windy out there and it must have blown up against the roof. I pulled it out and then climbed up and gave the top panel a thump and they snapped back together again.'

Robbie decided not to ask him how he'd managed to climb up onto the roof in the pouring rain. It probably wasn't all that difficult—he could have stood on the windowsill and levered himself up from there.

'Thank you. I'll get someone out to have a look at it in the morning, but at least it's stopped for now.'

His smile was just for her. But when he strode to-wards her, Robbie turned her face away from him be-fore he could kiss her, aware that Clara's and Joan's eyes were on them.

His mouth twitched downwards, but he gave an im-perceptible nod and stopped at a respectful distance away from her. No one owned up to a relationship this new, did they? Didn't keeping that secret for a little while just add to the heady excitement of it all?

Not for Joel. He'd been hurt by secrets, and he probably didn't find keeping this secret quite as deliciously exciting as she did. She grabbed his hand, pulling him close.

Are you sure? He mouthed the words at her. It was a bit late for that now—what she'd done could hardly have escaped Joan and Clara's notice. And she didn't want it to.

She stood on her toes, kissing him. Maybe that would show him how sure she was. How she could leave her own doubts and fears and need to be in control behind, in favour of making him feel more comfortable. Although she knew there were still things she needed to tell him…

As he drew away from her he was smiling. He mouthed *Thank you* and then turned away, but not before Robbie had caught an exchanged glance between Clara and Joan. By morning, the news would probably have reached everyone in their small community, but Robbie couldn't bring herself to care.

'The boat a little further up, painted red and green. That's Roy's, isn't it?' Joel's smile still lingered, but there was a note of concern in his voice now.

'Yes?'

'It's just that all the other boats have covers at the back and front, but he hasn't pulled his across. Should we go and wake him?'

'I can't imagine anyone hasn't been woken by this storm. And it's not like Roy, he's usually the first to keep his boat protected from the weather…' Robbie glanced round at Clara, who gave her an innocent look, as if she really hadn't been watching every move that she and Joel made.

'Have you seen Roy? Joel says he hasn't covered his front and rear decks.'

'No. Come to think of it I haven't seen him all day. Is he on the boat, Joan?'

Joan shrugged. 'He didn't say anything to me about going away, and he usually does, so we can keep an eye on his boat.'

'We'd better check on him.' Robbie glanced up at Joel. 'It'll only take five minutes. We can put the answerphone on.'

'I'll answer the phones. I've always rather fancied being a Nightshifter,' Clara volunteered, and Joel gave her a smile.

'That's great, thanks. Just a name and number is fine, but if you can find out what they need and write that down that'll be great. If it's one of the drivers, then tell them they can come back here, we've no outstanding calls.'

'Gotcha. Can I sit at your desk, Robbie?'

'Of course. There's a packet of fruit gums in the top drawer.' Robbie eased on her jacket, and followed Joel out into the pouring rain.

The towpath was illuminated by a string of bright streetlights, but Roy's narrowboat was in darkness. Joel switched on the torch, and Robbie saw dark shapes of furniture and seating inside as the beam of light played across the windows.

'This isn't right, Joel. He hasn't even closed his curtains.'

'I don't see anyone in there. Where's the bedroom?'

'It'll be near the back.' Robbie walked along the tow-path to the approximate place. 'About here.'

Joel shone the light at the windows again, bending down to get a better view. Robbie could see the shape of what looked like a man, on what looked like a bed.

'I can't see properly. But this isn't right, Joel. We should go inside and check on him.'

He nodded, hurrying back to the bow of the boat and stepping across onto the small deck. Reaching back, he coiled his arm around her waist, almost lifting her over the gap between the towpath and the boat. Then he turned, banging on the door and calling Roy's name.

Nothing. No lights, no answer. Joel started to look around the deck, obviously trying to find something to force the door. That might not be necessary. Robbie gave it a push and it slid open.

'Really?' He stepped inside, looking around him.

'People often don't lock their doors during the day, when they're up and around.' Robbie shoved the door closed behind them with her foot then slid her hand along the wall and found the light switch.

Nothing. She flipped the switch on and off a couple of times, to make sure.

'The boat's batteries must be drained, Joel. There's no light.'

He nodded, calling out again, and this time there was a reply, an indistinct but agonised mumble of words. The lights outside were reflecting into the boat and were just enough to see their way forward. Robbie followed Joel, stumbling as the boat rocked in response to a gust of wind outside, and feeling his arm around her waist before she could fall.

'I've got you.'

The words might be possessive and protective and all the other things that she'd rejected over the years. But Joel turned them into the fierce heat that she'd seen in his eyes when they were making love, and she couldn't forget that he'd revelled in *her* possessiveness, her protective instincts too.

'Yes. You have.' She murmured the words as they moved forward, Joel's arm around her to steady her.

Through the sitting area into a well-equipped kitchen, and then past that into a study, the books held in place by rails across the front of the shelves. The narrowboats afforded a surprisingly big living area once you were inside, and the unsteady rocking motion meant they had to take care, but finally Joel slid back the door to the bedroom. In the half-light all Robbie could see was a shrouded figure on the bed, and a hand raised against the beam of the torch. She hung onto the door frame, while Joel moved forward towards the bed, making sure to keep the beam of the torch from shining directly at its occupant.

'Hey, Roy. It's Joel and Robbie, we've come to see if you're okay.'

'Feeling pretty groggy…' The sound of Roy's voice attested to that better than his words, and the disorder and stale scent of the cabin was a world away from his usually spotless narrowboat.

'Okay. How long for?'

'This morning…'

'And what's the matter?' Joel laid his hand on Roy's forehead to check for a fever, and then his fingers felt for the pulse in his neck. Crude measurements, but that was all he had right now.

'Legs hurt…everything hurts. Can't keep any food down… Thank goodness you're here…'

Roy was as self-sufficient as anyone living on this stretch of the river. If he could move, he would be doing so and would probably have made his way up to the Tin Tabernacle with the others, and be drinking peppermint tea to calm his stomach. Joel glanced over his shoulder at Robbie and she shook her head.

'This isn't like him. He's really sick.'

'Roy, I'm going to have to just check you over to see if I can find out what the matter is.' He reached for the torch and Roy caught his arm.

'My head hurts…'

'Okay. I hear you. But I need to be able to see a little more. I'll shine the torch away from your face.'

Joel tried to calm him, checking his head for any bumps or bleeding as he did so, but the boat lurched again and he only just managed to snatch his hands away from Roy before he slid back against the cupboards lining the other side of the narrow cabin. This wasn't going to work.

'Joel, we need to get him out so that we can see what the matter is. There's a basket stretcher in the storeroom, go and fetch that and find someone to help you. Chloe and Grant are two boats along from here, see if you can find Grant. I'll stay here with Roy.'

If Joel was thinking of arguing, he dismissed the idea quickly. Getting to his feet, he helped her to the low cabinet beside the bed, clearing the top of it so she had somewhere to sit securely.

'Okay, hang on. I'll be back as soon as I can. You've got your phone?'

'Yes, I'll call you if he takes a turn for the worse.'

There wasn't much that Robbie could do here, other than to use what movement she had in her shoulder to try and check Roy's breathing and heartbeat, while she hung on with the other hand. But the sound of her voice seemed to soothe Roy and she kept talking, telling him Joel would be back shortly and that he'd be more comfortable when they got him up to the Tin Tabernacle. Sooner than she'd even dared to hope, she heard voices outside and the sound of someone boarding the boat again.

Stretching forward, she could see along the whole length of the boat. Joel was coming towards them, struggling to stay on his feet and manage the stretcher and behind him Grant was carrying the vinyl-covered insert and a couple of blankets.

Leaving the stretcher in the doorway to the bedroom, Joel wedged himself in next to Robbie at the side of the bed. 'How is he?'

'Low-grade fever, pulse seems steady. I can't find any bleeding and his breathing seems okay.' Robbie shook her head silently, and Joel got the message. It was impossible to tell exactly what was going on in these conditions, and Roy was clearly very unwell.

'We'll move him?'

'Yes, we'll move him.'

'Out of the way, then.'

Robbie squeezed past him, finding yet another reason to be grateful that last night had happened. If it hadn't Joel might have thought twice about putting his hands where they were resting right now, and it was actually the best way to stop her from falling over.

'Grant, will you put the vinyl insert into the stretcher…?' She helped Grant prepare the stretcher while Joel carefully sat Roy up on the bed.

'That's great. Now we'll slide it forwards towards Joel.'

What might have been a desperate, fumbling exercise turned into a well-executed manoeuvre. Joel helped Roy to swing his legs over the side of the bed, and carefully supported him down into the stretcher tucking the blankets and then a waterproof sheet over him, and fastening the straps around him.

Robbie went first, the torch tucked into the crook of her elbow, to leave her other arm free for the handholds along the way. The men followed, with the stretcher steering it carefully behind her to the front of the boat. When she reached the sliding door at the other end of the boat, she pushed it back with her foot, moving out onto the small deck.

Willing hands grabbed her, bearing her off the boat. A small crowd had gathered on the towpath, standing in the pouring rain, waiting for news of Roy. That was both good and bad.

'All right—everyone stand back, please, give us some room. Chloe, will you go on board, please, and give Joel and Grant a hand? Ollie and Rachel, would you come and wait with me? They'll be passing the stretcher off the boat and as soon as you can reach it you grab hold of it.' Robbie looked around and saw that Joel was already beginning to manoeuvre the stretcher round. 'Great. Perfect. Anyone got an umbrella I can borrow?'

She took the closest of three umbrellas that were offered, and turned to find Rachel leaning forward, almost climbing onto the boat in her eagerness to help. Robbie took her arm, guiding her back. 'It's okay, we need to have a safe footing up here on the towpath. They'll pass the stretcher over to you and you take it when you can reach it.'

'Ready?' Joel called across to her, and Robbie gave him a thumbs-up. The stretcher was passed smoothly and easily onto the towpath, Joel stepping across with it. Robbie shielded Roy's face from the rain as best she could with the umbrella, as they walked across the towpath and up to the Tin Tabernacle.

Inside, there was the evidence of activity as well. Geoff, one of the Nightshifters, had returned and was monitoring the phones and Joan and Clara had clearly been busy moving furniture. The desks had been pulled forward, and an old curtain draped from the rafters, to provide a space next to the storeroom that afforded some measure of privacy. The dozen or so people who followed them into the Tin Tabernacle formed a tight group at the other end of the office, talking amongst themselves in hushed tones.

Joel grinned at her as he set the stretcher down on the floor and took off his jacket. One hand briefly went to his heart and Robbie nodded. This community could be rambunctious and argumentative and the reason many of them lived here was that they didn't much like doing as they were told, but the care they showed to one of their own when they were hurt was touching.

He undid the straps that secured Roy into the

stretcher and Chloe and Grant helped him get Roy onto the camp bed that had been set up ready for them, while Robbie shrugged out of her jacket and fetched the medical kit from the storeroom. Roy was moaning, shading his eyes as if the light hurt them.

'Roy, we need the light to examine you. Just close your eyes, and try to relax. We'll let you know what's happening.' Robbie knelt down beside the bed and Joel opened the medical kit, squirting a dab of hand sanitiser onto his hands and then another onto Robbie's outstretched palm. Then he grabbed two pairs of surgical gloves, holding hers open for her to slide her hands into, before putting on a pair himself.

'I'll do the history—you do the exam?' She grinned up at him.

'Yep.' He popped his head around the side of the curtain asking for a pen and paper, and Robbie took them, ready to write everything down.

It was a lot quicker with two, working together without getting in each other's way. Roy had been suffering from vomiting and abdominal pain for the last six hours, along with severe muscle aches, a headache and a fever. When Joel uncovered his feet, there were the telltale signs of a rash.

Joel glanced at Robbie and she nodded. They didn't need to discuss what he should check next. 'Roy, I'm going to need you to open your eyes for a moment, so I can take a look at them.'

Roy shook his head, and Robbie cupped her hand on his forehead. 'I'm shading your eyes. But you have to open them just for a moment.'

Roy opened his eyes, blinking against the light. It took one look to confirm what Robbie had been thinking and Joel clearly didn't need any more than that either.

They left Roy to rest, walking a few steps to the corner of their makeshift booth. Each of them opened their mouths at the same time, and Joel smiled.

'After you.'

'I reckon the first stage of leptospirosis. He has most of the symptoms and the rash suggests it as well. And the conjunctival redness and jaundice…' They'd both seen the whites of Roy's eyes, and the yellow and red splotches were characteristic of leptospirosis.

Joel nodded. 'I agree. I'd say it's a mild case, he's a little dehydrated but no more than you'd expect from having been sick, so he doesn't need intravenous fluids. And he's definitely not in the second stage yet.'

If leptospirosis didn't resolve on its own, the second stage was Weil's disease, which was much more serious. But they'd caught it early and Robbie was confident that with a course of antibiotics to prevent the onset of the second stage, Roy would be feeling much better soon.

Joel didn't seem as happy about it all as she was. 'Normally I'd take a blood sample to confirm our diagnosis, and prescribe antibiotics and rest. But we can't just let him back onto the boat. He needs someone to keep an eye on him.'

'He has someone.' Robbie smiled at Joel's expression of surprise. 'Roy has a really big house about ten minutes' walk from here. His daughter and son-in-law live in one side of it, and Roy mostly lives on the boat, but he pops in and out of his side of the house whenever the mood takes him.'

'Ah. So if we call the daughter…?'

'She'll take good care of him. They're really close and I've met her, she seems sensible. We've got blood-sampling kits here, so we can do that now.'

'And I can take the blood sample straight to the hospital and write a prescription while I'm there. Do we know who his GP is?'

'Yes, it's one of the doctors who comes here twice a week. I can give him a call in the morning.'

'That's everything sorted, then.' Joel jerked his thumb towards the curtain. 'I'm rather hoping you might know what to say to the assembled well-wishers…'

Robbie chuckled. 'I'll say what we'd say if they all turned up with him in A & E. We expect him to make a full recovery, and he should be back on the boat soon. If someone wants to go and sit with him, that would be nice, but they're to keep quiet.'

'Rather you than me.' Joel didn't seem entirely confident that just saying no if anyone asked for more details would work. 'Do you have any idea how he got it?'

'Well, it's a waterborne infection. Most people here know how to avoid it and our clinics always emphasise the need for precautions, even if it's not likely you'll get it just living on the water. I'll see if I can find out a bit more while you're at the hospital. Roy may have fallen in and got a mouthful of the Thames at some point.'

'Okay.' He smiled at her, taking her hand. 'You go and talk to the assembled neighbours, and I'll do the easy part and take some blood.'

CHAPTER ELEVEN

IT WAS NINE in the morning. They should be gone by now, but Joel and Robbie were taking advantage of a few moments' peace, and were sitting back in the two office chairs, their feet on the desks, sipping coffee.

'So… marine rescue.'

Joel gave her a pained look. 'Can you really call it that? We were within a few metres of the towpath at all times.'

'On the water is on the water. Ask anyone here.'

'Okay. In that case breaking and entering.'

Robbie chuckled. 'No, I'm not going to give you that, the door was open. Diagnosis, treatment and family liaison.' Roy's daughter Kirsty had come to collect her father at six this morning, and while he was sleeping Joel had taken her through exactly what was needed and which symptoms she should look out for.

'Yep. Howling winds and a roof repair.'

Robbie looked up at the wooden ceiling cladding, which was drying out nicely. 'Yes, and I'd like to compliment you on the effectiveness of your repairs.'

'Thank you. Public health education because Chloe was really worried about having dangled her feet in the water three weeks ago. And then several hours on the phones with Nightshifters. That counts as two, by the way.'

'Absolutely. Although Clara made a fine job of covering while you were at the hospital and I was sitting with Roy. She said that once you've got someone to measure their five-year-old for a sweater, over the phone, this was a piece of cake.'

Joel grinned. 'Did you mention that you could do with a few more volunteers?'

'Yes, I did actually. She said she quite enjoyed being involved, and she's thinking about it. As long as she can bring her knitting with her.'

'Then that's recruitment as well. Have we got everything?'

'I think so.' Robbie thought through the events of the night and decided that it was more than enough to prove her point. 'So since we've done all of those things since we were first together, I think we can classify ourselves as *going steady*.'

The look on his face told her that he didn't mind that at all. 'Yes. I think we can.'

'Oh, and Clara asked me if you'd like a jumper. She and Joan do these random jumpers from all the leftover wool, and they're great. I said thanks but no.'

'You're managing my wardrobe now?' Joel raised his eyebrows. 'Feel free, it could definitely do with it, and it's a pretty sure sign of going steady.'

'No, neither of us are managing each other's wardrobes.' Robbie had had quite enough of that with Rory and her relationship with Joel was different. 'It was a nice thought, and meant as an acknowledgement that you're one of us now, but I happened to mention that they hadn't knitted *me* a jumper and Clara said she'd do a matching one for me. We'd have to wear them, and we'd never live it down with the Nightshifters.'

'Sensible. Yeah, that was a good call. Matching jumpers is a step too far.' His eyes softened suddenly. 'You don't mind that they know about us?'

It had obviously been important to Joel, and although Robbie had had her reservations, she was glad she'd put them aside. 'No, I don't mind. Although, maybe we'll keep quiet about it at the hospital for a little while.'

He chuckled. 'That's definitely a good idea. We don't need to run round telling absolutely everyone. It was just a really nice gesture of yours to tell people that you care about. I'm assuming that everyone probably knows by now?'

'Roy might have missed it, but only because he wasn't feeling well.' Robbie smiled at him. 'I suppose this all makes it quite all right to say, *Your place or mine?*'

His smile broadened. 'That would be more than all right. And although I'd love to say mine, I think I have laundry and shopping to do first. That's as long as it's not too presumptuous of me to hope that you may consider coming in contact with my sheets and my soap.'

'I was planning on getting you in contact with my sheets at the earliest possible opportunity. So no, it's not presumptuous at all. And if you'd like to go back to yours we could always swing past my flat first and I'll get sheets and whatever else I need.'

'Do you mind?'

That was what was so refreshing about Joel. He considered that if he was asking her to his home, it was his responsibility to make sure that his sheets were washed in detergent that wouldn't affect her skin, and that he had the right soap in his bathroom cabinet. It was the ultimate in gracious hosting, and made his house the most luxurious place on earth. Rory would never have understood that.

'I love that you don't mind if I bring my own things. And that you thought of it before I had to say it.'

He smiled at her, and suddenly everything was rosier than the most flamboyant sunset. 'Are you ready to go, then?'

Robbie looked around. The storm had abated at four in the morning, but everyone had stayed to tidy up and see Roy safely off before they went back to their boats, and the Tin Tabernacle showed no sign of all that had happened that night.

'Yes. I'm ready.'

They'd been together a week, and still the lustrous sheen that accompanied something new and precious hadn't dulled. Robbie was beginning to feel that it was made of strong stuff and that maybe it would never completely disappear.

'What do you think about switching to the day shift?' They were lying on his bed, watching the sun come up, when Joel asked the question. Robbie raised her eyebrows.

'Days? But we're Nightshifters, aren't we?' In more ways than just being *actual* Nightshifters. They both enjoyed the rush of working nights. The city at night.

Working in their own little bubble when everyone else was sleeping.

'We are. But we're not vampires, we won't fry if we go out in the sun.'

'I go out in the sun all the time—it's important to get your Vitamin D. And sunshine's good for the skin and helps boost your dopamine and serotonin levels. I probably get more sun than most people in the winter, because I get home from work and the sun's just coming up.'

'That's true. But right now, I just want to get up and go out and enjoy the day.' He raised her hand to his lips, kissing her fingers. 'Or maybe make love with you one more time. Then go out and enjoy the day.'

'You could make love with me one more time. I'd like that.'

Joel chuckled, rolling over onto his side, and propping himself up on one elbow.

'Your wish is my command. Particularly when you have such nice wishes.' He ran his fingers from her neck, down between her breasts and had reached her stomach before Robbie caught his hand, stopping it from going any further.

'Let's not be those people. The ones who stop talking about things because we want to have sex.'

'You don't want to have sex?' He shot her a look of exaggerated dismay. 'I'm crushed.'

'You can un-crush yourself right now, Joel. You know full well how much I love having sex with you. I also want to know why you think it's a good idea to switch to the day shift.'

He smiled. 'I just think that people work nights for

lots of different reasons, because it's better paid or more convenient…whatever. But you get paid more for working unsocial hours because that's what they are. Unsocial.'

'You think we're unsocial?'

'For me, working nights was always a great excuse to keep my relationships casual, so…yeah, that's pretty unsocial. There's an awful lot to be said for working at night, and I know there's always a need for it in A & E departments. I'm just wondering whether days aren't an option as well. Better CPD opportunities, more contact with specialists who work days.'

Robbie thought for a moment. 'I suppose… I started working nights when my confidence was at a really low ebb and I just wanted to disappear.'

He grinned, leaning over to kiss her. 'How's your confidence now? Anything I can do to boost it?'

She pushed him over onto his back, shifting to prop herself up against his chest. 'Like I said. We're not people who stop talking about things in order to have sex.'

'No. We aren't. So what do you think?'

'You've made a really good point, we both started working nights for lots of different reasons, but some of those reasons have changed now. We could think about changing with them. Only—we'd have to do it together. If I'm working days and you're working nights we'd never see each other.'

'Yeah, we'd do it together. And we can't stop working with Nightshifters, either.'

'No, but Nightshifters needs volunteers for the evenings just as much as for the early mornings. More probably. And there's a move to expand as well. The board's been scouting out a few places around Oxford.'

Robbie bit her lip. That was substantially true—her father had been doing most of the preparatory work for that, and he was on the board. 'There's something I should tell you, Joel...'

'That you're going to be involved with the expansion? That's great, you should take on more responsibility for the running of the place.' He grinned at her.

'No...well, yes and...'

His fingers were running down her back, making those patterns of sensation that she loved so much. Robbie shivered. She couldn't help it, she was going to be one of those people and put off talking about something important in order to have sex. Maybe that was the right thing to do, because she was still getting used to feeling warm and safe in Joel's arms. A little warmer, a little safer, couldn't be a bad thing when she took the step of sharing those last secrets, that had protected her for so long.

'We'll talk about the details later?'

He nodded, rolling her over onto her back and kissing her. 'Yes. Later...'

Plans. He had plans. *They* had plans, things like going away for the weekend, and seeing friends for dinner. Robbie had talked about a weekend in Ireland to meet her sister and brother-in-law, which everyone knew was a preamble to meeting her parents. Joel was unable to reciprocate on that score, but Robbie knew why and she understood.

It all felt tantalisingly normal, as if he was finally

starting to leave all the guilt behind. Robbie had gently suggested that going to see Aunt Carrie might be a good idea, just to open the channels of communication between them, and Joel was seriously considering it. It wasn't simply that Robbie had given him a new perspective on things—being with her had given him the desire to change.

Two weeks. That was all it had taken. His life had been turned upside down, and he was happier than he'd ever been.

Robbie had told him on Saturday morning that she'd be cooking and had gone home to make a start while Joel had stayed behind to follow through on a patient. When he arrived at her apartment and she buzzed him up, the kitchen was already in complete chaos.

'What are you cooking?' It was impossible to tell from the assortment of kitchen equipment spread across the worktops.

'Pizza. I've got a quick and easy recipe from Carla. And garlic bread and salad…'

'Right.' He could see a salad spinner, and it seemed to have something in it. 'Want a hand?'

'No, I'm cooking for you. You cooked for me last Saturday.'

Roast chicken with all the trimmings hadn't been quite as much trouble as this obviously was. But Robbie had a large and efficient dishwasher and cooking always made her happy, whatever the results, so he wasn't going to argue.

'Right then. Anything else you want me to do?'

'No! This is off-duty night. We eat, we talk we make love.' She grinned at him.

'Sounds good. In that order?'

She walked across the kitchen, kissing him. 'Yes. There's something I want to talk with you about, but I've got to… Oh!'

The kitchen timer pinged and she looked around. 'I'm not sure what that's for. I'll have to consult Carla's list.'

'I'll leave you to it.' Robbie seemed a little on edge tonight, and it was probably best to let her get on without interference.

'Yes, please do.' She was scanning a piece of paper that was held to the door of the fridge by a magnet. 'Prove the dough. I'm already doing that. By the way, I looked out my thesis from medical school, the one we were talking about the other day about kids in A & E. It's in the snug. In a blue binder to the right of the fireplace…'

'Okay, thanks. I'll take a look.' Robbie's work on her thesis was undoubtedly measured and perceptive, just like everything else she did medically. Cooking provided her with the opportunity to indulge in a bit of chaos, and it fed her soul in a different way. Joel was well aware of the fact that showing him these out-of-control moments was a sign of how far they'd come together in the last two weeks.

He walked into the book-lined snug, scanning the bookcases that occupied the deep alcove to the right of the fireplace. There were three or four blue binders, on two different shelves, and he pulled the nearest one out, opening it.

It was a photograph album. There were pictures of two little girls, on a beach somewhere, one of them unmistakeably Robbie. He smiled, wanting to see more but resisted the temptation to turn the page and put the album back onto the shelf.

The next blue binder had photographs in it as well, a slightly older Robbie who was just as entrancing. As he closed the cover, something fluttered from between the pages onto the floor. It was a newspaper cutting and when he picked it up, Joel couldn't help but see the headline.

Everything was under control. More or less. The pizza dough was proving and the toppings were prepared. Robbie had put everything she didn't need back into the cupboards, and she might pour herself a glass of wine before going on to the next stage.

Tonight was going to be the night. She'd suggested going to see her sister and brother-in-law, to give herself a deadline for telling Joel about her family. She was going to come clean, and tell Joel that Nightshifters was her brainchild, and that it was in the main funded by money from her trust fund. She'd tell him that the plans to expand to Oxford were already under way, and…

He'd be excited. It was something they could share and look forward to together. The little quiver of uncertainty in her stomach was just her old fears coming back to haunt her. Joel didn't care two hoots about the money, she knew that. But she'd kept it from him. Kept her family's money from him.

She saw him in the doorway, standing very still. 'Hey, did you find it? I was just about to open a bottle of wine.'

'I'm really sorry, Robbie. I was looking for the blue binder but ended up with a photo album instead.'

'Ah... No, my thesis is on the next shelf up from the albums. Same kind of binder but it's got pocket inserts instead of photo pages...' Suddenly she froze, because he was holding a newspaper cutting in his hand. *That* newspaper cutting.

It was okay. Everything was going to be okay. She'd been going to tell him anyway and she might even have shown him the newspaper cutting, even if she hated it for all the agonies of embarrassment it had caused her. But there was something about the look on Joel's face that said everything *wasn't* okay.

'I didn't mean to look at your photographs, but when I closed the album this fell out. I couldn't help seeing it and... I don't understand.' He laid the cutting down on the counter.

'That was what I wanted to talk to you about. It wasn't just my grandparents who had some money and left me this place. My dad's rich as well.'

Joel nodded. 'I've heard of him. David Hampton-Hall. And you're Olivia Hampton-Hall.'

'Yes, that's right. Roberta's my middle name...' A lot of people shortened a double-barrelled name or used middle names. Robbie felt herself blush because that hadn't been the reason. She'd deliberately tried to distance herself from the public image.

'And Nightshifters. Is that one of your father's charities?'

'No, it's *mine*. I saw the need, and I set it up from my trust-fund money. Dad's on the board of trustees, but I asked him to help because he has a lot of experience in running a charity and I wanted his advice. There's always been an understanding between us that Nightshifters is my responsibility.' Her father had told her that he was proud of the way she'd built Nightshifters and that had meant a great deal to Robbie.

'So Glen's not really the boss, is he? It's you.'

'Yes, he is the boss. North London Nightshifters is his, and when I'm working there I do what he tells me. My side of things is... I facilitate. I make sure that Nightshifters has the financing it needs, and I'll be dealing with our plans to expand.' Robbie heaved a sigh. This wasn't going as well as she'd hoped.

'And you're on the board of trustees. Along with your father.'

'What? Well...yes, every registered charity has to have a board of trustees, and I appointed people who could help steer Nightshifters in the right direction. There's my father, a couple of his contacts from the charity sector, and a solicitor to help us with any legal issues. What does that matter, Joel?'

He was so still. His face impassive as if he wasn't feeling anything. She wanted to hug him, or shake him, or anything that would provoke a reaction.

'It matters because you lied to me. About something I was getting involved with, and which I'd started to really care about.'

'No. I didn't lie. I just didn't tell you. I have no clue what your father does for a living or who he is, because you haven't told me. I don't know your brother's name and I dare say I won't be introduced to him any time soon. I accept that, Joel, because it's your family and it's up to you what you tell me.'

'That's not the same, Robbie.' A flicker of anger showed in his face. Robbie was almost relieved to see it because at least it was something. 'I can't know everything about you, and you can't know everything about me. But you deliberately withheld information that you thought would make some difference to how I felt. You acted with purpose.'

'That's not true.' Okay, so it was a bit true. But Robbie was feeling more than a little defensive now. He was standing in her kitchen accusing her of things and he just wouldn't listen to what she was saying to him.

'All right.' She held her hands up. 'Yes, okay, there were things I withheld, and I did it deliberately. The guy I told you about, Rory, who almost ground my self-confidence into dust, do you know why he stayed? He stayed because of the money, and what he thought it could do for him. He never wanted me and…'

Robbie took a breath, trying to still the panic in her chest. 'I was afraid, Joel. The secret was my way of protecting myself from all of that, and I just didn't want to let go of it.'

'And you think I care about the money?'

'No, I don't. I *know* you don't care about it, and that was why I was going to tell you. After we'd had pizza.'

His gaze searched her face. 'Yeah, I believe you.'

'Well, thank you for that. I'm so thrilled and happy that you believe me because it's the truth.' Robbie rolled her eyes.

'But… It doesn't make any difference. You still kept it a secret. You didn't tell me the whole truth. I… I can't do this, Robbie.'

'Why not? Because I happen to have money that you don't even care about?'

Suddenly his lip curled. She'd got through to him but all she could see in his face was anger now.

'No, it's because I know all about other people's secrets and how they can twist your life. How many people know about your family at the hospital? Your father's a prominent advocate for a lot of different medical charities, I expect most people there have heard of him and some might have even met him. Has it ever come up in conversation that he happens to be related to you?'

'No one, okay? It's my business.'

'No, it's your secret and you were going to ask me to keep it. What about Nightshifters? Who apart from Glen knows that you fund the place.'

'No one.'

'So that's another secret you wanted me to keep for you.' Anger was bursting from him now. 'I'm sorry, Robbie, I know why you did it. But I can't do this for you. It's the one thing I can't do for anyone. Didn't that ever occur to you?'

'And doesn't it occur to you that the person you need to say this to is your father? Not me. I just happen to be standing in the way of all the anger you're carrying around.'

'Can't you even see what you're doing? You're trying to control everything and everyone around you, by giving them half-truths. I can't do it with you, Robbie. I'm sorry but I can't.'

She turned her back on him, so that he couldn't see the tears. 'Stop saying you're sorry, will you? Because

I really don't think you are. You're just trying to hurt me because you're angry.'

Silence. She heard his footsteps and then jumped as she heard the door slam. Robbie ran out into the hallway, not knowing whether to be angry or dismayed. His coat was gone and so was the bag he usually brought up from the car, with a change of clothes and his shaving bag. She got as far as the front door and then stopped. If he was still outside, waiting for the lift, what was she going to say to him?

They were both too damaged. She'd tried to step out of the shadow of her own fears, to strip away the protective secrets, but she'd done too little, too late and she'd hurt Joel. And now he was hurting her, because he couldn't let go of his own guilt and pain over having to keep a secret.

She wouldn't cry yet. Robbie couldn't cry, because that would mean that it was really, truly over. She'd picked up her courier bag and walked from her crashed bike, hoping to find safety, and she'd found Joel. Now she had to find a different safety, and for the life of her Robbie didn't know how she was going to do that.

CHAPTER TWELVE

'Hey. You okay?'

Glen was alone at the Tin Tabernacle when Robbie arrived that evening and it was the first question that he asked. And it was the wrong question, because she really wasn't okay.

'Just a bit tired, I didn't sleep much today.'

Glen nodded. He had two kids. He knew all about not sleeping much. 'I heard about Joel.'

Tight pain gripped at her heart. She'd been hoping against hope that Joel would walk into the Tin Tabernacle tonight, as if nothing had happened. But something *had* happened, and it was impossible that life would just go on in the same way.

Robbie didn't need to go through all the palaver of keeping her shoulder quite still while she shrugged off her jacket any more, but she did it anyway because it hid her tears.

'What about Joel?'

'He called me, a couple of hours ago, and said he can't make it in this weekend. Whatever's come up, I reckon it must be pretty big, because he doesn't know when he'll be back.'

It would have been very easy to take that sentence and pick the one strand of false optimism from it. Not knowing when he'd be back implied that he might be. Or even that he was intending to be.

'What did he say exactly?' Robbie tried to hide the quiver in her voice.

'Not for the foreseeable future.'

That was more like it. Joel couldn't foresee a time when they'd be able to work things out enough to even be in the same room. Robbie wasn't sure she could either.

She took a breath. 'Shame. We can do with all the volunteers we can get.'

'Yeah.' Glen was eyeing her thoughtfully. 'I'd assumed that you would know all about what was going on with him. Since you two are an item.'

Robbie was busying herself with the coffee machine now, making two cups. That was the problem with telling people about a new relationship—when it went wrong everyone knew it.

'Sometimes it's difficult to know exactly what Joel's thinking. He keeps things close to his chest.'

'Hmm. I might give him a call during the week. Just to see what's going on with him.'

'Maybe you should leave it.'

'Yeah, okay.' Glen always made sure that anyone on the Nightshifters team who was going through a hard time was supported, and that was the glue that held them all together, but he was taking her word on it this time. Robbie put his mug of coffee down in front of him, and sat down at the other desk.

'The phones are quiet?'

'We had a busy patch an hour ago and everyone's out. Since then, nothing.' Glen took a sip of his coffee. 'So am I going to have to put a rumour around? Something to the effect that you two have changed shifts?'

Robbie puffed out a breath. Changing shifts just about summed it up, because it was unlikely she'd be seeing him again. He'd retreat back into his corner of the world, and she'd retreat into hers.

'Yes. Sorry, Glen, I seem to have driven one of our new volunteers away.'

Glen puffed out a breath. 'Forget about that. I'm just sorry to hear that it didn't work out for you. He seemed like a really nice guy.'

'He is. I'm just not a very nice girl.'

'Hey. None of that…' Glen frowned at her. 'I'll accept that it's a no fault on either side situation.'

'Okay. No fault on either side.' That at least allowed for some hope, even if it seemed unfair that two people who weren't at fault could manufacture such pain together.

'Bakewell tart? I saved you some.' Glen reached into the desk drawer and brought out a plastic box. 'Nothing better than Bakewell tart to mend a broken heart.'

That might be true in most circumstances. Sadly, Robbie felt it was going to take a little more than that to get over losing Joel.

'Thanks. My favourite. Can I save it for later?' She put the box next to her coffee cup. 'Shouldn't you be getting home soon? It's nearly eleven o'clock.'

Glen leaned back in his chair. 'Nah. Think I'll hang around a bit longer. Just in case you decide to tell me what the guy did to you to make you so miserable.'

Robbie shook her head. 'You may as well go. Joel didn't do anything, it was me. And I don't feel up to the details tonight. We'll do that another time.'

Glen shrugged, grabbing the phone when it rang, in a signal that he was staying anyway. Robbie took a sip of her coffee.

It really wasn't Joel's fault, however much Glen wanted to jump to the conclusion that it must be. Joel might have disagreed with her and been appalled by the secrets she'd asked him to keep, but he'd never said that he didn't love her. He'd just said that he couldn't be with her.

Maybe that was the answer she'd been searching for. Joel had given her the self-confidence to step away from things that had hurt her, things she'd already held onto for too long. To be what she already knew herself to be. He'd never asked her to change because she didn't need to. She just needed to believe in him a little more.

The phone rang again, and Robbie reached for it.

'Hello, Nightshifters. How can we help?'

Joel had spent a lot of hours staring at the wall this weekend. Wishing that the world would just stop, because he didn't have any further use for it.

But it kept turning. Glen had been understanding when he'd called him and said he couldn't make it in this weekend and probably not any other weekend either. But he had to pitch up and do his shift in A & E because there would always be a queue of people who needed him there.

He'd wondered whether he'd see Robbie, even hoping that he might. He'd thought about how she might smile at him and how he'd have to smile back, because he'd never been able to ignore Robbie's smile. And then he'd thought about how he was hard-wired in a way that made it impossible to accept what she was asking of him. However much he understood, and however much he loved her.

But Robbie wasn't anywhere to be seen when he turned up to work on Monday evening. He'd done his best to make his enquiries as to her whereabouts sound casual, and heard that she'd been cleared to see patients now, and so was working back in the paediatric A & E unit.

It was all for the best. He went to see his supervisor and put in a request to work days for a while, which was readily accepted because he'd already worked more nights than were required of him. And then he gritted his teeth and got on with it.

The first weekend without her had been the worst— until the second came around. He had to find something to fill the void that she'd left, but that was difficult when everything he did reminded him of her.

He wept furious tears. And then, hidden deep inside, Joel found grief. Grief for his mother, and guilt for everything he'd done to shield her from the truth. The deeper he delved into his own heart, the more he missed Robbie, because she'd been his guide. He missed everything about her, the way she made him feel and the way he knew he made her feel. Her courage, her determination and the way she made him laugh. Her cooking...he even missed Robbie's cooking.

And then, on the third weekend, Robbie had led him to the place he should have gone to a long time ago. It was almost a year since Joel had seen his aunt Carrie and much longer than that since they'd really talked. When he'd called and asked if he might visit, she'd told him that he was welcome any time.

His uncle would be out with his sailing club on Saturday morning, and Aunt Carrie would be home on her own. She welcomed him with a hug, so like the ones his mother used to give.

He shouldn't think like that. Carrie wasn't a replacement for his mother, and she couldn't step in and forgive Joel in her stead. He was here for his aunt's sake, in the hopes that he could repair his relationship with her.

'Well.' Carrie settled down on the sofa opposite him. 'It's a treat to see my favourite nephew. What have I done to deserve a visit?'

He'd been away too long. Avoiding all of his family so that he didn't have to confront the issues that hurt so much.

'I'm sorry. I should come more often.'

'You don't owe me anything, Joel. You come and go as you please.'

'I *wanted* to come more often, then, because I miss you.'

'That's nice to hear.' Carrie beamed at him. 'Your mother would have loved to see the way you've turned out. She was very proud that you were at medical school. She used to talk about it all the time.'

Familiar pain almost took his breath away. 'I didn't visit Mum as often as I should have, either.'

'Nonsense, Joel. You were studying and making a life for yourself. That's exactly what Theresa wanted for you.'

This was the opportunity he'd told himself he would take. 'I was wondering… Would you mind if we talked a bit about Mum?'

'No, of course not. You have something particular in mind?' Carrie leaned back in her seat, with the same expression she'd had on her face when he'd challenged her to board games when he was little. *Bring it on, kiddo.*

The secret hovered on the tip of his tongue. Instinctively Joel swallowed it back down, and it felt as if it were choking him.

But Carrie seemed to have none of his reservations. 'I don't suppose you've seen your father, have you? The last time I bumped into him, which was admittedly some time ago, he said you hadn't been in touch since Theresa died.'

'No. I haven't.'

'I'd be interested to know why that is, Joel. Your father said he had no clue, but I could tell that he knew a lot more than he was saying. He never was quite as clever as he thought.'

Carrie had asked, and he'd answer honestly; he owed her that much. 'A lot of reasons. One of them was that I didn't think he treated Mum very well.'

The silence in the room bore down on him like an oppressive mist. He and Carrie both opened their mouths to speak at the same time, and Joel smilingly indicated that she should go first.

'I think it's about time that we levelled with each other, don't you?'

He wanted to. Joel knew that he had to take the first step.

'Sometimes it's less hurtful to let the past stay where

it is.' He should prepare Carrie for what was coming. Let her just nod her head in agreement, and drop the subject if she wanted to.

'I don't think so, Joel.' Carrie's mouth was quivering with emotion now. 'In my experience, pretending that things never happened doesn't make them go away.'

Carrie was right, and she'd issued him with an ultimatum. Whatever the consequences, whether or not his aunt could accept what he'd done, Joel had to tell the truth.

'I found out that my father was having an affair, when I was seven. He swore me to secrecy, saying it was for Mum's sake because the family would break up if I said anything…' He felt himself flinch as Carrie's hand flew to her mouth. 'Carrie, I'm so sorry.'

'Oh, my goodness. You *knew*?'

'Did you?'

'Yes, your mother told me. You know she had a habit of thinking the best of everyone, especially your father, but she wasn't stupid. She used to come round and drink tea and tell me that she loved your father and that it would all blow over. No one would know that anything was ever the matter…'

Suddenly everything was coming into sharp focus. Joel was finally beginning to see it all through an adult's eyes, and not a child's.

'I'm pretty sure that Andrew didn't know—he was only two years old. I did, though. My father used to take me out in the afternoon and leave me in the park to play on my own for hours. When he got back, he'd tell me that I had to tell Mum that we'd been together the whole time.' Joel shrugged. 'I never told her. I felt very guilty about that.'

A tear dribbled down Carrie's cheek. 'That never should have been allowed to happen. *I* should never have allowed it to happen.'

Joel shrugged numbly. What had all of his guilt and soul-searching been for? 'There was no way you could have known. No way that Mum could have known.'

'Theresa was my sister, and you know how much I loved her. How much I still do love her… But I should have realised that a lot of what she said was just wishful thinking. You never should have had to bear that burden.'

Joel got to his feet, moving over to the sofa to sit next to Carrie. When he put his arm around her shaking shoulders, trying to comfort her, she clung to him, crying. 'I'm so sorry, Joel.'

He knew now exactly what to say. Robbie had shown him the way and given him the strength to take that path.

'Carrie, listen. This was never my fault and it was never yours. We got caught up in something that wasn't of our making. It's not too late for either of us to make our peace with that.'

They talked for a long time. He stayed for dinner and when he left Carrie hugged him and demanded that they make a date for dinner at his house. His uncle's parting words to him convinced him that he'd done the right thing.

'Thank you for coming, Joel. Carrie's been needing to talk about this, for a long time.'

* * *

Robbie was nervous. Actually, nervous didn't cover it.

Glen helped her write the press release, striking out all of the parts he said were too apologetic, and replacing them with a succinct history of how Nightshifters had been founded. Robbie added short profiles of Glen and the members of the board, and details of the expansion plans.

'There. That'll do. When we actually get around to releasing it, we'll add a couple of case studies. But the Nightshifters don't need those, they just want to know what's happening.'

'And what I've done.' Robbie pulled an agonised face.

'What you've done is to build something we're all proud of, Rob, and it's about time you took some credit for it. Going public is the best way to expand, and we're ready to do that now. We're telling our own crew first, so they don't read it in the papers later on.'

Robbie wondered if the Nightshifters would see it the same way. But she emailed a copy of the press release to each of the volunteers along with an invitation to a meeting at the Tin Tabernacle.

By the evening of the meeting she was feeling sick with worry. Carla had said she'd be there, which meant that two people would be talking to her, at least. The Tin Tabernacle was filling up quickly, and Roy popped in to announce that he was back and feeling in the best of health, accepting a plate of sausage rolls from the food and drinks table to take back to the boats.

Then Glen roared for silence, and everyone sat down on the rows of chairs that had been put out.

'All right. I don't need to tell you what's going on, you've all had the information by email, and the plans for Oxford are over there on the wall. So I'll go straight to questions and comments.'

Glen sat down again. Robbie would have preferred that he'd talked a little longer, but he was right. Everyone had the information, and this meeting was about their thoughts and ideas. Saying anything more was just putting off the moment that Robbie was dreading.

Rosie stood up, brandishing her copy of the press release. 'I want to propose a motion.'

'Sure. Knock yourself out, Rosie.' Glen nodded.

This was it. Rosie had been a good friend over the years, and she didn't mince her words. Losing her now, losing any of the people here, would tear Robbie's heart out. But they deserved to know.

'If I'd been financing this place, I'd make sure everyone knew about it…' Heads nodded in agreement. 'But Robbie just went ahead and did it. I don't know about you, but I'm pretty fed up about that.'

Here it came. Rosie was clearly working up to a sting in the tail, which was exactly what Robbie deserved. She felt herself flush with misery.

'So I'm going to put things right. I'm proposing a vote of thanks to Robbie, for everything here that means so much to so many people. And for being a complete dunderhead, because she didn't sit back and reckon she'd done enough already, but pitched in and worked as hard as any of us.'

'Yep!' Glen's hand went up, but it wasn't the first.

Hands were being raised thick and fast, and Robbie felt tears of relief spring to her eyes. Glen stood up and tried to count them, and then gave up.

'I think that's unanimous. Apart from Carla…' He shot his wife a querying look.

'Oh. Do I get a vote as well?'

A groan ran around the hall and Rosie spoke up again. 'Carla gets two votes. On account of the mince pies, last Christmas.'

Carla beamed at Rosie and held up two hands.

'Right, then. Consider yourself well and truly thanked, Robbie, and thank you to Rosie for proposing our first motion.' Glen turned to Robbie mouthing, *I told you so.* 'Now, let's settle down and have some questions about the expansion, shall we?'

There was a lively discussion about the new branch of Nightshifters, and quite a few good ideas. Glen was taking notes and fielding the questions, and Robbie sat still and silent. Carla slipped from her seat and came to sit next to her.

'You okay?'

'Yes. Thanks. I'm just a bit overwhelmed.'

Carla nodded. 'You deserve it. Does this make a difference to you?'

Robbie thought for a moment. She'd be going to Oxfordshire tomorrow for two weeks, and when she got back the press release would go out. Joel might still be too angry with her to take any heed of it, but even if she never saw him again, she'd know that his love and hers hadn't been for nothing, because it had brought her to this point. She'd done it for him, and for herself and for the Nightshifters. And if she did see Joel again, she could at least look him in the eye, and tell him that she'd done her best to be worthy of his love.

'Yes. It makes all the difference in the world.'

Change was hard. It had its good times, being able to phone Carrie and talk when he wanted to, and hearing that she'd been in touch with his brother, Andrew, and that he'd asked after Joel. It would take time, and maybe Andrew would never know about what he'd been too young to understand, but Joel was beginning to see a possibility of change.

And it had its bad times. Waking up in the night and reaching for Robbie was the worst of them, because the cruel disappointment when he remembered that she wasn't there was like losing her all over again.

Joel didn't dare try to see her, but he was hungry for news of Robbie. And the gossip he overheard from the hospital grapevine was always happy to oblige.

'I heard that Nightshifters are expanding their operation and setting up another office in Oxford.'

'I heard that too. Good thing, I'd say. And David Hampton-Hall is involved with the project. I didn't know he was Robbie's father, did you...?'

'I don't think anyone knew. You've got to respect her for keeping quiet about it and not trying to trade on her family name. By the way, did you know that Josie's gone over to Paeds for three weeks?'

'No. I knew she wanted to make the move.'

'It's just temporary, she's filling in while Robbie's on leave. But at least Josie will be getting some experience there, and it'll stand her in good stead if she applies for a transfer...'

Robbie was moving on. No…she was moving out, coming out of hiding and spreading her wings. And if he'd needed any reason to remind himself that he still loved her, it was the warmth that he felt at that thought. Almost in a daze, he went to his supervisor and asked if he might have a week's leave, to deal with an urgent personal matter. And when his request was granted, he knew what he had to do.

He drove home and fell into bed, bone weary from so many sleepless nights. He slept for fourteen hours, then woke with the kind of resolve that he hadn't felt in a while.

He needed coffee, lots of it. Plenty of carbs, some stretching exercises, and a map of Oxfordshire. Then, ninety-two phone calls later, he hit gold.

'Good afternoon, The Cloisters Hotel.'

'Hi. Olivia Hampton-Hall, please.'

A pause. Joel lay on the sofa, staring at the ceiling and replaying the inevitable answer in his head. Always starting with *I'm sorry…*

'May I take a message, sir?'

Joel sat up suddenly, scattering crumbs and knocking his cup over. Robbie was capable of disappearing from his life, but she just didn't have it in her DNA to stay completely out of reach, in case someone from Nightshifters needed her. He'd reckoned that she would probably be out all day working, and that she would have instructed the hotel's reception to take messages.

'No, I'll catch her later. Thank you.'

He grabbed the map. He'd painstakingly worked his way out from the centre of Oxford, calling every hotel he could find. The Cloisters Hotel, was a little over eight miles from his starting point, and now he knew where Robbie was. Tracing his finger across the map, from London to Oxford, made the distance between them seem inconsequential. Tomorrow he'd be facing a much more difficult journey.

CHAPTER THIRTEEN

JOEL WAS UP early and on the road before nine o'clock. He got stuck in traffic in West London, and then the day became bright and clear, with an open road in front of him. The Cloisters Hotel was just outside Oxford, and it lived up to its name.

The main reception area was modern and sleek, complementing the old stone arches that he could see at the far end, which revealed a carefully kept courtyard garden beyond. It was quiet, the kind of place you'd go if you were searching for respite. Joel had the uncomfortable feeling that respite was exactly what Robbie had been searching for, and that it was from him.

'Olivia Hampton-Hall, please.'

The receptionist's lips moved automatically into a professional smile. 'May I take a message, sir?'

'No, that's okay, I really need to see her. Do you know when she'll be back?'

'I can pass on a message…' That was clearly all the receptionist was authorised to do.

'I'll call her. Thanks.' Joel wondered whether sitting in Reception and waiting for her was the thing to do, and decided that he might be there all day. Not that he'd mind, but it might elicit a few questions.

He went back out to his car, and got in. It made sense to just wait until Robbie returned to the hotel. It actually made sense to wait until she returned to London, but he had no idea when that would be or even if she was going to be back. She didn't have to consider the practicalities of a place to live and a job—her trust fund meant that she could just leave everything behind and disappear if she wanted to, and Joel feared that this was exactly what she was doing.

But Robbie was practical. The hotel was nice— gorgeous actually—but she was perfectly capable of staying anywhere as long as it was close to where she needed to be. He had to just trust in what he knew and think. If Robbie was setting up a new regional office for Nightshifters it would be somewhere near one of the major routes into the surrounding towns. Probably somewhere that satisfied her fascination with the unusual and her commitment to communities…

Fifteen minutes later, he threw his phone back down onto the passenger seat and started the engine. It was only a ten-minute drive, and as soon as he turned off the main road and onto the newly tarmacked lane he knew he was in the right place.

Tin Chapel Field was right ahead of him. And although there was no Tin Tabernacle there, there was a new structure that resembled one, with the same arched wooden doors and wooden-framed windows. The walls and roof looked as if the original corrugated iron had been replaced with a modern high-performance material that wasn't quite so susceptible to rust as the Tin

Tabernacle in London. But at a distance the two looked much the same, apart from the fact that this one was sky blue. Joel stopped the car on the paved parking area, next to three others.

He walked over to a man who was perched on a ladder, painting the wooden eaves. 'Hi. Is Robbie around?'

'You've just missed her.' The man put one last finishing touch to the bright, white gloss and climbed down the ladder. 'She won't be long. She's gone to fetch lunch.'

That was just like Robbie. She didn't care about being the boss, she just did whatever was useful. The thought prompted a wave of intense yearning, coupled with terror at this uncertain enterprise, and Joel choked both back.

'Nice place…' He nodded towards the building and the man beamed.

'Yeah, it's come out all right. Took us three days to put it up. It came in a flat pack from the manufacturers.'

'There used to be one like it here?'

The man laughed. 'The Tin Chapel rusted away years ago, terrible old thing it was. The name survived, though. It's nice that there's going to be something like it here again.'

And this place was an ideal location, both beautiful and practical. There was easy access to a main road, but it was surrounded by open fields.

'Plenty of space.' Joel was trying not to think about beautiful and practical, because those were words he connected with Robbie, and his heart might tear into little pieces, right here and now.

'Yeah, the land goes right down to that boundary

there.' The man pointed towards a fence that circled a wide area of grass, along with copses of trees and what looked like a small stream.

The sound of a car approaching made them both turn. Robbie looked as if she might be about to ram his car with hers, but at the last moment she reversed, parking on the other side of the paving. No doubt she'd seen sense and decided that when she told him to go, he was going to need some form of transport.

Joel swallowed hard, trying not to think about it. In his determination to find her, he'd been able to put aside thoughts about what was going to happen when he actually did find her, but now he was facing the biggest challenge of his life.

She got out of the car, reaching in to collect a cardboard tray of drinks and a large carrier bag. The sunshine reflected in her hair as she walked towards him and surprisingly she didn't have a scowl on her face. But it was possible that was just for the benefit of the man standing beside him. Another couple of men had appeared at the door of the building and Robbie handed over the lunches and watched them walk away towards an old picnic table that had been set up on the grass. When she turned, her face was grave.

'How did you know I was here?'

That hurt, because it meant that Robbie must have deliberately covered her tracks, so that he couldn't find her. He gestured towards the grass on the other side of the building, out of sight of the workmen. If she was going to punch him, then he really didn't need anyone to rush over and save him, because it was what he deserved. And if he was going to get down on his knees and beg, he'd rather do it without the distraction of an audience.

She walked to the spot he'd indicated and then turned to face him.

'What is it, Joel?'

Not being able to believe that this was really Joel, when she'd first caught sight of him, was less to do with the realities of the situation, and more to do with what had been going on in Robbie's head. She'd thought about him. Dreamed about him. Once, the hairs on the back of her neck had prickled, when she'd thought she'd caught his scent, but when she'd looked round he wasn't there. Hallucinations weren't such a big step away from that, even if they were a concern.

But you couldn't hallucinate this. The way he stood, the fine balance of his body and the way he smiled as he chatted to Dave. It had been something akin to the shock she'd felt when she'd been catapulted off her bike and hit the ground, and in her consternation she'd almost rammed her car into his. Robbie had wiped the tears from her eyes, picked up the lunches and faced him, but she was trembling all over.

She wrapped her jacket around her, folding her arms across her stomach. Maybe that would keep her in one piece for a while.

'What is it, Joel?'

'I'm sorry. Truly sorry.'

He looked sorry. She was sorry too, but Robbie couldn't bring herself to believe that it would change anything. The press release hadn't even been sent yet, so there was no way that he could know what she'd done.

'Apology accepted.'

'What?' That was clearly the last thing he'd expected her to say. And the sudden flash of warmth in his eyes made her want to cry.

'I said things I regret too.' Maybe she should tell him that there were no more secrets any more. Or maybe she should wait, and let him say what he wanted to say first.

He nodded, looking down at the grass. 'You had every right to say what you said.'

This was harder than she'd thought it would be. How could he stand there, looking so beautiful, and not realise how agonising this was?

'Is that all you wanted to say, Joel?'

His jaw hardened. 'I wouldn't have come all this way if there was nothing more to say. If I felt the same as I did then...'

So what's changed? Robbie couldn't get the words out, she just stared at him dumbly. Something at the back of her mind was insisting furiously that if this was the last time she would see him, she wanted every second of it to keep, because however awful things were between them, it was better than being without him.

'I went to see Aunt Carrie... We talked for a long time.'

So he was finding some healing. That was good. She'd found some too, but maybe what she'd done wasn't going to be enough for him...

'I've realised something. Neither of us can change what happened in the past, but we can change how we choose to deal with it.'

'I...' Robbie hardly dared say anything. If this

sounded too good to be true it probably was, but Joel was here, and that must mean something.

'I'm sorry too. You were right, I shouldn't have asked you to keep my secrets. I'm doing my best to leave them behind.'

He smiled suddenly. 'I heard. Hospital gossip's got a lot to say about Nightshifters and how you turned out to be David Hampton-Hall's daughter. Robbie, I'm not asking you to come back to me…'

There it was. It *was* too good to be true after all. Disappointment tore at her savagely, and then suddenly Joel fell to his knees. Robbie jumped back, yelping in surprise.

'I love you, and I'm asking you to talk to me. Just to find out whether we can work through this, because I really believe that we can leave the past behind and find a future.'

'Joel. Get up.' She could feel tears on her cheeks.

'So I can walk away from you?' He shook his head. 'Sorry, Robbie, not a chance. Not this time. If there's any walking to be done, then you'll have to do it.'

That was just fine, because Joel was the best thing that had ever happened to her, and she'd never leave him. She flung herself at him, hugging him awkwardly.

He was trembling too. Holding onto her as if she was the one and only thing he'd ever wanted. Robbie wasn't sure how long her legs were going to hold her, and she pulled away from him, dropping to her knees.

Better. He could hold her and kiss her now, the way she wanted him to, and he did just that.

'Please, Joel. Tell me you mean this…'

He dropped back onto his heels, holding her hands between his.

'I love you, Robbie. I'll do everything to prove that to you—'

'Just tell me. Then I'll know I can believe it.'

'I mean it.'

'I love you too, Joel. I mean it.' This felt like a lasting promise, one that opened up a future for them both.

He grinned. 'Will you come on a date with me, then?'

That would be perfect. She wanted to share everything with Joel and the one thing they hadn't had time for was a romantic first date.

'Yes.'

'Now?'

Now was going to be a problem…

'I really want to. But Dad's been helping out with some of the fundraising and publicity and he and Mum are driving down to see how the Tin Tabernacle's going, and take some photographs. They'll be here in a couple of hours…' She reached forward, trying to smooth the look of sudden panic on Joel's face.

'They'll love you. Not as much as I do, but…'

He grinned. 'I can face the terrors of being introduced to your parents. As long as you love me.'

'I do. But if I'm going to introduce you to them, we'll have to be going steady. At least.'

That wicked look that she loved so much crept into his smile. 'You're right. Going steady it is, then. Officially.'

Robbie had wondered aloud whether going back to the hotel, for an hour alone before her parents arrived, would be possible and Joel had vetoed the idea. Clearly he felt that frustrated yearning was a better look than smug satisfaction when greeting her parents, and perhaps he was right. Although, that hadn't stopped him from accompanying her on a tour around the land attached to the new Tin Tabernacle, when he knew full well that as soon as they were out of sight of the workmen and among the trees they'd be kissing and making all of the promises that Robbie so wanted to hear.

Her dad liked him. What wasn't to like? Joel was affable and smiling and knew a lot about some of the medical issues that her dad's charities were involved with. Before long the two men were taking a stroll around the boundaries of the property, talking animatedly together. Her mother joined her at the window of the Tin Tabernacle as she stared out at them.

'Don't look so worried, Robbie. They'll manage if you take your eye off them for one minute.'

They probably would, but then that would be one minute that Robbie missed out on. 'You think Dad likes him?'

'That would make any difference?'

'Yes, because I want them to like each other. No, because *I* like him.'

Her mother laughed. 'Yes. I can see that. Of course your father likes him. Joel's clearly devoted to you, and that's a very good start. His being a doctor gives them something to talk about, and... Ah, yes. See, they're pacing out the area for the new community centre...'

Dad was gesturing to show the scale of the proposed building, and Joel was nodding, obviously asking a few questions. Robbie had been otherwise occupied when they'd reached the trees that would surround the community centre, and had forgotten to mention it to Joel.

'Is there a nice pub near here?' her mother asked.

'Yes, there are loads of them.'

'Good. I could do with a G & T and a sandwich before we go.'

Robbie hid the smile that sprang to her lips behind her hand, not wishing to give the impression that she didn't want to see her parents. 'I thought you were staying for dinner at the hotel.'

Her mother frowned. 'For goodness' sakes, Robbie. I'll be happy with a thank you, for taking your father off back to London while you do whatever it is you're impatient to do with that young man of yours. I don't blame you, he's rather gorgeous.'

Mum had never talked like that about any of her boyfriends. But then none of her boyfriends had been Joel.

'Thanks, Mum. We'll do dinner another time. Very soon.'

Joel wasn't due to go back to work for another week, and their time together here had been idyllic. Working hard during the day, at the new Tin Tabernacle, and playing hard and sweet at night. Robbie was happy and that was really all that Joel cared about, because she never failed to make him happy.

He'd promised to take her on the belated 'first date' on the Saturday evening before he left and the hotel's conservatory-style restaurant was the perfect place. Robbie was in the bathroom, getting ready, and Joel was pacing their hotel room.

'What are you doing?' She appeared in the doorway, in a sleeveless blue and white dress that fell softly around her legs. Her hair was pinned up in an artfully messy arrangement at the back of her head, and her smile was the most beautiful thing he'd ever seen.

'Pacing. Isn't that what you're supposed to do on a first date?' He came to a halt. 'You look gorgeous. It's a nice dress, as well.'

She laughed, pleased with the compliment. Robbie didn't much care about things but she cared about people. And she knew that this particular person belonged to her, and always would.

'You look particularly delicious, too. Very undressable.' She looked around the room. 'Have you seen my shoes? The blue suede ones.'

'Under the bed. Let me get them for you.'

'My Prince Charming. How many phone calls was it to find me again?' Robbie plumped herself down onto the bed.

'More than two.' Joel reached under the bed, grabbing her shoes.

'I heard you scoured the kingdom for me. Followed the clues to the Tin Tabernacle.' She grinned, holding her foot out.

'Not really. I had the advantage of an online map.' He dropped her suede court shoe over her toes. 'Too bad. It doesn't fit.'

Robbie pulled a face of mock horror, reaching for her foot and pulling the shoe on.

'Yes, it does.'

'Well, that's a relief. May I kiss you now, princess?'

Now. He'd been planning to do this later, but he was already on his knees in front of her and he just couldn't wait any longer. Earlier in the week, Joel had driven back to London to fetch some clothes and drop some papers that Robbie had signed in to the charity's solicitor. He had used the opportunity for a more important errand. He'd gone from shop to shop, knowing that he couldn't afford the kind of ring that Robbie really deserved, and then he'd come to his senses. She didn't want the sizeable rocks that he'd been wishing he could buy her; Robbie would find such a thing bulky and impractical.

She'd told him that she wanted his love, and he'd promised she'd always have it. And when he'd found a jeweller who would put the stones of his choice into an eternity ring and then courier it down to the hotel, he'd thought carefully about what he wanted to say to her.

He kissed her, a little nervous now. But love could do anything it wanted, it had brought them back together, and sealed their whispered promises. It could do this, too.

'Olivia Roberta Hampton-Hall…'

She smiled at him. '*All* my names. I'm listening carefully.'

'Good start. I never had a choice about falling in love with you, but it *is* my choice to love you a little more each day. Will you marry me?'

'Joel. Yes!' Robbie squealed with delight, throwing her arms around his shoulders. Joel resisted the impulse to stay like this, just kissing her, and felt in his pocket for the ring.

'I have this…'

She looked down at the ring, resting in the palm of his hand. 'Oh! Joel, it's beautiful. Aquamarine…'

'For the colour of your eyes in the sunlight.'

'And sapphires…'

Joel smiled. 'The colour of your eyes after dark. Diamonds for the promises we make, and platinum for the strength to keep them.'

'And in an unbroken circle for eternity. Joel, this is so perfect.'

She laid her hand in his and he put the ring onto her finger. Different shades of blue, blending together as she turned her hand in the light. Robbie took a moment to look at it, and then cupped her fingers over her ear.

'I can hear it, Joel. Everything it's saying to me.'

He couldn't stop smiling. Joel held her tight, feeling her heart beating against his.

'Are you ready for our first date?'

When Robbie turned her gaze up towards his, her eyes were as blue as the sapphires on her finger, promising him everything for the night ahead. Everything for the rest of their lives.

'Yes. I do believe I am.'

EPILOGUE

ONE YEAR. ONE WEDDING. One baby. One true love who would never let her down.

Robbie sat in the garden of their new house in Oxfordshire, watching Joel with their eight-week-old son. Daniel seemed to be growing by the day, and she'd never seen Joel so happy.

'They'll be here soon. Why don't you give Daniel to me?'

'In a minute...'

'Now, Joel. Stop monopolising him. I'm sure I haven't had my share of cuddles this morning.'

Joel came to sit next to her on the bench, curling his arm around her and holding Daniel between them. 'Will that do? I can't let go of him just yet. You get all day to hold him when I'm at work.'

'This is good. Two for the price of one.' Robbie kissed him. 'And don't tell me that you don't love your new job.'

Joel chuckled. 'I love my new job. Not as much as you and Daniel, and it's less of a challenge, but I do love it?'

'*Less* of a challenge? Making your mark as head of

A & E in a brand-new hospital? Moving down here three weeks before Daniel was born? I'm pleased and proud to be more of a challenge than that,' Robbie teased him.

'Always. You'll always be my first and best challenge.'

A car drew up on the hard standing beside the house. 'He's here, Joel. Your next challenge.'

Joel nodded. 'I'm still not sure what I'm going to say to him.'

'*Hello* will do for starters. Then you introduce him and his wife to your wife and son, and then you show them around the garden, while I cook lunch.'

'I was thinking about doing the cooking myself.' Joel leaned over and kissed her. 'I can do something quick and easy for today, and tomorrow, when we have the place to ourselves, we can let rip and you can devastate our new kitchen.'

Robbie chuckled. 'I'm looking forward to it already. In that case, you men can share culinary tips, and Daniel and I will be on garden duty.'

'And then?' Joel's brow creased.

'And then you take everything as it comes. You don't have to even think about the past, because we have a future to concentrate on.'

'Yeah. Thanks. I needed to hear that one more time.'

Robbie watched as Joel got to his feet, walking across the grass to the car. A man and a woman were getting out, and the woman hung back while the man strode forward to meet Joel. There was one moment of hesitation and then the rather formal handshake turned into a bear hug. Robbie let out a sigh of relief.

'There, Daniel, see that?' Daniel seemed half asleep now, and he hadn't seen anything.

But Robbie had seen it. Aunt Carrie's diplomacy and Joel's careful determination had borne fruit and Joel had finally got to hug his brother again.

* * * * *

COMING SOON!

We really hope you enjoyed reading this book.
If you're looking for more romance, be sure to
head to the shops when new books are
available on

Thursday 31st March

To see which titles are coming soon, please visit
millsandboon.co.uk/nextmonth

MILLS & BOON ®

Coming next month

FORBIDDEN FLING WITH DR RIGHT
JC Harroway

At Darcy's front door, she fumbled with her key in the lock, her heart pitter-pattering in anticipation and fear of them being alone in her empty house.

Darcy breathed through the panic of her ill-judged invitation. Already she had a head full of erotic visions involving Joe, except now that they'd worked as a team to save Holly, that he'd needed her in moment of alarm... that meant something more to her than the physical attraction there since that first day they'd met.

Did he see her as an equal...?

In the kitchen Darcy dropped her bag, flicked on the lights and then the kettle. She reached overhead for two mugs with jittery fingers, the hair at the nape of her neck rising with awareness of Joe in her kitchen, filling her personal space with his magnetic aura. When she turned to face him, prepared to fake a bright smile and make small talk or resurrect the personal conversation they'd begun in the car, he'd stepped closer.

Face to face, a mere pace apart.

Darcy fell into the depths of Joe's stare and all thoughts of conversation dispersed.

Heartbeats pulsed through her like lightning strikes, marking the seconds they stood in tense silence.

He raised his arm, slow and steady to brush back that stubborn lock of her hair determined to reside on her cheek.

As if conditioned to his touch, Darcy turned her face into his palm, part of her craving more, craving it all. 'Joe…' His name passed her lips all breathy and pleading. For what? She wanted him physically, of course, but they had complication written all over them, the space between them an emotional and professional minefield.

He was still grieving the death of his daughter and perhaps even the demise of his marriage, and before meeting him, she'd sworn to focus on her career, a career she stood to jeopardise if they started something personal. Even sex would be a far from straightforward exchange between two people who shared insatiable chemistry, for good or bad. Come Monday morning she'd have to face him, he'd still be her boss. She needed his reference for her consultant position applications.

Could she risk clouding their work dynamic just for sex?

'I want you,' he said, his expression starkly open and honest.

Overwhelming need built inside Darcy, its pressure centred between her legs.

'I've tried to resist,' he said, his voice full of gravel, 'but I'm failing badly.'

Darcy wavered. Joe's eyes brimmed with repressed emotion. He was clearly experiencing the same conflict tugging Darcy in two different directions.

Continue reading
FORBIDDEN FLING WITH DR RIGHT
by JC Harroway

Available next month
www.millsandboon.co.uk

MILLS & BOON

THE HEART OF ROMANCE

A ROMANCE FOR EVERY READER

MODERN

Prepare to be swept off your feet by sophisticated, sexy and seductive heroes, in some of the world's most glamourous and romantic locations, where power and passion collide.

HISTORICAL

Escape with historical heroes from time gone by. Whether your passion is for wicked Regency Rakes, muscled Vikings or rugged Highlanders, awak the romance of the past.

MEDICAL

Set your pulse racing with dedicated, delectable doctors in the high-pressure world of medicine, where emotions run high and passion, comfort an love are the best medicine.

True Love

Celebrate true love with tender stories of heartfelt romance, from the rush of falling in love to the joy a new baby can bring, and a focus on the emotional heart of a relationship.

Desire

Indulge in secrets and scandal, intense drama and plenty of sizzling hot action with powerful and passionate heroes who have it all: wealth, status, good looks…everything but the right woman.

HEROES

Experience all the excitement of a gripping thriller, with an intense romance at its heart. Resourceful, true-to-life women and strong, fearless me face danger and desire - a killer combination!

To see which titles are coming soon, please visit

millsandboon.co.uk/nextmonth

JOIN US ON SOCIAL MEDIA!

Stay up to date with our latest releases, author news and gossip, special offers and discounts, and all the behind-the-scenes action from Mills & Boon...

 millsandboon

 millsandboonuk

millsandboon

It might just be true love...